POISON ORCHIDS

SARAH A. DENZIL & ANNI TAYLOR

POISON ORCHIDS

SARAH A.DENZIL & ANNI TAYLOR

COPYRIGHT

PART I

1

THE DRIVER

The long-haul driver squints at the milky haze created by his headlights and spots two teenage girls. But the figures are swallowed up by the dark again.

His eyes are playing tricks—surely. He's been on the road too long tonight. No one would be out here in the middle of this lonely highway. Must have been an effect of the heat and rain. The bucketing showers of the past hour have subsided to a drizzle, and he can almost hear steam hissing from the hot road. January is in the wet season in Australia's Northern Territory.

This is the kind of night his wife worries about the most. She hates the thought of his petrol tanker being out on a slippery, obscured road. The Stuart Highway stretches for almost three thousand kilometres across the dead centre of the country, from top to bottom. Right now, he's somewhere near Kakadu, at the top end.

Just as he has himself convinced he saw a mirage, two figures tear away from a deep, black patch beside the glow of his headlights.

The girls.

Running straight for his tanker.

Cuts and bruises on their faces. Blood spattered on their short white dresses. There's a man too. Chasing them.

Hell.

He can't stop—

He swings the tanker off-road, the tons of fuel-laden steel behind his cab jackknifing and skidding on the uneven ground and rocks. Then comes an unholy grinding noise as the tanker rolls hard on its side.

Five hundred litres of fuel explode into an orange fire that mushrooms into the sky.

The next thing he sees is an abbreviated view of rocky ground through the only clear spot in his smashed windscreen, and two pairs of bare female legs racing towards him.

2

MEGAN

Psychologist Megan Arlotti walked along the hospital corridor, pausing briefly as she passed rooms 43 and 44. Through the plate glass sections of the doors, she glimpsed each of the two girls she'd been asked to come here and see.

Hayley, a fair-haired English girl from York, slept while a daytime soap ran on the TV. She was tanned for a Brit, with a golden glow across her forehead and freckles clustered around her nose and cheeks. And Gemma, an Australian girl from Sydney, was curled up tightly on the bed, chocolate-brown hair strewn across her face.

All Megan knew about them was that they'd been picked up on the highway late last night by emergency services and that a tanker had gone up in flames near them. Both girls were suffering from smoke inhalation, cuts, and minor burns. Hayley had suffered a blow to the head, resulting in a concussion and some memory loss.

Megan poked her head inside a small office that was shared between the psychologists and counsellors who visited patients at the hospital. She was there to meet with the two detectives who would be briefing her before she spoke with the girls. This situation must be very different to the usual, as she wasn't normally asked to come in so early on a case. As a clinical psychologist working in a local practice, she normally saw victims of crime only after the police were done with their questioning.

Detective Bronwen McKay and Detective Joe Kouros stood to shake hands with her. She'd known them both for over a year.

As a pair of detectives, they were an odd couple. Bronwen was smallish, her bronze skin coming from her Aboriginal mother, her eyes sharp and inquisitive. Joe was a mountain of a guy with permanently flushed skin and a weary expression. "Have you seen the news about the girls, Megan?" Bronwen asked.

Megan gave a half shake of her head as she sat in an exhausted heap on the nearest chair. "Only what you told me over the phone. I just flew in half an hour ago. My sister had a baby last night—a home birth. I was her support person."

Bronwen's eyebrows shot up almost comically. "Hell. Hope my sister never asks *me* to do that. How'd it go?"

"It was damned terrifying," Megan conceded. "But incredible at the same time. She had a little girl."

"That's great. Huge congrats to your sis'." Joe handed Megan his computer tablet. "We'd better catch you up."

A news page displayed photos of the two girls she'd just seen in their hospital beds. The story's headline was gaudy: *Backpacker Girls Escape Murder Plot.*

The news site was known for its sensationalist headlines. But as Megan read on, her shoulders sank and her brow furrowed, and she had to admit that for once, the headline matched the story:

Backpackers Hayley Edwards and Gemma Lucas, both 19, allege they were held captive by Rodney White in a large bird aviary at his home in Bowman's Creek, Northern Territory, for the past two-and-a-half months. The girls say that late last night, Mr White drove them to a remote spot alongside the Stuart Highway to carry out his plan to murder and bury them.

Managing to escape from Mr White, the girls fled onto the

highway to flag down the only vehicle on the road at that time—a fuel tanker driven by a Mr Adam Johnson. Mr Johnson blindly drove the tanker off-road to avoid hitting the girls. The tanker rolled and exploded into flames. Allegedly, Mr Johnson managed to crawl out of the cab of his tanker, only to be set upon by Rodney White. The two men wrestled for a short period, before ending up close to the blaze. Mr White's clothing caught on fire, and he died shortly after of heart failure due to his third-degree burns.

Hayley and Gemma are recovering in hospital after their ordeal. Rescue services found the girls covered in cuts, bruises, and blood. Tanker driver Adam Johnson lapsed into unconsciousness before the rescue services arrived and remains in a coma at present time.

Megan raised her eyes to the two detectives, struggling through several layers of disbelief and astonishment before speaking. "That's... shocking. The media are going to have a field day with this."

"They already are," Joe muttered, taking back his tablet and handing her a cup of coffee. "That's why I've instructed hospital staff not to let anyone visit the girls without clearance from us. We don't want anyone talking with them before we finish our questioning."

"How are they?" Megan gave Joe a smile for the coffee. He always remembered how she took it. Milk with no sugar.

"Doing okay, considering," said Joe. "The English girl had a concussion. That's the worst of it."

A flash of anger heated Megan's skin. That man—Rodney White —had kept two girls imprisoned for months and then coldly tried to murder them. Megan's sister had just given birth to a tiny girl, and the thought of someone in the future wanting to hurt her like that was hideous. Without thinking she took a gulp of hot coffee. The liquid burned all the way from her throat to her stomach.

Megan spluttered for a moment then asked, "And the trucker—is he still in a coma?"

"Yeah," Joe told her.

"He's a hero, right?" said Megan. "Crawls out of a burning wreckage and then wrestles with a murderer?"

"We don't know if Rodney White has ever gotten to the point of actually murdering anyone," Bronwen stressed. "But yes, you could call the driver a hero, I guess. He certainly showed up at the right time."

"Okay." Megan slowly exhaled, gathering herself mentally. "You have to wonder if these girls are his first victims."

"Things are pointing to him being a serial rapist," Joe told her. "Last night, Bron and I did a check of his house to make sure he didn't have any other girls locked up there. We sighted quite a few items—rope, duct tape, blindfolds. And also underwear and wallets."

"Oh, God." Megan shook her head.

"Yeah." Joe's heavily lidded eyes squeezed shut for a moment. "I think we're at the tip of the iceberg. Right now, we're waiting on forensics to go over everything, then we'll be heading back over there."

"I don't envy you." Megan suppressed a shudder. "Okay, so, is there any area you want me to focus on specifically when I talk to the girls? I think I have enough background information to begin."

Megan sensed a hitch in the air, hesitation brewing in the eyes of the detectives. "There's something else I should know, right?"

Bronwen bent her head in affirmation then shot Megan her trademark direct gaze. "The girls are basically telling two different stories. Probably due to mental trauma and memory loss. We don't know which story is the right one yet. But we don't want to push too hard. I've had victims completely shut down on me before. We're hoping you can untangle the knots a bit, and then we'll take over."

"You say their stories aren't adding up?" Megan queried. "You mean just small things? Or—?"

"No, that's the trouble." Bronwen puffed up her cheeks and blew out a breath. "The main discrepancy is not a small thing. Hayley's very fuzzy, but she seems to think that they only spent a couple of weeks as a captive of Rodney White. She claims that they spent most of the three months on some fruit farm, working alongside a large group of backpackers. But she's not totally certain." Bronwen raised her eyebrows. "Very hazy. Gemma, on the other hand, says they were only at the farm for two weeks, and then they met Rodney—while hitchhiking from the farm into town. Gemma says he locked them away in the cage for a period of two-and-a-half months."

"Hmmm, okay." Megan flicked her gaze over to Joe, who was shaking his head.

"And here's the rest of it," he told Megan. "Hayley's hands don't match her claim of picking mangoes for over two months straight. I've seen what the hands and arms of mango pickers look like—mango sap is very acidic, and the skin tends to get a bit beat up. Burns and blisters. Even when they're careful and wear gloves, just a slip up now and again does that kind of damage. But Hayley's hands look pretty pristine. It's Gemma's hands that look beat up. The other thing is that the girls both have good tans. And tans don't come from being locked away in a dark shed for over two months. Gemma's story doesn't match with those tans, but hers is the story that the media is running with—probably because it sounds more dramatic if the girls were locked up for two months rather than two weeks."

Megan gave them both a tight smile, already reeling—how was she going to unravel this? "Shall I get started?"

3

HAYLEY

Hayley drew circles with her finger over the surface of the table next to her hospital bed. They started small, stretching wider and faster until her fingernail grazed the edge. It was bright under the fluorescent lights and white walls. Everything was colorless and sterile, including the bedsheets. How long had she been here? For some reason she kept losing track of time. Had she slept here one night or two?

When the door opened, her circling stopped and her head snapped up to see the woman gently closing the door behind her. It wasn't the female detective, Hayley knew that much, but it also wasn't anyone from the hospital because the woman wasn't wearing a uniform or white coat. Whoever it was, Hayley felt herself shrink into the sheets away from her, away from yet another stranger. She was sick of strangers by now.

"Hi, Hayley, my name is Megan Arlotti, and I'm a psychologist. I'm here to have a chat."

Hayley watched with suspicion as the psychologist gave her a friendly smile. The woman, Megan, was dressed smartly in black trousers and a white blouse. She was blond, perhaps thirty-five or so, and carried a coffee cup in one hand and a file in the other. There were dark circles under her eyes, and her blouse, though clearly expensive silk, was a little crumpled.

You have to look hard to find the imperfections, but they're always there. The words had popped into Hayley's mind from a place she didn't recognise, and that alarmed her.

Hayley tried to pull her thoughts back as Megan grabbed a chair on the far side of the room and dragged it closer. Megan set her coffee cup down on the table and opened a file.

What was in that file? Was it about her?

"Are you here to ask me more questions?" Hayley asked. Her voice croaked towards the end of the sentence, forcing her to clear her throat to speak again. "I've told the police everything I know."

"Would you like some water?" Megan reached across to the jug, but Hayley snatched it out of her reach.

"I can manage, thanks." Hayley poured the water into the plastic cup and avoided the psychologist's gaze.

"Of course," Megan replied. "I have the statement you gave to Detectives McKay and Kouros here. What you've been able to tell us so far is really good, Hayley, but there are a few gaps, and I wanted to go over them with you. Maybe we can retrace your steps, if that's okay?"

Even though Megan had posed the question in a relaxed, informal way, Hayley got the impression that the 'chat' would go ahead whether Hayley was okay with it or not, so she nodded. She sipped on her water, more to give her hands something to do than because of a pressing thirst.

"What brought you to Australia, Hayley?" Megan crossed her legs and smiled encouragingly. Her voice was soft, gentle from sympathy, and she tilted her head slightly to the right. Hayley got the distinct impression that Megan was a hugger, and she'd never quite known what to do with people who were demonstrative in that way. Growing up with reserved parents made her uncomfortable around people who showed their emotions and carried their hearts on their sleeves.

"I was travelling with my boyfriend." Hayley licked her lips and stared out of the hospital window. "We started in Tokyo then went to Seoul." She paused. She didn't really want to tell this stranger all of this, especially not the part where everything had gone wrong after Seoul. "Then we went to Thailand. David stayed in Thailand, and I came to Sydney on my own."

"Why was that?" Megan asked, her voice soft and kind.

"He dumped me," Hayley replied, still staring out of the window. She sighed. "I was running out of money, and we were working in bars to pay for our hotel rooms. David got bored of me and called the whole thing off. I didn't have enough money to go home, but I had enough to get me here, so here I am." She smiled bitterly at the psychologist, wishing for her to go away and leave her alone.

What she hadn't told Megan was how David had found her a job in a back-alley massage parlour and expected Hayley to prostitute herself to earn extra money. *"Just give them a happy ending,"* he'd told her. *"You'll earn triple what you're earning from the bar."* But she'd refused, and he'd turned psycho, hitting her across the face and throwing her out of their dingy little room into the street, her suitcase falling open with her belongings spilling out next to the sandaled feet of passers-by.

"That was around three-and-a-half months ago, wasn't it?" Megan asked.

Hayley shrugged. "I guess so."

"Don't you remember the day you got here? Don't you remember the date of your flight?"

"It's... blurry. The doctors said I have memory loss or something." She shrugged and looked down at the bedsheets. Not remembering things made her feel strange and not herself. It was almost like someone had altered her mind and she didn't know how to make it normal again.

"Okay, well, the detectives can check the flights to ascertain your arrival here."

"What does it matter?" Hayley asked. "Don't you just want to know about Rodney White?"

"We're going to build a timeline together," Megan replied. "Which will come to Rodney White. Don't worry, everything helps towards the case, and you can take as much time as you need. How long had you been in Sydney before you met Gemma Lucas?"

"Pretty much the next day. I needed money, so I went around a few bars and asked for work. Gemma was working in a place called Sam's. Before we took off, I worked there for a few days. But it turned out Sam was a dick. I walked in on him trying to cop a feel of Gemma, so we stole the money from the till and got out of there. We found out about this farm next to the most beautiful waterfalls and landscapes. We followed the directions on the leaflet and went there."

"Let's just back up a moment. Did you take off right after you witnessed Sam sexually assault Gemma?"

Hayley shook her head. "No. He stopped when he saw me and passed it off as though it was nothing. We didn't do anything at first, but later on during my shift, I asked Gemma if she wanted to go to the police. She didn't want to, and that was when I found the advert about the farm near Kakadu. The next day, we met at the bar, legged it with the cash from the register, and hitched."

"That's almost 4000 kilometres from Sydney." Megan raised her eyebrows. "You hitchhiked the entire way there?"

"Pretty much," Hayley said. "In and out of lorries mainly. We walked a fair bit. We stayed in some god-awful motels along the way."

"How long did it take you to get there?"

"I don't know. Three, maybe four days."

"And where did the leaflet come from?"

Hayley paused. She thought back to the day in the bar when she and Gemma had talked about going, but Gemma's face was slightly out of focus, and she couldn't hear all of the words that came out of Gemma's mouth. She remembered grabbing the cash from the register. She remembered the sound of Gemma's laugh as they'd run through groups of tourists near Sydney Harbour. It was clear as day, as though Gemma was in the room with her. But why couldn't she remember everything? Her chest felt tight as she struggled to focus her mind.

"Hayley?"

"Is there a reason why I can't visit Gemma? The detectives wouldn't let me. Is she all right?" Hayley felt as though Gemma was the one with all the answers to what happened before the tanker blew up. But Hayley felt strangely conflicted. There was part of her that didn't want to see Gemma ever again, but she didn't know why. She kept telling herself that it was stupid, that she was confused from the concussion and couldn't rely on her memories, but at the same time, she couldn't deny that she was relieved the police hadn't taken her to see Gemma yet.

"She's fine. The detectives have decided to keep you apart until we can get all of the facts. We want a clear picture of what's happened, okay?"

Hayley nodded along, but inside she was screaming. She'd had enough of being in this hospital room, talking to strangers. She'd never missed the narrow streets of York as much as that moment.

"I don't know," Hayley said eventually. "I can't remember it all, not properly."

"That's okay," Megan said. She reached forward and patted Hayley's hand. "We'll take it slowly."

At least Megan didn't put pressure on her like the short detective with the piercing eyes. Maybe this wouldn't be as awful as she'd thought.

"I wish I could remember things better. This concussion... I hate what it's doing to my head."

"That must be hard," Megan said.

"It is," Hayley mumbled. "I wish I could remember everything. I want to. It's horrible not knowing what might have been done to me." She closed her eyes and took a deep breath.

"Take your time."

"I'm okay."

Megan smiled. "Good. Try to remember as much as you can from this point on. What was the farm like when you got there? How long were you there for?"

"It was a fruit farm, with fields of mango trees. There were dorm rooms, like a hostel, with, I don't know, a few dozen other travellers. The guy who ran it, Tate, also grew beautiful orchids. We were there all summer I think. Picking mangoes."

"What do you mean by all summer? How long is that?"

"I don't know. From when we left Sydney to about two weeks ago. But it's all kind of hazy." Hayley frowned, trying to remember dates and times and days, but everything merged into one messy lump of time.

"How long were you held captive by Rodney White?"

Hayley wrapped her arms around her body. They kept asking her this, and she kept giving her answer, but she didn't want to talk about Rodney. It made her stomach churn. "About a fortnight."

Megan paused, staring at Hayley with puzzled grey eyes. Hayley kept getting the sense that she was giving them the wrong answer, but she didn't know what the right answer was.

"And who is this Tate person?" Megan asked.

"Tate Llewellyn," Hayley said, relieved to not have to talk about Rodney anymore. "Some of the guys at the farm called him The Chemist because his family owns a pharmaceutical company. He was growing orchids to make perfume. But mostly he grew mangoes."

Megan narrowed her eyes. "What sort of perfume was he creating?"

Hayley shrugged. "I can't remember. The backpackers mostly

just pick mangoes, and that's it." Her head hurt when she tried to remember more. It was as though she had locked some memories away and couldn't find them anymore. All she knew was that the summer at the farm had been the best weeks of her life.

"When did you meet Rodney White?"

Hayley shook her head. "It's all so fuzzy. I... I just remember waking up in a small room. Gemma was there. We were tied up." Her heart began to beat a quick tattoo against her ribs as she brought up the painful memories. "I had tape over my mouth. It was so hot. The sweat kept stinging my eyes. I couldn't wipe it away." She paused, catching her breath. "And the birds. Always squawking. They wouldn't shut up."

"And you were there for two weeks?"

"I don't know." Hayley felt the burn of tears as she forced herself to talk about the darkest time of her life. "I was too scared to sleep. He'd come into the room and..." She couldn't say the words. "Then he took us in his car, and I think he was going to murder us. That's all I remember."

"You're doing well, Hayley, but are you sure there isn't anything else?"

There was something about this kind psychologist that encouraged Hayley to try harder. Even though every part of her body was begging her to stop this line of thought, she forced herself to think as hard as she possibly could.

The memories hit her hard and fast, coming at her in quick flashes. She gasped.

"What is it? Tell me?"

"I don't know why I saw this."

"Tell me," Megan urged.

Hayley brushed a tear from her eye. She felt weak, as though all the life had been sucked out of her.

"You're safe here, you can tell me what you saw."

"It was so cold. I was shivering. The cold... it was... it got into your bones." Hayley dropped her face into her hands and sobbed. "Don't make me... it's a nightmare, that's all. It's not real. It's a nightmare."

"Where was cold?" Megan asked, leaning forward with her brow furrowed in confusion.

Hayley couldn't stand looking at the woman's confused expression. She couldn't stand knowing that everything coming out of her mouth was jumbled and made no sense. She just wanted to go back to before she came to Australia. She wished she'd never come here.

"It was the cold place," she said. She could feel it now, as though the cold air was brushing her skin. Nausea churned at her stomach, and her mouth filled with water.

"It's okay, Hayley. Everything is all right now."

Hayley stared down at her hands and realized that she was trembling.

4

GEMMA

Sitting on the hospital bed, Gemma gulped a glass of water that made her gag. The petrol tank explosion last night had blasted searing hot smoke everywhere, burning her throat ragged. But no matter how much water she drank, she couldn't rid herself of the horrible taste in her mouth—of fuel and smoke and gritty desert dirt. Worst of all was the taste of Rodney White the last time he forced his tongue inside her mouth.

I'm glad he's dead. Some people deserve bad things to happen to them. He deserved to burn alive.

A woman entered the room, introducing herself as Megan. Even before she said why she was here, Gemma knew she was a psych. Her eyes were tired but searching—eyes that could look inside people and examine the faulty wiring in their brains. Megan positioned herself on a chair by Gemma's bedside and asked how she was feeling.

"Like my body's here," Gemma answered, "but my mind is off floating somewhere else."

Megan pressed her mouth into a sympathetic line. "It must be very difficult for you to process all the things that happened."

Gemma nodded, drawing her knees up to her chest and locking her arms tightly around them.

"We're just going to have a little talk," said Megan. "Is that okay?"

"I guess, yeah."

"First of all, is there a place you'd like to start? Anything you'd like to tell me?"

"I just... hurt all over. I feel raw and exposed... and dirty. I want to make all that go away." Her throat rasped on every word she spoke. She poured herself another drink and sipped the water, being careful not to gulp it this time. "But I don't know how to make it go away." Gemma could almost smell Rodney's breath on her face, feel his touch on her skin. Shivers travelled up the length of her back and needled her arms.

Megan caught the glass as it half dropped from Gemma's hand and placed it back on the tray. "Gemma, although we can't change the past, we can learn to lessen the pain. Often the best way is simply to tell others what happened. Little by little, the raw parts begin to heal."

"That's the trouble. I don't know if I *can* heal from what happened. If I can't change the past, then I want to make *myself* go away."

"You want to make yourself go away?"

"I want to die. So I don't have to feel this anymore."

Megan straightened and leaned forward, giving Gemma's shoulder a gentle squeeze. "Are you willing to trust me? You will come out the other side of this. I promise. You will. I can give you medication to get you through the worst of it."

"I don't want medication. Rodney used to medicate us. He drugged us all the time."

Megan nodded, shifting back again. "Okay... I understand. No meds." After a pause, she spoke again. "How about we talk about your life before the whole thing with Rodney? Were you working? Studying?"

Turning, Gemma faced the wall. "There is no *before*. That girl is gone."

"Gemma, that's not true. You just—"

"She's *gone*."

"I understand that you're feeling lost. I spoke with Hayley a little earlier. She's feeling very lost herself. Her memory is patchy."

"I remember everything. I wish I didn't. What did Hayley say?"

Megan sighed. "Not a lot. She remembers you two hitchhiking to a farm near Kakadu. She said you went there to work on the farm, but she's fuzzy on the events that followed."

"Yes, we went to work on the farm. We were only there for a couple of weeks when we decided to hitchhike into town to buy some things. Like some shampoo and deodorant. That's when Rodney stopped and offered us a ride."

"Okay," Megan said softly. "And did you accept the lift?"

"Yeah. We did," Gemma told her, each word landing leaden and monotone in her ears. She needed to get this out. She needed to say it. Something about talking to the police had made her shut down. But Megan was different.

"I hitchhiked all the time," Gemma continued. "It was always okay. Until that day. After he offered us a lift, he said he'd forgotten his wallet. He drove us to his property at Bowman's Creek. And then he asked us in for a cold drink. It was stinking hot in Rodney's car— the air-conditioning wasn't working. Not to mention it just plain *stank*. Looking back, I think he probably just lied and said the aircon didn't work so that we'd be sweating and desperate to get out of his car. Hayley and I went inside, and Rodney gave us some orange juice. It tasted kind of chemical. I felt sleepy straight away. Hayley felt sick and went to use the bathroom. Rodney said he needed to check on his birds—he had an aviary in a shed out back. I fell asleep for a little while, and when I woke, Hayley was still gone. I knocked on the bathroom door, but no one was in there."

She stopped, scratching at the mango sap burns on her hands and arms, anxiety cramping her stomach. "So, I went out to the yard, thinking maybe Hayley had gone to see the birds in Rodney's aviary. I found the aviary in the shed. It was huge—about the size of a small room, and full of large, squawking birds. I felt sorry for the birds, trapped in that dark shed in that dingy cage and unable to see the sky. I was about to leave. But then..."

Gemma's voice choked in her chest. She grabbed the jug of water and poured herself another drink. *People can drown if they drink too much water—I heard that somewhere. That doesn't sound like a bad thing right now. I can drown myself... drift away.*

"Take your time." Megan touched her shoulder again. "Really. There's no rush. And you don't have to tell me any of the details now. We can concentrate on the timeline instead, and—."

"No." Gemma tried to settle her breathing. "I need to tell it all."

The psychologist drew her eyebrows together, seeming to deliberate on something. "If you're going to go further with this, we might need the detectives present in the room. Are you ready for that?"

She gave Megan a nod, her cheeks wet from sudden tears. "I want people to know what he did to us."

Rising, Megan hurried from the room. She returned with Detectives McKay and Kouros. Gemma had spoken to them briefly the night before.

"Gemma, Joe and Bronwen will be sitting here behind me," said Megan. "You'll be talking with me, just as before. But they might need to clarify some things that you say. Are you okay with that?"

"Yes," she told her.

Megan quickly filled the detectives in on what she'd been told so far then turned back to Gemma, giving her a reassuring smile. "Are you ready to continue?"

Gemma sucked her lips in, brushing her hair away from her eyes with fingers that felt numb. "I'm ready."

"Okay, then tell us what happened after you first saw the aviary," Megan said.

Gemma inhaled the cool hospital air—so different from the air where she'd been imprisoned for months—and let her eyes close. "I was about to head back into the house when I saw... Hayley and Rodney. In a large cage next to the aviary. Rodney had her tied to a post. He'd taken all her clothes from her. He... was doing things to her. I screamed and ran. But whatever drug Rodney gave me earlier made me too woozy. I stumbled and fell. Rodney was there before I could even get to my feet. He dragged me and shoved me into the cage with Hayley. I untied her, and we tried to find a way out. But we couldn't get out. Two hours later, he came back. He made me take off my clothes... *everything*... and... he..."

Gemma shook her head, unable to continue, fixing her gaze furiously down at her lap, twisting the glass of water around and around.

"It's okay," came Megan's soothing voice. "I know it's difficult for you to tell us these things."

When she raised her head, she saw Megan exchange glances with the detectives.

What are they thinking? Do they think Hayley and I did a stupid thing in accepting a ride from Rodney? Should we have guessed that there was something evil about him?

"Gemma," said Detective McKay, "During the two-and-a-half months that you say you and Hayley were kept at Rodney's house, where exactly were you?"

"The cage," she answered. "In the shed. That's where he kept us. He called us his *little birdies*. We no longer had names."

"Just to be clear," said Detective McKay, "did he ever let either of you out?"

"Just... Hayley. She was his favourite. But he never let her out for long." Her mouth grew dry, and she finished the glass of water. "He kept us there and used us when it suited him. Until he decided it was time for us to die."

"And that's the night we picked you both up on the highway, isn't it?" said Detective McKay.

Gemma nodded.

"Can you tell us about that night?" asked the other detective —Kouros.

"Okay." Gemma felt nausea rise in her stomach, her fingers clenching into fists. "Rodney decided that his new birdies must die —*us*. He was tired of us. We complained too much. We were looking sickly. His drugs made us vomit and made us stink like a sewer. He said that when one of the birds in his aviary got sick, he'd take them out and bury them alive." Gemma heard Megan's low gasp. "He tied us up and gagged us and took us one by one to the back seat of his car." Her voice choked, and she paused.

"Can I ask something?" said Detective Kouros after a moment. "You were both in dresses the night we found you. *Clean dresses.* Apart from the blood. Where did those dresses come from?"

"The dresses?" Gemma stared at him for a moment, not understanding the question. Until she remembered. "He gave them to us. To die in. Mostly, he didn't let us have clothes." Why was it so important to the detective to ask about the clothes they were wearing? Did they even care about what had happened to her and Hayley?

He nodded. "Okay. Thank you. You can continue."

Gemma breathed deeply, feeling the air fill her lungs. She took another gulp of water then set it down on the tray. "He drove for a while then pulled the car off somewhere on the highway. He removed the gags and kissed us each goodbye."

"Did he say anything at that point?" asked the female detective, her gaze intent on Gemma's face.

"He said he was going to make us fly away now. And he pulled out his knife."

"And then?" asked Detective McKay.

The detectives were starting to fire questions at her—in a way that Megan hadn't. They really didn't care about her. They just wanted all the sordid details for their case file. Get the details, wrap it up. Onto the next rape and murder case. But she'd started the story, and she needed to finish it. *She had to do this.*

"He was going to kill me first," Gemma continued. "Because he said Hayley had been his *best birdie* and he was going to save her until last. He put the knife to my throat." Instinctively, her hand reached across her neck, protecting it. "He was telling me to get out of the car because he didn't want my blood messing up his car. I guess I got a bit frantic at that point. I acted like I was going to do what he said, but instead I swung my legs around and kicked his groin. He... he got angry. Like an animal. He reached into the car to grab me, but I was able to get hold of the knife. He lunged at me. And the knife got him in the neck. His blood was spurting out everywhere. All over Hayley and me."

Detective Kouros's eyes grew large, and he breathed out a whistle. "Jesus."

The other detective had a different reaction. She tilted her head, her eyes sharpening. As sharp as the blade that Rodney had come at her with. "You say you got the knife? But your wrists were tied?"

Gemma put her wrists together then rotated them in opposite directions, like a bird's wings outstretched. She made a grasping motion with her right hand. "Like this."

Detective McKay made an affirmative sound under her breath. "Thank you. That makes it clearer. What was the next thing that happened, after Rodney was stabbed?"

"He was shocked," Gemma answered. "He went away, swearing his head off. Maybe to check how bad the wound was. I don't know. I cut the string around Hayley's wrists with the knife, and then she cut mine off."

"You're doing well," said Megan in a tone that was as persuasive as it was gentle. Megan was on the same side as the detectives. This was just a job to them. None of them would ever know what it was like. To them, it would only ever just be a story.

Gemma still had her hands in the shape of a bird in flight. She wished she could fly out of there. Instead, she twisted her fingers around and threaded them together, locking them tight.

"Hayley opened her door, and we got out that way," Gemma said. She could picture Hayley's terrified face, darkly illuminated by the faint glow coming from the headlights. "Rodney must have heard the car door. He came out of nowhere. We ran off. He chased us onto the road. A tanker came over the hill. We thought we were saved. But then the guy crashed the tanker, and it went *boom*." She could taste the acrid smoke and feel the burning sting in her eyes. "The driver was able to crawl out. Rodney attacked him. They wrestled for a few minutes, and then Rodney ended up getting too close to the flames."

Closing her eyes, Gemma breathed easier now. That was the best part of the story. The part where Rodney got what he deserved.

The psychologist and detectives sat in silence for a time. They already knew parts of the story, but it was obvious to Gemma they hadn't heard all the things she'd told them right now. She wondered what Hayley had said.

Megan nodded at Gemma, her eyes wet. "Are you okay?"

A shudder passed through Gemma's body. "I... can't... talk anymore. I don't—"

Detective McKay held up the palm of her hand, a warm smile briefly altering her serious expression. "That's okay, Gemma. We can stop there with the details of that night. I just have a couple more questions on a different matter. I know that we already asked you these things, but we need to go over them again, just to be sure. Okay, so Hayley seems to think that you were both kept in a very cold place. Are you certain that you were never kept anywhere like that?"

Gemma shook her head. "I don't know what she means. It was hot in the cage. It only cooled down during the night, but it was never cold." She poured herself another drink of water from the jug on her bed stand. Rodney had never given them enough water—making them beg for the little he let them have each day. "Wait, he used to take Hayley away sometimes, into the house. Maybe he had an air-conditioned room in there. I don't know. He never took *me* into the house."

"Hmmm, okay," said Detective McKay. "My second question is, are you certain about the time frame? Hayley thinks you were only kept at Rodney's house for about a fortnight. But you told us that Rodney kept you and Hayley in the aviary cage for two-and-a-half months?"

"Yes. Give or take a few days," Gemma told her.

"Can I ask how you knew that?" she said.

"Every morning when I would see sunlight coming through the gaps of the shed roof, I'd count off another day," Gemma answered. "And I tried to keep track of the time—and days of the week—to see if there was some kind of pattern to when Rodney would come in and out. Because if he ever got sloppy and left the key somewhere we could reach it, I wanted to be ready. I wanted to know if he'd be out for the day and we could get away."

Detective McKay studied her face for a moment before speaking again. She had an unnerving habit of doing that. "Thank you for telling us those things. It helps us understand things a bit better. Well, we'll probably need to have one more chat before we reunite you with Hayley. You can see her sometime later today."

Gemma tipped the glass of water on its side as she replaced it on the tray, her fingers fumbling as she grabbed it and stood it straight again. "Sure, that would be nice."

Megan frowned. "Gemma? Is everything okay?"

Gemma swallowed, nodding. "Yeah. I'm okay." She didn't want to admit to them that she didn't want to see Hayley—*ever again*. She wouldn't tell that part of her story. Maybe Hayley did what she did just to get through. And if Hayley had forgotten everything, maybe that was a good thing for her sake. And for Gemma's sake. Because a Hayley who remembered everything could be dangerous.

5

BRONWEN

Bronwen chewed on her lip in the hospital cafeteria. The pressing question of the moment wasn't whether to go for the tuna or egg sandwich—neither of which appeared particularly appetising—but whether she could trust anything the two victims were telling her. The psych had managed to get more out of both of them than either her or Joe had, but their stories were still muddled, and she wasn't sure she could put it all down to concussion and pain killers; some of it had to be manipulation and lies. But why? Why would either of these girls lie? What did they have to gain?

Rodney White fit the profile down to his pants size. They'd found the chains and the ropes in his car and at his dirty little house in Bowman's Creek. Theoretically, this case should piece together perfectly, but these two girls were screwing everything up. She wasn't even sure the girls had been with Rodney for the summer. Gemma claimed they were while Hayley claimed they were living the dream on a mango farm. If the girls couldn't get their stories straight, she couldn't close this case and sleep at night. What if there was more to it? What if there was an accomplice out there? She had to discover the truth.

There was definitely something not right about either girl's story. Hayley was a fair-headed girl from England. How likely was it that a girl like that would have a bronzed tan after spending the summer kept in a cage by a psychopath? But at the same time, Hayley didn't have any of the telltale signs of manual labour—like calluses on her hands—and her recollections were hazy at best. The truth had to be somewhere in between Hayley's romantic summer on the farm, and Gemma's torturous months in captivity.

She grabbed the tuna, took a coke, and carried her tray to the table where Megan and Joe already sat. The doctors were with Hayley and Gemma, and they had an officer watching the rooms. It was time for a much-needed lunch break, but Bronwen knew they wouldn't be able to stop talking about the case.

"So, Hayley mentioned this 'cold place', which seemed a bit odd," Megan started the conversation, jumping right in, just as Bronwen had thought.

Bronwen sighed. "I'll be honest, I don't know what to make of the two stories. You've spent some time with the girls. What do you reckon?"

Megan rubbed her temples and stared at the coffee cup on the table. "It's not unusual for victims to remember things differently to how they really happened, due to the trauma of everything. And sometimes victims don't tell the whole story because they feel shame. I mean, sometimes rape victims won't talk about all of the things that are done to them because of that. Gemma was able to give us more detail about what happened at White's, even though she seemed to be holding back some details. Whereas Hayley still seems to be suffering with memory loss. It's possible that she's created this happy summer at the farm as a way of blocking out what really happened to her. She certainly seems the less traumatised of the two, which could be some sort of defence mechanism. And if that is the case, it could be possible that this memory of the cold place really is some sort of nightmare. Perhaps it's the buried trauma trying to force its way out of her subconscious."

That was an interesting take on the two stories. Bronwen hadn't thought of the idea of Hayley's idyllic mango farm being a way to psychologically cover up the shock of what she went through. "If it is because of the trauma, how long until Hayley starts to remember what really happened?" Bronwen asked, pulling the crust off her sandwich. It was soggy anyway.

"You can never tell with psychological issues," Megan replied. "Some people never repair the broken aspect of their mind."

"Shit," Bronwen said.

"We can't discount Hayley's story about the cold place completely, though, right?" Joe added. "Because there really isn't much else to go on." He shrugged.

Bronwen had to agree. Rodney, their main suspect, was dead. The trucker was in a coma. The two main witnesses had wildly varying stories. They had to jump on whatever information they could get, and right now that meant checking out the mango farm, and actually putting some thought into the *cold place*. What could she mean by *cold*?

"What about an air-conditioned room of some sort?" Bronwen said.

Megan chewed on her bottom lip. "That could work, but it would need to be powerful. She seemed to actually grow colder just thinking about this place. She said it got into her bones and made her freezing."

"Well, she's a Brit," Joe said. "Not used to an Australian summer. Going from the hot air outside into an air-conditioned room might be a shock."

"That's true," Megan admitted. "Was there anywhere at White's like this?"

Bronwen leaned back in her seat. She'd briefly been up to Rodney's place to check the place over for more victims, and it hadn't been some-where she'd want to visit twice. It certainly hadn't been air-conditioned. The place stank of stale odour, stifling and disgusting. The kind of smell you can taste. But had she missed something? "We'd have to check again."

"A hidden room, you reckon?" Joe added.

"Stranger things have happened," Bronwen admitted.

"I guess we're going back to White's then," Joe said.

"Sounds good to me," Bronwen replied, pushing away the half-finished sandwich and turning back to Megan. "We'll be back to the hospital later."

"What, now?" Joe complained. "I haven't finished my burger yet."

"Bring it with you." Bronwen shook her head and walked away from the table with her coke.

―――――

On the way to White's house of horrors, Bronwen watched with dismay as Joe dropped lettuce on the passenger seat of their unmarked police car, regretting her suggestion that he bring the burger with them. They'd been partners for three years, and during that time, she'd watched him drop bits out of any and every food item you could think of, from burgers and fries, to kebabs, to pastries, to ice cream; the man was a walking rubbish bin. It must take 3000 calories to fill him up. If he wasn't working out every hour not on duty, he'd be bursting out of his clothes.

White's place, on a small acreage about fifteen minutes out of Katherine, was dotted with junk, tree stumps, and broken, rusting vehicles.

Bronwen heard the raucous chatter of the birds before she even parked the car. So much for this being some sort of aviary—most of them were flapping around the place, completely free to roam wherever they felt like it. During the time it took her to get out of the car, one of them had already shit on the windscreen.

"Would you look at that?" she exclaimed gesturing at the white gloop spreading over the glass.

"The little bastard," Joe said. "Hey, is anyone looking after these birds? Reckon we ought to find them new homes?"

"Never mind the birds, what about my car?" But as Bronwen locked up, her anger faded. "We'll get one of the officers to find an animal shelter nearby."

As Bronwen strode towards the run-down shithole of a house White lived in, Joe took his last bite of burger and followed her. Forensics was just finishing up on the place, packing their equipment into a van and removing their white cover suits. She hoped they'd found enough evidence to clear this case up, but Bronwen had a sneaking suspicion that there was more going on than what happened to the two girls. This was only the surface, and the more they scratched at it, the more dirt they'd find. And besides, they had a duty to keep scratching. This case had so many holes it could go in any direction, and she couldn't stop wondering if White had an accomplice somewhere doing God knows what. If another girl out there ended up hurt because she hadn't followed through on a lead, she wasn't sure she could live with herself.

Bronwen nodded at the forensic team as she and Joe ducked beneath the police tape and made their way into the house. There was no need to go into the aviary again. Forensics had already been through, and there was little else in the outbuilding than bird shit. But if the house search proved fruitless, she would need to go back. Even the thought of it made her blood run cold. She remembered the sight of the cages, the smell of the place, the straw floor the girls slept on. She pulled on disposable gloves before touching anything. Even if forensics had finished for now, she didn't want to leave any prints here.

Stepping into the dim light after suffering the bright, dry sun outside made Bronwen disorientated as she gingerly made her way through the entryway. White had lived in filth. Every window was painted over to block out the sun, and every pane was covered in grime. There was no high-powered air-conditioning here. The air was stale and hot. She made her way through the corridor, trying to ignore the stacks of old porno magazines and boxes of crap. Every time she moved another cloud of dust caught the back of her throat, and the place smelled of must and rot.

"Where are we even going to start?" Joe asked. "And what are we looking for?"

"Well," Bronwen said, trying to think through what she knew so far. "We need air-conditioning units. We need to check the wall and roof cavities. Hey, Stevie, where you going, mate?"

The crime scene officer stood frozen in his white coveralls, between the cramped hall space and the door. "We're just finishing up here—"

"Yeah, yeah. So, what have you got for us, Stevie? Any hidden rooms? Bodies in the walls?"

He shifted from one foot to the other, clearly impatient to finish up his job and get out. Bronwen couldn't blame him for it. She wanted to get out, too, and she'd only just arrived. "Nothing like that."

"You checked *everywhere*?" Bronwen never quite trusted anyone else's ability to do the job. She knew it was annoying and that they all thought of her as a bit of a jobsworth, but she needed to know everything was aboveboard, nothing had been missed, and everyone had done everything they were supposed to, especially on a case like this. "Nothing in the walls? What about air-conditioning?"

"The unit in the living room doesn't work," he said. "We were fucking roasting in this place. Tried to turn it on and nothing happened. It's dusty too. I think it's been out of action for a while. As for hidden rooms... Well, we've checked for any hidden doors and so on. The cadaver dogs have been in. Nothing. Just junk."

Bronwen slowly nodded her head. "Cheers, Stevie. We're going to do one last sweep. Not that I don't trust you guys." She winked.

Stevie just rolled his eyes. "There'll be reports soon, you know. And we've bagged enough shit to fill the van."

"I'll take upstairs, you start with the lounge," Bronwen said to Joe. "If there aren't any hidden rooms or working air-conditioning units it could be that Rodney was hiring a place elsewhere. Not sure where or what, but..."

"You know, that girl is probably just in such a state that she's mixed up or... making stuff up. I dunno."

"Yeah," Bronwen admitted. "I know. But, look, what if there is another place out there? What if he's hurt other girls?"

Joe's eyes fell to the floor. "Yeah, yeah." Then he looked up and wagged his finger at Bronwen. "Don't you come breathing down my neck again. I can perform a search just as good as you."

Bronwen held up her hands. "Oh, I know, Kouros."

As Bronwen made her way up the stairs towards the bedrooms, it occurred to her that she'd always taken charge with Joe as her partner. He was a good detective. He always had a good read on people, and the man was an intimidating interrogator, but she was the one who organised them at crime scenes. She suddenly felt pretty good about this case and getting to the bottom of what the hell was going on.

The upstairs stank as badly as downstairs, forcing Bronwen to cover her nose as she passed the bathroom. Dead bodies didn't stink half as bad as Rodney White's uncleaned shitter. The place gave her the creeps like no other, and she'd been to countless murder scenes. This man was a whole new level of disgusting, and now it was her job to search through his filth.

Get on with it, Bron.

She started by the door of White's bedroom and searched systematically towards the bed. He had an old TV resting on a chest of drawers, layered with dust. It was so old an antenna poked out of the back and it had a built-in VHS tape player. She pressed the eject button and examined the tape inside. *Anal Sluts 3*. Nice.

She opened the top drawer to find it filled with dirty underpants and socks. Did the man ever clean anything? The next drawer was just as fruitless, filled with stained vests and shirts. The bottom drawer rattled with dozens of used batteries.

The room had nothing on the walls, no pictures or paintings. The wallpaper was faded, but the pattern had once shown tacky green palm trees. There was only one photo in the entire room, placed on the bedside table. The photo was old and grainy, but it showed a chubby toddler holding hands with a dead-eyed teenage girl. Was that White's mum? If it was, she could only have been eighteen, maybe even younger, and the kid was perhaps three years old judging on the size. She couldn't quite make out the facial features, so she didn't know for sure that it really was Rodney. Bronwen lifted the photograph and examined it. The young girl was skinny, with two thin chicken legs poking out of her dress.

She placed the picture down. What good did it do to start feeling sorry for the criminal?

Bronwen pried open the top drawer of the bedside table and tried not to focus on the sex toys and lube inside, instead she went straight to the back of the drawer where there were a few papers, White's passport, and Chapstick. She grabbed the papers and the passport first.

There was nothing unusual about White's passport, except that he was an ugly brute of a man with stubble and multiple chins. Looking at his photograph she found herself imagining what those two girls went through. Though she didn't want to, she couldn't stop her mind thinking about what it would be like to have White forcing himself on top of her, pawing at her body, tearing her clothes. She could smell him, putrid and sour, leftover ketchup on his face, mustard on his dirty vest, BO emanating from him like toxic gas.

Those poor girls.

The scraps of notepaper didn't appear to be anything interesting, but she bagged them anyway. There were a few scrawled phone numbers that could lead to something. Bronwen imagined that White had friends in low places.

Next, she flipped the mattress, tossing stale bedding and cushions onto the ground. Nothing. She placed her hands on her hips and tried to imagine she was Rodney. Where would a piece of shit like him keep a secret item? As she stood there, her gaze fell back on the photograph of Rodney's mother. She chuckled to herself. Could he be that much of a cliché?

She strode back to the table, grabbed the frame and slid the back out. Now this was interesting. Two keys taped to the cardboard, both similar to the kind that come with a padlock. And a note, faded and crumpled. When Bronwen laid it flat, she was absolutely sure that the writing had once been a full address.

Well, she thought, at least that part was easy.

6

BRONWEN

Bronwen and Joe continued on with their bird-shit marked car. They had another place to check out today.

It wasn't often that Bronwen was completely sure of someone's guilt, but this guy had been an obvious pervert. However, it was clear there was more to this case than just Rodney and his perversions, and Bronwen had decided to pay a visit to Tate Llewellyn's mango farm to see if the man recognised the girls.

If she could pinpoint a timeline, perhaps she could figure out what was going on.

They drove towards Deep Springs—a remote place about an hour north, close to the Kakadu National Park. From what Bronwen had discovered about Tate Llewellyn, he was the multimillionaire son of a guy who owned a major pharmaceutical company. When she asked around the town, most people reiterated the same thing—he offered lodgings, food, and a wage to backpackers willing to pick fruit on his farm. The farm was spread out over a hundred acres and was situated in a picturesque location between waterfalls and lush vegetation just outside Pine Creek, not far from the Kakadu National Park. It was paradise for travellers, and many passed through the farm from year to year.

As they approached Llewellyn's place, Joe let out a low whistle. "How much money does this guy have?"

"Millions. All family money though. Lucky bastard."

"I'm not jealous at all," Joe said, staring up at the three-storey house with a glass front.

"What do you mean? What about that sweet police pension we'll get in thirty years?"

Joe smirked. "Yeah, you're right. We're really winning at life."

Despite the jokes, Bronwen couldn't help but be impressed with the place. The house was stunning, reflecting the mango fields in its long windows. The building lay in the midst of the fields, with a myriad of outhouses and greenhouses around it. It was more like a luxury hotel than the residence of a farmer.

She pulled the car into a small carpark close to the glass building, leaving it under the shade of a tree. It seemed that Llewellyn must have a garage somewhere, because the carpark had only delivery vans and pickup trucks parked within the bays. You'd imagine that a man like Llewellyn would have at least a few expensive sports cars.

Bronwen pulled at the collar of her shirt as she slammed the car door shut. As always, she was on high alert, scanning the area for anomalies, danger, anything that stood out, but this place was unlike any other she'd been to. This kind of wealth was unusual everywhere, but it was especially alien to her, having grown up in a single-parent household with a mum who worked two jobs to make ends meet.

After Rodney's disgusting abode, the glass mansion was a stark contrast. It was one extreme to the next in this occupation.

"So, where do you reckon we find the boss around here?" Joe asked, sliding a pair of sunglasses onto his face. The gravel crunched under his hefty boots.

Bronwen looked around, searching for some sort of reception or at least someone who appeared in charge, but all she could see were young people carrying piles of mangoes through the fields, laughing, and a few others boxing up fruit ready to pack into the utes. There was a relaxed atmosphere about the place. It all seemed too wholesome to be a business. How was Llewellyn making money on this place? Maybe he was some sort of eccentric millionaire who wanted a hobby and this was it. Or maybe Bronwen didn't have much of a clue about farming.

There was a tattooed teenager with a deep tan, those Thai trousers that travellers always seemed to wear, and his long hair pulled up into a top knot, walking through the carpark carrying a box of mangoes.

"Hey," Bronwen called to him. "Where can I find Tate Llewellyn?"

"That greenhouse over there," he replied, adjusting the box to his left arm in order to point towards a glass greenhouse adjacent to the main house. There was an awful lot of glass on this farm.

"Thanks."

Bronwen and Joe made their way over to the greenhouse closest to the house and entered through the door into a fragrant room bursting with colour. It was the tallest of the greenhouses, with a whirring air-conditioning unit and narrow panes of glass letting the sun in above. Long tables ran the length of the building, each one filled with orchids of different colours. It was like walking through a rainbow, with the stunning flowers leaning over towards her. Bronwen had never been a flowers-and-chocolates kind of woman, but she couldn't help but appreciate the beauty of these.

In the centre of the greenhouse, a dark shadow amongst the rainbow of colours, was a man leaning over a purple flower holding a pair of secateurs. He was younger than Bronwen had imagined, no older than thirty-five, with jet black hair and a growth of designer stubble along his jaw. He wore a casual grey shirt tucked into chinos and seemed to be humming to himself.

Joe cleared his throat.

"Mr Llewellyn?" Bronwen raised her chin as she approached. "Detective Bronwen McKay and Detective Joe Kouros." She flashed her Northern Territory police badge. "We're here to ask you a few questions about two backpackers who worked at your farm a few months ago."

Tate didn't lift his head until Bronwen was half a step away from him. "Good afternoon, detectives. My apologies, I really must finish up here. It won't take a moment." He had long fingers, pianist's fingers, that caressed the luscious green leaves of the orchid plant. After hesitating for a moment, he clipped one of the leaves and stood back with one finger on his chin, examining his handiwork.

Bronwen watched him with interest, taking in his fluid motions and his intensely dark eyes. He was a pretty boy, there was no doubt about that—a man who would fit in well in Hollywood. He did not look like a farmer at all.

Eventually, he turned to Bronwen and offered his hand to shake. "I'm sorry if I seem rude. Orchids are tricky to maintain. I like to take my time; it seems to help."

"Of course. We appreciate you giving us your time." Bronwen smiled thinly. She'd seen these kinds of delay tactics before when a person was confronted with a police officer at their premises. Some tried so hard to act naturally that they either came across as obnoxious, or they went the other way and practically bowed at her feet. Llewellyn was clearly the obnoxious kind. She pulled two photographs from her pocket and handed them to him. "Do you recognise either of these girls?"

Llewellyn examined the pictures with a frown. "Yes, I do. Let me think." He pointed to Hayley. "She was English, wasn't she? Hayley was it?" He lifted his head and smiled, revealing perfect teeth. "We get a lot of young people who work on the farm for a few weeks and then leave so I don't always remember names." He slipped a hand into the pocket of his chinos and Bronwen made a note of the more relaxed pose. Perhaps he was getting used to their presence now. Or perhaps he really did care that much about trimming an orchid.

"That's all right," Bronwen said. "Whatever you remember is useful to us."

"The other girl was with her. Australian girl. Think she might have been from Sydney, but I'm not sure. I tend to chat to as many of the travellers as I can, but I don't run the day-to-day operations here. I have staff for that." His smile was apologetic, as though he felt embarrassed by his wealth. "I don't remember her name, though, I'm afraid."

"Do you remember how long they stayed here for?" Joe asked, leaning his hip against one of the tables. This didn't go unnoticed by Llewellyn, who frowned at Joe but didn't say anything. "Do you or a staff member keep a log of who works at the farm?"

"Yes," Llewellyn replied. "Speak to my assistant, Sophie. She'll give you all the details. The computer system records everyone working here."

"And how are the workers paid?" Bronwen asked.

"Mostly via a standard bank transfer, but for some, especially those travelling from unusual places, we pay cash or cheque."

Bronwen nodded and made a note in her book. There was a lot of opportunity for evading the system here. What if assistant Sophie was asked not to log a worker? What if those being paid cash gave a false ID? It'd be an easy place to hide if you didn't want to be found. She wondered how often Llewellyn's farm was checked out.

There were certainly plenty of air-conditioning units in this greenhouse, currently regulating a balmy temperature in the greenhouse, but certainly capable of chillier temperatures. An eccentric millionaire like Tate Llewellyn would have more than enough resources to create some sort of cold room. But searching the place would mean obtaining a warrant. Besides, it was a leap to think this man and this place was involved in what happened to the girls, especially as the girls had not indicated they were linked in anyway. She reined in her thoughts, keeping an open mind.

"Can I show you something?"

Bronwen lifted her eyes from the notebook to see that he was looking right at her with those disconcerting dark eyes. "Me?"

"Yes."

Perhaps it was Tate Llewellyn's arresting gaze, the heat of the greenhouse, a combination of the two, or the fact that the man didn't seem to blink, but for some reason, she felt her face flush. This was work, and Llewellyn had hardly suggested that the two of them should dance horizontally together, but the man was magnetic, and she couldn't help but respond to it. All of this was a strange new feeling for Bronwen, seeing as she didn't particularly like rich pretty boys. But she had to admit that the pretty boys she'd known at school —like Dom Kelly and those sweet blue eyes of his—didn't have a patch on farmer Brad Pitt here.

"Sure," she answered.

Ignoring Joe's eye roll, Bronwen followed Llewellyn further into the greenhouse until they reached a section that had been partitioned away from the rest of the plants. Llewellyn unzipped the plastic partition and opened a flap to allow them through. Bronwen stepped through, not entirely sure what to expect, before holding the plastic open for Joe to follow.

Once they were inside, she got a good look at why this particular section was separate from the rest of the greenhouse. There was just one flower here, growing inside a tray that was connected to various tubes. She saw that some of the tubes intermittently sprayed the plant with water. The flower was another orchid, but rather than being colourful, like the ones in the rest of the greenhouse, this one was almost completely devoid of colour. Its petals were velvety black, like the sleek fur of a panther, with its eye a pastel pink in the centre. She'd never seen a flower like it, and for the first time she understood exactly why other people loved giving and receiving flowers so much. She had never seen anything so beautiful.

"The rare black orchid, part of the *Bulbophyllum* genus. This one is native to Papua New Guinea and extremely difficult to grow. The conditions must be just right. There are times when I come here just to stare at it. To drink in its beauty." Llewellyn paused, staring at the orchid right at that moment. Then he pulled himself out of the spell. "I like to show visitors because chances are they've never seen a black orchid before."

"It's certainly very beautiful," Bronwen admitted.

"Yes. Yes, it is." He smiled, his eyes flitting between Bronwen and Joe. "Sophie is usually on the ground floor of the house. We have a couple of office rooms in there. She'll get you everything else you need."

Bronwen tensed. She didn't like the way Llewellyn was dismissing them, not the other way around. Somehow, though she couldn't pinpoint the exact moment, the power had shifted into Tate's hands. Rich people were slippery buggers to deal with.

"Thank you for your time," Bronwen said, stepping carefully back out of the plastic.

Llewellyn remained with the orchid.

"Well," Joe said as they made their way out of the greenhouse and towards the main building. "He's creepy."

"Hmm."

"Had you wrapped around his finger."

Bronwen turned sharply towards Joe. "What the hell are you on about?"

"Oh, come on. You were practically in a puddle on the floor talking to him. If you ask me, the guy's all suave and no trousers. Seems like a total weirdo. Who puts this much effort into flowers?"

Bronwen shook her head and pressed the buzzer on the main house. "All suave and no trousers? Where do you get these phrases from, Joe?"

But her partner just shrugged.

The receptionist, Sophie, confirmed that Hayley and Gemma had worked on the farm for a couple of weeks before leaving. There were pay slips for a couple of weeks but beyond that nothing. The girls hadn't given notice or any kind of resignation. Instead, they just hadn't turned up on the mango fields one day. Apparently, it was common for that kind of thing to happen, and they didn't usually think anything of it. Travellers were known for being flaky and spontaneous.

They tried asking Sophie a few more questions but didn't discover anything useful. Leaving the house, they walked under the burning sun back to where the greenhouses stood. Llewellyn was gone.

It seemed clear that the girls had only had a brief stay at the farm. But Bronwen wanted to be sure, so when she spotted the tattooed guy with the top knot, she retrieved her photographs from her pocket and approached him again.

"Excuse me, how long have you been working here?"

"Oh, six months or so," he said.

"Have you seen these girls here?" Bronwen handed him the photographs.

He leaned into the photograph and frowned. "I dunno, I recognise them, but..."

Bronwen examined him and realised his pupils were far more dilated than they should be. Top-knot guy was high.

"Hayley and Gemma," he said. "I know them, but I'm not sure how I know them, do you know what I mean?"

"Not really," Joe said.

Top-knot guy just shrugged. "Sorry, dudes. Gotta get back to it."

Bronwen looked at Joe and raised her eyebrows. "How is it possible to be so high you can't remember where you know someone from, but at the same time know their names?"

"Seemed weird," Joe admitted.

"I mean, people are never reliable when they're high, are they? But, even still." Bronwen watched top-knot guy pick up a crate of mangoes and walk towards a ute in the carpark. "Look. He's capable of packing fruit. He's not exactly drooling on the ground or incoherent. Why didn't he just say the two girls used to work at the farm?"

"Want to question him some more?" Joe asked. "Or some of the others?"

Bronwen turned back to the house to see Llewellyn watching them through the window on the second floor. He nodded once in recognition but didn't move from his position. While they'd been talking to Sophie, he must have gone up there. Did that mean something? Had he finished in the greenhouse anyway? Or had he wanted to watch them?

"I think if we linger, we might be overstaying our welcome," Bronwen said. "Probably best to check with the boss to see what we can get away with without a warrant."

"Yeah, probably best," Joe added. "These rich fellas always have connections."

Bronwen looked up at Llewellyn one more time before they made their way back to the car. Joe was right. Something did seem weird.

7

HAYLEY

The air was dark and dry. When Hayley breathed in, her throat burned and her lungs ached. She was weak, and her head throbbed. She felt like she couldn't move her arms and legs. There were no shoes on her feet, and her hip was sore pressed against the floor, but every time she tried to adjust her weight, she found it impossible to get comfortable. The restraints prevented her from moving very far anyway. She licked her dry lips and longed to be anywhere else. Even back in that bar in Sydney with skeevy Sam, or on the street in Thailand with David standing over her, his angry, disappointed eyes making her feel ashamed.

A small crack of light fell across her face as the door slowly opened. Her body reacted even before her mind did, as she huddled up as small as she could go.

It was no good. She saw his shape move through the door. He was here, and he was going to hurt her again.

"Hayley?"

Her eyes snapped open, wide and panicked. She winced at the bright hospital light above her head, surprised again to be plunged into brightness after spending so much time in the dark. Her throat was still raw from the smoke inhalation. For a moment, she'd imagined it was from the dry air in Rodney White's aviary.

"Would you like some water, Hayley?"

As Hayley's sore eyes adjusted to the brightness, she made out three figures: the psychologist from that morning and the two detectives. Megan, the psychologist, was the one who was talking. She nodded to Megan, wishing they would all disappear and leave her alone.

"Did you say my parents were coming? When are they getting here?" Hayley croaked. Her palms itched, and her insides squirmed. She didn't want to see anyone; she just wanted to be alone so she could try to piece together the flashes of memories she'd been having. There were times when the chill on her skin felt so real that she thought she was back in the cold place, but then she forced the memory away, knowing that it would only bring her pain to remember.

She wanted to be back on the farm, washing the mango sap from her hands, eating the sweet flesh when she got hungry, or messing around with Gemma and the others. She missed the kiss of the sun on her skin and the tickle of the grass on her ankles. But it alarmed her that even those memories were in fragments. Sure, she remembered the taste of the mangoes, waking up in the cabin with Gemma in the other bed, and Tate Llewellyn's smile... but that was it. It was broken. She was broken.

"I'm sorry, sweetheart, I didn't hear you." Megan turned back and handed Hayley a glass of water.

She drank it down greedily, forgetting that the doctors advised her to be careful not to gulp. She winced at the pain in her throat and placed the water on the small table. No, she certainly wasn't at the farm anymore. She was here instead, bruised, sore, and sick of the people in her room.

"When are my parents coming?" she asked again.

"Soon." The female detective spoke up. What was her name?

Briony? Bron... Bronwen. "They just landed in Darwin, and they're getting the next flight over to Katherine. You'll get to see them tomorrow." She smiled and nodded as though it would fix everything Hayley had been through. Hayley, however, knew that it would not.

Megan pulled the chair closer to the bed again and leaned forward, just as she had that morning. Hayley wasn't even sure how much time had passed since she'd last seen the psychologist. Was it late afternoon? Evening? The next day?

"I'm so sorry we woke you," Megan said, "but we needed to ask you a few more questions about the cold place you mentioned."

"I told you, it's just a bad dream." Perhaps if she told herself that enough it would be true.

"Were you dreaming about it before we came in?" The male police officer asked. She'd forgotten his name. "You seemed frightened when we walked in."

"No," Hayley said. "I was having a different... bad dream." All these questions made her head throb even harder. Sometimes it was as bad as being locked away in Rodney White's cage. No, she wouldn't think about it. She wouldn't think about what happened there next to that disgusting man's aviary. The sound of bird wings echoed through her mind, and she blocked it out. Sometimes she worried that if she did think about it, she'd never come back and nothing would be left of her.

"I'm sorry, Hayley," Megan said. "I know this is hard for you. The detectives are just here to listen so they can make the best case possible against Rodney White. You remember them, don't you? Detective McKay and Kouros. You spoke to them yesterday."

"I remember them," Hayley replied. "What does it matter about Rodney White? I thought he was dead."

"We still have to get all the facts," Detective McKay said gently. "White could have had an accomplice, or he could have hurt other girls. If he has hurt other girls, they're going to need our help. Everything you tell us brings us a step closer to piecing all the clues together and making sure the victims are found and cared for."

For the first time, the enormity of what had happened hit Hayley, and she realised that it wasn't just her and Gemma who had been hurt by White. He must have done it to other girls before. Her memory was still hazy, but she knew that they'd been chained up somewhere. That meant he was prepared. He'd practised. She closed her eyes and leaned against the hospital pillow. This was so much more messed up than anyone knew.

"What can you tell us about the cold place?" Detective McKay asked.

"I... I swear it isn't real. It *isn't real*."

"Hayley, do you recognise these keys?"

Hayley lifted her head from the pillow to see Detective Bronwen McKay produce a plastic bag with some old keys inside. She shook her head.

"What about this?" Bronwen proffered a small note with scrawled letters on it. The note was old, damaged, and only a few letters remained.

"I've never seen it before," Hayley said.

"Okay, this might be difficult for you to do after everything you've been through, but it's really important that you think as hard as you can," Megan said. "Do you remember anything else at all that might help us?"

"I don't know if I can... the concussion—"

"I know," Megan said. "But you've had flashes before. I really think that if you concentrate you can remember something. Will you try for us? For the other girls that Rodney may have hurt?"

Hayley nodded her head. Then she took a deep breath and closed her eyes.

Perhaps the doctors were wrong about her concussion. Maybe she could force her memories to the surface. She made herself go into that terrible dream where she'd felt the cold all over her body, and a chill swept over her arms and torso.

She could smell the cold, like blood mixed with ice, and feel it creeping up her neck, prickling the fine hairs there. Her breath came out in a cool vapour. She was frightened and freezing, and her hands trembled at her sides. Even though she was still in the hospital bed, part of her was afraid that she didn't know the way out or that the door was locked. She wasn't sure which it was; all she knew was that she was terrified she'd never get out of there alive.

The light was dim, but she stumbled forwards, needing to move to keep warm. That was when her eyes began to adjust to the dark and she realised there was something in the room with her.

"Hayley?" Megan leaned closer. "Are you all right?"

Her eyes opened, pulling her from the dark, cold room to the bright, warm hospital room. She lifted a shaking hand to rub her temples, trying to stem the throbbing pain that had taken up residence in her skull.

"Hayley?" Megan prompted in a gentle tone. The psychologist reached for Hayley's arm but seemed to think better of it, dropping her hand.

"It was like I was there." Hayley reached for the glass and gulped down a couple more mouthfuls of room-temperature water. When she was done, she gazed down at her forearms expecting to see goose pimples spread across her skin. But there was nothing.

"What happened?" Megan asked.

"It was a dim room, and I could barely see. No windows. It was cold, so cold. I didn't know if I could get out. I think I was afraid that someone had locked the door behind me. But I walked forward, and that was when I felt like there was something or someone in the room with me."

"Rodney White?" asked detective Kouros.

"I don't know. It was so still, like nothing was moving, not even the air. But I felt like I was being watched. And there was this smell, I think it might have been blood, but I don't know."

"What kind of room were you in, Hayley?" Detective McKay took out her notebook and jotted something down. "You say it might have smelled like blood? And with no windows? Hmmm, could it have been a freezer? A cold room? Like a type where they keep animal produce?"

"I think you're right. It was a freezer room. It was too cold to be anything else."

The three pairs of eyes staring at her made her feel ashamed that she couldn't remember more. Everything was a jumble inside her head, and she wished she could tell them what they wanted to hear.

"Where is the freezer room?" McKay asked.

"I... I don't know. When I have those... dreams, I always see a dirt track and... I can't remember." She paused and tried again. "I think there's some sort of barn there too."

"What do you remember about the barn? What colour is it?" Detective McKay was still scribbling in her notebook.

"It was just wood, with a sliding door. The cold place, the freezer room, had no windows, and I think the door had a padlock on it. I don't remember anything else. Can I go back to sleep now?"

"Soon, Hayley." Detective McKay smiled at her, though it wasn't a particularly warm or reassuring smile. "Can you tell us more about this mango farm you and Gemma stayed at?"

"Yeah," she said. "It was this place where you could work in return for lodgings. Lots of backpackers went there. Tate, the guy who runs it, grows mangoes mostly. He has a room just for orchids, they're the most beautiful flowers you've ever seen. He used to take me to see them every now and then. But mostly I worked with a group harvesting mangoes."

"It's a beautiful place. Joe and I took a drive up there today. We spoke to Sophie, Tate's assistant, do you remember her?"

Hayley nodded, excited to be thinking of Tate and his mango

fields rather than the cold place. "Yeah, I remember her. She sorted out all the financial stuff and organised the rooms."

"According to Sophie's records you stayed at Llewellyn Farm for a total of fifteen days."

"What?" Hayley's jaw dropped. "That's not right. We were there for months. Can you check again? There must be some sort of mistake."

"We can check again for you." Detective McKay smiled. "A lot of backpackers pass through the farm, lots of young people. I bet there's quite a bit of partying going on."

"Yeah, all the time. I can't remember everything right now. There was a campfire though. And drinking, I guess."

"Sounds like a Friday night at Joe's house," Detective McKay joked, flashing her partner a cheeky grin. "Did you see any drugs at the farm?"

Hayley felt the blood drain from her face. "Weed, I think. Look, it's still hazy after my head injury. Like I said, there are huge chunks of my memory that are just gone. I remember dancing, and I remember how sometimes people passed joints, and..." She trailed off, remembering how she occasionally took a joint to smoke. And... well, there was more she remembered too.

Detective McKay's jokey tone was gone. She remained stern-faced as she made notes in her little book. "Just weed?"

"Some pills," Hayley admitted.

"I know this is hard," Megan said. "But it really helps us if you're honest. You won't get in trouble for talking about the drugs at the farm."

Hayley glanced from Megan to Detective McKay and hoped the psychologist was right.

"Did you take any drugs, Hayley?" Detective McKay asked.

This was it. They wouldn't take her seriously now. She reluctantly nodded, knowing that they'd think she was not only a crazy girl with a head injury but a junkie too.

"I didn't take that many, I swear. Just a few joints and a few pills and only at night."

Megan reached across and squeezed her hand. "It's all right, Hayley."

But even with the best of intentions Megan could never know if it was going to be all right. What did she know?

"Okay, let's move on," Detective McKay said. "Tell me more about what you remember about your stay there."

"I... I remember working on the farm. I shared a room with Gemma." Hayley tried to sort through the fragments of memories in her mind. "The Chemist, umm, that was what we called Tate, showed me the orchids. He said he was working on some sort of perfume, and he had a laboratory." She was getting tired. Nothing was making sense anymore, and she was beginning to wonder what was real and what wasn't. One thing she could remember clearly was Tate. She remembered walking with him through a field of grass, and she remembered being happier than she'd ever been in her life.

She remembered the day he'd taken her into the greenhouse filled with stunning orchids in every colour imaginable. He'd placed a gentle hand on her waist, but she'd liked that. Everyone loved Tate, and why wouldn't they? He was a generous, thoughtful, gorgeous millionaire who wanted to make the world a better place. Even though there were lots of backpackers working on the farms, Tate still took the time to remember everyone's name. He often brought coffees to the fields and let people take long breaks to cool off in the natural waterfalls in the nearby Kakadu Park.

Gemma would come to bed telling Hayley all about how Tate had smiled at her, how he'd brought her an extra coffee, or complimented her. The two girls would lie there giggling about his dazzling smile and tanned arms. Some evenings they went camping with the other backpackers, and all the girls would gush about him over their beers and joints.

Did you see The Chemist in that V-neck T-shirt? Hot!

He brought me a pastry today. I'm officially his favourite.

But suddenly the memory soured, leaving Hayley with a strange sense of anxiety and shame. That anxiety was directed at Gemma, but Hayley couldn't remember why. Gemma had done something, she was sure of it. Gemma had upset her, and it had something to do with Tate.

"What is it, Hayley?" Megan asked, picking up on Hayley's change in expression.

But Hayley just shrugged. "I think I'm getting mixed up again. If you want to know more about Tate, go ask Gemma."

8

GEMMA

Three sets of footsteps shuffled in through the doorway. Gemma, sitting cross-legged on the floor and facing the wall, didn't turn her head. She was out of words, couldn't speak anymore. Megan was right. She'd told too much too soon. The things Rodney did to Hayley and her—

I'm inside Rodney's cage again, but this time, the cage is in my mind and I'm trapped there.

"Gemma..." Megan's hand came down on her shoulder. "You okay?"

She recoiled from the touch. "Please, I'd just like to be alone."

Megan's voice softened. "I'm sorry, but we really need to talk. Detectives Bronwen and Joe are here too. It's urgent."

The three of them remained standing behind her. It was obvious they weren't going away until they got whatever they came for.

"We just want to show you something," said Megan. "Two keys. We need to know if you've seen them before."

Why is Megan trying to force me to look at keys? Keys keep you locked up tight. Locked in the dark. Locked away where no one—

"Gemma, listen..." It was Detective Joe Kouros's voice this time.

"There have been other missing girls over the past months and years. We need to know if there are any girls that Mr White is—or was—keeping locked up somewhere."

Inclining her head, Gemma rested her forehead on her knees. She felt Megan's hand slip away from her shoulder and heard her softly sigh.

"If you won't talk to us," said Megan, "maybe you'll talk with Hayley? We're going to bring her in here, okay?"

An involuntary shiver rained down Gemma's back, and she stiffened. She knew no one would notice that. All her life, no one had noticed her pain. Her family wasn't even bothering to come and see her.

Someone stepped away. A moment later, the door swung open again.

"Hello, Gemma." The voice so small and uncertain. Hayley's voice.

Gemma edged around. Hayley barely resembled the girl she'd been when Gemma last saw her. Her blond hair was clean and falling in neat waves around her face—instead of caked with dirt and blood. Her expression was aloof—instead of crumpled in terror. The cuts that Rodney had inflicted were starting to heal over.

Fear began pumping through Gemma's body. She'd tried hard to block out what Hayley had done, and she'd felt safe—*almost*—with the police and guards around. But now that she was forced to face her, it was different.

Detective McKay brought two chairs over. "Please, sit. Both of you."

Reluctantly, Gemma rose and took the seat that was offered.

A nervous smile flickered across Hayley's face but didn't reach her pale, almost colourless eyes. "How are you?"

Keep it vague. Act like you remember nothing. "I'm not sure how I am. I'm not sure I even know who I am anymore. How about you?"

Hayley drew her lips in. "That's exactly how I am too. I don't even remember—"

"Don't you?" Gemma said sharply. Too sharply. She had to learn to control that. They'd forced her to see Hayley, and now she had to deal with it. She couldn't let Megan and the detectives know about Hayley, because Hayley was too good at playing innocent. She'd talk her way out of all accusations, and then she'd come after Gemma.

Hayley twisted her fingers together, her eyes darting away as she shook her head.

The room fell into silence. Gemma was reminded of the kind of thick, blanketing silence of a church after the priest asks his parishioners if any of them are without sin. Her mother had dragged her to the local church a few times when she was a kid. "Show me someone who never did anything wrong, and I'll show you a damned bold-faced liar," her mother used to say.

"Gemma." Bronwen stepped across and sat on the bed in between them. "Can you tell me about these?" She opened the palm of her hand out to display two small metal objects. The keys.

Gemma felt her throat pulling tight. She'd heard the jangle of keys clinking, clinking, *clinking* in Rodney's hand every day—for the first month after he'd locked them in the cage. After that, days could go by in which they didn't see him. In which they had no food. Just darkness and suffocating heat and the never-ending screech and caw of the birds in the cage next to theirs.

"They're Rodney's, right?" Gemma heard herself state. "Why do I have to see them again?"

"We just need to know what they're from," Bronwen told her. "They don't fit the cage in Rodney White's shed or anything else there that we can find. We found half an address or something along with the keys. A road that ends with the letters O N. That could describe a thousand roads between here and Darwin."

Gemma let herself focus on the keys. "I don't know. I don't know about that or the keys. Please, take them away from me."

"The cow skull," Hayley whispered to herself. "The cold place."

Bronwen turned her attention to Hayley, her eyes suddenly razor-sharp.

"The road to the freezer room—it's a dirt road. I remember a skull on the front gate," Hayley breathed. "A cow skull, with the biggest horns I've ever seen."

Bronwen raised her eyes to Detective Kouros momentarily before resting them on Hayley's face again. She leaned forward in guarded anticipation. "Tell us what else you remember..."

Hayley folded her arms in tight against her chest, shivering as if a chill wind had blown in through the room. Her eyes were distant before they closed. "Nothing. I can't..."

"Can you see a sign, Hayley?" Bronwen prompted. "A street sign? Or any kind of signs on the house—anything at all?"

Hayley exhaled slowly. "I... no." Her eyes snapped open, and she gaped at Gemma. "You... you took me there once. You opened the door to the cold place..."

Gemma was unable to look away, trapped in that gaze that was icy beneath the layer of confusion. "What are you saying? Hayley, don't do this. Don't—"

Megan and the detectives watched on with a new intent in their expressions, the air in the room suddenly seeming sharp, like it could cut you to pieces if you moved even just a fraction.

Gemma made herself stop. She couldn't tell the truth without telling everything. And if she told, maybe Hayley would be triggered to remember the terrible things she'd inflicted on Gemma. *Yes, there had been a freezer room.* God, she'd almost succeeded in pushing the memory of that place away. A place so terrible, it was almost easy to make herself believe that it wasn't real. It was better that no one ever knew about it. Because if people knew about it, then she'd have to admit to herself that it existed. And she'd have to remember the times that Hayley had forced Gemma into the freezer room. And worse, if Hayley suddenly remembered it all, that would put Gemma in direct danger. Through Rodney, Hayley had made connections with bad people—people who wouldn't think twice about murdering you. Even Hayley herself was capable of hurting Gemma. She'd already tried. Thank God that truck driver had crashed his tanker on the road that night. He'd stopped Rodney and Hayley from carrying out what they intended to do. Maybe she could still stop this—stop the detectives from looking for Hayley's cold place.

She swallowed, her throat as parched as old carpet left out in the sun. "You're remembering it wrong, Hayley. I was there, but I was forced to be there. I was forced to open that door."

A pucker formed on Hayley's brow. "*He* made you do that?"

"Yes," Gemma answered quickly. "Of course he did."

"So, the freezer room," said Detective McKay to Gemma, a quiet tone masking the urgency in her eyes. "You *do* know about it? Tell us where it is."

Gemma gathered her breath before she answered. "Yes, of course I know about it. No one asked me about it."

Detective McKay frowned. "We asked you about a cold place that Rodney took you to."

"I didn't understand. This was just a freezer room. Not somewhere that he kept us. I don't know what was in there. Dead kangaroos or livestock maybe. He always kept the lights off. He took us in there to scare us. He liked scaring us."

"Who is *he*?" asked McKay carefully. "Just to be certain."

"Rodney." The name felt like sawdust in Gemma's mouth, almost making her gag.

"Thank you," said McKay. "Gemma, can you tell us where to find this freezer room?"

She shook her head. "I—I can't tell you that. He always blindfolded us. He never let us see."

McKay shot a glance at Hayley.

Hayley gave a nod of confirmation. "Except once, when I pulled the blindfold off. That's when I saw the skull. And the farmhouse. There was a blue house, I think."

"Hmmm," said McKay. "Well, if we're talking about a skull with massive horns, that's a bull skull." She turned to Kouros. "Buffalo?"

"Right on the money." Detective Kouros began browsing the internet on his phone. "There's a couple of different types around here. Hayley, do you remember if the horns were curled or kind of straight?" Turning his phone around, he showed her a couple of buffalo pictures.

Hayley frowned in concentration. "Straight. Huge and straight. Scary."

"Good work," he said. "Okay, so that's a swamp buffalo. The water buffalo have curly horns." He sighed, eyeing the female detective. "We're still looking for a needle in a haystack. It's the Wild West around this area. Feral buffalo horns are plastered everywhere."

McKay bent her head, silent for a moment. When she spoke, her voice sounded tight with frustration. "If we put all the fuzzy bits together, do we have anything? Swamp buffalo, big property, farmhouse painted blue, freezer room, street name ending in *on*?"

Kouros kept flicking through screens on his phone. He gave a small yelp of victory. "We might have found it. A freezer room could mean a farm with a slaughterhouse on-site." He stood, turning the screen around to McKay. "Here's a property that used to farm swamp buffalo. They had facilities for slaughter. And the road checks out—it ends in *on*. Denton Road."

Detective McKay whistled. "That's it."

9

BRONWEN

Bronwen had never been fond of pessimistic people, but she couldn't control the creeping feeling of negativity as she drove the police car down half a mile of dirt track. The tyres kicked up clouds of red dust as she followed the narrow drive to the property.

In the passenger seat, Joe appeared completely oblivious to her worries as he tapped along to the music on the radio, driving Bronwen mad with his nails against the dashboard. Her mind continued to dwell on the words spoken to her by the superintendent at the station. *Finish this case up, McKay. We've got a media circus about to erupt, and the press want blood. Give them the fucking blood.*

There'd been enough blood recently, what with the increase in violent crimes spreading through the area. Superintendent Jones didn't want any more eyeballs on his department than there already were, which put her and Joe under pressure.

They already knew Rodney White was the perpetrator. He had to be. The girls had identified him, and forensics had found their DNA evidence all over Rodney's aviary and the disgusting cage he kept them in. So why did she feel like this case was going to turn out far more unpredictable than anyone else seemed to think? Why was this feeling of negativity weighing down on her, as though she was waiting for the kick in the teeth to come along and knock her over?

There was the strangeness at the mango farm too. Sure, everything seemed normal on the surface. Llewellyn's assistant Sophie was willing to cooperate, and the computer system matched up with Gemma's story. But why had that spaced-out kid made her so suspicious of the entire set up? Bronwen had met a drugged-out teenager a time or two, but she'd never known one high enough to forget meeting a couple of girls but sharp enough to know their names. It was certainly unusual. If only Llewellyn hadn't been watching them, they might have been able to poke around the farm some more. Perhaps if there was enough evidence of illegal drugs, they could get a warrant to search the place.

Never make assumptions, she thought. A good police officer had to know when to stand back and view the case as though from the outside. That was what she had to do today, which included forgetting all about Superintendent Jones and his warnings.

Could she do that? And more importantly, would she be allowed to do that? With the super breathing down her neck, the case could be pulled from her at any time.

"Looks like this is it," Bronwen noted as the property came into view. Her blood ran cold when she caught sight of the bull skull that was wired to the gate and when she realised that the farmhouse was blue, just like Hayley described.

Joe nodded, whistling softly.

Bronwen clenched her jaw as she regarded the scrapped trucks, old tyres, discarded petrol drums, and tethered dogs around the yard of the house. If these were the people they needed to deal with, she had to approach with caution. She knew the type, and she knew these isolated people were wary of police, preferring to live by their own laws.

After Joe had figured out the name of the road, they'd done some digging, and come up with a property owned by a woman called Wendy Williams.

The dogs growled at them as they exited the vehicle, stretching chains as they snapped their teeth. Bronwen pulled at her tight pony-tail before letting her fingers brush the holster of her standard issue firearm, reminding herself that she was the one in the position of power here.

Joe walked beside her as they sidestepped the remains of a bonfire to get to the front porch. Bronwen rapped on the door and waited. Inside, the house erupted into more barking.

"Sure this isn't a kennel?" Joe raised his eyebrows.

"More like a dump," Bronwen said quietly. Her boots were already covered in the red soil of the area.

Inside the house, she heard heavy footsteps followed by the sound of jangling keys and a female voice yelling at the dogs to be quiet. When the door was yanked open, she caught her first glimpse of the owner. The woman was short and wide. Her face was hard, lined, and dust-white. The only colour on her face came from the broken blood vessels around her nose.

"What do you want?" croaked the woman.

When the door opened a further inch, Bronwen noticed she had curly, grey hair that was red at the ends, a hair dye that had grown out months ago, and wore cheap polyester clothing covered in faded flowers. Her large breasts hung low beneath the dress.

"Good morning, ma'am. My name is Detective Bronwen McKay, and this is Detective Joe Kouros. We'd like to talk to you about Rodney White. Are you Mrs Wendy Williams?"

"I am," she answered.

"Can we come in for a few minutes?"

As the woman opened the door a little wider, one of the dogs tried to escape, which led to a scuffle of fur, a wagging tail, hoarse shouting, and a yelp.

"Rodney White, you say?" Mrs Williams narrowed her eyes at

Bronwen. "What about him?" She didn't offer to allow them into the house, which raised Bronwen's suspicion, but didn't surprise her.

"That's right. How do you know him?"

"Well, he rents from me," Wendy replied. "A few outbuildings out by the top field. My son used to live in the cabin up there until he passed five years ago. Got it all kitted out with internet and whatnot."

Bronwen took out her notebook and scribbled down her description of the outbuilding. "Was Rodney White living in the cabin?"

"Living?" She laughed. "I have no idea *what* he was doing in the damn thing. I barely saw the man. Oh, his truck would be parked out in the yard blocking me in every now and then, and he had a habit of waking the dogs up at all hours of the night with his coming and going, but whether he was living there or not, I couldn't tell you."

"You sure we can't come in for minute, ma'am?" Joe flashed her his most charming smile, the one he thought women over a certain age turned to melted butter for. "It's hot out here, and we'd kill for a glass of lemonade."

"Well, all right then," she said. "But you'll have to watch the dogs."

Joe turned his triumphant grin to Bronwen as Wendy waddled through the door into the kitchen. Bronwen only rolled her eyes as they stepped into the house, at the same time trying not to step on a paw or a tail. It was hard to count how many dogs there were, as none of them wanted to be still for even a second. The kitchen floor was lined with dog bowls. Even the counter was stacked with bags of dog food, one bag almost spilling out to eager dogs ready to pounce on a stray bit of kibble. Bronwen grimaced at the stench as they made their way through the kitchen into the living room.

"I'll get the lemonade," she said.

"Reckon she's lying about Rodney?" Joe whispered. "An isolated old farm like this sounds like a pretty good spot for raping women. But do you really think this old bird didn't hear anything?"

"She knows he was dodgy," Bronwen admitted. "But I don't think she knew anything about any attacks. She needed the money, so she kept her mouth shut and rolled over at night when Rodney's truck set off the dogs."

"Do you live here alone, Mrs Williams?" Joe asked, raising his voice over the sound of barking dogs and heavy feet shuffling around the kitchen.

"Yes, it's just me now," Wendy slowly entered the living room carrying a tray of lemonades. "My old man passed seven years ago now. Cancer. My son went the same way five years ago."

"This is a big property for a woman on her own," Bronwen said. "Do you have any help with the dogs?" Or the cleaning, she thought, though the answer to that was an obvious no.

Wendy shook her head as she passed around the lemonades. "That was one of the reasons why I rented out the place to Rodney. He was a tall guy, not too old for odd jobs. I thought he might help out around this place. But I hardly ever saw him."

"How long have you been renting the property to him?" Bronwen asked.

"About three years now," she said.

"And what about the other outbuildings?" She asked. "You mentioned that there were a few."

"Oh yes, well they're pretty close to the cabin so they came as part of the package seeing as I'm not using them. Rodney thought he might park a few cars in the old slaughterhouse."

Bronwen exchanged a glance with Joe. "Slaughterhouse?"

"Uh-huh."

"Is there a freezer room in or near the slaughterhouse?" Joe asked.

"Yes," said the woman. "Of course there is. Where else would we store the buffalo meat? This used to be a fully working farm, you know."

It certainly seemed they were at the right place. "And are you aware that Rodney White is dead?"

The woman's jaw dropped. "Dead? No. When did that happen?"

"About three days ago." Bronwen noted that Wendy's reaction appeared to be genuine. It didn't surprise her that the woman didn't read any local news.

"I guess that explains why he was late with the rent payment this month," she said. "Well, I suppose you'll be wanting to look over the place." She heaved her weight back on her feet, huffing and puffing with the effort. "I'd better find you the keys. I hope you're not wanting me to come with you. It's quite a walk, and my ankles aren't up to the strain."

"Mrs Williams, may I ask how you buy food, drink, and other supplies for the house?" Joe said.

"Online shopping of course," she said, frowning at him. "I'm not a complete idiot you know."

Bronwen couldn't help but smile at Joe's red face.

———

With Wendy's detailed instructions, Bronwen set off with Joe through the fields at the back of the farmhouse. Slowly, they made their way up another narrow track towards the old outbuildings. If this was indeed a place for Rodney White to commit terrible crimes, he couldn't have found a more isolated area. Bronwen thought of the 'cold place' described by Hayley and wondered what they might find here.

She had to admit, she hadn't been convinced by the girls' stories. Sometimes she wondered if it made any sense at all. Maybe they were both suffering some sort of hysteria. Maybe the trauma of what they'd been through had caused them to exaggerate everything. But the mention of this slaughterhouse had changed her opinion almost completely.

"You know, for the first time, I have absolutely no fucking idea what to expect," Joe said.

"Me neither," Bronwen replied.

Bronwen's hand brushed her gun instinctively at the sight of the outhouses, her senses on high alert. There was something about the atmosphere here that made her think of trouble. Maybe it was some sort of police officer's intuition, but the place had that feel to it. Beyond a five-bar gate was the small cabin Wendy had described, which seemed normal enough. A short distance away from the cabin was a large facility. The slaughterhouse.

Sucking in a deep breath, Bronwen opened the gate and walked through. As they approached the slaughterhouse, her heartbeat quickened.

"Let's try one of the keys then. See what's in this place." Bronwen ignored the keys Wendy had given them, and instead reached in her pocket for those retrieved from Rodney White's home. She hadn't checked whether the keys were the same, deciding to wait for the big surprise.

It was a padlock on a thick chain. Rodney must not have wanted anyone getting into this place. But why?

The first one fit.

"Here goes nothing," Bronwen said, pushing open the door.

It slid back with a shuddering, metallic scrape, revealing the silent machinery of the once-working farm. Though Bronwen liked to think she had a fairly strong stomach, even she flinched at the thought of the bellowing of dying animals that once must have sounded out from this place.

They made their way past the still conveyer belts and hooks, towards what appeared to be the freezer room at the back of the facility. It was the only part of the place that had a door, so it had to be it. On the outside of the room, next to the door, she noticed a display panel with a minus temperature displayed.

"This is it," she said, exhaling. As the door opened, the smell hit her at the back of her throat. They were in the dark, with only the light from the doorway to show them the way in.

"Something doesn't smell right," she said, as she retrieved the Glock from its holster.

"Not ripe enough for a body," Joe observed.

He was right. She didn't detect the stench of decomposition. But at the same time, they were in a freezer. Despite the chill, Bronwen felt a trickle of sweat work its way down her spine. "It's still cold in here. If there was a body, it wouldn't be ripe."

As she continued into the freezing cold room, her stomach twisted up. There was a set of short steps leading further down into the room. She took the steps at a steady pace, careful not to trip. At the bottom of the steps, Bronwen reached a second door with another padlock. She turned to Joe, and he nodded, still holding his handgun. Bronwen holstered her own weapon and retrieved Rodney White's second key. Her ears were filled with the incessant buzzing of the fans as she tried the key in the padlock. It unlocked.

She retrieved her Glock once again and opened the door, keeping her gun high. It was unlikely anyone was here, but she couldn't take any chances, and she didn't like the feel of the place.

As the door swung wide, the chill hit her with its full force.

The cold place.

Bronwen was only vaguely aware of Joe moving behind her, despite his heavy footfall, she could barely hear them. Down here the sound of the fan was loud, blocking almost everything else out. She was on high alert now, listening carefully.

"Make sure that door stays open," Bronwen called out, suddenly imagining the two of them trapped inside this place. Who knew they were here apart from the rather unreliable Mrs Williams? Had she told anyone at the station?

The place was pitch-black, so Bronwen groped in her belt for a torch, but just as she was removing it, Joe hit the light switch and the place lit up.

"Holy fuck," Joe exclaimed, taking the words out of Bronwen's mouth.

"We need forensics in here," Bronwen said, trying to stay calm.

But it was hard to stay calm as she looked at the sight of the room. The room was square, windowless, and suffocating. In the space around her, Bronwen counted a dozen bodies. It wasn't the sight of the bodies that disturbed her, it was the way they were arranged. Every single one had been placed on a chair, held in position by restraints. They sat with their hands on their laps, with their clouded eyes open. Staring at her.

10

HAYLEY

Hayley watched Dr Hibbett scribble something down on the clip-board, but she wasn't thinking about the doctor or whatever he was writing—she was thinking about Gemma. It was a couple of days since they'd both identified the keys as the ones that open the door to the cold place. What the police had found inside... she shuddered and tried to block it out.

Gemma had made things sound different to what Hayley remembered, not that she was sure about anything anymore. Her memories still refused to emerge from the fog in her brain, and names and faces got all mixed together.

Did Gemma go with her to the freezer? Or was it Rodney? Or was it someone else? She wasn't sure, but what she did know was that seeing Gemma had made her feel stressed and afraid. Why did Gemma make her feel afraid? She knew there was a memory deep down in her mind. She wished she could push her hand through her skull and pull it out.

She closed her eyes and imagined she was back at the farm with the sun on her skin. She felt calm and happy as long as she was back there. The cold place and Rodney White and everything else could be blocked out as long as she thought about the happiness she'd once felt.

"Your vitals are good," the doctor said, pulling Hayley from her thoughts. "But I'm still concerned about your memory loss. I think it's best that we keep you in for a little while longer."

"All right."

"Tomorrow we'll try out some cognitive tests. See if we can get the ball rolling."

"Fine."

Dr Hibbett placed the clipboard down at the end of the bed and crossed his arms. For the first time, Hayley really looked at him. He was young, mid-thirties, with a square jaw and green eyes. He was handsome, and that only made her feel even more uncomfortable, because now she could only think about what it would be like to have his hands on her skin and his mouth on hers, but all of that made her feel dirty. Why would she think of him like that so soon after what happened with Rodney? Was she sick and sadistic? Or just a slut?

"Don't you want to get better?"

"Not particularly," she said. It was true. Why would anyone want to remember the horrible things that had happened? Why should she have to relive everything that Rodney White did to her? Every day she fought this battle. Part of her desperately needed to know what had happened and why, but at the same time she was too afraid to remember.

And then there were those detectives and the psychologist forcing her to remember, making her feel guilty for not remembering. Making her want to help them. Every time they came into this room they helped her recollect yet another terrifying memory that her mind had blocked out. What else was lurking deep inside her mind?

"This must be very difficult for you. But I know if it was me, I wouldn't want that man to have taken anything more than he already had from me. Especially not my memories."

"He hasn't taken anything from me," Hayley snapped. "I'm still whole. I just don't want to remember." Her words may have sounded strong, but deep down she felt fragile, and she wasn't even sure the words were true. "Besides, I didn't ask for your opinion."

But what did it matter now anyway? The police had basically closed the case, Rodney was dead, the bodies from the freezer room had been found, and they were working on identifying them. She felt sick every time she thought about the bodies. Why didn't she remember them? All she could remember was the way that place had made her feel, and that was pure panic, like all her muscles were about to seize up.

"Your parents are going to be here soon," Dr Hibbett reminded her. "In less than twenty minutes in fact, depending on traffic. Are you looking forward to seeing them?"

But Hayley didn't answer because her skin was hot all over and she felt like a porcupine was prodding her arms and legs. No. *No. No. No. No.* She couldn't face them. Not now, not like this. A deep sense of shame rippled through her, and she balled up the bedding in her fists. Suddenly, a searing pain ripped across her skull.

"Hayley?"

She was vaguely aware of Dr Hibbett rushing towards her and his hands on her shoulders.

"Hayley, are you okay? Tell me where it hurts."

"Head," she mumbled.

"Have you hurt yourself?"

His fingers probed her skull. As his fingers touched her, she pulled herself away, her stomach roiling with nausea. Her muscles tensed at his touch, and that feeling of shame returned. Shame because a man had his hands on her and instead of being repulsed, she almost felt comforted.

He stepped away, and she tried to relax. When the pain was finally over, Hayley leaned back against the pillows and wiped away sweat with the back of her hand. The headache wasn't anything to do with the head injury she suffered—this was different. It came from stress.

"Can you describe the pain for me?" Dr Hibbett asked. A nurse had also rushed into the room ready to administer extra pain relief should it be needed.

"Sharp. Radiating over my skull," Hayley answered. "It doesn't last very long though."

"Have you ever felt pain like this before? Before the accident, I mean."

"Yes," she said. "I used to get bad headaches when I was at school." She hesitated, not wanting to relive those awful years. "I went to the doctor, but he told me they were stress related and to take ibuprofen. But they never worked. Sometimes I'd be in bed for hours at a time with the curtains drawn because sunlight hurt my eyes."

Dr Hibbett retrieved his clipboard and started writing again. "Did you notice any stiffness in your neck? Loss of vision? Visual phenomena, such as seeing shapes? Difficulty speaking or numbness?"

"None of the above. Don't worry, they checked the migraine checklist too. No, it was really bad tension headaches. Exam stress, that kind of thing. I guess I'm just *that* uptight." She gave a lopsided smile, feeling more and more like an idiot as Dr Hibbett assessed her with his eyes. "They tested me for everything—brain tumours, eye problems, the lot."

"Perhaps these headaches are your body's way of dealing with stressful or traumatic events. I'm sorry that we can't do much for them, but if your doctor in England had you tested for a physical cause, it sounds like it might be psychological. I would firmly suggest seeking help from a trained therapist." He raised his eyebrows to convey seriousness, no doubt used to receiving an eye roll whenever the word 'therapist' was thrown into a conversation.

"I will, thanks," Hayley replied.

As Dr Hibbett turned to leave, Hayley leaned forward in her bed and reached out as though to grab him. "Wait."

The doctor turned around with a neutral smile on his face. "Yes?"

"I don't want to see my parents yet."

"They've travelled a long way, Hayley."

There were voices in the hallway, distracting him. He kept glancing at the door. Her head hurt again. It was all too much, and she couldn't cope.

"My head still hurts," she said. Her hands flew up to her face, rubbing tears from her hot eyes before catching hold of her hair and tugging on it.

The door opened.

"Hayley?"

There was her mother, five foot six, her face made up with precision, and her hair volumized to perfection. There was her usual skirt suit in stylish tweed and a silk scarf around her neck. There was her dad, with his left hand in the pocket of his smart chinos, and a polo-neck shirt open at the collar. Both of them were tall as houses to her, and she couldn't bear them staring down at her.

"Hi," Hayley said quietly. She tugged on her hair again, without realising, and her mother reached out to take her hand in a firm grip.

"Hayley, stop that right now." Pamela Edwards knew how to raise her voice in a classy way. Hayley never heard her mother scream or shout, but she'd seen her raise her voice to command respect and fear. "What is this nonsense?"

"I... I can't see you today. I'm sorry." She forced herself to place her hands on her lap.

"What are you talking about, sweetheart?" Her father tried to place a hand on Hayley's cheek, but she turned her head away.

The look of hurt on her father's face made Hayley wince, but only for a moment. She thought about her headaches, and she thought about the day she'd run away from home to get away from them. From their schedules, and their private tutors, all the mounting university pressure. They'd expected so much of her, and she'd failed. Here she was, broken and dirty, a failure as always.

"Please. Make them leave," Hayley begged.

"But I thought you wanted them to come?" Dr Hibbett stared at her in surprise.

"I was wrong." Hayley pushed her blotchy face into the palms of her hands. "I was wrong." She rocked back and forth. "I was so wrong. So wrong."

Somewhere at the end of the room, Dr Hibbett said, "Perhaps it's best you wait outside for now."

11

MEGAN

Megan sat at the desk in her office, trying to avoid looking at the towering pile of folders. She'd put everything that she could put on hold aside, so that she could concentrate on the *freezer room* case.

The attention surrounding the case had been like an avalanche. Media from around the world had descended on Katherine. They were universally flustered to find a small town of friendly people in the middle of vast, empty plains—not some hotbed of murder.

The two girls were at the centre of it all. They had to know so many of the shocking details about the freezer room, but they were largely unable to tell anything. Megan fiercely wanted to protect them. But at the time, she knew the police had their job to do and they needed the girls to talk.

The problem was, the more she spoke with Gemma and Hayley, the more a divide was appearing—not only in their stories but between themselves. They were even blaming each other. What really happened in the months before they were picked up on the highway? Were they the victims that they seemed? Neither of the girls exhibited the classic signs of lying, but at the same time, there was something worryingly artificial in a few of the things they'd said.

She began a file on the girls, writing up a quick summary of what she knew so far. She always started a file on a client by jotting down what she thought intuitively—more of a mind map than anything else. The clinical analyses would come later.

Hayley: Suffering from a head injury and memory loss. Head injury was diagnosed as minor. Unable to give much of an account of what happened to her. Her mentions of the farm where she worked seem unrealistically glowing. Her hands and arms don't show the same kind of damage from mango sap that Gemma's show. Changes her story slightly under suggestion. Is she lying or just confused? Is she pretending that her memory loss is much worse than what it actually is?

Gemma: Was able to give an account of what happened to them both, but some details are hazy or missing. Her story about being locked away in a shed for months doesn't match with the girls' tans. Appears afraid of Hayley but won't say why. It's possible that Hayley chose or was forced to do things that hurt Gemma in some way. Gemma shows distinct signs of avoiding a traumatic memory in relation to the freezer room. Is she telling deliberate lies or shielding herself from further pain?

Opening her laptop, Megan tried looking up the girls on social media. She wanted a more rounded view of them, which was something she'd been unable to gain. So far, there'd been no one else to talk to who knew them.

Hayley was on Facebook. But there were scarcely any of the usual teenage-girl pictures—no images of her blowing *duckface* kisses with groups of girlfriends. Instead there were photos of her at expensive European resorts with her parents. There was one photo of her in a one-piece swimsuit and oversize sunglasses, lounging on a yacht in Sorrento, Italy. She looked bored.

Who could possibly be bored *there?* Megan would have died and gone to heaven to have gone somewhere like that when she was in her teens. But she had to admit that she had no idea what Hayley's life had been like. Things that looked good from the outside were sometimes rotten underneath.

One of the most recent images was of Hayley with her arms clasped around a young man. Megan guessed he was the guy who Hayley said had ditched her in Thailand. Her Facebook profile hadn't been updated for months. Megan peered at the man. He had the look she despised—rich and smug. Hayley was also on Instagram, but those photos were mostly of her pets—a dog and cat that were both white fluffy balls of fur.

She looked up Gemma next. Gemma proved much harder to find, but Megan eventually found some of her old accounts. She'd uploaded a few illustrations to art sites when she was a few years younger. There was one picture of her camping by a river with what looked like her father and brother—Gemma hugging a cattle dog.

Her phone buzzed. It was Bronwen, wanting to know if she could go and chat with Hayley's parents and fill them in on everything. They'd just been in to see Bronwen, but she hadn't had much time available to spend with them. Bronwen added that Hayley's reunion with her parents had been hairy.

Megan jumped at the chance. She put away the file she'd been working on and headed straight over to the hospital.

The hospital café was empty but for a few people. An elderly woman knitted in a corner. A youngish man in work overalls sat with a gaudy, cellophane-covered gift basket filled with teddy bears on the chair next to him. Megan guessed he'd just become a father. And there was an older couple sitting hunched together, anxiously stirring their cups of tea.

The couple had to be Hayley's parents. She could easily spot the mother-daughter resemblance.

Introducing herself, she joined them at their table and then proceeded to fill them in on what had been happening with their daughter over the past few days. They'd already heard the most sordid of the details in the news and from the British police officer who'd first contacted them.

"I'm at a complete loss," said Mrs Edwards, toying with a spoon with her manicured nails. "This isn't like Hayley at all."

"Tell me, what is Hayley like?" Megan held her in a direct gaze. "I've only known her in the aftermath of this awful thing. I'd like to help her, and to do that, I need to know more about her."

Mrs Edwards nodded. "She's a very driven, academic young girl with a bright future. Goodness, we have a whole room filled with awards she's won."

"What about her personally? Her character?" Megan asked.

"Well, she can lose focus at times, which is why we have to keep her on track." Mrs Edwards's chin dimpled as her mouth turned down. "Like this whole business about running off with that boy. I mean, she didn't have time for that. She was meant to be finishing her second year of university. But the two of them ran away together leaving us worried sick. We haven't heard from her for months and now she's here, in Australia. How did any of this happen?"

Mr Edwards sipped at his tea, his face screwing up into a bitter expression that Megan guessed wasn't caused by the tea. "This whole episode has been rather tawdry. From start to finish. I can't believe our girl got mixed up in it."

"It wasn't Hayley's fault that she was abducted by Rodney White," Megan hastened to say.

But his expression remained unchanged. "She was hitchhiking. *Hitchhiking!*"

Megan expected Mrs Edwards to admonish her husband, but she merely nodded at him. "It's like she just threw away everything we gave her."

Megan decided it was best to change the topic—as much for her own sake as anything because she felt anger swiftly rising inside herself. Maybe Hayley wasn't exaggerating about her parents after all. "So you didn't hear from Hayley after she started working at the mango farm?"

"No, she was very neglectful," Mr Edwards told her then frowned. "But come to think of it, I did hear a couple of things secondhand. I bumped into a friend of hers at the shops—Alice. Hayley and Alice were best of friends all through their schooling at Queen Margaret's, you see. Hayley told her she'd been picking mangoes with a terrific bunch of people. I can't imagine why a bunch of random backpackers were so terrific, but there you have it. Hayley was apparently worried that the mango season was ending in a couple of weeks and she didn't know what she was going to do after that. She should have just come home, that's what she should have done."

Megan's head tilted to the side instinctively. There was something in what he'd just said that'd struck a chord. What was it? *Mango season.* Yes, that was it. Due to Hayley's memory loss, she'd had a lot of trouble trying to gain solid time frames from her. But this could be a clue.

"Mr Edwards, do you know when Alice had that conversation with Hayley?" Megan asked.

His eyes had a distant sheen as he stared at her. "No, I'm afraid not. Is it important?"

"Would you excuse me for a moment?" Taking out her phone, Megan looked up *mango season, Llewellyn Farm, Northern Territory.* The results came back with *October to late-December.*

Megan rubbed the back of her neck, a spot that seemed to have been constantly damp and sweaty ever since the hot weather arrived. She tried to put things together. If Hayley had been worried about mango season ending in a couple of weeks, that meant she'd made the call to Alice at the start of December. And that meant she was still at the farm owned by Tate Llewellyn in December. Which meant she hadn't been in the shed at Rodney's house at that time. According to Gemma's timeline, the girls had arrived at Tate's farm in early October but had only been there for about two weeks before being abducted by Rodney. That didn't match up.

Did Hayley have a reason to lie to Alice, or was something else at play here? If Hayley was correct, that meant Gemma was lying. But Hayley's arms didn't show signs of having been fruit picking for almost three months. If Hayley hadn't been fruit picking and hadn't been trapped by Rodney for most of that time, where had she been and what exactly had she been doing?

"I have to go," Megan told the Edwardses. "Please give your daughter some time. I still can't say why she's had the reaction to you both that she has, but sometimes severe mental trauma can result in some very unexpected effects. We don't even know yet the extent of the trauma that she underwent. In time, her memory loss should improve and we'll know more."

It was more than they deserved to hear. But perhaps they were just highly stressed and being unusually critical of their daughter.

Excusing herself for a second time, she left them both in the café and headed out of the hospital.

The fiery midday heat began cooking her through her blouse as soon she stepped outside. Megan had grown up in the snowfields of Victoria, down at the other end of Australia. After more than a year, she still wasn't used to these temperatures.

She hiked up her car's air-conditioning onto full blast as she drove towards the police station. Katherine might only have a population of ten thousand or so people, but the actual area was large and sprawling—and the station was a good fifteen minutes away.

On the way, she debated with herself whether mentioning Hayley's phone call to Alice to the police was the right thing to do. She'd hate for the case to be taken in the wrong direction just because of one small factor.

She only made her final decision as she was parking her car outside the station. Sometimes, during her counselling sessions with clients, a tiny revelation could be the catalyst that changed everything.

The police should know.

12

MEGAN

Megan was lucky to catch Joe and Bronwen at the police station. They'd been at the site of the freezer room discovery at Denton Road all morning and had briefly stopped back in at the station, due to head out again. Right now, they were having a quick lunch in Bronwen's office.

"What's up, Meggie?" Joe bit off a full half of a long salad roll, his eyebrows shooting up. He was the only person in her life who ever called her *Meggie*.

"I just... could I have a minute?" she started.

Bronwen paused at her paperwork, taking a quick gulp of her bottled water. "Were the Edwardses okay? Pretty rough visit they had with Hayley." She shrugged.

Despite Joe and Bronwen's casual voices, a ragged tension showed in the lines of their faces. She couldn't imagine exactly what they'd been dealing with over the past two days.

"The Edwardses are confused." Megan closed the door behind her. "Look, I'm a little concerned about something. According to a friend of Hayley's—Alice—Hayley was stressing about the end of mango season coming up in two weeks' time. Mango season ends in late December, apparently. Which means Hayley was still at Llewellyn Farm."

"Oh yeah?" Bronwen scrawled a quick note inside the open folder on her desk.

"That's interesting." Joe pushed the rest of the roll into his mouth. "Our visit to the farm didn't turn up anything like that. The farm's office manager said that the girls were there and gone in the first two weeks of October."

"But then, how do we explain that conversation Hayley had with Alice?" Megan asked, scratching now at the bumpy skin beneath her ponytail, the heat outside having made her even itchier.

Joe balled up the paper from his bread roll and tossed it clear across the room into the bin. "Hayley's a bit scattered. Maybe she was scattered even before Rodney picked the girls up. Might explain the bust-up she had with her boyfriend too."

Megan felt herself crumple a little. Another thought came to her. "What about the girls' tans? You both said that doesn't fit with being kept in a dark place for two-and-a-half months, right?"

Bronwen shot her a look that was hard to decipher. "Well, sounds like they got taken out to the old buffalo range a few times. Maybe they were allowed to walk around out in the sun there."

"Like some sort of game before Rodney forced them to go into the freezer room? Boiling hot and then freezing cold?" Megan wondered if she was trying to convince herself.

"Maybe," said Bronwen. "What we've seen inside that freezer is about as strange as it gets."

Megan's stomach lurched. "You're going to have to brief me on that room. I think it's important for me to know what the girls actually saw in there."

Bronwen glanced at Joe before answering. "Picture a room with chairs in a circle. And bodies strapped to those chairs. Men and women. All aged in their late teens and very early twenties, except for one. All completely dressed. All frozen solid. We don't know if the victims underwent sexual assault or torture in the time leading up to their deaths, but so far, there's no sign of those things. We're unsure how they died. Forensic pathology is going to take quite a while due to the number of bodies and having to thaw those bodies out first."

"Hell." Megan felt herself recoiling from Bronwen's description, despite her matter-of-fact tone.

"A vision of hell for sure." Joe's eyes and voice had a sudden weight to them. "The important job now is the process of ID'ing the bodies and getting the pathology done. Then it'll be time to return them to their families to have proper funerals. That's the worst of it. Having to tell parents that their missing son or daughter is dead—and worse, that they ended up in the hands of a psycho."

"I'm guessing quite a few missing person cases are going to get solved." Megan gave a wry, sad sigh.

Joe nodded then exchanged a wary glance with Bronwen. "Ah, Meggie," he said in a low tone, "nothing's certain yet, but we should prepare you—there could be someone among the bodies that you knew. From our town."

"God. *Who?*" Megan asked. "One of my clients?"

"We can't say yet," Bronwen told her. "Until the IDs are done. Sorry." She shot Megan a quick, warm smile. "We wanted to let you know in case it gets out to the media before we have a chance to tell you. The super will decide when we start making statements about the identities. Also, if you want to know all the nitty-gritty of the whole case, we'll be doing a full media briefing in a few days. Up in Darwin."

"I'll be there." Megan nodded. She decided that the body in the freezer room must be one of her psychotherapy clients. She didn't have any family or close friends in town. Her mind strayed to which one it could be. Her clients were mainly teenage criminal offenders, and she often grew close to them.

Joe flexed his fingers—a habit of his after he'd eaten. "Bron and I are putting together a profile on White for the superintendent right now. At least people are going to be breathing easier knowing he got burned to a crisp."

"So, it's a definite that Rodney White is the perpetrator?" Megan said.

"Yup," Joe replied. "We've got pretty clear evidence so far. And it all points his way. With a big flashing neon sign."

Finishing her bottled water, Bronwen glanced out the window. "Shit, there's Jones already." She focused on Megan again. "I'll get Alice's contact information from Hayley's parents and follow up. Truth be told, things are a little strange out at Llewellyn's happy farm. A little *too* happy, maybe."

"Oh yeah?" Megan returned her gaze with interest.

"Yeah." Bronwen exhaled. "But nothing Joe and I can pin down."

Megan angled her head to watch as the superintendent headed into the building. "Okay. I'll wish you both luck."

She drove home to her little unit in Katherine. The first thing she did was to switch on the aircon. It was a blessing the place was so tiny. It cooled down fast. After peeling off her clothes, she stepped across the floorboards in her underwear. She grabbed a yogurt from the fridge and settled on the sofa. She was done for the day.

Afternoon TV was crap, but she needed something to focus on other than Rodney White and the identity of the freezer room body. She watched a game show for a while then succumbed to sleep. The heat, the intensity of everything, had drained her. She hadn't been sleeping well the whole week.

It was late when she woke again. Heading towards night. A thin black trail of ants marched to and from the discarded yogurt container on the floor.

Sleepily, she flicked through the messages on her phone. There were two photos of her sister's newborn baby. She smiled at the squashy little pink face. And a message from the guy she was dating, Jacob. Jacob worked as a microbiologist for the Northern Territory local government. The message was just a cute picture that Jacob had snapped of a koala and baby in a tree. He must have been working out in the field today. There was no text with the photo. She had no idea where things stood with Jacob. He would go radio silent for days at a time. But that was okay. She wasn't ready for anything serious yet.

In her early twenties, she'd had two boyfriends in a row who'd cheated on her and made her swear off men for years. And then she'd met Simon. Simon was the complete opposite of Jacob. He'd tried to push the relationship towards marriage within the first weeks and at the same time constantly getting defensive and telling her to quit analysing him. She hadn't even realised she'd been doing that. Maybe, at some point, she'd stopped enjoying his company and started analysing why he was in such a crazy race for commitment. Analysing people's behaviour came as second nature to her.

A sudden news broadcast on the TV took her attention away from her phone.

They'd identified the first of the bodies. The first five. Three men and two women.

Megan held her breath.

Photos began flashing up on the screen. The families must have already been informed and consented to the victims' names and images being given out.

Theo Kostas, Mike Reid, Clayton Durrell, Eleonora Pinto, Leah Halcombe.

She felt an invisible sucker punch to her chest at hearing the last name. Leah had been the senior clinical psychologist at the office where Megan worked.

How did Leah manage to become one of Rodney's victims? She'd mysteriously left town months ago, leaving only a quick note to say that she needed some time away for personal reasons. Megan had taken over the senior role at the office in Leah's absence.

Leah had been an intelligent, forthright sort of person who

cared about her clients. Her leaving had been a huge loss to the town. Megan knew that her husband had died and she'd lived alone. Had Leah been coerced into writing that note about needing time away?

The more Megan thought about her murder, the stranger it seemed.

Maybe the question wasn't *how* but *why*.

Why had Leah been targeted? A sixty-something psychologist didn't fit with the other victims. Had Rodney White been one of Leah's clients perhaps? If so, Megan didn't remember him among Leah's client files. But he could have been a client from before Megan started working at the practice.

Megan thought of something. Leah kept a set of personal files in her office. She had been a little secretive about them, closing them quickly on a number of occasions when Megan had entered the office. A couple of times, Megan had seen her locking them away in a metal cabinet that was labelled *office stationery*.

Did those files hold a clue? She hadn't thought to peer into those files before—Leah had obviously wanted to keep them private. And Megan had expected that she'd return soon. But now she knew that Leah was never coming back—she'd been murdered.

Shivers rained down Megan's arms.

It was past six at night. The office where Megan worked would have been locked up an hour ago by one of the two psychologists who she worked with.

After a quick shower, she dressed and ran down the stairwell to her car. A tropical storm was beginning to blow along the streets, palm trees bending to-and-fro, a cover of deep grey clouds making the world prematurely dark. Everything felt urgent and somehow much bigger than it had this morning. As if the horror of the freezer room wasn't yet over.

A dead frond dropped from a tall palm tree, skidding across her windshield as she parked her car outside the office. She hurried inside, tapping the numbers on the keypad that would stop the alarm from sounding.

She switched on the light inside the office that used to be Leah Halcombe's.

Megan rifled through the drawers, searching for the key to the locked stationery cupboard. She had to try several different keys until she found the right one. She flung open the door and pulled out the files. Carrying the pile to the desk, she sank into the swivel chair.

What the hell was she going to find inside these files? Was it going to be Rodney White practically confessing to the cold room murders? But surely Leah wouldn't have kept something like that secret?

She glanced up, looking out past the client waiting area to the dark street. She realised that she probably shouldn't be alone, doing this. If it ended up being that there was more than one cold room killer, then the evidence could be right here. And she was putting herself in danger. But she was here now, and she had the files in her hands. She felt compelled to see what she could find out.

Her heart began to hammer as she opened the top file.

The client's name was Clay Durrell.

Clay. *Clayton.* That was one of the names from the freezer room. *Oh God.*

She quickly read the summary on the first page. He'd been twenty years old. An American backpacker who'd lived in Texas and then Mexico. He had very little money, and Leah had been seeing Clay for free. He'd been suffering from strange delusions for months. *Dead people sitting on chairs in a circle. A man following him.*

He'd apparently been worried about the safety of several of the others that he knew—including Eoin, Dharma, Ellie and Hayley. He'd wanted to head back home but delayed going because he was trying to convince his girlfriend to go with him. So far, she'd refused. His girlfriend's name was Gemma.

Megan's skin chilled under her blouse.

Gemma. Hayley.

Dead people on chairs.

Being followed.

Clay hadn't been having delusions—the freezer room was real. He must have seen the freezer room at some point before he was killed.

Gemma hadn't mentioned having a boyfriend. Why hadn't Gemma mentioned Clay?

Bronwen and Joe needed this information *pronto*.

She tried to remember the other names from the TV news broadcast. The only other name she could remember was that of a dark-haired, pretty young woman named Eleonora. She'd been from Portugal, apparently. Was she the *Ellie* that Clay had mentioned?

A sharp ring emitted from her pocket, making her flinch and drop the files.

She answered her phone to find Bronwen on the other end of the line.

"Megan, have you been back to the hospital to see either Gemma or Hayley this afternoon?" Bronwen's voice carried a sharp, urgent note.

"Was I meant to?"

"No. We're trying to find out where they are. Because at the moment, they're both missing."

Megan's throat dried as she struggled to answer. The girls were gone? A horrible sensation began drumming in her chest. Someone had taken them—she was sure of it. Someone who wanted to hide the truth about the freezer room.

"The police officer didn't see anything?" Megan remembered there'd been one there watching on the days she'd spoken to the girls.

Bronwen sighed heavily. "He was taking a short break in the café. Anyway, he was just there to prevent the media or any other weirdos from getting to them. We didn't expect that the girls would leave."

"God," Megan replied. "We need to find them."

13

GEMMA

She stiffened with pain as she roused and woke fully.

Where—?

She was lying face down on a dirty floor, the smell of petrol and solvent saturating the air. Everything was dark. A small grille-covered window above let in the glow of street lights. Beneath her, the floor rattled and bumped. Greasy spanners and toolboxes clattered against walls so close she could reach out and touch them. Except she couldn't reach out—something held her tight.

I'm in someone's van. Tied up. God, how did I get here? I was in the hospital—and then?

Raw instinct took over. Jerking herself onto her back, she thrashed against the ropes that dug into her wrists and ankles.

The ropes refused to budge. A scream rose in her throat, but only a muffled sound reached her ears. It was only then she realised some kind of cloth had been wrapped around her mouth and tied at the back of her head. It didn't smell dirty like the rest of the van. Raising her hands together, she clawed at the cloth. It broke away. A hospital bandage.

Gemma rolled onto her side then to her knees. Raising her chin, she peered through the grille.

Two people sat in front. Both of them wearing caps that obscured their heads.

Who the hell are they, and where are they taking me? Should she demand that they tell her? She twisted her head, looking back at the van interior. *No*—better to plan an escape instead. These people had to stop sometime, didn't they? She'd find a handsaw that could file the ropes free and sneak out. Or if one of them opened the back of the van, she'd be ready and waiting with the sharpest tool she could find. The guy in the passenger seat looked small for a man. Whatever —she'd make them both pay. After what happened to her in the past, she was going to do whatever it took to remain free.

She froze as she met eyes with the smaller guy in the rear vision mirror.

He turned his head sharply. "It's okay, Gemma, I'm taking you back to the best place for you."

The *man* wasn't a man.

"Hayley." The name dropped leaden from Gemma's lips.

The larger person, at the wheel, twisted their head around then.

Eoin. It was Eoin from the farm, black hair sweeping above pale eyes.

After a slight swerve, Eoin righted the van, switching back to watching the road. "Only a few minutes to go. You've been asleep."

"What did you two do to me?" Gemma cried, her bravado dissolving.

"Just a little injection. Eoin brought it with him," Hayley told her. "You were pretty drowsy, but not too hard to get out of there when the guard went to get a bite to eat. Eoin helped me walk you out."

Gemma gasped. They must have come in while she was sleeping. "You fucking bitch."

"Oh, Gemma, this is for your own good," she said.

Gemma struggled against the ties again. "Turn the van around, take me anywhere else. *Anywhere*. Whose van is this anyway?"

She shrugged. "One of the vans from the farm. Eoin parked where no one was likely to see it."

"Please," Gemma begged Hayley. "You have to remember what happened to us there. We can't go back."

In response, Hayley fumbled with the radio, switching it on and turning it up full blast. It was an old song that Gemma only knew because her music teacher made the class learn it—*Here Comes the Sun* by The Beatles. Gemma could only just hear Hayley singing along above the music.

Through the grille, she caught sight of the view ahead. A plantation of medium-sized trees, all swaying in the breeze.

They were here.

The farm.

Ice-cold threads tugged and knotted in her chest.

Eoin turned off the music.

In stone-cold silence, they drove in through the open gates.

Crawling to the back of the van, Gemma kicked at the door. In desperation, she looked for a tool to arm herself with, but the van had nothing good. Just spanners and screwdrivers. And the toolboxes were all locked up.

She crawled back to the grille as Eoin parked the van. Someone was closing the gates.

Eoin jumped from the van, stretching.

"Hayley," Gemma urged. "Please listen to me. I know that we grew apart. You went one way. And I went the other. But we can fix this. Quick! Slide across into the driver's seat and start the engine. If you reverse and swing the car around now, we can get out. Slam through the gates. It's our last chance. Once you get out of the car, we're as good as dead."

"What are you talking about?" Hayley snapped.

"*Just do it*. We can go anywhere you like. Back to Sydney even.

Or Cairns. It's directly East. You'd like Cairns. It's on the ocean and it's all tropical and—"

"Gem, don't be silly. This is the only place either of us really felt safe. Rodney can never hurt us ever again. You'll be happy here, once you get used to it again."

Gemma tried to think fast. Maybe if Hayley recalled who she was before they came here, she'd realise what terrible danger they were in. It was risky, because memories were unpredictable. But they were out of time. She had to try.

"Try to remember," Gemma cried. "Quick. Remember back to when we looked out for each other. Before we ever came to the farm."

Hayley angled her head around to Gemma, a frown pulling at the centre of her forehead like a needle tugging at cotton. "I... can't think clearly..."

"You have to."

She shook her head. "Sorry. It's all fuzzy. I don't know why."

Gemma's wrists burned from pulling against the ties. "Hayley, please..."

Behind them came a sharp clanging sound as the farm's metal gates were shut tight.

PART II

THREE MONTHS EARLIER

14

HAYLEY

"I don't think you should be doing that."

Sam froze, with his meaty paw still underneath Gemma's shirt. He had his head turned towards Hayley, who had nipped back to ask Sam about an extra shift at the weekend. She hadn't expected to find her colleague pushed up against the wall of Sam's office, his mouth an inch away from her neck, and her face turned away, screwed up in disgust.

The moment hung in the air, and Hayley wished she hadn't opened her mouth at all. But she couldn't stand there and watch what was happening. Finally, Sam dropped his hand, and he broke out into a grin.

"Whoops! Red-handed," he said with a laugh. "Looks like she caught us, Gem. We'd better be more careful next time." He backed away from Gemma, who hurried away from him towards the door. "What did you want to talk about, Hannah?"

"It's Hayley," she said. "Erm, can I knock off early today? I have a doctor's appointment." There was no way she was going to sit in Sam's office with him after witnessing that. She watched as Gemma hurried past her to get out of the room.

"Sure. It's quiet enough. You go."

"Thanks," she said.

His attempts at making a joke out of the whole thing hadn't worked. She'd seen the look on Gemma's face. There was no way they were in a relationship, that man was trying to force himself on her. He was sexually assaulting her. She made her way out of Sam's office and through the bar to catch up with Gemma as she left.

"Hey, are you okay?"

When Gemma saw Hayley approaching, she slowed down slightly, but her expression was hard, as though she wanted to be left alone. There were tears in her eyes, but she sniffed and wiped them quickly away. "I'm fine. It was... it was nothing. But... thanks for what you did in there."

"You didn't look like you were enjoying that at all. He made all that stuff up about you two, didn't he?"

Gemma just nodded. They walked together along the street, passing cafés and fast food restaurants. It was boiling hot as always, and Hayley worried about the sun. She worried about everything. But then she lived in a dirty little room in a shared house with three students who didn't care about leaving dishes in the sink for weeks and who never knocked before entering a bathroom.

"We could go to the police, you know," Hayley suggested.

The shake of Gemma's head was barely noticeable. Instead, she said, "Want to go to the beach? I snuck a bottle of vodka out of the bar." She gestured to her bag. "That'll teach him for copping a feel."

It didn't seem like enough justice to Hayley, but at least it was something. Plus, she wasn't sure about leaving Gemma alone. "Okay, sure."

Gemma immediately seemed brighter, and she broke into a grin. They turned off at the end of the street and made their way down to Bondi Beach, passing the pavilion on the way. As usual it was crowded—Bondi's famous beach was a mecca for Sydneysiders and overseas backpackers alike. Today, it was a place for herself and Gemma to run away from Sam the sleaze.

It was a beautiful beach, but Hayley had never felt completely comfortable here. She couldn't strip down to a bikini and play volleyball like so many of the other girls she saw. They were all her age, but they seemed so much happier and together. She wasn't ashamed of her body, but she didn't have the same confidence as the others. Maybe that was the difference between English and Australian girls. Maybe it was the confidence. Or maybe it was the pale skin underneath her T-shirt that she was ashamed of.

As they reached the sand, she kicked off her flip-flops and let it flood in between her toes. At least she was here. At least she was living.

"You're from England, right?" Gemma flopped down onto the sand and reached into her bag for the drink.

"Yeah."

"Thought so. How long have you been here?"

Hayley tensed up. She hated talking about herself, and she hated thinking about what happened with David in Thailand. "A week."

"You're not on holiday though, are you? Are you travelling alone?" Gemma took a swig of the vodka, wiped her mouth and passed it to Hayley.

She took it and sipped from the bottle. "Yeah, I guess so."

Gemma's brow furrowed, and her eyes narrowed. Hayley squirmed against the sand, realising that she sounded crazy.

"Well, I guess I need a new job," Gemma said.

The change in subject was a relief for Hayley. She took another sip from the bottle and passed it back to Gemma. "I guess we both do."

They started to laugh. Gemma took a long swig, and then Hayley did the same. Before long the bottle went down to a quarter full as they talked about music—Gemma also loved live DJs more than listening to music at home. And they swapped travel stories—Hayley told Gemma about the beaches in Thailand and trekking through the jungle on an elephant. Hayley felt a warm glow spreading all over her body from the alcohol, but bringing up Thailand just reminded her of David.

"We ran out of money there," Hayley said. "And then he wanted... he wanted me to do something awful that I just wouldn't do." Her throat clogged up as unshed tears built behind her eyes. "When I said no to his... plan, if you can call it that, he threw my suitcase out on the street and called me worthless."

"The fucking arsehole," Gemma said, reaching across the space between them to rub Hayley's arm. "He's not worth those tears." With her other hand she brushed one away.

"And now I'm stuck," Hayley said. "I don't have enough money to fly home. I can't ask my parents after running away from Uni. I live in the most disgusting shared home you've ever seen. And now I guess I'll need a new job."

"That's my fault," Gemma said, shaking her head.

Hayley took another swig. "No, it fucking isn't. It's that... that... pig's fault."

Gemma laughed a little. "I'm liking angry Hayley." She took the bottle back and drank some more. "But seriously, I do owe you for what you did today."

There was dew on her eyelashes as she thought about the incident again. "We should just get out of here, you and me. Fuck Sam and his dingy little bar."

"I'll drink to that." Gemma raised the bottle in the air.

Hayley dug around in the depths of her bag and fished out a creased, crumpled piece of paper. "Hey, remember those leaflets someone left at the bar a week or so back? About fruit picking?" Already tipsy, she fumbled as she unfolded it. "Most of the farms on this list sound pretty basic. But what about this one on a mango farm? Sounds too good to be true. Hot springs and waterfalls. Kayaking.

Parties. Says it's near a place called Deep Springs, near Kakadu. Hmmm, can we catch a train there?"

Gemma snorted. "Kakadu? That's right up at the top end of Australia. And we're both out of cash. No can do."

With a huffing sigh, Hayley grabbed the bottle from Gemma and downed the rest of the vodka. "Shame, it sounded perfect. So, we're stuck."

Gemma's face was hazy now, and every time she shook out her hair, the edges of her face blurred. She was drunk.

Gemma frowned. "Maybe we *can* do it. I've got an idea. Everything is going to be okay."

"Well, if you say so," Hayley said with a grin. "Hey, look, the sun's setting."

An orange glow began to spread its way along the sea, broken only by deep red clouds. It was stunning. Hayley would never see anything like this stuck at her parents' house in York. And what would she get to see in Kakadu? She'd never kayaked before. She'd never swum beneath a waterfall.

"Why don't we just sleep on the beach?" Gemma said. "It's going to be a beautiful night."

———

Gemma said we'd be okay, Hayley thought. We're going to be just fine. Just fine. Just fine. It was her new mantra. But as they walked along the side of the Stuart Highway with the early summer sun beating down on her pale English skin, she wondered if she'd been foolish to throw all of her trust into this girl who she hardly knew, who had remained unnervingly quiet since they'd left Sydney.

They'd run out of cash pretty quickly, despite stealing as much as they dared from the till at Sam's. Hayley had nothing left after her abrupt departure from Thailand, and she was too ashamed to call her parents back in the UK and admit how destitute she really was. She was such a failure.

They'd taken a bus out of Sydney with tickets to a town en route to South Australia, but they'd stayed on way past their stop before the new change-of-shift bus driver realised they'd stayed on longer than the ticket they'd bought. Then they were turfed out on the side of the highway. Hayley was forced into her first experience of the Australian outback, terrified of snakes and spiders emerging from the dusty roadside.

"We'll hitch," Gemma had said. "Hey, don't look so scared. I do it all the time. It's perfectly safe." She'd wrapped an arm around Hayley's shoulders and squeezed her.

At least Gemma had rung ahead and told whoever runs the farm that they were on their way. Maybe when they finally got there, they'd have baths waiting for them. Or a meal. Or an air-conditioned room at the very least.

Hayley glanced dubiously at her sunburnt arm and frowned. "We're nearly out of sunscreen, and I'm not used to this heat." She didn't have a hat either, and they were short on water. For once she longed for the drizzly summers of York and hoped she wasn't too close to sunstroke.

That was three hours ago, and the girls had been walking without a break for almost all of that time. Every time a car or truck came past, Gemma stuck out her thumb and Hayley held her breath. She was no longer afraid of creepy drivers, now she just wanted to get out of the heat. The sun was the real danger. Her feet were dirty, they had no water left, and she'd thrown away the empty tube of sunscreen on the side of the road.

From the distance, Hayley heard the quiet rumble of a large truck and pushed her sweaty hair out of her face.

"Gemma." She gestured towards the truck, an enormous blue monstrosity with a steel grille.

They both stopped walking, and Hayley dropped her bag to the ground sticking out her thumb as far as it would go, but when the truck showed no sign of stopping, she began waving her arms and jumping up and down, pleading with her eyes for the driver to stop.

"Please," she whispered. "Please."

"Come on!" Gemma joined in the waving, her flip-flops slapping against the dusty tarmac.

When the truck started to slow, both girls cheered and hugged, before Hayley reached down and snatched her bag from where it rested next to her dirty legs. They wasted no time hurrying to the cab. Hayley was terrified that the driver would change their mind and drive off, leaving them at the mercy of the sun. Even Gemma had been struggling with the heat over the last few hours, and at least she was used to the Aussie climate.

"Where you girls heading?"

Hayley craned her neck up to the driver who had swung open the truck door. To her surprise, the driver was a woman, and she immediately felt a surge of relief. A woman was safer.

"Up to Katherine," Gemma replied.

"Well, I'm not going that far," said the trucker. "But I can take you as far as Port Augusta. You can get a Holiday Inn or something there, right? It's gonna take you a while to get as far as Katherine."

"That'd be great. Thanks," Gemma said.

But as Hayley followed Gemma into the truck, a sense of panic washed over her. This journey was going to take far longer than a day, and they had no money left. Where were they going to sleep?

The woman let out a low whistle. "You girls look like shit. What, have you been walking along here all day?"

Gemma nodded.

"No sunscreen? No hats?" she shook her head. "Ladies, really."

"We were in a hurry to get out of Sydney," Gemma explained. "And... well, we ran out of money."

Hayley gave Gemma a sharp look, wondering what she was playing at telling a stranger that they had no money. But perhaps that was the Brit in her, always reluctant to talk about money because it was *tacky*. It didn't make much difference if this person knew their circumstances.

"What are your names, girls?" the trucker asked.

"Gemma."

The trucker turned to Hayley, and she shrank back in her seat under the piercing gaze of her grey eyes. "Hayley."

"English?"

Hayley nodded.

"Well, I'm Eileen. I'm sixty-five years old. Too old for this job, it has to be said. And I don't think I've seen a sorrier pair of kids in all my life. I've got grandkiddies a few years shy of you two, and I wouldn't want to see them sunburnt and sweaty on the highway. There's water in the cooler and bananas too. Help yourselves."

Gemma reached across, eager to get to the water. Hayley noted the way her fingers trembled and helped her lift the lid from the cooler box.

"Thank you," Hayley said, holding those piercing grey eyes for a moment before Eileen turned back to the road. And she meant it. As her life had been spiralling out of control over the last few months, she held onto these small moments of kindness. First it was Gemma befriending her at the restaurant, and now it was eccentric Eileen in her truck, which she now realised was decorated with Oriental charms hanging from the rearview mirror, and a gold and red cat on the dashboard.

Eileen saw Hayley checking out the ornaments and said. "My dad was Chinese. He passed last year. It's funny, I never liked any of this crap when he was alive, but when I was clearing out his stuff with my sister, I found I couldn't let any of it go. It's a mystic knot. A good luck charm."

Hayley smiled, understanding how absence made the heart sentimental. It reminded her of how much she longed to go home but how when she was at home she couldn't wait to get away. There were times when she dialled home from her mobile and let her thumb hover over the call button, daring herself to press it. But then she thought of everything that had happened between her and her parents and the way she'd run off with David, and she couldn't do it.

"So why are you heading to Katherine with no money instead of going home to your families who probably miss you?" Eileen tapped the side of her steering wheel with her index finger and sighed heavily, as though exasperated with the girls.

"No home to go to," Gemma said. "No family."

Hayley turned to her friend in interest. She knew Gemma had a story, but she hadn't opened up yet. She felt a pang of guilt about her own situation.

"I need the money," Hayley said. "And there's a farm hiring up there. And I've always wanted to see Kakadu."

"What's this farm thing?" Eileen asked.

"A fruit farm," Gemma replied. "Mangoes, mostly."

"Well, I'm sure you don't need an old fart telling you to be careful, but I'm going to say it anyway, because someone needs to."

Hayley bit her lip and tried to stop her eyes from watering. She was tired, sore, and worn down from the last few days. Part of her wanted to snuggle into Eileen's bosom like a child and stay there. But Eileen was not her mother, and Hayley needed to grow up. This was the path she had chosen, and if she was going to survive it, she needed to be an adult. She had chosen to escape, to travel, to find who she really was, and it was experiences like backpacking through the Australian outback that would reveal her true character.

She pulled herself together, ate a banana, and drank a bottle of water. Then she settled into her seat, calmed by the thought that Eileen wasn't going to hurt them, and watched the arid landscape whoosh by through the truck window. An hour into their journey, Eileen cranked up the classic rock station and the three of them sang along to Bon Jovi and Journey, and every other cheesy classic that her friend Alice's dad used to listen to. Not *her* dad, though, because he preferred Bach to Bon Jovi and Puccini to Pink Floyd.

Hayley wasn't ready for the hotel outside Port Augusta. Part of her wanted to stay in that truck cab where she knew it was safe. She glanced at Gemma, whose expression was tense, her skin pulled tight, her lips turning white. They were both worrying about what they were going to do next. Camp out somewhere? With no tent? Hayley imagined waking up to find a snake on her chest, its jaws wide open and dripping with venom.

But then Eileen climbed out of the cab. "Come on, girls."

"What's going on?" Gemma asked.

For the first time, Hayley was concerned about Eileen's motives. Did the woman expect something in return for the lift? Her stomach rolled over with hungriness and worry. Was Eileen going to stay with them in the hotel?

"Well, you two obviously can't afford a room, and I'm not leaving you out here in the dark. I'll check you in on my card, and you get a bed and a place to clean up. I'd take you all the way to Katherine if I could, but I'd lose my job and I need it. Actually, I'd take you girls home, but I know you wouldn't want to go there, and I'm not about to force you."

"Eileen, that's..." Gemma hugged the trucker, and Hayley joined in.

"It's bad luck to make an old woman cry," Eileen said. "Now come on. Let's go spend my money."

———

They had a room, a small room, but nevertheless it was a room for them to freshen up. It was safe, warm, and relatively clean. They also had $200 in cash that Eileen gave to them before they left the carpark. They both decided to save most of the money and ate a meal of vending machine treats before making the most of the free breakfast. Then they took turns to shower, got into bed, and passed out.

Hayley woke up to see that Gemma's bed was empty, and for a moment she panicked, until she saw that Gemma had left her bag behind. She'd probably just gone for breakfast without her.

After coming out of the shower, Hayley realised that she was right. Gemma burst in carrying pastries in napkins, which she emptied out onto her bed.

"I'm guessing you like croissants, because, you know, who doesn't?"

Hayley grabbed a pastry and pulled it apart with her fingers. "Thanks."

"Good news," Gemma said, with wide eyes. "I've got us another lift. There's a bloke heading out towards Alice Springs. It's a long drive, but he needs to get there soon as apparently. Bet he won't even stop to sleep. We're just a couple of days away now."

"Sounds good," Hayley replied, wondering when the hitching would end. The good night's sleep hadn't eradicated her weariness, but they'd bought sunscreen from the small kiosk in the lobby of the motel, a couple of baseball caps, and bottles of water. "You didn't find another female trucker, did you?"

Gemma laughed. "I think Eileen was a one-off. But this guy seems nice. He was chatty, normal. I dunno, I guess it's hard to tell if someone is a rapist from a five-minute conversation." She let out a hollow laugh.

"What did you do? Hover around the breakfast buffet waiting to chat to truckers?"

"Pretty much," Gemma said. "Worked though."

Hayley couldn't argue with that.

The guy was called Bob. He was older than Eileen, covered in white hair from his bushy beard to the wiry little hairs that poked out of his nose. His cab was dusty, and there were photographs of his family on the dashboard, which made Hayley feel a little better.

They travelled quietly, snacking on the pastries from the breakfast buffet, staring out of the windows, watching the scenery flash by. After twelve hours of naps, polite conversation, and a few toilet breaks, Bob dropped them off on the road in Alice Springs in the dark.

Hayley squinted to see if there was anything around them, but all she could see was tarmac and dust. They set off walking again, sticking out thumbs every time a truck flew past, but no one stopped. Eventually, as the night crept in ever darker, and they hadn't eaten for hours, Gemma suggested they get off the highway and find a place to stay the night.

This time it was a hostel, and they had to share a room with a group of blond Swedish guys around their own age. They'd split the money up between them, and Hayley clung to her bag all night as she tried to sleep with the sight of a size-eleven foot dangling from the upper bunk. They seemed like nice enough lads, but Hayley barely slept, worrying about their safety all night. There were times, deep in the early hours of the morning, when all she could think about were the strangers around her.

Gemma lined up another lift at breakfast by finding a diner frequented by truckers. Hayley scarfed down bacon and eggs as Gemma worked her charms on the truckers. This time, she found a young man heading into Kakadu who was particularly enamoured with Gemma's bright smile. Hayley just hoped that Tim, their new driver, was honourable despite clearly fancying Gemma big-time.

And then she wondered why she was so suspicious? Had her experience with her ex-boyfriend completely erased her trust in others? Gemma didn't seem nearly as apprehensive about getting into the vehicle of a stranger. She chatted happily to Tim about nightclubs in Sydney as they got into the cab. And, as Hayley sat sullenly staring out of the window, Tim told Gemma all about the countries he'd visited before he had to get a job.

"That's why I'm doing this," he said with a laugh. "I spent all my cash."

"Same," Gemma replied. "That's why I'm hitching."

It was obvious to Hayley that this life suited Gemma, but it didn't suit her. She wasn't the same free spirit that Gemma was, and she wondered if she'd made a terrible mistake in agreeing to travel from one end of Australia to the other without money. And the farm probably wasn't the least bit like it said it was in that leaflet. She leaned back in the seat, closed her eyes, and tried not to cry.

Tim didn't just drop them off in Deep Springs—he stopped and asked locals for directions and drove them to the gates of the farm, going a few minutes out of his way to help them. There was more vegetation here, with palm trees and dry grass, but the roads were still just as dusty, and the sun continued to beat down. Gemma took his mobile number at the end of the journey and gave him a kiss on the cheek. Hayley even shook his hand, marvelling at the good fortune they'd found on their way here.

As she pulled her rucksack onto her shoulder, she took in the long drive that wound through the mango fields, with the last of the late evening sun reflecting on the brilliant yellow of the fruit on the trees. It was a beautiful sight, and a welcome one after the journey they'd had.

"I can't believe we're here," Hayley whispered. "Can you?"

Gemma hooked an arm in hers. "Nope."

"They all helped us," Hayley said. "Every last one of them helped us to get us here."

"You know, babe, the world isn't actually out to get you," Gemma said with a laugh. "I know you think it is. You underestimate people. There are some good folk out there."

"I guess I do." Hayley took a step towards the farm and felt convinced that her bad luck was about to change.

15

GEMMA

The first thing she noticed about the farm was the music. That was what always struck Gemma first about a place: the sound. A Lady Gaga song blazed from loudspeakers. Green trees were studded with golden mangoes, and throngs of young people buzzed about. The scene was saturated with the pink-red blush of the coming sunset.

It occurred to Gemma that maybe they kept the music pumped up loud to mask the fact that there was nothing but empty space in every visible direction around the farm. It was so... *isolated*.

Hayley didn't seem worried. She'd looked distinctly tense for the entire journey, but she was smiling now.

People stopped and gave them friendly waves as they entered, pointing for them to keep heading along the gravel road. A house—*a mansion*—stood in the distance, the sun sparking off the enormous expanses of glass that made up the entire front of it. The mansion seemed completely out of place here. A low-set farmhouse with a wide, generous porch would have fitted in a lot better.

A thin girl came running up to them, her thick waves of brown hair making her face small and almost childlike. At first, Gemma thought she was about sixteen, but when she spoke, she sounded a few years older than that. "Are you Gemma and Hayley?"

"That's us." Gemma raised a hand in greeting, unable to place the girl's accent.

"Tate sent me to greet you—Tate Llewellyn, the owner of this farm." She nodded firmly, dark eyes large and serious. A set of keys hung from a belt on her hip. "I'm sure you'll like it here. We're all a family, and..." She trailed off, as if distracted, then blinked. "Welcome, our home is your home. *Bem-vindo à nossa casa.*"

"That's Spanish, right?" Hayley smiled. "I've been to Spain with my parents a couple of times."

"Portuguese," answered the girl. "I'm from Portugal—right next to Spain. My name's Ellie. Short for Eleonora. I'll be your guide while you're here. You can come to me at any time with questions or suggestions you may have."

She greeted each of the girls with a quick, rigid hug, almost as an afterthought. As soon as the hugs were done, she dug her hands deep into the pockets of her shorts—like she didn't know quite what to do with them. "Tate told me you travelled all the way from Sydney. I'm so happy you made it here to us okay."

It didn't seem to Gemma that she was actually happy that they'd made it to the farm or happy in general.

"As you can see," Ellie continued, "we have the mango fields to the far left and right. We also grow pineapples and chocolate pudding fruit. In the greenhouses"—she pointed to a set of low buildings—"we grow many vegetables and varieties of mushrooms to feed the workers. We have chickens here for fresh eggs every day. To your immediate right, you'll see the accommodation. It can get quite hot sleeping at night, but just be sure to keep your windows open and check carefully that your insect screens have no holes in them."

"Sounds great." Hayley glanced at Gemma, a look of relief on her face. "Right? I think we struck gold. Once I get used to the hot nights, that is."

"Yeah. Looks good enough." Gemma cast a long look at Ellie. Who was this tiny, nervous girl that the farm's owner had instilled such trust in? And why hadn't he come to greet them himself?

Ellie seemed to shrink from Gemma's gaze. "I'm sure you'll both enjoy your stay here. There's just one restricted area. And that's the orchid glasshouse. You may only visit there if personally invited or instructed by Tate himself."

"What's so special about the orchids?" Hayley eyed Ellie with bemused interest.

"Tate likes his orchid glasshouse kept sterile," said Ellie stiffly. "He grows his own collection there. Perfume is distilled from the flowers. It's all experimental at this stage, and it hasn't been taken to market. Basically, it's no more than a hobby. But the equipment is all very expensive and quite fragile, and also Tate naturally doesn't want any contamination in the flower essence. So, I'm sure you can understand why that greenhouse is not part of the general operation of the farm."

"Got it." Hayley looked bored by the answer, glancing across at a group of shirtless guys who were hoeing at a patch of dirt, the sweat dripping from their brows caught by bright bandannas. She sharply turned away, her face flushed bright red.

"Well, you both look a little... dusty," said Ellie. "How about I send you off to the showers and then bring you to the food hall for dinner? We have dinner early here at the farm. The workers are always famished by this time of day."

"I'll show the girls to the showers, if ya like," boomed a voice behind them.

Gemma spun around.

A rangy-looking guy in a tie-dyed shirt and blond hair in a ponytail grinned widely at her, a hoe in his fist. "I'm Clay. I'm at the end of my shift, so I can give you girls a tour. Showers included."

Gemma returned his smile. His accent was broad with a slight drawl—American. She couldn't help but wish that he'd been chosen by Tate to be their guide instead.

"Now, Clay," Ellie admonished, "you know that's not true. It's not tools down for another half hour. I'll take the girls to the shower block."

Clay gave a lazy shrug. "See ya at dinner. Wait, what are your names?"

"They're Hayley and Gemma," Ellie answered before either of the girls could. "Okay, let's go."

Alongside Hayley, Gemma followed Ellie along the dirt road, past a well and a scattering of outbuildings. She walked at such a quick stride she was soon way ahead of them.

"She's so serious," Hayley whispered. "We'll have to ditch her if we want to have any fun here."

Gemma screwed up her face. "I don't like her." She looked quickly back over her shoulder to where Clay had been standing, but he was gone.

Ellie guided them to a long concrete block. Stands of bamboo and banana plants draped their fronds low over the ceilingless shower cubicles. The entire shower block was completely open to the sky, even the toilets.

Hayley gazed at the showers in horror. "They're not very private."

"You'll get used to them," Ellie told her. "Just limit your night-time showers, when the bats and flying foxes are out. They come hunting fruit and insects and might drop down on you by mistake. They carry viruses, and you don't want to get scratched by one of them."

Hayley shivered, crossing her arms over her chest. "Has that happened to anyone here?"

Ellie shook her head. "Not that I'm aware of. They're pretty easy to avoid. Also, you don't want to roam about anywhere at night because you never know when you might come across a spider or a snake in the plantations. The mouse spider is a pretty scary looking character, and the males are about at the moment looking for mates."

"Funny, none of this was mentioned in the job description," Gemma joked to Hayley under her breath.

If Ellie heard, she didn't react. Unlocking a cupboard inside the shower block, she took out two large towels. "Do either of you have phones with you?"

"I have mine, but Gemma lost hers back in Sydney," Hayley said.

"Oh," said Ellie, directing her gaze to Gemma. "Are you sure? It's just that we keep them in the big basket in the hall. Tate prefers it that way. Phones get in the way of peace and cohesion at the farm. People are welcome to call home, though, once a month after the meditation on Mondays. But people rarely seem to want to call home, once they're here. Shows how much of a family we are." Her voice stretched thin on her last words.

Then she reached her hand out towards Hayley, prompting Hayley to start rifling through her bag in a panic.

"You can frisk me if you think I'm smuggling my phone in," quipped Gemma.

A weird, embarrassed bark of a laugh burst from Ellie's throat. "I'll believe you." She took Hayley's phone before handing them the towels. "Here you go. I'll wait while you shower." She locked the cupboard again and returned the keys to a hook on her belt.

Gemma and Hayley exchanged glances while they chose their cubicles. It seemed like a scene from a prison. The shower cubicles didn't even have doors or curtains for privacy.

"Are you going to watch us *shower*?" Gemma demanded.

Ellie blushed. "Gosh, no. I'm sorry." She stepped outside, keys jangling on her hip.

"She's kind of dorky, isn't she?" Hayley disappeared inside a cubicle.

"Times one thousand," Gemma agreed.

Forgetting the talk of bats and spiders and the restricted orchid greenhouse, Gemma sloughed off her dress and underwear. Naked, she stepped under the water. She soon realised that she didn't need to turn the hot water on—the water was warm enough without heating it. Above, through the bamboo leaves, she could see the first stars in a brassy blue sky that was tinged with sunset colours. Not long now to twilight.

Closing her eyes, she luxuriated in the tingly feel of the water running over her body. Washing everything away.

She dressed in clean underwear, shorts, and a halter top. Tugging her fingers through her wet hair, she wondered if she'd see Clay at dinner. Grabbing her backpack again, she rummaged through until she found her tiny makeup case and applied a light layer of lip gloss, tinted moisturiser, and eye pencil. Those were the only makeup items she owned.

Across from her, Hayley pulled on a sundress, her back and shoulders red and sunburned through the crisscrossing straps. She ran a comb through her fair hair and then twisted it up into a loose knot, leaving long tendrils to fall free around her face. Gemma noticed it was a style she wore a lot—it made her seem somehow delicate.

"I'm starving." Hayley applied lip gloss, smacking her lips together.

"Me too. I wonder what's for dinner?"

"Mango stew?"

Gemma laughed as she buckled her sandals.

Ellie was waiting patiently outside. "Feeling better, girls? Come on, I'll take you to your accommodation, and you can offload your bags. Then I'll have to take you to the office, where Sophie can sign you onto our books. Have to make everything official and explain the pay and workplace conditions. Next, I'll show you the areas you'll be working in tomorrow and where the tools are to be found. After that, we'll head to the food hall, okay?"

Hayley obediently trekked after Ellie like a lost child. Gemma took her time, studying the house as they entered the ground floor and then into a large office. The only person in there—a blond woman of about twenty-five—swivelled around on her chair. She introduced herself as Sophie.

Sophie greeted Gemma and Hayley with businesslike hand-shakes and a rundown of their working day schedules. She had them sign a register and took their banking details.

"Thanks for taking us on at such short notice," said Hayley.

"Oh, it's not set in stone yet," Sophie replied coolly. "But if every-thing works out during your trial period, we'll offer you a stay of three months. Which is the entire mango season."

"I hope we work out then." Gemma meant it as a little joke, but it came out awkward.

Sophie cast her a sharp look. Everything about Sophie looked kind of sharp. Her pinched features, the angled cut of her hair, the icy-blue eyes that gazed out from beneath her straight fringe.

"Come on," said Ellie, ushering them out. "Time to eat. I bet you're hungry."

Ellie guided them out of the house and across to the food hall. Other backpackers were already streaming inside, all wet-haired and fresh from their showers. Scents of soap and shampoo mingled with the cooking smells coming from the kitchen. Everyone seemed inter-ested in Gemma and Hayley, each one asking the same questions. *Where are you girls from, and how long are you planning on staying?*

Large metal bain-marie were set up on a table near the kitchen, filled with vegetable lasagne and a variety of salads. It seemed that a group of farm workers had made the meal. People filed across to fill their plates.

Someone bumped her arm. "Meet you after dinner—near the well?" Clay flashed a smile at her.

She turned her head to where Hayley was ladling salad into her bowl. "Do you have a friend to bring along? I can't leave Hayley alone on her first night."

"Sure thing. A pretty girl will always have guys wanting to meet her."

"Just... pick someone nice."

He chuckled.

"So, where's the bigwig?" Gemma asked. "The dude who runs this whole shebang?"

"The Chemist? Up in his ivory tower, I think."

"The Chemist?"

"Yeah, that's what my buddy Eoin and I call him. He doesn't like you to call him that though—so don't."

"Okay. Doesn't he have dinner with the workers?"

"Not usually. You'll probably see him about tomorrow."

Gemma caught sight of Ellie staring hard in her direction. She couldn't quite put a finger on Ellie's expression—was she anxious or angry?

"Are you and Ellie, um..." Gemma started. "I mean, have you and Ellie ever been together?"

"Me and Ell? No way. She's as uptight as they come."

"Oh yeah? Any reason why she's like that?"

"No idea. She's always snooping around and checking up on what everyone's doing. Hard to sneak a snooze under a shady tree when she's around." His right eye crinkled in a wink.

Ellie stayed close to Gemma and Hayley during dinner, and she even insisted upon walking them to the activity lounge afterwards. "You can play cards or read or just hang out here. Go and meet some of the crew. I have some things I need to do right now, so I'm sorry to say I can't stay with you." She paused. "But don't go wandering off. Everyone needs to be back in their cabins by ten. And that's strict."

Gemma yawned. "I'm pretty tired already."

"Well, you're welcome to go and sleep right now if you want. Early to bed, early to rise." Her voice ended on a high, upward inflection as she gave an awkward smile. She was a strange mix of stern and nervous.

"Are you really going to bed now?" said Hayley quietly as Ellie walked quickly away.

Gemma shook her head. "Uh, nope. Just wanted to get her off our backs for a minute. C'mon, let's head for a little walk."

"Out there? With the snakes and spiders? No thanks."

"Just as far as the well." Gemma started walking before Hayley could ask any questions.

Clay was waiting there with another guy.

Hayley shot Gemma a wry look when she spotted the men. "Okay, so we're getting to know a couple of the other backpackers? You planned this, didn't you?"

"Yeah," Gemma admitted sheepishly.

The heavy scent of pot carried itself through the sultry air.

Clay passed Gemma a joint as the girls stopped at the well. "This is Eoin. He's Irish, so no Irish jokes, okay, girls? Unless you can't control yourselves. Then it's okay."

Hayley's cheeks dimpled. "My grandmother's Irish."

"You just went from pretty to perfect," Eoin told her, flicking back the mess of dark hair that brushed his shoulders. Even in this darkness, Gemma could tell that his eyes were a vivid colour.

Gemma inhaled the joint and then passed it to Hayley. Hayley did the same and passed it onto Eoin, with a slightly shy inward curl of her shoulders.

"What do you think of the farm so far?" Eoin asked in his Irish brogue, emphasising each R.

"It's amazing," Hayley breathed, her eyes bright despite the long day they'd had. "I mean, kind of scary with the critters and everything. But apart from that, it looks like fun."

"And what do you think of *me*, Hayleee?" Eoin raised his eyebrows suggestively, drawing out her name on his tongue. "I'm the icing on the cake, no?"

"You're not bad, Owwww-en," Hayley answered, giggling,

drawing out his name in the same manner. It seemed to Gemma that the single puff of pot had already affected her.

Gemma raised her eyes to the distant glass frontage of the mansion. A tall figure slowly walked up the flights of stairs that were clearly visible through the plate glass.

"What about you, Gemma?" Clay prompted. "What do you think of the farm?"

She snapped her head around to him. "Oh, uh... I'm not sure yet. We've only been here three hours."

Clay tilted his head, frowning deeply. "It's great here. What's not to like?"

She laughed nervously. "Ask me again tomorrow, once I've had more of a chance to look around. And once I've had a chance to talk with *The Chemist*. I'm not exactly impressed that he didn't come to meet us himself."

Eoin laughed derisively at her answer, handing the joint back to Clay.

Clay sucked hard on the tiny nub of joint between his thumb and forefinger before blowing a puff of smoke high into the air and tossing the nub to the ground. He seemed vaguely annoyed.

"Who—?" Hayley started.

"Apparently that's Tate Llewellyn," Gemma cut in. "That's what Clay and Eoin call him." An uneasy feeling crawled down her back, like unseen fingertips. The people at the farm were a bit odd. She couldn't be sure yet whether coming here was a good idea or not. But they were here now, and all she could do was to make the best of it.

16

HAYLEY

She hadn't slept well. The weed she'd smoked with Eoin and Clay had made her paranoid, and it didn't help that in the middle of the night she'd crept onto the communal computer and Googled what mouse spiders looked like. While she was there, she'd decided to try to log onto Facebook to see what her friends were up to. Were they missing her? Had any of them tried to message her?

But when she'd tried to load the site, it was blocked. She tried Gmail, Twitter, Instagram, Hotmail... all blocked. Ellie wasn't messing around about outside contact. It was worrying, but at the same time it did make sense to block everything out while she was here.

After shutting down the computer, she'd tiptoed back to bed staring at the ground beneath her feet, convinced that the enormous spider was going to leap out into her path. Then she'd checked the duvet and under her bed before settling down to sleep. But the damn spider worked its way into her nightmares. Gemma, now with eight legs, pounced on her bed in her dreams, and she'd woken with a start.

Why was Gemma the spider? Maybe it was because she'd sprung that whole double-date thing on her without asking. It was their first night in a new place, and all Hayley had wanted to do was curl up in bed, alone, and sleep. Instead she'd ended up spending time with two guys she didn't know.

Eoin seemed all right. He was attractive, dark haired, and that Dublin accent was a bonus, but he just reminded her of home, her Irish cousins, and the family she'd left behind in York. She liked being immersed in a new country because it made her forget, but all she saw when she looked at Eoin was the boyfriend who'd left her in Thailand, the parents who'd pressured her into being top of the class, and the country she'd run away from, as well as all the negativity she'd tried so hard to leave behind.

She hadn't come to Australia to smoke weed with boys. She'd come to find herself.

Maybe Gemma didn't understand.

She glanced at the clock on the wall of their room. Seven. Good. Work didn't start until 8:30, which meant she could hurry to the shower block before it got busy. Gemma was still snoring in the bed next to hers as she gathered a few things and rushed out to the shower, checking the ground for spiders.

One thing she knew for certain as she quickly undressed and showered was that she was completely out of her comfort zone now. If she'd wanted a change from her private school in York, she'd certainly found it in an Australian mango plantation. The old Hayley was gone, shed like snakeskin, and this new and improved Hayley would stop seeing the worst in people or thinking the worst was going to happen. She was going to grasp this opportunity in both hands and not let it go.

She changed quickly, throwing on a dress with spaghetti straps. It was all she could wear in this heat, especially after losing a few pounds during the journey up to the farm. Her jeans and shorts hung off her frame like sacks. After combing her wet hair, she smeared sunscreen onto her skin and left the showers to go back to her room.

But as she made her way back, the fine hairs on her arms stood up in warning, and a prickling sensation spread over her body. She felt eyes on her back and turned around to see a tall guy walking away. There was nothing sinister or strange. He was just a guy walking in the opposite direction, probably on his way to another part of the farm. But she'd felt as though he was watching her.

He had dark hair and walked with a straight back. She hesitated for a moment, but the guy didn't turn to face her. One thing she did notice was that he was dressed differently to the other backpackers at the farm. He wore a shirt tucked into chinos. It seemed far away from the Caucasian dreadlocks and lip piercings she'd seen on the farm so far. Hayley shrugged and ignored her gut. She was being paranoid. It was all leftover from the weed last night. A little of the old Hayley kept rearing its ugly head every now and then, demanding to be listened to.

"You're in Field B."

The harsh European voice squeaked up, making Hayley start. She spun on her heels to see the small shape of Ellie staring at her, unblinking. "You can come with me if you like. We're in the same field."

"I should probably tell Gemma—"

"No need," Ellie said. "She's already on her way out to Field C."

"We're not together?" Hayley asked, surprised that whoever organised the workers would split them up on their first day. Maybe Ellie had done it herself. Perhaps it was a way to make sure the workers actually worked and didn't stand around chatting.

"No, You're with me. Are you ready?"

"One sec."

Hayley rushed back towards her room to dump her toiletry bag, thinking about how Gemma seemed to be fitting in here well. She'd already met a guy she liked and appeared to be comfortable moving around the farm on her own. Or it felt that way.

"All set," Hayley said brightly, still determined to maintain this new persona of optimism.

"We'd better go. Lots to do. The farm supplies all the local shops and restaurants. Some of our mangoes are even shipped further. We supply a few supermarkets in Sydney too." Ellie slipped through the communal area, turning sideways past a group of tall backpackers in tie-dyed elephant pants and flimsy vests cut down way past the beginning of patchy chest hair. Their upper arms were already slightly damp with sweat.

"Why do they call him 'The Chemist'?" Hayley asked, squeezing her way past the group of lads, who all seemed to be speaking French.

"Because of his father's company," Ellie replied. "Didn't you know?"

"Know what?"

"Tate Llewellyn is the heir to the Llewellyn corporation. It's a huge pharmaceutical company worth billions of dollars."

They made their way out into the sunshine where the compound bustled with the early morning crowd heading to the food hall. Ellie hadn't even asked if Hayley wanted any breakfast, and her stomach was rumbling. At least she could snack on mangoes out in the fields.

"Then why does he spend all his time here? At a mango farm full of backpackers?" Hayley asked, still bemused by the set up.

Ellie shrugged. "I guess it's what he wants to do. He has a lab here too. He does work on his own projects as well as run the farm."

But nothing about this place looked like a pharmaceutical company. Not that Hayley knew what one looked like. But surely it would not look like a state-of-the-art farm sprawling with outbuildings, a glass mansion, fancy greenhouses, and mango fields full of complicated machinery. Tate had obviously had this place built to his own specifications. Why go to all this trouble to pick fruit?

Hayley watched as the workers yawned, stretched, and raised their faces to the sun. They climbed into pickup trucks, or utes as they called them here, and sped off towards the fields in groups, laughing, joking, and rubbing sleep from their eyes. The vibe was chilled and easygoing, yet somewhere on this farm was a laboratory for a billionaire. It was certainly a strange setup.

Perhaps that was the old, suspicious Hayley again. Why was she questioning a place that so obviously made people happy? The entire farm was filled with happy people.

Ellie drove them a short distance away from the outhouses to a field of mango trees heavy with fruit. Dotted amongst the trees were people with long poles and a few hydraulic ladders, like the kind firemen use to assist people out of burning buildings. When the fruit was picked, the people threw them onto a vehicle that was rigged up with tarpaulins. The mangoes rolled down the tarpaulin through some sort of liquid and out of sight. Hayley was surprised to see people in the fields already, thinking that the hours were from 8:30 onwards. Perhaps it was best to get ahead of the hot sun and begin work early.

"Not a great job if you hate heights, then?" Hayley said.

To her surprise, Ellie's face broke into a grin, and high-pitched hee-hawing sounds like mating foxes emitted from her tiny body.

"No," she said between bouts of her alarming laugh. "Not good at all."

Hayley found herself joining in with Ellie's laughter as the truck was parked. Even as they piled out of the cab, Ellie continued to chuckle at the joke.

The oddness of Ellie's sense of humour broke the awkwardness and made the rest of the morning fly by. Ellie taught Hayley how to use the extendable poles, and where to break the stem of the low-hanging fruit so that the sap didn't get onto her skin. Then they'd take the buckets of mangoes over to the harvest aid—the vehicle rigged out with tarpaulins—and put the mangoes through the strange liquid, or 'mango wash,' to get rid of any sap. While they were working, Hayley learned that Ellie was from Lisbon.

"I've never been to Lisbon," Hayley said. "But my parents took me to the Algarve twice."

"All the tourists go," Ellie noted, as she peeled a mango with a knife. "It's pretty. But too English." With a giggle, Ellie took a long slice of mango peel and placed it under her nose like a moustache. "Oi. Mate. Sausages. Beeeeeer." Her terrible mash up of a cockney and Portuguese accent had Hayley doubled over in laughter. "LAGER!"

Hayley almost choked on a piece of mango at the last one, snorting as she laughed. "That sounds like the English all right. So how did you end up here, Ellie?"

With that last question, the laughter stopped, and Ellie let the mango peel drop to the ground. She avoided Hayley's gaze and cut another piece of mango.

"It's... not a good story," she said with a shrug. "But it doesn't matter anymore. I like it here. This is my home now. Tate... he's like a father—to us all, I suppose. Some of us don't have families anymore. We made our own because we had to. We need each other."

Hayley nodded, understanding the idea of making a new family. Even though she missed her parents, there had been so many days when she felt as though she didn't fit into her family. She'd needed to get out. To breathe. And she had. By running away. How many more of the people here had done the same? How many had run away from their families? Run away from their problems?

"Is it safe here?" Hayley asked in a quiet voice. "I know you say it's like a family, but families aren't always... nice. Are they?"

Ellie's eyes finally met hers, and the seriousness was back. "This is your new home, Hayley. We will keep you safe. Tate will keep you safe."

A shiver ran through Hayley. Ellie's earnestness had touched her, but it also made her feel uneasy. Was she right in thinking Ellie was a little odd? Just eccentric? Or was she more vulnerable than that? Someone who shouldn't be working alone so far away from home for instance. Or was it just the accent and the serious demeanour? Hayley got back to work and couldn't stop thinking about what

Ellie's background might be. But at the same time, she couldn't stop thinking about her own future too. Now that she was here, what was she going to do?

17

GEMMA

Gemma reached inside the collar of her shirt to scratch her shoulder. Sweat and mango stem sap was making her itch like crazy. She was already sick of the sweet smell of the fields, and she wasn't even that fond of mangoes in the first place. Most of the mangoes they were picking were slightly underripe, but the mangoes at the very tops of the trees had ripened enough to emit cloying scents everywhere.

Ellie had sent her out here to Field C, pairing her with a guy who seemed high on drugs, who laughed at his own bad jokes and barely taught her what she was supposed to be doing. His body had the doughy softness and puffy round cheeks of an overgrown toddler.

He said his name was Freddy when she asked him, but he wouldn't tell her where he was from, insisting that his life was on *the farm* now. She wasn't good with accents, but she guessed he was British, just with a different accent to Hayley—a harsher, more nasal tone.

The only relief from Freddy was the music that constantly blared out from speakers in the fields. She tried to focus on the songs she liked and block out the guy's inane chatter.

By eleven in the morning, she was wilting like lettuce in a day-old salad. She was used to heat, but not heat like this. This heat made her feel like her skin was in danger of melting from her bones.

A voice came over the loudspeakers—echoing through the fields —announcing it was time for lunch. Exhausted, she followed the streams of tired backpackers to the food hall.

Hayley was waiting for her outside the hall, her face red and flushed from the sun. "How was it?"

"I'm dying for a shower."

"Definitely. Every muscle in my body is throbbing. And my head too." She gave a groaning sigh, pulling the bucket hat from her head. "Ellie's kind of strange. One minute she's fun, and the next she's bossing me around. Maybe she's just trying to do a good job here and she doesn't know how."

"You were paired with Ellie this morning?"

"Yeah."

"She *is* strange. Her brain seems a bit *understaffed*, if you know what I mean. I have no idea why she got put in charge."

Hayley nodded in agreement. "Who did you get put with?"

"Dude named Freddy. A complete weirdo."

They stepped inside the hall. Hayley turned to Gemma in surprise—the layout was nothing like it'd been the night before. Large, Moroccan-style floor cushions were scattered in a loose semi-circle—the tables and chairs all neatly stacked along a wall. The shades were drawn, making the daylight disappear except for a rich, multihued sunlight spilling in from the high stained-glass windows.

A rich aroma of coconut and spices filled the air. Gemma and Hayley swung around, watching a group of people busy at work in the kitchen. A long line of bowls was lined up on a bench.

Everyone was dead silent as they entered. There was none of the jostle and banter of dinner last night.

Hayley looked around. "Why is everyone so quiet?" She motioned towards a big wicker basket at the front of the room. "Look, that's where they're keeping everyone's phones."

"Shhhh!" a small redheaded girl cautioned them with an annoyed expression.

Gemma and Hayley exchanged confused glances, shrugging. They chose cushions near the back of the semicircle and sat cross-legged. The entire farm of workers was now sitting quietly, like a class of compliant children.

Gemma furtively eyed the crowd, trying to see if she could spot Clay. Finding him sitting next to the Irish guy, Eoin, she shot him a smile. His eyes met hers, and he returned the smile. She swivelled around again to face the front, trying to get comfortable on the cushion. After hours of fruit picking, her muscles felt like they were seizing up.

A small group of workers moved out from the kitchen with trolleys laden with steaming bowls of soup, and they began distributing them among the others. The soup was a Thai dish—thick, spiced coconut with strips of ripe mango. Despite Gemma not being a fan of mangoes, the soup tasted wonderful.

As she sipped at the hot soup on her spoon, she felt her muscle pains begin to fade away. She felt *good*.

When the people around them finished their soup, they placed the bowls in front of them. But they remained silent and didn't move.

Gemma and Hayley copied the others, putting their bowls down and waiting.

"What are we waiting for?" Hayley said in a low voice.

Gemma shrugged, frowning.

A tall figure walked in, his stride and posture oozing confidence. He wore his loose, casual clothing like a runway model. His hair was clipped short, a light covering of facial hair accentuating the handsome angles of his face.

There was no denying that the man had a strong presence. She watched him walk through the hall, unable to take her eyes from him.

"Has to be the big boss guy. Tate Llewellyn," Hayley muttered under her breath. "I saw him earlier."

Gemma nodded. It made perfect sense that he was the farm's owner. The way he stood and looked at all of them, she could believe that he owned the entire world.

Tate stood silently at the front of the semicircle, beaming.

"I trust you all enjoyed your lunch. We work hard, and then we replenish. It's yet another perfect day at the farm," he began.

Another perfect day, came the immediate chorus. Every worker in unison.

Hayley stared at Gemma with wide eyes.

"We give thanks for the harvest and thanks that we are all here together. Every day is a celebration," he continued.

The chorus followed with *every day is a celebration*.

"Freaky," Hayley said in a whisper so low she barely caught it.

"Yeah," Gemma whispered back.

Tate paused for a moment, inhaling a deep breath. The entire room did the same. He seemed to have them in the palm of his hand.

"We've come a long way since our beginnings," he said. "I'm proud to offer not only a farm in which to work and earn a living but a haven. A place away from the stresses of everyday life. Many of you have troubled pasts. You had people who didn't love and care for you in the way you deserved. But here, you leave them and those troubles behind. We are a family and will remain your family after you leave us." He paused. "And now," he said, "it's time to welcome two new members of our family. You know who you are. Please come to me."

Hayley tugged on Gemma's sleeve. Awkwardly, they unfolded themselves from their sitting positions and then rose and picked their way through the group, taking care not to step on anyone's bowl.

Tate greeted them with open arms. The next minute, they found themselves facing the group, Tate's arms around each of them.

"Introduce yourselves, girls, so that we all may know who you are."

Hayley spoke first. "I'm Hayley. I come from York, England. I went to school at Queen Margaret's and—"

"Hayley," Tate gently admonished. "None of those things are *you*. They are things *about* you. But they are not *you*. Tell us things that would remain true about your soul, no matter where you happened to be born into this world."

"Oh... uh," Hayley faltered. "Well, I like to travel, I guess that's why I'm here so far away from home. I'm *really* hoping none of those mouse spiders come out at night. Um, I dunno what else." She shrugged and sighed. "I guess I'm here to get away from it all, you know? I'm not sure what I'll find here, but I hope I find what I need." Hayley's smile turned shy, and she wrapped her arms protectively around her body.

Welcome home, Hayley, everyone responded. *The farm is your home. We are your family.*

"Um, thank you." Hayley's voice was small and seemed to be laden with as much confusion as emotion.

Gemma tried to swallow the hard lump in her throat, a lump that felt as large and firm as a mango seed. Tate squeezed her shoulder in encouragement.

"Okay, so, I'm Gemma," she began. "I grew up in a country area, running around on my own a lot. I wasn't one for console games and computers. Couldn't keep me inside. I used to like watching things grow and becoming something else. Like tadpoles to frogs. I'd keep them in an old fish tank and watch it happen." She thought for a moment. "Storms make me anxious. And animals with teeth. When I was three, a dog bit me. I still have the scar."

"Good girl," whispered Tate, his lips almost brushing Gemma's ear. A shiver turned warm as it made its way down from her neck to encompass her entire body. For a split second, she imagined herself with Tate, alone. She could almost feel herself in his arms and hear him talking in that low, reassuring voice.

The chorus echoed around the hall. *Welcome home, Gemma. The farm is your home. We are your family.*

Gemma bowed her head to hide the rush of heat in her cheeks.

"Thank you, girls," said Tate. "Now, everyone, what day is it today?"

Harvest Friday, came the swift response.

"Indeed it is." Tate smiled widely, like a Sunday School teacher impressed with his students' knowledge. "And what do we do on Harvest Fridays?"

We harvest, they replied.

"Yes, that's exactly what we do." He sighed warmly. "I have business to attend to, but I'll be with you all again at tomorrow night's celebration. Please, let's give thanks for everything we have."

We give thanks for all we have, came the chorus yet again.

Dropping his arms from Gemma and Hayley's shoulders, he gave a slight nod to each of them and then walked from the hall. Gemma watched his tall frame as he exited.

The atmosphere relaxed, people taking their bowls to the kitchen and quietly talking among themselves.

"What's *Harvest Friday?*" Hayley asked Gemma nervously. "I mean, we were harvesting all morning, right? Sounds like they're going to work us even harder or something."

"God, I hope not." Gemma sucked her lips in. She didn't want to admit it, but the sensation of Tate's touch was still drifting in her mind. She shoved the thought away. "What did you think of that loopy little welcome ceremony?"

"Felt like we accidentally walked into some kind of support group."

"Yeah. Exactly."

Ellie walked up and commandeered Gemma and Hayley into the kitchen. "Families help each other," she told them. "I always get the new people into the kitchen to clean up. It helps them to settle in more quickly. Giving and receiving is what we do here."

"Ellie," said Hayley in an uncertain tone, "what was all the chanting about?"

"It's just something we do." Ellie flashed her a smile. "It's calming. Didn't you find it calming?"

"I don't know," Hayley replied. "It was just *weird*. I didn't expect anything like this."

Gemma hung back at the doorway. "It was super weird."

"I'm sorry..." Wincing, Ellie hesitated for a moment then smiled brightly. "Look, you'll soon get used to the rhythm of things around here. Okay, I'll show you where everything is."

Ellie pointed out where the plates, cutlery, and food were kept around the kitchen.

"Why so many of these?" Hayley indicated towards the bottom drawer she'd just opened. It was filled with disposable eye droppers.

"Oh, they're just used on the odd occasion when we happen to use the expensive spices." Ellie flicked the drawer shut lightly with her foot. "Any other questions?"

She was quick to leave, before Gemma had time to put the questions in her head into words.

Watching Ellie scurry away into the hall, Gemma began rinsing the mountains of piled-up bowls. "Did she seem a bit nervous to you?"

Hayley carried a pile of bowls across to the bench nearest to the sink, her eyes anxious. "Yeah, she did. And what kind of spices was she talking about? I hope it's not magic mushrooms or something."

"Magic mushrooms? Are they even a spice?"

"It's just... I feel a bit spacey."

"I feel really relaxed." Gemma frowned. "You don't think they put something in our lunch, do you?"

"Just to be sure, why don't we have a look and see what they've got in that spice cupboard that Ellie showed us?"

"Might as well. We're supposed to familiarise ourselves with the kitchen, right?"

She helped Hayley drag a stepladder across and then climbed up the stairs.

"Hmmm, lots of chili powders," Gemma reported, peering into

the high cupboard. "Uh, vanilla bean extract, cardamom, star anise, pepper... cloves, turmeric, garam masala—I think that's a mix. Um, and liquid saffron—"

"Saffron's super expensive," said Hayley, standing close behind her. "I know because I go with my mum to the Indian food shops when she's stocking up her kitchen. The type she buys costs about seven thousand pounds per hundred grams. Maybe that's what Ellie meant?"

Gemma twisted back to Hayley, pulling a dubious expression. "How can a spice cost that much? Jeez, you could practically sell that on the street like a drug."

Hayley giggled. "Yes, but they'd probably cut it with cheap curry powder."

Gemma laughed, almost tripping as she stepped down from the ladder. Reaching up to catch Gemma, Hayley had another fit of giggles.

"Okay, so maybe saffron's the spice that's so super-duper expensive they've got to dole it out in eye droppers," said Gemma, smiling and shrugging. "I guess we'd better get some of these dishes done before they wonder what we're doing in here."

Gemma drained the sink and then refilled it with hot, soapy water.

Hayley sobered, drying the bowl that Gemma handed to her. "I was overreacting. The spaciness I'm feeling is probably just a bit of heatstroke."

"Yeah, I guess. It was hot as hell out there. But what about that chanting? Did you think that everyone looked a bit zoned out?"

"Yes, I noticed a bit of that. But mostly, I was just so nervous being made to stand there in front of them all."

Gemma eyed her friend. "They were *so* zoned out. I mean, they're a bunch of fruit pickers. But they're sitting around chanting like meditating monks."

"It's crazy when you think about it. Just what kind of place *is* this?" Opening a cupboard, Hayley shoved the bowl inside. "I know we practically just got here, but something doesn't feel right."

"Yeah."

Hayley's forehead pulled into a tight frown. "I don't want to feel like that. This is supposed to be an adventure."

"Hey, I'm feeling it too," she said gently then hesitated. "So, we'll hit the road again and see where it takes us?"

Hayley shook her head emphatically, flicking the cupboard door shut. "I... I can't. Wild horses couldn't drag me back there."

Gemma pushed back hair from her face with the heel of her hand, trying and failing not to get suds on her skin. "The road's not so bad."

"Yes, it is. It's *bad*."

"Well, it's all we've got. The other farms on that fruit-picking leaflet brochure you had were all full up. And we don't have a backup plan."

"Why'd this place have to be full of weirdos? After coming all this way, the last thing I thought is that we'd have to turn around and take off again." Hayley crinkled her eyes shut, drawing her arms in tight around herself.

Gemma didn't know whether it was frustration or anger that suddenly needled her. She scrubbed a dish in fierce circles. "At least you have options."

Hayley blinked her eyes open. "What options?"

"You're a rich girl from a rich family," she blurted. "Not me. I've got nothing. I spent my last cent on that bus trip. But I bet the shoes on my feet that your parents would send you money or pay your way home if you asked them to."

Hayley physically recoiled from the stinging words. "That's not fair, Gemma. They *would* send money if I was desperate. But that would mean giving up, wouldn't it? It'd mean going back to York."

"If you told them what your ex-boyfriend did to you—"

"No. I'm doing this alone, without them." She shook her head. "I don't want to even think about this anymore."

Gemma stopped scrubbing the dish, her shoulders sinking as her anger dissolved. She cast a look of sympathy at her friend. "Sorry for bringing all that up."

"It's okay." Taking a deep gulp of air, Hayley met eyes with Gemma. "Look, maybe we're both spinning out. It's only our second day here. You know, when you mentioned my parents, the people here suddenly didn't seem so bad. At least they're welcoming. That has to be a good thing, right? Seems like they want us to be one big happy family."

Gemma chewed her lip, turning her attention back to the dishes. "Maybe. But I don't need a family. I never needed one."

"Okay," Hayley said gingerly. "But they haven't been awful to us or anything. So... we'll stay for a while and see how it goes?"

"We'll stay." Gemma nodded. She shouldn't have called Hayley a rich girl, even if it was true. Hayley was here trying her best to survive on her own. She had to admire that. "Hey," she said, attempting to lighten things up, "even if the scenery isn't quite what they promised, at least the guys here are kind of easy on the eye."

But Hayley's face creased into a questioning look. "You wouldn't end up going off with one of them and leave me on my own... right? Like, you'll keep sharing the cabin with me and everything?"

"Of course. We came here together. We stay together. And if we've had enough of this place by the time we get our first pay packets, we can take off then."

Hayley hugged her.

Half an hour later, the dishes were done. They emerged from the dimly lit hall, blinking in the harsh sunshine. Gemma felt even stickier now, soap suds and mango tree sap making her crave a shower.

"Are we about to be sent straight back out to the fields, or what?" Hayley cupped a hand over her eyes to shield them from the glare. "Where did Ellie disappear to?"

The redheaded girl who'd told them to shush in the hall stepped up in front of their faces. She turned to Gemma. "Mr Llewellyn wants to see you up at the house."

"Me?" said Gemma in surprise.

"Yes, you. He's busy, so let's go."

Shrugging at Hayley, Gemma followed the girl to the house.

The girl cast an odd look at Gemma before pointing to the staircase. "Up there."

"Is everything okay?" said Gemma, starting to worry.

"Of course. Everything's always okay here." Her voice rose in an upward inflection that sounded as if she were asking a question.

Leaving her behind, Gemma ascended the stairs. She felt as if the girl were still watching her.

All the doors were shut on the second floor. Where did Tate expect her to meet him? Then she spotted his tall frame, just in front of the enormous glass wall that overlooked the farm.

"Gemma," he said.

She took self-conscious steps across the marble floor. The intense light coming through the glass highlighted his sculpted cheekbones and beautiful eyes.

"How was the trip to the farm?" he asked her. "I haven't had the chance to ask yet. Any problems?"

"No, no problems. We made it in one piece."

"Good. That's good to hear. How's your friend settling in?"

"We're doing okay." She laughed nervously as she realised that Tate had only asked about Hayley, not about both of them.

He didn't seem to notice her nervousness. "I hope our Ellie is being helpful? I've trained her to ensure new people feel comfortable, but she can be a little... scatterbrained... at times."

"I've noticed."

Tate studied her face in surprise, and then a smile cracked across his face. "Honesty is the best policy."

He asked then if she'd like a cup of tea or coffee, and she

accepted. The woman from the office—Sophie—brought them up two cups and then left again.

Gemma sipped her tea, looking out at the farm's expanse with Tate.

For a moment, she had a view that sent a pack of tiny shivers down her spine. It wasn't the view of the farm—it was her mind's eye view of Tate and herself standing here together having tea. It seemed intimate, as if they were a couple, and as if they owned all this together. The image felt secure and thrilling at the same time.

———

Hayley was waiting outside the hall when she returned. "What did he want?"

"Just a chat," said Gemma lightly. She'd almost forgotten what they'd talked about. The mental picture of herself with Tate looking down on where she was now crowded everything else out.

A line of large vehicles passed them, kicking up dirt. All battered SUVs and utes.

Clay and Eoin stopped in their car, both with their heads out the windows.

"You girls coming or what?" called Clay.

"Coming where?" Gemma called back in confusion.

"It's a surprise. Wear swimsuits."

Eoin grinned. "Make that bikinis."

"I thought we were supposed to be doing some sort of harvest?" Hayley shrugged at Gemma.

"That's right." Clay nodded. "Go grab your gear and jump in."

"Whatever this is, it has to beat mango picking," said Gemma as she and Hayley dashed back to the cabins for their swimsuits.

When they returned, the boys were still waiting. They climbed up into the high seats of the SUV.

"Woo-hoo!" Eoin howled from the front passenger seat.

"So, there *is* actually somewhere to swim around here?" muttered Hayley. "I know there was supposed to be water nearby, but I can't imagine it. Feels like we're in the middle of a desert." Tugging her hat down over her eyes, Hayley wriggled down in her seat as if she were going to nap.

"That's where you're wrong, city girl," Eoin told her.

"Didn't you say you were from Dublin?" Hayley said in a dry tone, from beneath her hat.

"Hayley's got you there." Clay jerked the car to a stop as an enormous red kangaroo bounded out of nowhere and crossed the road, making them all slam forward.

Hayley pulled off her hat, watching with wide eyes as the kangaroo hopped away, kicking up dirt as it went.

"I'll be a Dub boy 'til the day I die." Eoin shrugged. "But I've been here for a few months now. A lot of the city's been knocked out of me. You girls just need to stick close to me 'n' Clay, and you'll be right."

"We don't need anyone looking after us, thanks." Gemma yawned and settled back in the seat as Clay drove away again. It'd already been a long, strange, and exhausting day.

Hayley nodded. "We got ourselves all the way here on our own. I think we can manage this. You guys seem to have it pretty cushy, anyway, with your meditation and gourmet meals."

"Yeah right," Eoin said then made a derisive sound through his teeth. "You chicks get it easier here than us guys do. The Chemist works us harder. But being pretty gets you girls a long way. 'specially on Harvest days."

"Why's that?" Hayley demanded. "What *is* Harvest Day?"

"You'll find out soon enough." Eoin ignored the sharp glance that Clay shot him.

"Shut it," Clay warned. He twisted around to the girls, shaking his head. "It's not like that. Girls work just as hard as the guys do on the farm. You'll earn every cent that you make." He threw Gemma a quick smile before he turned around again, correcting the slight swerve that the car had taken.

Eoin's a big jerk, Hayley mouthed at Gemma.

Gemma nodded. Eoin *was* being a jerk, but it was just banter. He wasn't being weird in the way that the people at lunch had been weird. Everything was going to be okay. And Clay seemed like one of the good guys.

Hayley angled her hat over her eyes again and leaned her head against the seat.

Gemma followed suit, though trying to sleep through the bumps and bounces of the SUV proved almost impossible.

It took an hour or so to reach their destination. Gemma woke in time to see the sign for the town, Katherine.

The SUVs and utes from the mango farm parked near a river, and everyone jumped out. Gemma and Hayley stepped beside Clay and Eoin to a long, separate body of water that ran alongside the river.

"Katherine thermal springs, ladies," said Eoin. "Come on in with us. We'll keep you safe from the crocodiles."

The clear, turquoise-coloured springs had square-cut stone walls and stone steps leading in, overlapped by palm and paperbark trees. The water flowed underneath a small bridge.

Throngs of tourists milled about, snapping photographs and swimming. Lots of families and middle-aged couples but also groups of young backpackers.

Another SUV pulled up, this one new and unscratched. Ellie stepped out, wearing a sundress and sunhat, looking more like a tourist—instead of that safari-suit gear she wore back at the farm.

"Hayley, Gemma, there you are," she exclaimed running up. "Thought I'd lost you." She cast a sharp glance in the direction of Clay and Eoin. "I'll take care of the girls, thank you."

"Are there crocodiles in there?" Hayley pointed at the springs, her face anxious.

"Yeah, we don't want to be a croc's lunch." Gemma glanced across at the shadow-speckled areas where the springs vanished around a bend.

A short, raucous laugh burst from Ellie's throat. She covered her mouth in sudden embarrassment. "No. No crocs. I mean, I wouldn't trust the river, but the springs aren't connected to the river. The water bubbles up from underground."

"Hey, Eoin and I can show the girls the ropes, Ellie," Clay said.

"No. You'll only distract them," said Ellie primly. "Do I need to remind you this is still part of our working day?"

Clay and Eoin slunk away.

Ellie laid out a picnic rug on the grass, placing containers of cut fruit, towels, and an insulated container of water on top.

"Can I ask why we're here?" Gemma couldn't keep the disappointed note from her voice. It'd seemed like fun until Ellie showed up. "How are we supposed to be *working* here?"

"We... recruit," Ellie explained, her gaze darting away to the tourists surrounding the springs. "We let people know about the farm —to bring in new workers. About half of our workers are long-term, but we have a high turnover with the other half—as you'd expect. Almost all of our workers are backpackers. We try to find the ones who'll stay long term."

Hayley shrugged. "So, can't Tate just advertise for fruit pickers?"

"Mr Llewellyn likes a special kind of person," Ellie told her, each word firm and precise "We don't accept just *anyone*."

"What kind of special person?" Hayley asked curiously.

"Someone's who's likely to stay with us for a while and be loyal. Someone who needs us as much as we need them. We're a family..." Ellie's voice faltered. "Anyway. Watch and learn. Welcome to your first *Harvest Friday*."

She pulled her sundress over her head, revealing a startlingly skimpy red bikini underneath.

18

HAYLEY

Ellie didn't seem the sort of girl to wear such an outfit on her own volition, and Hayley immediately felt a niggle in her tummy that something wasn't right. She shared a bemused glance with Gemma and frowned.

"What's going on?" Hayley asked. "Were you told to wear that, Ellie?"

Ellie gave one of her hyena-chorus laughs and slapped Hayley on the shoulder, which definitely stung after a morning in the sun. "Don't be ridiculous. You think we get a checklist of what to wear? No. But part of Harvest Friday is talking to tourists, finding out more about them, and presenting the farm in a certain way."

"Are we supposed to flirt with them?" Hayley said. "Isn't that... honey trapping?"

Ellie rolled her eyes. "You don't get it. The preservation of the farm is important because Tate's work is important. It's a small... what is the word? Sacrifice. It's a small sacrifice. It does no harm. Come on. It's a bit of fun. You're not prudes are you?" She wrinkled her nose.

Gemma recoiled from the insult. "You don't know me."

"Gem." Hayley placed a hand on Gemma's arm, worried that her friend was getting worked up. She turned to Ellie. "Maybe we should go. I... I'm not good at flirting like that."

"No, no, wait," Ellie said. "The outfit is my choice. You don't have to do all that. Look, stick around and wait. Watch. It's not as bad as it sounds." She smiled nervously before skipping off towards the group of backpackers lounging around the springs. Clay and Eoin were already chatting to some of the girls, stripped down to their shorts, revealing toned, bronzed bodies.

"What do you make of all this?" Hayley turned to Gemma hoping she was feeling just as uncomfortable.

"They're taking liberties. But, I dunno, it gets us out of mango picking. And it's only for a few hours. I'd be in a bikini in this weather anyway, so I guess it's not that different."

"Yeah, but." Hayley couldn't find the words to explain how she felt about the situation. She was downcast that Gemma didn't see anything wrong with it. Maybe she *was* a prude. She knew she had issues after her boyfriend left her in Thailand. But this was different, wasn't it? She had a choice. She didn't have to do anything sexual. All she had to do was talk.

Hayley found a patch of shade to sit and watch Ellie, Clay, and Eoin chatting with the young backpackers. They were all around 18-19 years old, relaxed, tanned, and nodding along to whatever Ellie and the others were saying.

"Hope Clay doesn't end up hooking up with one of those girls. Because he is *fine*," Gemma said, flopping down onto the grass next to her. She let out a sigh like a teenage girl with a crush, and Hayley was jealous of the way she was so open to the idea of a new relationship or fling or whatever.

"Don't you think the name is creepy? *Harvest Friday* sounds... I dunno, dystopian or something, like we're harvesting people."

Gemma laughed. "What, like there are people growing on stems and you have to pluck them?"

Hayley raised her eyebrows. "It looks like we'd be doing more than *plucking* them, given the outfits."

Gemma laughed harder, then she quietened after a moment. "I get it. Like we were saying in the kitchen, this place is a bit odd."

"Yeah," Hayley said. "But where else are we going to go? What else are we going to do? We could just see how it goes."

"I guess we can stay for a bit longer," Gemma replied. "Do you think we have to join in?" She nodded towards the others.

It was a relief to see Gemma as dubious about the creepy Harvest day as Hayley felt. But she didn't want Gemma to give up and for them both to leave. The thought of being on the Stuart Highway again horrified her... or worse, having to phone her parents and admit how much of a mess she'd got herself into.

Hayley let out a long breath. "Maybe it won't be so bad once we get chatting to them?" She scratched at a patch on her arm trying not to cringe at the thought of talking to strangers. There was no chatting to strangers in a swimming costume in England.

"I think one of us will have to. Otherwise it looks like we're being... I don't know, hostile about the whole thing?" Gemma said.

Hayley avoided her eyes and continued scratching her arm. "I'm a bit hot, Gem. I think I need the shade for a bit."

"All right, but you owe me one." Gemma got to her feet and pulled the dress she was wearing over her head before walking over to Ellie and sitting down next to her. Hayley watched enviously as Gemma reclined next to the springs, stretching out her long, tanned legs. Within seconds she was shaking hands with the backpackers. She fitted in here. But Hayley never fitted in. She was always on the outskirts.

———

The ute had been packed to bursting on the way back with the addition of the new backpackers, and Hayley had been squashed in next to Clay, who was chatting intensely with a petite blond girl to his left. The girl's loud laugh made Hayley wish she had a glass of water and an ibuprofen for the headache it was giving her. No, actually she longed to be alone in her room, on her bed, reading. She was worried that her tension headaches were going to start up again. At school and university the headaches could be debilitating at times, so bad that they felt like a sledgehammer taken to her skull. Sometimes, even at the slightest twinge, she became terrified that one of the terrible headaches was going to come back, and anxiety would build up through her body like coiled elastic.

As they'd crammed into the truck, Ellie had leaned close to her and said quietly, "It's fine for you to watch the first time, but next time you must help. Okay?"

And Hayley had nodded like a good little girl. But inside she wasn't sure whether she would or not.

"You okay?" Gemma whispered.

"Yeah, it's just hot in here."

"You seem a bit quiet."

"It's just been a long day," Hayley said, trying not to put a dampener on the afternoon. Gemma was glowing, her smile wide. She'd found it so easy to chat to the guys at the springs. Hayley felt stupid and inadequate for not being able to join in. She pulled her dress over her knees and crossed her arms over her chest.

Ellie leaned over and said brightly. "There's a party tonight. Everyone at the farm goes."

"I thought you were all about the work, El?" Gemma replied with a laugh.

"Oh, I can... umm"—she paused, searching for the words—"let my hair down."

Gemma laughed and the two of them continued talking while Hayley tried to relax on the hour-long journey back, trying and failing to rid herself of the negativity she'd woken up hoping to combat.

After arriving back at the farm, Hayley jumped in the shower to rinse away the dust and sunscreen. Then she squeezed the water out of her hair and went back to the room still a little damp. Gemma was dancing around the room in her underwear, waving two dresses in the air.

"Which one?" she asked breathlessly.

Hayley regarded the red mini dress with polka dots and the long floral maxi with a plunging neckline. "The maxi. Clay will be weak at the knees."

"What are you wearing?" Gemma asked.

"I'm not sure. Most of my clothes are covered in patches of dried sunscreen." Hayley looked at her pile of clothes in dismay. Maybe after a couple of drinks she wouldn't care what she was wearing.

"The red dress," Gemma said. "Definitely wear that." She reached into Hayley's pile of clothes and pulled out a halter-neck dress with an A-line cut. "You look gorgeous in this. Eoin will love it."

"You think?" Hayley held it up to her body. "Honestly, Gem. I don't know if I even like Eoin."

"Really, how come? He seems nice enough. And that accent!" She raised her eyebrows.

"We didn't click, I guess. I'm glad you and Clay are hitting it off so well."

Gemma made a sound of derision. "Not anymore. Did you see him with that tiny blonde?"

"Oh, he's just doing that to get her to stay at the farm. He's definitely more into you."

"You reckon?"

"Totally."

Gemma grinned and slipped the maxi dress over her body. "You'd better be right."

Hayley followed Gemma out of the cabin and wandered through

the maze of outhouses. The location of the party was an easy spot, as people filtered out and made their way to the event. All they had to do was follow. As it turned out, the party was at the glass mansion itself, next to a wall that looked into a modern living space with white walls and floors. A long dining table was the centrepiece of the living area, and accessible through open glass doors. On the table, which must have easily been ten feet long, were a number of snacks, appetisers, and fruit. Gemma grasped Hayley's hand and pulled her over to the snacks where they each took a plate.

After biting into a delicious avocado and tomato appetiser, Hayley realised she was ravenous and thirsty. She looked around for the drinks table, taking in the sights. She could see why Tate would want to host a party here. The place looked like something out of a Hollywood movie *about* Hollywood, with a large swimming pool stretching out next to a neat lawn and patio area. There were little tables and chairs dotted around, with more Moroccan-style cushions over the lawn. But what did appear jarring were the guests compared to the surroundings. Rather than glamorous people in expensive outfits, Tate's party consisted of just the backpackers from the farm in their tie-dye and piercings and scruffy beards. The juxtaposition of the two very different views gave her a strange feeling, and she couldn't help wondering why Tate had opened his doors to these people.

Was he really that charitable?

Sure, they worked for him, but he didn't need to provide this. He didn't have any obligation to the people who worked here apart from paying them a wage and providing food and shelter. Maybe he wanted people around him because he was lonely. Maybe Tate was some strange modern-day Gatsby who hosted the craziest parties but never revealed himself to the revellers.

"I'm going to get a drink," Hayley said. "I think I see some water bottles over there."

"I need a beer." Gemma frowned. "Are there any?"

"In that ice bucket near the swimming pool." Hayley pointed the beers out to Gemma.

"Ooh, Clay is over there too."

Hayley grinned and waggled her eyebrows. "Good luck."

As she made her way over to the water bottles, Hayley noticed that Eoin was now talking to the petite blonde from the hot springs. Good. That saved another awkward 'double-date' scenario happening with Gemma and Clay.

"Having a good time?"

Hayley froze with her fingers grasped around the neck of the bottle. She turned, holding the bottle, to find Tate standing behind her. Earlier that day at lunch she had obviously noticed how handsome Tate was, but now that he was stood here, in the dusk, leaning over her with his hands casually in his pockets, she noticed his good looks again. When he smiled, he revealed a perfect set of white teeth.

"Yes, thank you. I mean, I only just arrived so I haven't had time to do much, but it's really beautiful here."

He moved his head, surveying the scene. "I built this place with socialising in mind. It's a lovely spot, and I'm very blessed."

"It's so kind of you to open your house to us like this."

He took a step closer, and Hayley smelled the musk of his aftershave. "Thank you, but I really don't do it to be kind. It's actually quite selfish of me. I don't like to be alone, which I am quite a lot, and this house deserves the sound of laughter."

So, he *was* lonely.

Hayley opened her mouth to speak but a group of excited, tipsy backpackers came over and began talking to Tate, thanking him for the party in an overwhelming, gushing way. Hayley decided to slip away quietly and find Gemma. But first she went back to the food table and grabbed a mini veggie burger.

She finally found Gemma at the far end of the lawn, which edged onto farmland of rugged grass. There was a campfire here, giving off heat, and Gemma sat cross-legged next to Clay. Ellie was with them, too, holding a bottle of beer, leaning against a guy Hayley recognised from the springs.

"There you are!" Gemma jumped up and hugged her, which took Hayley by surprise. "Have you got a beer?"

Hayley gestured at the water.

"Seriously? Drink something proper! Here, take this." Gemma reached down and pulled a beer out of an ice bucket.

Now that she'd rehydrated and eaten something, Hayley didn't see the harm in having a few beers. She didn't want to drink so much that she'd have a hangover—she'd discovered quickly that hangovers in the Australian summer were no fun—but a couple wouldn't hurt.

"Clay is about to sing," Gemma announced.

It was then that Hayley noticed that Clay had a guitar on his lap. "I didn't know you were a musician."

"Hey, I'm not really," he said. "But I know a few songs."

"Cool."

He was actually quite good, and Hayley began to relax by the fire with her beer. She chatted to Ellie on occasion, mostly about mango stem sap, the hills of Lisbon, and the wall that circled the city of York. Gemma watched Clay play his guitar with an earnest intensity that worried Hayley. Was she getting too attached too soon? But before long she'd had a second and a third beer, and she no longer cared.

"I'm going to get more food," Hayley said to no one in particular, because they were all lost in their own conversations. When she stood, she felt a bit dizzy. With her recent weight loss she'd become even more of a lightweight than before.

By this time the party had spread out from the lawn to the fields. There were still plenty of people splashing around in the pool, and the surface rippled, highlighted by the sparkly lights on Tate's patio. She watched the lights dance on skin and water and thought it was really quite beautiful. But she didn't want to head towards the noise and movement. She wanted the quiet. So instead she walked towards the fields.

"Going so soon?"

When Hayley turned back, she saw Tate standing on the edge of the field. "Just for a walk." She hesitated. "Will there be snakes in this grass?"

Tate glanced down and frowned. "Maybe we should walk along the path instead." He gestured towards the path between the lawn and the field.

Hayley barely even picked up on the word 'we'. She just moved across to the path and walked by Tate's side. She wasn't sure whether it was the beer or Tate, but she felt at ease, which wasn't like her around strangers.

"I liked what you said at the introductions. It felt very honest." He pushed his hands down into his pockets. "A lot of people are here to find themselves. It's okay to feel lost."

"I don't know," she replied. "Sometimes I think I just need to grow up."

He laughed. "Why? You can be older and still feel lost."

She'd never thought about it like that before.

"I think you'll like it here," he said. "I know it's a cliché, but we really are like a family here, and everyone has a place and a purpose. Everyone is wanted and needed."

The way he spoke the words made it sound like he needed everyone. As though this place—the farm and the people working here—were personal to him. For some reason that felt comforting to Hayley, to be wanted and needed. She knew her real family wanted her, but it had always felt so overwhelming and intense. This was gentler. And more flattering.

"What made you want to start a mango plantation?" Hayley asked, feeling bold.

"I'm a gardener," he replied. "I love plants, flowers, trees. I love nature, and I wanted to be close to nature."

"But the others call you The Chemist, which doesn't sound very natural at all."

"There's nothing unnatural about chemistry, Hayley." He stopped walking and leaned closer to her. "Nature and chemistry are not mutually exclusive. They exist within each other." He was so close to her that she could feel his body heat. "I would love to show you my orchids one day. Would you like to visit my greenhouse?"

All she could do was nod.

19

GEMMA

Her cheeks stung hot from the blazing campfire, Gemma leaned her face back into cooler air, staring into a star-dotted sky. She'd been singing all the wrong words along with Clay's songs—she never knew the right song lyrics. She was all about the music, anyway.

Some guy stumbled forward drunkenly as he poked at the fire with a stick, the ends of his blond dreadlocks catching on fire.

Eoin poured a can of beer over the guy's head. Everyone clapped and cheered as if it'd been the best entertainment of the night.

The acrid smell of burned hair made Gemma's sinuses seize up and her eyes water.

Grabbing her hand, Clay led her away. She liked the feel of her hand in his.

Inside the house, the party was pumping.

Without Gemma noticing, dusk had stepped into night. She'd already had enough beers to sink a whale. She knew she should stop there. At parties, she always swore she'd quit when she got tipsy—but she always found herself drinking until she blacked out.

She gazed around woozily.

Everything at the party seemed to slide and smudge together. The driving beat of the music, people dancing, and the constantly changing light show of the pool. Body heat, sweat and perfume, and the sweet smell of mangoes saturated the air. Everyone who was wading in the in-ground pool—which stretched from indoors into the outdoors—was being baptised in the intoxicating elixir that was Tate's farm.

She sat herself down on a cushion next to the pool, her feet trailing in the water, feeling as light and free as birds.

Clay reclined beside her, lightly strumming his guitar, not caring when the occasional spray of water hit the strings. They talked. About everything. About deep things. Crazy things. Things they wanted to do. Who they wanted to be.

She'd never had a conversation like that with anyone before. He'd pulled things out of her head that she didn't even know were inside her. That wasn't like her. She never let people too far in. People always hurt her, sooner or later.

Boom, boom, boom, boom. The beat grew deeper, tunnelling in through Gemma's bones. Her gaze skated lazily between the dancers on the floor, trying to spot Hayley. Hayley'd been at the campfire earlier, but she'd wandered away. For a second, a vague stab of panic hit her in the stomach—could Hayley have taken something? She could be out cold on the floor somewhere, overdosed.

Tonight, it seemed that drugs were being passed around like chocolate. Party drugs and pot and LSD. Gemma thought that LSD was something that only baby boomers had dropped in their university days, but she'd seen it here, in tiny blotter tabs with angels printed on them.

But Gemma couldn't picture Hayley taking drugs. She was so *straight*. Nope, she'd probably gone back to the cabin, to sleep or read or something.

Gemma caught sight of the blond girl that Clay had brought back from the harvest. In an orange bikini, she was stunning. The girl shared a passionate kiss with another girl from the farm. Gemma was kind of relieved to see that she wasn't interested in boys.

People were peeling off from the main crowd in twos and threes, finding spots that were not so private to fling their clothes off. Or just jumping into the pool.

A guy with wild dark hair was going around offering the angel-stamped LSD tabs to everyone. When he crouched to offer them to Clay and Gemma, Clay waved him away. But Gemma sneaked a few tabs while Clay was twisting around to push his guitar beneath a nearby table.

"Just pop one under your tongue until they dissolve. They're only a tiny dose each." Winking, the guy stepped away.

She slipped them all under her tongue before Clay saw. She knew he took a dim view of drugs. He'd told her so in no uncertain terms when they were talking earlier. But tonight, she just wanted to get *away*—as far away from herself as she could possibly get. And she wanted to fit in with the people here. If she and Hayley were staying, they needed to do that, else they'd stand out like sore thumbs.

Clay kissed her while the drug dissolved in her mouth.

Things began rushing at her and then rushing away. Material-ising and vanishing.

Everything, *everything* was splintering.

"*Gemmmma?*" Clay's face appeared before hers, with a smile that made her heart thrum like one of his guitar strings. "Dance?"

Splinter.

She found herself in the middle of a jumping group of dancers on the marble floor.

Splinter.

Clay's mouth found hers. Warm. Exploring. Whispering things into her ear and temple. He felt solid and whole as his arms came around her.

Splinter.

Tate was kissing her instead of Clay.

No—that wasn't Tate. It was Clay in front of her. She'd just been imagining Tate.

Why am I seeing Tate?

When she opened her eyes, she was alone.

Clay was gone.

Gemma was left dancing by herself. She whirled around and around, dropping her head back and staring up at the glittering lights of Tate's ceiling. She realised she felt peaceful. The workers at the farm weren't weird. So what if they chanted during lunch? It was safe here. She and Hayley had been worried about nothing.

Hands grasped her body.

She whirled around to see a random guy in a Hawaiian shirt and dreadlocks trying to dance with her. He smelled awful—she realised he was the one who'd singed his hair in the fire earlier.

Over the guy's shoulder, she spied Clay and Eoin talking out on the patio. They were throwing their arms up as if having an argument. She frowned. What could possibly be wrong? Wasn't it Clay who'd told her that things were always happy here?

She walked off the dance floor, but by the time she reached the deck, Clay and Eoin had vanished.

Two people stepped along a corridor in the fields, but it wasn't Clay and Eoin. Gemma paused, squinting to see in the overhead light that streamed from the house. It was Tate and Hayley.

Tate was guiding Hayley by the arm and talking with her, as serenely as if he were a character of that book that Hayley was mumbling about at the campfire earlier. *The Great Gatsby*. Gemma had seen the movie. She'd never been one for reading books.

She ducked back, out of the light. Hayley had looked content. That was good, right? She and Hayley were both finding their place at the farm. This was what they'd come here for.

She imagined Hayley and herself later in the cabin, telling each other about the night they'd each had. Like sisters, sharing stories and giggling together.

Still, she couldn't help a burned feeling from creeping under her skin—a prickly, uncomfortable envy. Tate had singled Hayley out. Part of her wanted to be in Hayley's place. *With Tate.*

The image of herself standing beside him on the top storey of his house entered her mind. She bit down hard on her lip, confused. *Why can't I let that go?*

She watched Tate and Hayley until they vanished into the fields. She couldn't figure why Tate even was interested in Hayley. She was about as unsophisticated as they came. No, Tate's interest in Hayley couldn't be romantic. He was just showing her around and making her feel more settled. And why did she care, anyway? A guy like Clay was a lot more accessible than Tate Llewellyn.

Black, balmy air seemed as thick as syrup as she stepped through the night, but it was just fresh enough to wake her from the dreamy state she'd been in.

The sound of muffled cries drifted towards her. The sobs were coming from somewhere behind her. Rotating, she went looking for the source.

She found Ellie with her back against a palm tree, the glow of a spotlight just near enough to dimly illuminate her. Drooping palm fronds cast deep shadows across her face. Ellie spoke in a burst of fast, anxious Portuguese into a phone. She stopped and nodded, as if listening intently to the person on the other end of the phone line. Then the sobs came again.

She ended the call quickly as she noticed Gemma, wiping her nose and straightening herself. In the dark light, Ellie's eyes seemed swollen—she'd been here crying for some time.

"What's up, Ellie?" Gemma asked, stepping across to her.

"Nothing. It's nothing. Just talking with my mother."

"Feeling homesick?"

Ellie's shoulders rolled inward, and she sighed. "I'm *so* homesick. I had a big fight with my family, just before I left Portugal. I didn't think I'd ever want to see them again. But I was wrong. It was just a stupid fight. *I* was stupid." She sounded like a child, almost whispering the words.

"Can't you just go home, then?"

"I will... soon." She jammed her eyes shut for a moment. "Please don't tell Tate that."

Gemma shrugged nonchalantly. "Why would I tell Tate?" She watched as Ellie slipped her phone into the pocket of her shorts. "I thought we weren't supposed to have phones?"

Ellie paused before she answered, her hand freezing in place on her pocket. "We're not. I just needed to hear Mama's voice."

"I don't have any family worth calling."

"I don't know who is luckier. You or me. I miss my family so much it hurts." Ellie made a fist and knocked it against her chest, on top of her heart. She made a cringing face then, throwing Gemma a sympathetic look. "Oh, of course you are not lucky. Everyone should have a family who loves them." She peered at Gemma. "You've had a troubled life, *sim*?"

"Sim?"

"Portuguese word for *yes*."

"What makes you think I've had it tough?"

"I can see it in your eyes. And you're so private. Hayley has told me some things about her life and family, but I haven't heard you say a peep about any of that."

Gemma's head was starting to ache now, the drugs and alcohol she'd had making her feel unsteady. She didn't like talking about *them*—her family. Or her life. She'd been hoping to start again here, fresh. As if her old life never existed.

Ellie's fingers trembled suddenly as she threaded her hands

together. "Gemma, I shouldn't tell you this. But I'll feel bad if I don't. If you've had a hard life then you deserve some happiness. If I were you, I'd leave the farm. You and Hayley. It's your first week here, and it's easy to leave *now*."

Gemma's brow tightened. The sudden turn of conversation confused her. Had she heard right? "Why would we want to leave?"

Ellie hushed her voice, eyes darting about to see if anyone was listening. "This farm isn't what you think it is. *Nothing* here is what you think it is."

"You don't like me much, do you? From the minute I stepped foot on this farm, I could tell."

"No, Gemma. It's not like that. Please—"

Gemma spun around and walked away. She wasn't going to listen to *that* any longer. For the briefest of moments, she'd let herself believe that Ellie cared. But it had just been a ruse. She didn't care. She was just like everyone else in Gemma's life who hadn't cared.

A small, sharp stone dug into the flesh beneath her sandal. Stepping behind a palm tree, she leaned her back against it and dug the stone out. *That stone is you, Ellie.*

Clay and Eoin came jogging from the opposite direction. She was about to step out and join them when they ran straight up to Ellie.

None of them could see Gemma where she was now, in the middle of the thick clump of palm trees. She decided to stay and listen.

"Where's Hayley?" Eoin demanded. "You're supposed to be watching her."

"She's fine," Ellie said defensively. "I *am* watching her. She's in the fields with Tate. *You're* supposed to be watching her with me. You don't seem to be doing a good job of that."

"I was busy indoctrinating the new chick from the harvest." Eoin shrugged, exhaling loudly.

"He didn't do a good job of *that*, either," Clay joked at Eoin then grew serious. "Freddy was meant to be watching Gemma, but we just found him passed out drunk in the field. Hope the snakes get him, the fat fuck."

"What about *you?*" Ellie said. "Aren't both you and Fred assigned to Gemma?"

"Yeah." Clay shoved his hands into his pockets. "But I've got other stuff to do tonight. We're waiting on a delivery."

Gemma listened, incensed. Why were they watching her and Hayley? Who asked them to do that? She eyed the two-way radios that the three of them wore clipped to their belts. She guessed that they used those to keep track of the new workers at the farm.

"Anyway," Clay continued, "Gemma seems happy. I was just with her at the party."

"Did you race her off for a quickie?" Eoin asked.

Clay frowned. "Nope. She looked like she'd taken something."

"All the more reason." Eoin waggled his eyebrows.

Shaking his head, Clay groaned. "You're a deviant."

Eoin grinned. "Wait." Ellie's voice sounded tense and shivery. "That delivery guy is coming here now?"

"Yep," Eoin told her, seeming oblivious to her frightened tone. "Rodney's dropping off some chemicals and other stuff."

"I'm heading back to the party. Hayley's okay. She's with Tate. I'll look out for Gemma too." Ellie started to walk.

"Just a minute." Eoin reached to grab her wrist. "You're scared of the delivery guy, aren't you?"

"No. I'm not scared of him." Despite Ellie's denial, it was obvious to Gemma that she was.

Eoin peered closely at Ellie's face. "Something's wrong here. We're going to have to tell Tate."

"You don't need to tell Tate anything. So, don't," said Ellie quickly.

"Actually, you look like you've been crying." Eoin rummaged in Ellie's pocket and pulled out her phone. "Well, *this* is trouble. Thought I could see something in there."

"We're allowed to call home sometimes," Ellie said rigidly.

Eoin made a whistling sound through his teeth. "Yeah, when Tate says so. Once a month, when we're all together at Monday meditation." He pushed the phone into his own pocket.

The headlights of a small truck flashed at the top of the farm's driveway, just beyond the gate.

Clay nudged Eoin. "Leave Ells alone. Anyway, we gotta go."

Eoin jabbed a finger in the air at Ellie before heading off with Clay. "I'm keeping an eye on you."

Eoin and Clay headed off towards the gate while Ellie continued on her way back to the house.

There was no way Gemma wanted to return to the party now. Clay wouldn't be there, and Ellie would be watching her—for some crazy reason that Gemma didn't understand. And the conversation between the three of them had been damned strange. So, Clay had only been cosying up to her because he was *supposed* to be? Like he'd been assigned to her or something?

The mix of foods she'd eaten earlier at the party rolled in her stomach until she wanted to vomit.

Everything had seemed good—*stupidly glorious* even—just minutes ago. Now it was all lying in a big stinking ruin.

Gemma remained where she was, looking on as Clay and Eoin unloaded boxes from the truck in the distance, carrying the goods into a large supply shed. She could only see a silhouette of the truck driver. What had he done to make Ellie so afraid of him? Maybe she'd been a bitch to him and he'd retaliated. Yeah, that made sense. She could be pretty snippy.

Gemma decided to go and confront Clay—let out the anger that was now lying low in her belly.

Gemma crossed the grounds, stopping just behind one of the farm's many SUVs that were parked up near the gate. She still couldn't see the driver clearly. But she could hear him, speaking in low tones to Clay. Eoin had stepped away and was talking into his two-way radio.

"Make sure you stack these carefully," the driver warned. "It's chemicals in glass vials. They'll smash like a china shop if you drop them."

"Keep your hat on, Rodney," Clay told him. "We'll be careful. Hey, one of the farm's supervisors seems to have a problem with you. *Ellie*. What's that about?"

Rodney paused with a box in his arms. "Mate, that's none of your business. Drop it."

Clay didn't drop it. "She seems pretty cut up. I'm going to let Tate know."

Placing the box on the ground, the man advanced towards Clay. "I'll tell him myself. Nothing happened. She's just a hysterical kid."

Clay stood his ground. "What the hell do you do on the farm, anyway—apart from the deliveries? You're always coming here at odd hours. I see you sneaking around the grounds at night. Does Tate even know about that?"

Rodney clutched Clay's shoulder. "What I do around here is between Tate and me. Even *he* doesn't know everything that I do. And that's the way it's going to stay. If you get in my way, then things are not going to go well for you."

The cold, menacing tone in the man's voice made a shiver rain down Gemma's back.

Eoin moved in between the driver and Clay. "Clay, lad, maybe you should back off."

Gemma glanced behind her. Hayley came walking out of the fields, her blond hair lifting in the light breeze. Gemma decided to head her off and make sure she stayed well away from the strange delivery driver.

Staying out of sight of the three men, Gemma slipped past the supply sheds and met up with Hayley.

Hayley's eyes held a contented kind of sheen in them, her cheeks glowing. "I was just with—"

"I know. You were with Tate."

"Why aren't you at the party?"

"Why aren't *you*?" Gemma felt nothing but lost and irritated now. She wished she'd been the one waltzing about the fields with Tate and didn't hear all that she'd just heard. The night had gone from bad to worse.

Hayley sounded deflated when she said, "I was hoping you were having a good time. Sounds like you weren't."

"No, I'm not."

"Come and dance with me at the party. Let's have some fun. I'm not ready to go to bed."

"You do what you want. I'm heading off to the cabin. But don't wander around the grounds. Someone just said they saw a red-bellied black snake up that way." She pointed in the direction of the driver and his van.

Hayley shuddered. "Ugh. Yeah, I'll stay at the party."

She debated whether to tell Hayley about what she'd just heard Clay and Eoin say. If she told her, Hayley might freak and want to leave the next day. And she didn't want that. She had no money and nowhere to go.

Gemma and Hayley looked up abruptly at the house as two figures walked up the stairway. Through the all-glass frontage of the three-storey mansion, it was easy to see that the pair were Tate and Ellie.

Tate led Ellie inside a thick white door at the top of the stairs and closed the door behind them.

Inhaling sharply, Gemma crossed her arms. Was Ellie sleeping with Tate? Of course she was. What else would they be doing in that room together? All of that nonsense with Ellie looking shy and embarrassed in her skanky red bikini today was just that—nonsense.

And all that stuff about her being scared of the delivery guy was just Ellie trying to cover up her affair with Tate.

Gemma knew exactly what Ellie was now.

A conniving, lying little snake.

Ellie had told Hayley and herself about the venomous snakes here on the first day they'd arrived—but Ellie was the real snake they should be looking out for.

Now Gemma knew how Ellie had scored a cushy job as a farm supervisor. She'd been throwing herself at Tate.

20

HAYLEY

She woke with a headache that seemed to radiate from the back of her skull until it settled behind her eyes into a dull, thudding ache. What had happened after Gemma had left the party? It was blurry now. She'd obviously drunk too much and blacked out, but she knew she hadn't been drinking a lot at the beginning of the party. Why did she drink so much in the end?

What an idiot. Her mouth was dry as a bone, fuzzy, and tasted like stale beer. And in this heat? She was going to wilt. Or puke. Probably both.

Gemma was gone, and Hayley realised that she'd slept in later than usual. It was Saturday, and Hayley wasn't sure whether she'd be mango picking today or not. Did they work weekends here? She cast her mind back to her first day but couldn't remember.

Gently, very gently, she swung her legs out from the bed and sat upright, with her head spinning and her stomach lurching. When she rubbed her eyes, last night's mascara coated her fingers. It was all over her pillowcase too.

What happened after Gemma left?

She remembered getting a drink. After her long chat with Tate, she had been in a good mood, and she wanted to dance for a while. At this point she was mostly sober and a little afraid of the writhing bodies that had broken away from the others. She saw several people in varying stages of undress at different places in the fields and quickly glanced away. But instead of her feeling like a prude, she found it kind of funny and adventurous. Like the holiday feeling people get away from home, more likely to throw caution to the wind. Maybe it was like that. Maybe that was why she'd started drinking more than usual. And then headed to the dancefloor...

There was a guy in a tropical shirt. She'd danced with him for a while. Eoin had tried grinding against her, and she *thought* he'd given her a drink.

How long had the party gone on for?

She glanced down at her body. She was still dressed in the clothes she wore to the party. After closing her eyes for a few moments, the room finally calmed, and she felt a little better. Her head still ached so badly she felt like there was a drill boring through her skull, but she was at least able to get her makeup bag and begin removing her eye makeup.

Halfway through the second eye, there was a knock on the door.

"Yeah?" Hayley croaked. She barely bothered to straighten herself up, expecting Ellie to step through the door. But to her surprise, it was Eoin.

"Morning, lush." He grinned at her. "Feeling spritely this morning by the look of ya."

Hayley just groaned. "What time did I leave last night?"

"Oh, I dunno," he replied. "But I think the morning birds were singing. I had no idea you were such a party animal."

"I'm not." Hayley pulled the duvet around her protectively, hiding her crumpled dress.

"Well, whatever. You'll have to pull yourself together, I'm afraid. The boss wants to see you."

"Tate?" Despite the awful hangover, she felt her mood brighten and her back straighten in surprise.

"He wants to show you his greenhouse. If I were you, I'd down some coffee, boot, and rally." He cringed. "Maybe not in that order. And have a shower, yeah? I'll meet you near the food hall and take you across."

An hour later, Hayley had not booted, but she had managed to keep down a breakfast of dry toast and a large cup of coffee, showered thoroughly, and applied foundation to hide her dark circles. There was still no sign of Gemma. Maybe she'd gone for a walk to clear her head. Hayley remembered Gemma seeming a bit drunk and emotional before she'd left the party. And then... oh, of course! They'd seen Ellie walking up to the farm with Tate.

Hayley's shoulders slumped. She'd forgotten all about that. Maybe seeing Ellie with Tate was the reason why she'd started drinking so much after Gemma left. Perhaps it was irrational to think this, but after her walk with Tate, she'd felt a definite connection and had hoped it was romantic. But if Ellie was with Tate, she must have misread the signs.

No, surely not. She couldn't imagine Tate with a girl like Ellie. Ellie was a little... off? A little odd. Immature, maybe. And Tate was so sophisticated and together. No. It wasn't possible.

But why else would Ellie be with him late at night?

As she came out of the food hall, Eoin nodded to her, and then his eyes roamed over her body.

"Looking better already," Eoin said, his grin lopsided and mischievous. "I'll take you up to see the boss."

Hayley flanked his right as they made their way through the compound to the mansion. On the way she couldn't help searching for Gemma, worried that she'd upset her somehow during the party last night.

"Have you seen Gemma this morning?"

Eoin shrugged. "A bunch of people went to check out the springs this morning. Maybe she went with them. I saw one ute heading to the town too."

Well, if Gemma went with them, at least she wouldn't be on her own. "How long have you been here, exactly?" Hayley asked, trying to pass the time.

"Six months or so."

"Don't you miss home?"

"Nah. Here's much better. Decent craic, good people, good food. And then there's the girls... Well." He wiggled his eyebrows suggestively. "We have a laugh here. It's more relaxed. I actually moved to London to work in a bank before I went travelling. To be honest with you, I was sick of England, even sick of Ireland. Sick of the traffic, the people, the way everyone is so fucking uptight. You don't need to worry about any of that here."

"And Tate? Do you know him well?"

"About as well as everyone else." Eoin directed them through the carpark towards the farm where the long greenhouse was adjacent to the glass walls of the house. "He mostly keeps himself to himself. Apart from during the meditations."

"What are those about?"

"Mindfulness mainly. I don't think I have the words to explain it," he said. "But I feel better after them."

Hayley frowned, wondering what *better* meant. Better wasn't good, or amazing, or brilliant. It was just *better*. Better than what?

"Here. Just through that door. Don't touch any of the orchids. Seriously." Eoin nodded and raised his eyebrows to show just how serious he was, before he turned around and walked away, not giving Hayley an opportunity for any more questions.

It sounded like Tate was pretty intense about these orchids. Eoin's warning had spooked her a little, unless it was the hangover paranoia creeping in. As she opened the door, she had nerves bouncing around her belly and her mouth had gone dry again.

The scent of the orchids was like spiced vanilla and cinnamon, but with a subtle, floral note to it. They were in rows atop trolleys, with a watering system rigged above them, colourful and bright against the glass and chrome of the rest of the greenhouse. Back in York her mother had been given an orchid from a friend, but it'd wilted and died quite quickly after her mother failed to look after it properly. All Hayley remembered of that plant was its strange little bud at the centre of the petals. A little button on its face, like a nose.

She dared not touch, but she did lean in for a closer inspection. Red, pink, white, yellow... They each had a separate scent too.

"I wish I had a camera," said a low, silky voice.

She hadn't heard anyone approach, and the sudden sound of Tate's voice seemed discordant in the echoing space.

"What?" Her jaw fell open, and she felt stupid. Her face flushed with heat, and she longed for the ground to swallow her whole.

Tate took a step towards her, with his hands pushed deep into his pockets, his shoulders relaxed. He was just as suave and smart as last night, in a light-blue shirt and grey trousers. Despite the hot day he appeared cool and collected, whereas Hayley could feel her hair sticking to her neck with sweat.

"I said, I wish I had a camera. Because the image of you witnessing this greenhouse for the first time is beautiful."

Blood rushed to her cheeks, and she felt like a child next to this man. He wasn't that much older but he seemed so much more *together*. She was a mess. A hot, tangled mess of a girl. *Fuck*. What was she doing here? And now she had to reply, but she didn't know what to say.

"Thank you for coming this morning," he said. "I know it's Saturday and you girls like to throw on a swimsuit and head to the springs." He smiled knowingly, as though imagining the sight. "But I like to show some of the new recruits my greenhouse. Many have never even seen an orchid, if you can believe it." He moved closer, but all Hayley could think about was that word 'some'. She had been chosen out of many. Why?

"This is a Moth Orchid, or *Phalaenopsis*. One of the most popular varieties. The flowers resemble a moth in flight. That's how they got their name." He steered her away from the white and pink flower to another, with pretty little yellow petals. "We call this the Dancing Lady Orchid, or *Oncidium*. The sprays of flowers are so intense that the plant often can't hold its own weight and they sag downwards. I find that incredibly sad, that a flower can't support its own beauty. Luckily, this one has me to help it grow."

"I love that colour," Hayley said, relaxing as she leaned in to inhale the scent.

Tate smiled wider to reveal his white teeth "It suits you. The yellow reflects off your gorgeous golden skin."

A shiver ran down Hayley's back. The good kind that tingles on its way, that sends butterflies into your stomach, that prickles your flesh with excitement.

"I don't normally do this." Tate's wide smile turned into a mischievous grin, making Hayley feel as though she was in on a secret. "But I think you need this." He picked up a pair of secateurs from a trolley next to the plants and carefully, very carefully pruned a flower from the Dancing Lady Orchid. Then he gently placed the flower in Hayley's hair, tucking it above her ear. "Beautiful. You're just beautiful, Hayley."

That slight lean forward and the touch of his fingers against her skin made her heart pound. There was no denying that he was the most attractive man she had ever seen outside of her television screen, and she couldn't believe he had singled her out of everyone else at the farm. She felt her knees weaken as he showed her around the rest of the greenhouse. Her mind couldn't stop focusing on the moment his skin brushed hers and the magnetism she'd felt emanating from him. She was gone. Completely gone. Like a puddle on the floor. And Hayley never fell for guys like this. She'd never had the goosebumps and the tingles and the inability to focus on anyone but *the guy*. Her boyfriends in the past had usually progressed from a few drunken fumbles to a full-on relationship without any real fanfare or knee-weakening action. Tate was different. He was a man, and when he graced her with his focus, she felt like the only girl in the world.

"I think it's perfect," Hayley said, turning back to the orchid on the trolley, but thinking more about the man next to her.

"Nothing is perfect," Tate replied. "You have to look hard to find the imperfections, but they're always there."

"Really?"

He stood behind her and leaned over her shoulder as he pointed to the centre of an orchid flower in front of them. There, next to its stamen, was a tiny tear in the petal.

"I didn't even see it," Hayley remarked.

"That's because the bright colour distracted you," he replied. "Come on. I want to show you everything we do here."

As they made their way through the greenhouse, he talked to her like she was an adult, and that was new for her. She was used to being pushed and prodded around by her parents, always kept in a little bubble to make sure she did the *right* thing. Go to school. Do your work. Pass your exams. Thailand hadn't been the remedy to all of that structure, but it had led her away from it. And now she was here, with a man who treated her so differently to anyone else. Tate spent time explaining the different orchids to her, but not in a patronising way, more in an enthusiast's way. He even showed her his lab, which was nestled away in a large building attached to the greenhouse.

"This is where we extract chemicals from the orchids," he explained. "It's a lengthy process using solvents, which I won't go into." Tate stopped to nod and wave at an assistant through the glass. "But those chemicals are then put into perfumes and so on." The corners of his lips rose quickly then dropped, and his gaze moved away.

Hayley felt like she should be paying attention, because she'd been so intrigued by the laboratory and what went on inside. She'd been so suspicious of the place, and she was still interested, but Tate had blinded her with his charm, and now she just wanted to be back in the greenhouse with him, smelling the orchids. But she did force herself to concentrate on what she was seeing. There was a stack of large glass bottles wrapped in cellophane in one of the corners. There were two lab workers, one male and one female. She didn't get close enough to see their faces because Tate informed her that they couldn't go further due to possible contamination. The lab workers wore goggles and blue gloves and held test tubes.

"Is this your passion?" Hayley asked. "I mean, I know you have the mango farm, but you seem to really love the orchids. So is this what you're most passionate about?"

"I think it is, yes," Tate said. "Because it's exciting. I'm creating something new and original. Something the world hasn't seen yet." He paused. "I know it's silly to feel that way about perfume, but I think you'll agree with me when you learn more about what goes on here."

"I'd love to learn more."

Tate wrapped an arm around her shoulders. "I can't wait to show you. But it'll take time. You need to settle in first."

21

GEMMA

Gemma had been stuck with Freddy again all morning, assigned to weeding. Tate liked the grounds pristine.

She wiped sweat from her forehead and where it trickled along her nose. Today the farm seemed sandwiched between layers of blue sky and red earth, being cooked as if in a grill. The temperature soared even higher than yesterday.

Freddy shovelled dirt to cover the holes left after they'd pulled out the bellyache bush. Ellie was supervising, occasionally taking loads of it away in a wheelbarrow. Gemma was glad to see two of the supervisors doing some work. She'd been shocked to discover last night that Freddy was one of the farm's leaders. He seemed like a large, naughty child.

Clay had come up behind her three hours ago and put his arms around her, and she'd reacted as if she had been stung. She told him she'd heard everything he'd said to Eoin. She hadn't seen him since.

She hacked at the bellyache bush. The stubborn weed had purple leaves and was toxic to humans and livestock. Gemma thought wryly that it was giving her a bellyache just from the effort of digging it out of the ground.

Leaning on his shovel, Freddy began telling a dirty joke, snickering uncontrollably as he paused just before the punchline.

Gemma shot him a glance that was halfway between mocking and withering. "Say it and die."

Looking cheated, Freddy dropped his mouth shut. Gemma ripped a weed from its moorings to show that she meant it.

No way I'm putting up with your lame jokes anymore, Freddy boy. You and Clay and Eoin and Ellie—you can all go to hell. Hayley and I are not children who need watching.

Where was Hayley anyway? She hadn't seen her all morning. Ellie simply said that Hayley had been given a task to do.

It was close to midday when Gemma spotted Hayley emerging from the orchid greenhouse. Hayley's cheeks were flushed pink, but it couldn't be from the heat of the day—she'd been indoors. Then Gemma saw Tate step out after her.

Gemma immediately felt deflated, brushing sweat-soaked hair back from her eyes and flexing her stiff shoulders. What task had Tate given Hayley to do in there? And wasn't it supposed to be restricted?

Ellie had an odd look on her face as her eyes tracked Tate returning to his house. But then she began humming, her eyes going blank.

Hayley headed off to the hall. Why was Hayley going there and not helping with the weeding? Maybe it was break time.

Rising, Gemma dusted off her dirt-caked hands and walked across to Ellie. She waved her fingers in front of Ellie's face. "Hello, anyone home?"

Ellie blinked as if distracted from a dream. "Gemma. Is everything okay?"

"Yeah. Just wondering if we're going to be doing this all day."

"No, of course not. Just a half day on Saturday. And Sundays are completely free." She began humming again.

Just then, a voice came over the loudspeakers: *Time to put down tools, everyone. Thank you for all your hard work this morning. Everyone to meet at the hall. Enjoy the rest of your day.*

The disembodied voice was Sophie's—Tate's office assistant. It was only ten o'clock. Were they all having an early lunch?

Leaving Freddy to put the tools away, Gemma headed off for a shower. She dressed in denim shorts and a halter top and made her way down to the hall.

Hayley was there, along with about a dozen others, packing food into small insulated containers.

"Gemma!" Hayley grinned in excitement. "We're going camping!"

Eoin, lifting a bag of rice, nodded at Gemma. "One of the perks of the farm. We're heading off to the gorge. We go almost every weekend, except in the rainy season. Too many crocs about then. Supposed to be the rainy season right now, but we've had a long dry spell."

"Cool." Gemma couldn't manage to dredge up any enthusiasm.

Clay was there too. He flicked his gaze towards Gemma, but she looked away sharply.

Standing back, Gemma watched them packing up the mountains of food. Everyone seemed to know what was going on around here, except for her. Even shy, reserved little Hayley had moved into the swing of things. Gemma wasn't used to that. She was used to being the one who people looked to for direction. But the farm had somehow turned the order of things upside down. Like gravity had suddenly been switched off.

As soon as the insulated food containers were stuffed into backpacks, everyone piled into the SUVs again. Gemma, Hayley, and a girl named Dharma ended up in the car that Ellie was driving.

Dharma was one of the long-term residents of the farm—an Australian. Her frizzy blond hair framed a pixie face that was punctuated with nose, eyebrow, and lip piercings. She was annoyingly positive and bubbly, talking about how great everything was.

Ellie continued to be strange, barely speaking. Switching on the radio, she hummed along to the songs with her own tune, as if she could only hear music playing in her head.

The drive to the town of Katherine was hot and dusty. Instead of the line of cars stopping in the town this time, they peeled off and made a left-hand turn onto Gorge Road. The road took them all the way to a tourist centre.

A park ranger met with them all as they emerged from the cars. His name was Pete, and he had deeply brown skin. He introduced himself as a descendant of the native Jawoyn people.

"Who are the new people here today?" Pete asked.

Dharma gently pushed Gemma and Hayley forward. A few of the new recruits from the hot springs stepped forward alongside them.

"Hello and welcome, newbies," said Ranger Pete. "Hope you'll enjoy your time here. This place used to be called the Katherine Gorge, but it's now known as Nitmiluk, in respect to the traditional owners—the Jawoyn and Dagomen people. Nitmiluk means *place of cicada dreaming*. Many of my ancestors' rock paintings can be found throughout the area. The Katherine River carved out the ancient sandstone millions of years ago. It's a series of thirteen gorges, separated by rapids, and about fifteen kilometres long, with sheer cliffs of sixty to ninety metres high—uh, any Americans among you?"

A wiry, muscled black guy put up his hand. "Yo."

"Okay," said Pete. "For you, that's roughly ten miles long and almost three hundred feet high. Your group can kayak freely between the gorges and pull up and camp wherever the mood takes you. You won't find better swimming holes anywhere in the world. As usual, the boss at your farm has arranged the overnight hire of kayaks and camping sites with a tourism operator."

His voice switched from friendly to stern. "You are to stay with the others at all times. They know where to go and where not to go.

Stay clear of freshie breeding grounds. To the best of our knowledge, there are no salties."

"*Freshies and salties?*" Hayley asked hesitantly.

"Freshwater and saltwater crocs," Pete answered. "Breeding season for the freshies is over, but you are still to stay well clear of them. Kayaking at this time of year is not usually allowed, because the wet season can mean flooding and dangerously fast water—and salties. But we've had a stupidly long spell of the dry. So, we've been able to keep the salties well out of the gorge. Don't worry, we've got an excellent safety record."

One of the new recruits—a tall, spindly German guy—did a double blink at that information. "You're saying there are freshwater crocodiles are out there in the water right now? How big are they?"

Pete stretched his arms straight out, grinning. "About three times as big as that, mate. But they won't hurt you if you don't annoy them. You're not the tucker they're after. Please remember everyone, being here is a privilege. Don't mess it up by doing anything dumb. During your trip, just think, *what would Pete do?*" Crossing his arms, he smiled broadly, showing evenly-spaced white teeth.

People seemed to take that as a sign to start moving off.

Gemma hung back. Anything with large, snapping jaws terrified her. Whether it was sharks, crocodiles, or dogs. "What do we do if a freshie approaches us?"

"They won't approach." A troubled look entered Pete's eyes, and he lowered his voice. "You're from the *Llewellyn* farm and you're worried about the *crocs?*"

"I'm not sure what you mean."

"I've been to the farm. It's a very different animal to any of the other farms around these parts, that's all I'm saying. And as for that guy they call *The Chemist…*" He exhaled, a deep wrinkle indenting his forehead. "Anyway, you'd better scoot before they leave without you."

Gemma headed off after the others, casting a backward glance at Pete.

Down at the river, people were already paddling away from the stretch of sand. Hayley, standing by the bank, tugged Gemma's hand towards one of the kayaks.

Eoin jumped in front of them. "Have either of you kayaked before?"

Hayley shook her head.

"How hard can it be?" Gemma raised her eyebrows, annoyed that he wasn't among the people who'd already left.

"Try paddling up the river all day and then carrying a heavy kayak between the gorges," Eoin said. "Then you'll have your answer."

Shrugging, Hayley glanced at Gemma. "I'll go with Eoin. You go with someone with a bit of experience."

Gemma stared at her. Hayley was different. Before, she'd said she couldn't stand the sight of Eoin. Now she was jumping into a kayak with him. It seemed like the doubts about the farm that Hayley had spoken of were completely gone now. She was no longer questioning anything.

There were just three kayaks left.

Clay waited in one of them, expectantly. Throwing her backpack over her shoulder, Gemma stepped through the water and into a kayak with a muscly girl.

Gemma didn't look at Clay again as they pushed off.

The girl was Australian, Gemma discovered. From country Queensland. Her family used to own a cattle station until drought drove them from it.

The blinding afternoon sun tinted the soaring sandstone cliffs red. They paddled along a wide expanse of jewel-green water.

A crocodile with a long, narrow snout basked on the sandy riverbank. Gemma started rowing away.

"Don't worry," the girl told her. "He couldn't care less about you."

Further down the river, the group pulled the kayaks off at a tranquil water hole. Deep water lay between twin rock walls, a waterfall rushing down a steep wall at the end. Hayley dived straight in, trusting Eoin's word that it was safe.

For a while, Gemma sat on the bank, watching everyone wade in, her head throbbing from the heat. Even in the shade, the temperature was sweltering. Clay glanced across at her a few times, but she refused to meet his gaze. He'd have to give up sooner or later.

The water proved too enticing. Gemma slipped in and let herself float, her hair fanning out and encircling her. When she opened her eyes, cathedrals of cliffs seemed to form a safe place—a sanctum. Maybe things weren't as bad as they seemed. Everything could be rationalised. She was overthinking things.

She swam across the warm surface.

For a moment, her vision blurred with the sharp reflections of light in her eyes. At the far edge of the water hole, a large shape moved. Her vision focused.

A crocodile.

Her entire body tensed. This time, she wasn't in a kayak. She was in the water—crocodile territory.

The more she told herself to swim, the more she froze. Water lapped above her mouth. She could hear every breath she took.

Someone was stroking towards her. Clay. He put an arm around her shoulders, and she felt herself being tugged backwards.

Breaking away from him, she swam to shore.

Clay splashed out after her. "You okay? You were starting to go under out there."

Pushing her dripping hair back from her face, she breathed deeply. "No, I wasn't. I didn't need help."

She glanced across at the reptile in the distance. It was in exactly the same position. It hadn't gone into the water after her.

Clay followed her gaze and then turned back to her. "That's a freshie. Were you scared of—?"

"Just quit watching me, okay?"

"I'm not."

"You don't have to pretend anymore. You didn't have to stick on me like a damned leech last night just because Tate told you to."

"You think that's why I was hanging out with you?"

"Just... leave me be." She walked away, towards where Hayley was talking animatedly with a small group, all of them standing waist-deep in the water. None of them had even noticed Clay's rescue attempt. Hayley flashed her a smile.

The farm workers spent the rest of the day rowing and trekking in and out of gorges and diving under waterfalls. Close to sunset, Eoin and Fred decided that the group should camp overnight on a sandy riverbank. The sunset was insanely beautiful, making the sand glow a deep apricot colour, layers of burnt orange and purplish sky spread wide behind the rust-red rises of the gorge.

Dharma and a group of girls picked bunches of wildflowers that Gemma was sure they weren't allowed to pick. Dharma's group threaded flower garlands for everyone's hair and then made everyone sing sixties songs around a campfire. For a while, Gemma almost felt connected to the group, yelling out the lyrics to a song she'd just learned—Neil Young's *Sugar Mountain*. The song's lyrics were something about adolescence and having to leave a place called Sugar Mountain when you turned twenty.

But she couldn't completely lose herself to these people. Some of them were watching her—and who knew about the others? She had to stay vigilant. The same way she'd lived her whole life.

Gemma glanced at Hayley, who was singing louder than just about anyone, holding hands with Dharma and another girl. She had a blissful expression on her face, her eyes glistening in the light of the flames. Gemma realised that Hayley was exactly where she wanted to be.

Dinner followed. Sausages and mashed potatoes, and lentil rissoles for the vegans and vegetarians. Gemma was surprised that there were no drugs or alcohol on offer once dinner wrapped up. Dharma informed her that Tate strictly forbade it when they were out camping. He didn't want anyone drowning in the river or making stupid decisions.

People started putting up tents or walking off in small groups. Hayley wanted to stay in Dharma's group, singing songs around the fire.

Gemma wandered off on her own. She wasn't sure where she fit in now or who she could trust.

The singing sounded distant as she walked further away.

Sitting cross-legged on a rock, she plucked a wildflower from the garland in her hair and tore it to pieces, petal by petal.

Someone walked up next to her, carrying a light.

She knew it was Clay even before he spoke.

"When I was a kid," he drawled, looking upward. "I dreamed of seeing the Centaurus constellation. But I needed a Southern sky. And, bang, there it is. Centaurus. So clear. Half-man, half-horse."

She let the petals drop through her fingers. "People romanticise stars. They're just hot-as-hell suns. Not centaurs. Not twinkling little jewels to wish upon. Just suns."

"Aren't you a barrel of laughs?"

"Do you have to follow me *everywhere*? What if I'd gone off to pee?"

Climbing the rock, he came and sat next to her, so close that she could see tiny patches on his nose and cheeks where the sun had made his skin flake, and fine scars on his chin and below his lip.

"I'm not following you," he said. "I came to apologise. Tate told me to make sure you're okay, that's all."

"*I'm okay.* Put that in your report."

"There's no report. We keep a close eye on all new workers." He exhaled. "Can we start again?"

"Why?"

"Because I like you. I was hoping that you liked *me*."

She didn't answer, looking away into the patchwork of dark spaces.

"Hey, ask me anything," he said. "I'll answer it honestly."

She shrugged. "What're those scars on your face?"

"Dog bite. When I was ten. I patted a dog in the street—back in Sugar Land, where I lived until I was twelve."

"*Ouch.* That happened to me too."

"I know. I remember what you said when you introduced yourself in the gathering hall."

"But no one lives in *Sugar Land*. You just made that up."

"I'll take you there one day. It's not far from Houston. One set of grandparents still live there."

"Hmmm. Okay. Did you have fun when you were growing up?"

"Yeah. Apart from the dog bite, that is. It was a good childhood. But then my mom died and my dad ended up drifting from Texas down to Mexico. I spent most of my teenage years in Mexico. It wasn't the place that was bad—it was my father. All he did was drink."

"My mum died when I was a kid too. And my dad's an alcoholic, just like yours. How old are you now?"

"Twenty."

"Are you planning on working your way up at the farm—like, becoming a manager or something?"

"Nope. I was planning on heading off straight after the mango season. But I'm not sure now. There's this girl who just arrived at the farm, and I'd kind of like a chance to get to know her better..."

She ignored that. "How can a supervisor just *leave*?"

He hesitated. "Don't mention it to Tate, okay? There's a few things that I—" He sighed heavily, shaking his head. "Never mind. Can't see myself staying much longer, that's all."

"You sounded so happy about the farm that first night I spoke to you. Like nothing could ever be wrong."

"It was an act. For newbies."

She felt her forehead crinkle into a frown. "Why put on a big act?"

"It's just the way Tate likes it. He puts in a lot of effort to make everyone happy, so he expects a lot from his supervisors." He paused. "Can we drop this? Clean slate?"

She wanted to get up and walk away from him. But she didn't. Because maybe he was right and she'd just read too much into what she'd overheard. She wanted him to be right.

The look on his face was so damned earnest. Not many people were earnest. Maybe it *was* better to pretend that they just met each other and start again. Sometimes, pretending was easier. Reality was just someone's perception anyway.

"Clean slate," she echoed.

They shook hands.

He kept her hand in his. "Now, time for me to ask *you* any question I want. And you have to answer it."

Moving her face close to his, she switched his penlight off and kissed him. That was easier than telling him about herself. She'd already told him enough the night of the party. Telling people too much was always a mistake.

She surprised him with the kiss. But he kissed her back. And kept kissing her.

She watched the stars overhead. Stars that were suns. Or eyes. Or sparkly silver fucking jewels. It didn't matter. What you chose to believe was all that mattered. It was all that ever mattered. What you believed to be true in the moment.

It felt awkward at first when things went further. Two bodies that didn't yet know each other's curves and angles and scents.

They fell onto the still-warm sand together. Behind the rock, in the darkness, no one could see them.

They held each other, entwining, their breaths growing fast and hard.

"Can we?" he said, panting. "I mean, I have a condom—"

"Did you think you were going to get lucky tonight?"

"Better than getting caught without one."

She couldn't argue with that logic, but she wondered wryly if he took them everywhere he went.

He began kissing her again.

Unbidden, another face kept flashing in her mind. *Tate's.* One moment, it was like Tate was there—above her, murmuring her name.

It was only when Clay was done that she realised where she was and who she was with again. Clay mustn't have noticed her zoning out. She was glad for the cover of the darkness.

She moved in against Clay's chest, numb and confused.

How does Tate manage to push his way into my thoughts all the time? What did he even say to me at the farm yesterday? That conversation was now floating in loose threads in the air, along with the scents of sunscreen and humid earth.

Clay stroked her hair. "Did you get there?"

She shook her head on his chest.

"Do you want me to—?"

"It's okay. Next time."

"I'm happy there'll be a *next time.*" He continued stroking her hair, softly singing along with the group that were still shouting out songs back at the campfire.

She wanted to enjoy just being here with him, but she couldn't— not totally. They began talking again, until Clay fell into a deep sleep. She stayed awake for hours before she felt herself drifting.

They woke just before sunrise, on the other side of the rock, still wrapped up together.

Gemma startled as she noticed that people had gathered around them and one of them was tugging her hair. She angled her head backwards to see who it was.

Dharma was busily playing with Gemma's hair. "Hey, sleepy-head," she crooned.

Gemma gave a nervous, self-conscious smile and tried to sit. She discovered that her hair had been plaited together with Clay's and entwined with wildflowers.

Clay started laughing, sitting up with her.

"I hereby pronounce you two engaged." Lifting her chin, Dharma fluffed out her long, kinky locks.

"S'true," someone else said in a wise tone. "When Dharma ties two people together, it's official. She does this all the time."

The group of people clapped and cheered.

Clay dropped a kiss on her temple. "Sorry I don't have a ring," he quipped.

Hayley appeared from between the mass of people, not clapping or cheering. Her brow was deeply furrowed. "Gemma, d'you know where Ellie is? I couldn't find either of you. Now I've found *you*, but I still don't know where Ellie got to."

Gemma squinted up at Hayley as the sun peeked over the gorge walls, sparking long, gold-hued rays into her eyes. "Probably in her tent."

"No, I checked," Hayley said. "She's not. Ellie and I are supposed to be making porridge for everyone."

Gemma began untangling her hair from Clay's. "Maybe she went for a walk. Anyway, most people probably aren't even hungry yet."

Hayley bit her top lip. "I just want to do a good job. Show that I'm fitting in."

"Hey," said Clay. "Why don't we go look for Ellie? I need a walk and a good stretch anyway."

Gemma unpicked the last of Clay's locks from her own and pulled herself to her feet. "I have to go pee. Then we'll go."

In one direction, the way was blocked with a high rock wall. The three of them headed in the opposite direction, Gemma splashing her feet in the water, her fingers catching with Clay's. Hayley glanced across curiously.

The path was well-worn, from endless days of tourists. But there were no tourists here today.

Gemma felt the heat rising from the ground. It was going to be another hot one. Clay went to take a leak, his bare back shining in the sun. Gemma and Hayley rounded a corner, squeezing between two boulders.

At the base of a small waterfall—barely twice as high as Gemma—some wildflowers that their group had picked yesterday fluttered in the tight crevices of the rocks, squashed and trapped.

Curled up on top of the rocks was a girl, eyes closed, the ends of her dark hair floating in the trickling water. A trail of red liquid on her arm splashed red on a rock and was carried away by the water below.

"Ellie..." Gemma mouthed. Her first thought was that it had been a crocodile. But on closer look, it wasn't that. *Not anything close to that.*

Thin red lines marked Ellie's wrists.

In a blur that seemed to happen in slow motion, they rushed to Ellie.

Hayley pulled her shirt free and wrapped it around and around Ellie's left wrist.

Gemma inhaled a breath of air that didn't release. She wound her own shirt around Ellie's other wrist.

Ellie murmured, opening her eyes.

Hayley moved close to hear. "Ellie?"

"Don't take me back to the farm," Ellie said softly.

Shocked thoughts raced through Gemma's mind. Maybe she didn't like Ellie, but this was bad. Why had Ellie tried to kill herself? And why didn't she want to go back to the farm? She had everything well set up there, right? She was a supervisor. She was sleeping with the damned owner of the farm. Could the thing she'd told Gemma really be true—about something being wrong at the farm?

"You don't have to go back there," Gemma told her. "You can go home."

"It's too late. Too late to go home..." Ellie shook her head. "Don't let him..."

"Who? Don't let who?" Hayley glanced anxiously from Ellie to Gemma and Clay.

"That man." Her voice was weak but icy. "The man with the truck. Don't let him near me. Promise..."

22

HAYLEY

Hayley had never liked the sight of blood, even a paper cut made her wince, but the moment she'd seen Ellie lying like that on the rock, she'd acted before that part of her brain kicked in. What had Ellie done? Hayley tried not to look too hard at the cuts, worried she might faint if she did, but judging by the amount of blood flowing into the water, the cuts were deep.

Why here? Why like this?

"We need to get her to a hospital," Gemma said, and she was right.

"I have a satellite phone in my pack at the campsite," Clay said. "I'll run back and get it."

"Wait." Hayley placed a hand on Clay's arm. "Shouldn't we take her with us?"

"I don't think we should move her." Clay glanced at Ellie and then Gemma in a way Hayley thought seemed guilty, almost regretful. She watched Clay hurry away and frowned, concerned by Clay's hasty explanation. People with certain injuries couldn't be moved, true, but this wasn't a spinal problem. Perhaps he was worried that the effort of moving Ellie might increase blood flow and result in greater blood loss.

"Maybe we should hold her arms above her head," Gemma suggested. "And put more pressure on the wounds."

Ellie let out a cry as they lifted her arms, but she didn't quite pass out from the pain. She certainly seemed to be drifting in and out of consciousness. Whenever she stirred, she began to move her lips. Hayley bent lower, trying to hear what she had to say, but everything she mumbled was in Portuguese.

Hayley squeezed the shirt against the girl's thin arm, trying not to think about the blood seeping through the fabric. "Come on, Ellie. Don't give up now. Tell us why you don't want the man from the truck to come near you." She thought that maybe if she kept Ellie talking then she might stay conscious.

"Did you mean the man that made a delivery the night of the party?" Gemma added. "What was his name—Rodney?"

"Yes, him." Ellie closed her eyes and opened them. Her face contorted into a grimace, like someone mid-sob, her mouth opened wide and tears began to stream down her face. "You." She stared directly at Hayley with her large, piercing eyes, half-focused and manic. "You need to leave. It's not a good place at the farm. You *have* to believe me."

"Okay, I do," Hayley replied. "But tell us why. Tell us what happened to you. Maybe we can help. Especially when you're better... We can tell someone if he's hurting you."

"It was... I don't..." Ellie's eyes rolled back. "My hands feel numb."

"It's okay," Gemma said. "Everything is going to be okay."

"I don't remember things good." Ellie giggled. "That's not correct English. Bad Ellie. Must do better." She paused, seemingly losing consciousness again. Then she said, "He comes at night."

But Ellie had begun mumbling in Portuguese again. Hayley held Gemma's gaze. What had this man done to Ellie at night?

But her thoughts were interrupted by the soft swishing of the water. Clay and Eoin were on their way towards the waterfall in a kayak, both paddling quickly. Clay kept his head turned away, avoiding eye contact with anyone.

As the boat reached the rocks, it was Eoin who took the lead. "Quick, take these bandages and dress the wounds. Then we need to get her in the kayak."

"What the hell?" Hayley exclaimed, catching a bandage. "Now isn't exactly the time for a paddle."

"It's the quickest way back to the visitor's centre," he said, watching carefully as they fixed the bandages tightly around her cuts.

As soon as it was done, Eoin wasted no time, reaching down to scoop skinny little Ellie into his arms.

"What about Ranger Pete?" Hayley asked. "An air ambulance? There has to be another way. Isn't this dangerous?"

"Trust us," Eoin said. "We'll take her from here."

"But where are you taking her?" Gemma got to her feet, bloodied hands placed on her hips.

No answer.

"Eoin," Gemma said again. "Where are you taking her?"

It was Clay who answered this time. "Everything's going to be okay, Gemma. We're taking her back to the farm."

"She's fine," Eoin insisted. "Tate has state-of-the-art medical equipment at the farm. He doesn't like outsiders interfering."

"She doesn't want to go back to the farm," Hayley said. "Eoin, are you listening? She just said—"

"The cuts aren't too deep," he replied. "A few stitches, some rest, and she'll be fine. Tate can do all of that."

"Eoin!" Gemma called as the two men hoisted Ellie onto the boat. "Stop!"

But there was nothing they could do. Eoin and Clay were already paddling away.

Hayley sat on her bed and tried to make sense of everything

that had happened at the gorge. After Clay and Eoin had taken Ellie, everything had seemed like such a blur. They'd paddled their own kayak as fast as they could, reaching the carpark too late to stop Eoin and Clay taking Ellie away. Their truck was already gone.

Ellie hadn't wanted to be taken back to the farm and knowing that didn't sit well with Hayley, and she knew Gemma was angry about it too. She couldn't stop thinking about a barely conscious Ellie being bundled into a truck with Clay and Eoin. It wasn't right.

———

She looked down at her hands and found Ellie's blood still crusted over her skin. Her shirt, screwed up next to her feet, was covered in it. She kicked the bloody shirt under the bed so she didn't have to look at it anymore.

The door opened, and Hayley turned towards the sound. "Any news?"

"They won't tell me shit," Gemma said. Her words were strong, but her posture was stooped and defeated. "But guess what?" Gemma kicked off her flip-flops and slumped onto her bed.

Hayley just shrugged, in no mood to play guessing games.

"Tate wants to see us at the house."

"Isn't that a good thing?" Hayley asked. "Maybe he'll tell us what's going on with Ellie."

"Your guess is as good as mine. All I know is—I'm tired and pissed off and I want to know what's happened to her." Gemma ran her fingers through her sweaty hair before leaning back on the bed.

But Hayley didn't want to sit and mope anymore. She wanted to go to Tate, who surely would have a perfectly reasonable explanation for all of this. Tate would tell *her* what was going on. She and Tate had a connection. He would be straight with her.

But she couldn't stop thinking about what Ellie had whispered to them. That quiet, raw voice and those few words... *He comes at night.* And she shivered. It cast a shadow over this place, over Tate even...

"That man Ellie was talking about," Hayley said. "Do you think he hurt her?"

Gemma sat up. "Yes, I do."

Hayley could barely bring herself to say it. "Do you think he raped her?"

Gemma nodded. "Why do you think Ellie stayed? Maybe Tate wouldn't let her leave?"

Hayley was on her feet in an instant. "That's ridiculous."

"Is it?" Gemma said, still on the bed, but turning to follow Hayley as she paced the length of the room. "What do we know about him except he's a rich white dude with a bunch of young people taking drugs at his parties?"

"Yeah, and you took those drugs and danced the night away," Hayley pointed out.

"And? I didn't know what was going on."

"You still don't," Hayley said.

"No, but something isn't right," Gemma pointed out.

Hayley finally stopped pacing and stood by the door chewing on a thumbnail. When she'd first arrived at the farm, Gemma had seemed the one who fit in and she'd been the outsider. Now, after just a few days, their roles had reversed. But did Gemma have a point about Tate? After all, Hayley had only spent an afternoon with him. Had his charms blinded her to the unsavoury underbelly of the farm?

"Okay," Hayley said. "You might be right. We don't know Tate. We don't know the man in the truck, Rodney, or Ellie, or anyone, really. We've not been here long enough to make a judgement call, and I'm seriously confused about everything. But Ellie is our priority, right? She's a girl in pain, away from her family, and we need to make sure she's okay. So, let's storm up to Tate Llewellyn and demand to find out what's happening."

Gemma stood and brushed dirt from her shorts. "All right. But if we get even a bad *feeling* about Tate, and the farm... or... I dunno, *anything*. We're leaving. Right?"

"Okay. Deal."

Hayley chewed on her bottom lip as they left the room.

———

It was Eoin who took them up to the farm again. But this time he took them into the house, through the living area and up the stairs to what appeared to be a sparsely decorated white room with a built-in cupboard along the wall and three oversized armchairs.

"Take a seat. He'll be back soon." Eoin left without a smile. He'd been silent on the way there. Perhaps it was because of what happened to Ellie. Walking through the compound, Hayley had noted a more sombre air than usual.

"This is the room I saw Ellie come to with Tate," Gemma said. "So, it wasn't a bedroom after all."

Despite everything, Hayley felt relieved, and it annoyed her that she felt that way. Like she'd said in their room, *Ellie* was the priority. Despite her prominent position at the farm, Ellie had felt so alone that she'd slit her wrists.

"Hayley. Gemma."

Hayley hadn't even noticed the door open from the opposite side of the room. Tate stood in the doorway with his hands in his pockets, as always, and his head tilted to the left. His shoulders were low, tired, as though he was exhausted. His eyes were darker than usual. He lifted one hand out of his pocket to rub his temples with finger and thumb. How long had he been there?

"Thank you for coming."

Gemma didn't speak, so Hayley decided to not say anything either.

Tate walked at a leisurely pace towards the final chair, which was positioned on the opposite side of a coffee table. "You both must be feeling very upset. I've ordered chamomile tea for you both. It will be arriving in just a moment." He crossed one leg over the other and gave a thin-lipped smile.

"Poor Ellie. I was sad to see her in that way. Hurt and upset. I can't even imagine what was going through her mind at the time."

"She wanted to die," Gemma said with a hard voice. "Who is Rodney, the man in the truck? The man who hurt Ellie—who is he?"

Tate's brow furrowed, and he opened his mouth to speak, but there was a soft rap at the door. "Come in. Ah, thank you, Sophie. You can place the tray down on the table."

The receptionist walked in, smiled politely, and moved towards the coffee table in the centre of the room. She silently poured the tea into three cups before leaving again, closing the door quietly.

"You'll have to be more specific I'm afraid," Tate said as he handed a cup to Gemma. "I don't remember a Rodney, but then, I am bad with names." And then he handed the second cup to Hayley, who couldn't help thinking about how quickly Tate had learned *her* name.

"When we found Ellie," Hayley explained, nestling the fine china into her palm, "she kept mentioning this man. She said he came to her at night and she was afraid of him. She didn't want to come back to the farm, and I really don't think she should have been brought here. She needs to go to a hospital and see someone."

Gemma nodded in agreement.

"Girls, I know you're both upset. I am too. I hear you." He sighed heavily, and from the way his eyes cast downwards, he seemed in genuine distress. "Look, why don't we do a quick meditation to calm ourselves."

"What?" Gemma said. "Just answer our questions. We haven't come here to meditate."

"Even still. I believe in the power of meditation to heal emotional wounds. I'll answer every single one of your questions after the meditation. You have my word."

Hayley glanced at Gemma who was still scowling straight at Tate. She shuffled in her chair, turned back to Hayley, and shrugged in a way that suggested they should get it over and done with.

"Okay," Hayley said. "How do we do this?"

"The tea is important," Tate said. "Take a sip."

They both took a sip of the tea.

"Gemma," Tate said. "Relax a little. I swear all your questions will be answered in due course."

Hayley could see that Gemma was resisting, from the expression on her face. But something switched, she sighed, and drank a big gulp of tea. Her expression changed to something more neutral.

"Are you going to tell us why Ellie was afraid of that guy? Rodney?" Gemma asked.

"Gemma, the ancient Chinese were ritualistic about their tea. There are monasteries even now that use tea as part of meditation practises. This tea has been brewed for the perfect length of time. It's chamomile, to soothe your troubles," he said, ignoring the question altogether.

It had been a long time since Hayley had drunk chamomile tea because she'd tried it once and didn't like it. She preferred PG Tips with plenty of sugar and a digestive biscuit. But she took another sip to show her willingness to join in the meditation.

"Take a deep breath in," Tate said. "And out. In. And out. More tea."

Any more and she'd need the loo, but anything to get to the actual answers.

"I'm going to count to ten," Tate said. "Take another sip. Good. Now. When I reach the number ten, close your eyes, relax, and empty your mind. One... Two... Three..."

Hayley was still breathing deeply. The chair was soft, the room was warm. She felt her shoulders begin to relax. It was so simple, and yet this did seem to be helping her reach an uneasy kind of calm.

"Four... Five... Six..."

Gemma was quiet and still next to her. She was following it all with Hayley, which was surprising to see. Gemma was so angry, and yet her face was more serene now. Hayley stopped looking at Gemma and concentrated.

"Seven... Eight... Nine... Ten..."

Hayley closed her eyes.

"Another beautiful day on the farm," Tate said.

The girls echoed his words. It was like a reflex.

"You're safe here. You're home with family."

Home with family.

"Listen carefully to my words," he said. "Listen deeply."

We will.

"You went camping at the creek in hot weather. Unfortunately, Ellie tripped on the rocks and hurt herself. She had a touch of sunstroke from the heat. You helped her along with Eoin and Clay, but you were both struggling through sunstroke, too, which is why your memory of the event is hazy. Ellie is fine. She isn't afraid of anyone on the farm. No one has even met Rodney. You will forget that name and forget all of your trouble. Ellie has been treated now, and her injuries are healing well. But she decided that she wanted to go home and visit her family in Portugal. She loves you all. She loves her family at the farm. The farm needs to be protected at all costs."

At all costs.

23

GEMMA

Gemma sat cross-legged on the patio, hair hanging like a veil, sketching. She hadn't sketched since she was a kid. But there were dull stretches of time at the farm in which there was nothing to do. Time was slow here, embroidering itself into the fields like a spiderweb—a web that caught everything and held it tight.

A long week had passed since the day at the gorge. She and Clay had sneaked off to his cabin three times since then. She hated to admit it, but each time it'd been like something was missing. Actually, not *something*, but *someone*. Tate.

Today had brought a welcome cover of dark clouds, rain pelting down. For once, scents of red soil drowned out the ever-present reek of ripe mango.

The wet season had started in earnest.

She was alone on the patio. Everyone else who was awake was either still having breakfast or playing cards in the hall. There was no work today, due to the weather.

A girl raced across from the food hall, her arms overhead in an attempt to block out the rain. Hayley. She was drenched by the time she reached the patio, laughing as she shook her head, sending water spraying. She knelt beside Gemma, inspecting the drawing, her forehead and cheeks bright with sunburn. Sunburn was a constant risk here.

"What're you drawing?" Hayley asked, munching on the apple she had with her.

Rolling her shoulder into a shrug, Gemma erased the line she'd just drawn. "A wallpaper design. Stupid, huh?" Her design was of wildflowers floating in water, the stems making a repeated pattern.

"Not stupid at all." Hayley bit into the apple again. "It's good. But why wallpaper?"

Gemma exhaled silently, watching rain pour from the top of the roof for a moment. "When I was ten, I lived in a house with old, mouldy walls. I used to lie on my bed, wishing I could just cover them all up. So that I couldn't see the black spots anymore."

Hayley's mouth pressed into a sympathetic smile.

The rain intensified, moving across the fields in sheets, sending a fine spray of water across Gemma's work. Gemma tipped her sketch pad, letting the droplets of water run in thin lines. Spiderweb lines.

Hayley's brow puckered. "It's ruined."

"I don't care."

Unfolding her legs, Hayley stretched them out on the deck. "Gem, what do you think Ellie's doing right now?"

"Ellie? I dunno. Hanging with her family, I guess."

"Wish she was still here. I liked her. She was fun... when she let loose."

"You talked with her a lot more than I did. I didn't see her fun side."

Hayley chewed a piece of apple reflectively. "Maybe we should write Ellie a letter and try to send it to her. Because we didn't get to say goodbye. Tell her that we hope her scratches have healed up nicely or something. You could draw her some mango trees to remind her of the farm. She'd like that."

"*You* can. My drawings suck." Gemma tore out the page and

balled it up. The thought came to her that she hadn't liked Ellie very much, but she couldn't remember why.

Hayley flicked her apple core into the bushes at the side of the deck then looked guilty when a lanky figure appeared behind them.

"Good morning girls," said Tate. "Look at you both sitting there. Like a pair of lovely flowers waiting patiently for the sun to return."

Gemma put her sketch pad down out of Tate's view, the whole idea of designing wallpaper suddenly seeming childish. Tate looked unruffled as usual, his handsome face making Gemma's nerves fizz.

"I hope the rain isn't dampening the spirits of my little orchids," he added with a wink.

Hayley's face broke into an impish grin. "I'm all for it. It means we get the day off."

He laughed in response.

Gemma watched the exchange between them. Hayley had developed a rapport with Tate that she envied. If the farm operated on an invisible spiderweb, then the fine lines of the web were vibrating in ways that Gemma wasn't privy to.

"Actually, Hayley," Tate said, "I could use some assistance in the lab today. It's your choice though. If you have other plans..."

Hayley stood, dusting off her hands and then wringing her saturated hair. "No, no plans. Should I run back to the cabin and grab some dry clothes? There's an umbrella I can use for the run back here?"

"That's not necessary," he told her. "Just come as you are."

Shooting a nodding smile at Gemma, Tate stepped away with Hayley.

Picking up her sketch pad again, Gemma started furiously drawing again. Dark, jagged lines became a distorted mango tree, rotten fruit splitting and its flesh spilling out.

Why didn't Tate ever ask *her* to help him with special jobs? The thought of Tate and Hayley together in the lab made the inside of her chest burn. They'd end up sleeping together. She was sure of it.

Another person made a dash from the hall. A guy. He ran all the way to the entry of the farm—where the SUVs were parked—an oilskin coat over his head. Opening a door, he jumped up and into the driver's seat. He remained sitting there, gripping the wheel.

Gemma squinted to see better. The cars were a long distance from the patio, and the view was fuzzy through the rain. But she was certain it had been Clay—the wiry body had looked just like his.

Eoin emerged from the hall, jogging across to the patio as he noticed Gemma.

He brushed his wet black hair back with his fingers, his blue eyes less startling a colour in the dull colour of the air today. "Hey, seen Clay? We're meant to go out to the rifle range as soon as this rain eases."

Gemma glanced in the direction of the cars, watching Clay duck down. "Nope. Haven't seen him. Can I come out to the range? I'm bored as hell."

"Sorry. Gun prac is for the farm leaders and managers. No exceptions."

"Can't I just shoot tin cans? I used to do that with my brother when I was a kid."

He shook his head. "The rifles are all kept at the range." Muttering under his breath, Eoin ran off in the direction of the cabins.

Leaving her drawing pad on the deck, Gemma rose and padded over to the railing. Something was happening, and she was curious to know *what*. Eoin and Clay had been as thick as thieves since she'd met them. But today, Clay seemed to be trying to get away from Eoin. If she wasn't going to be allowed out to the range, she needed something else to occupy herself with.

A few stiff oilskin coats were hanging on hooks on a wooden patio column. Taking a coat, she checked it for spiders and then drew it overhead. She sloshed through puddles as she made her way across the ground to the cars. It was definitely Clay in the car. She climbed in beside him, pushing the wet coat to the floor.

Clay, slumping down to apparently avoid being seen, looked across at her with a mix of alarm and annoyance on his face. "Go back to the hall, Gem."

"What's going on?"

"Nothing. Look, I just... need to get out of here for a while. Clear my head."

"Eoin's looking for you."

"I know. I saw him."

A thought burned through her mind. "Tate told him to watch you, didn't he? *You're* the one being watched now. Tell me why."

He blew out a stream of air, his gaze darting about the farm. "Hold on, we're heading out for a while."

Taking out a set of keys from his shirt pocket, Clay started up the SUV and drove it through the open gate and out onto the road.

"Did you ask Tate for permission to take one of his cars out?" She glanced back at the rain-whipped mango plantation.

Clay shook his head, fixing his gaze on the road ahead.

Maybe Tate wouldn't be as strict about the cars as he was normally. He was busy this morning. And Clay was one of the farm's supervisors—surely Tate would give him more leeway than the others.

Besides, she was at a loose end. "Where are we going?"

"Into town. I've got an appointment."

"With who?"

He hesitated before answering. "A psych."

"A psychiatrist?"

"Psychologist, I think. I just need to sort some stuff out. You can come along for the ride. There are some things I want to talk to you about anyway. Maybe it's good that you're here."

"What kind of things?"

"Let me talk with the psych first. Get my head straight."

Gemma let her back sink into the car seat. She tried switching on the radio, but Clay wouldn't let her, insisting on wanting quiet. Fields of mangoes passed them on one side of the road—the other side empty except for a bull with enormously wide black horns.

Clay remained silent all the way into Katherine. Gemma eyed the main shopping strip with interest when they arrived. She hadn't yet seen the centre of town. It was small, with mostly single-storey buildings in an older style. Unlike the farm, many of the residents were Aboriginal. She wondered why Tate didn't employ more of the locals than he did. A darker thought edged in—maybe the locals didn't *want* to work at Tate's farm. Maybe they knew more than the new recruits. None of the workers seemed to have been there longer than a year.

But what was wrong with the farm? Nothing, as far as she could tell.

Thoughts of Tate moved back into her mind. Thoughts of him never really left. He was always there, occupying a corner. In some way that she didn't understand, she was obsessed with him. She knew it, but she couldn't stop herself.

The psychologist's office didn't advertise what it was from the outside. As Gemma walked in with Clay, she saw that there were three rooms in operation. The psych that Clay was seeing had a small, chipped plaque outside her room that said, *Dr Leah Halcombe.*

While Clay was having his session with Dr Halcombe, Gemma read cheesy celebrity stories in a women's magazine.

His appointment was only supposed to be an hour long, but it was half an hour past that point when Clay appeared again. The psychologist —a short middle-aged woman with red bobbed hair— cast a concerned glance at Gemma.

Gemma stared back, wondering if the psych thought she should come in for a session too. Maybe Dr Halcombe thought everyone could do with a bit of a head check.

Taking her hand, Clay tugged Gemma out into the street. "C'mon, let's get something to eat."

"I don't have any money with me."

"I do. How about a burger?"

"Sure."

Rain continued to pour down, running in tiny streams along the street. It was nice, walking like this and holding hands with Clay. Like they could be any couple—a happy young couple, like the ones you saw in adverts.

She tried to stop thinking of Tate. Clay just seemed so *pure*. Like he was a transparent room, and she could see that everything inside him was good. He'd even trusted her enough to bring her along to his appointment with the shrink. Tate was different. Tate was like a windowless room—you couldn't see inside him at all.

They ate their burgers under shelter, peering into an art gallery of Aboriginal paintings.

They kept walking. Clay tucked her hair behind her ear, kissing her temple as she examined the pictures of sunsets in the window of a tourism operator. She smiled at him, wishing they could go to the places in those pictures together. No one else. Just the two of them.

She was about to say that when a frown rippled across his forehead and she guessed that he was thinking about his discussion with Dr Halcombe.

"Your psych looked kind of worried when you came out of her office," Gemma commented.

"Come here." Taking her by the hand, he guided her to a private spot under shelter, down a small side street.

He swallowed, his eyes steady on hers. "It's the farm. Tate has got some strange things going on. I just don't know if I want to be part of it anymore. Gem, I don't think I'm going to stay to the end of mango season."

Bitter threads of disappointment pulled tight inside her. "You're leaving?"

"Yes. I don't have much to go home to, but I can't stay here. It's driving me crazy. You were right when you guessed that Tate asked Eoin to keep an eye on me. Tate doesn't trust me anymore... and I don't trust *him*."

She tried to speak, but her throat suddenly felt closed up.

People I get close to always leave me.

A whirlwind started up in her mind, louder than the rain.

They always leave me. Hurt me.

"Come with me," he said quietly.

"What?"

"Today. Now. You don't need to bring anything. I saw what you walked into the farm with a couple of weeks back—practically nothing but the clothes on your back. I've got some money saved up. We can hitchhike to the nearest city—into Darwin. And get a job there until we've got enough cash for flights to the US. We can stay with my dad for a while—"

"Clay. I can't."

"Why not?"

"I can't just dump Hayley and run."

"You can get a message to Hayley later on. Trust me. The longer you stay, the harder it is to leave."

"That's insane. It's just a fruit farm."

"I know. I can't explain it. It's like I know I want to get away from the place, but it keeps sucking me back. Gem, I'm having some weird dreams."

"What kind of dreams?"

He shook his head, swallowing. "Crazy stuff. Nightmare stuff. *Dead people.* Not just dead but sitting up on chairs and facing each other. And it's fucking cold. Like the dead of winter in the Arctic kind of cold."

"Maybe you saw a movie like that once. Sounds like a movie. Right?"

"Whatever it is, I want it out of my head. But I can't get it out of my head."

Moving close, she held him, feeling a tremor pass through his body. She didn't know what to say to him. He was having nightmares? How would running away help with that?

"The psych thinks... she thinks that the detail I'm seeing in the dreams isn't normal," he said. "And the fact that the same dreams keep repeating. I must have a disturbed brain or something." He gave a short, hollow laugh.

"What did she say?"

"I asked her straight out what was wrong with me, and she told me she didn't know enough yet to make that assessment. But she said if I keep having lifelike dreams about death, then I could be heading into a manic episode. Scared of me now?"

She rested her head against his shoulder, trying to calm him. "No. I'm not scared of you."

He breathed deeply. "She asked lots of questions about the farm. She was especially interested in Tate's personal meditation sessions."

"I think I went to one of those a week or so ago. With Hayley."

"Yeah, you did. In the room upstairs."

"I felt better... afterwards. It helped me."

Clay moved back, holding her in his gaze. "I don't want his help anymore. You shouldn't either."

Gemma looked out onto the street, evading Clay's intense eyes. The rain had stopped, but the storm had grown wilder.

Wind blustered along the street, whipping Gemma's hair around her face. A plastic bag caught in the storm, swirling and flying high in the air in a frantic dance. She'd felt... *good* in the meditation room with Tate. He'd made her feel better. Maybe he'd even made her feel whole. And she'd never felt like that in her life before. She'd always been scattered in a million pieces. After the session, she'd wished it could have just been Tate and herself. The thought of leaving him made a hollow space open up in her chest.

"Gem," he said, "there's one more thing."

"What is it?"

"*Ellie*. It's Ellie. She's one of the dead people in my dream. Her skin was mottled and blue, but it was *her*."

"Clay, Ellie's fine. Back with her family in Portugal. She's okay, and you're okay, and we're all okay. It's just dreams."

"Yeah. I know. It's dreams. But damn, it seems so real..."

"Ellie was silly to go off by herself that morning. Especially feeling so sick. Lucky she didn't hit her head and end up in the water."

He frowned. "Gemma...? You think Ellie fell?"

Gemma tilted her head at him, not quite understanding. "Yes, of course she fell. You don't think someone pushed her, do you?"

"She cut her wrists. *That's* what happened."

Gemma shook her head, watching the plastic bag tangle and tear to pieces in the tree. "Ellie wouldn't do that."

"She *did* do that. Why do you think her wrists were bleeding? Why do you think we bandaged her up?"

"No," Gemma told him firmly. "She grazed her arms. She fell onto rocks, after all. Heatstroke got to her. You're remembering it all wrong. Maybe you really are having problems."

Clay studied her face, holding his wind-blown hair back with both hands. "See? This is what I mean. This is *exactly* what I mean. Crazy stuff like this. Listen to me. Ellie tried to commit suicide. Bad things had been happening to Ellie for a while. I don't know what, but it must have gotten too much for her. After Eoin and I got her to the farm, we left her in Tate's hands. I don't know what happened after that. And neither do you."

Gemma recoiled. She could picture the grazes on Ellie's arms. There were no cuts. It'd been nothing serious. Clay was wrong. No wonder he was seeing a psych.

"Tate told us. She went home," Gemma said.

"What if she didn't?"

"What are you saying?"

"I don't know. Maybe we need to find out. We could try to contact Ellie's family. Make sure she got home safe and sound."

"This is kind of crazy."

"Is it? Consider this—you and Hayley had a session with Tate. And then Eoin had a session with him. And you all believe the same thing. You all think Ellie fell that day. But I turned Tate down and didn't do the session. Doesn't it seem strange to you that I remember a different version of what happened? I don't know what is going on, but—"

"Please," she begged, "let's just go back to the farm. I'll talk Hayley into leaving, and then we'll all go together, okay? Just a couple more days?"

She didn't mean a single word of it.

Even if she went to America with him, she couldn't stay there very long. Their government wouldn't allow it. Clay would return to his family and friends, and she'd have to return to Australia all alone.

He wasn't thinking ahead. He was going nuts and trying to take her into his crazy-land with him.

Tate had at least offered her somewhere she could belong.

24

HAYLEY

Hayley pulled the oilskin coat closer to her throat and glanced sideways at Tate. He appeared unconcerned by the downpour, moving as slowly and gracefully as always under the protection of a golf umbrella. He made her feel ashamed of the way she looked, slobbing around in cheap high-street dresses while Tate gave the impression that all his clothes were tailored just for him.

The change in the weather had been sudden, and yet the farm remained as oppressive as ever. The scorching hot sun had been transformed into a blanket of rain that made the place seem smaller. Hayley had been feeling claustrophobic all morning.

"We may need to get you a towel," Tate said as they stepped into the farmhouse. "Perhaps it's best to dry off upstairs before we head to the lab." He placed the umbrella in a rack by the door.

She couldn't reply because her throat was so dry. Going upstairs with Tate had been a fantasy of Hayley's since she'd first met him, though she had worried it came across as childish and silly, a girl with a crush on a film star. *This is how movies begin, isn't it? A gorgeous, elusive man, torrential rain, an isolated mansion.* She had to focus. Not let herself get carried away with the fantasy of it all. And yet her mind was never far away from the moment in the orchid greenhouse where she'd felt a spark between them both.

As Tate hung his coat on a rack near the door, Hayley followed suit, before letting him lead her up the stairs to the same room she had been in with Gemma. The room where Tate had let them know that Ellie was going home to Portugal after her fall at Katherine Gorge.

"The wet season has started," Tate said as they walked slowly up the stairs. "Sometimes it rains so hard here that the roads flood and cause chaos. It makes deliveries quite troublesome. In fact, it makes leaving the farm at all very difficult."

"Will it rain constantly now?" Hayley didn't mind not leaving the farm for a while. The place felt like home now. It felt safe.

"No." Tate opened the door into the upstairs room and strode across the lounge area. "It comes and goes. It's unpredictable. I'm not a fan of the unpredictable. Would you care to take a seat while I fetch you a towel for your hair?"

"Thank you."

Hayley chose the same chair she had sat in the day before and relaxed into it, feeling slightly guilty about her wet clothes against the expensive fabric. She closed her eyes and thought about Ellie for a moment. It was such a shame about her accident.

She'd dreamt about Ellie last night. It was strange. In her dream, Ellie was talking to her in Portuguese. Hayley had been holding a bloodied shirt wrapped around Ellie's arm. Dreams always exaggerated real life, didn't they? Then Ellie had said something about the night and Hayley had woken up.

"How's this?" Tate handed Hayley a soft blue towel. "Oh, your feet are wet too. You must be freezing. Shall we have some tea before we head to the lab?"

"That would be nice." Hayley rubbed enthusiastically at her hair before she realised how frizzy it was becoming and that it wouldn't be particularly attractive. She calmed down and combed it with her fingers instead. "You're so nice to everyone here."

"It's a family," he said with a shrug. "We have an ethos here that I'm keen to maintain. Everyone has a responsibility to make sure the farm remains up and running. Even you, Hayley."

"I do?" She smiled, pleased to be important.

"You have fitted in perfectly well here." A door opened, and the tea was brought in, exactly how it was yesterday. Tate paused to pour her a cup, and she took it from him and blew on the liquid. "Both of you have, but you in particular, Hayley."

"Thank you."

"Does Gemma enjoy it here?" Tate asked.

Hayley took a sip of her tea and thought about it. "She seemed sad today. I suggested that we write Ellie a letter, but it didn't seem to cheer her up. Ellie is in Portugal, isn't she? Have you heard from her?"

"Of course," Tate said. "She's with her family. How is the tea?"

"Delicious."

"Good. Like I was saying, everyone here has a responsibility to the farm. It's a wonderful place, isn't it? So much natural beauty. So much freedom of expression. We become our best selves here."

Hayley smiled. It was true. She quickly finished the last of her tea and leaned back in the chair, happy and content.

Tate looked her up and down. "Well, you really are wet as a cat today. I think you'll need to clean up a bit if you're going to work in the lab. Everything has to be sterile. Why don't you use my bedroom to shower and change? We have a box of spare clothes left over from previous workers, all clean and warm. Won't that be nice?"

"Yes."

Tate stepped over to her with one hand outstretched and helped her out of her chair. "It's good that you would do anything for the farm. And you *would* do anything, wouldn't you?"

"Yes. Anything." Tate's hand was warm inside her own. She leaned into his side.

"That's it, pretty orchid. Lean against me."

Hayley rested her head on Tate's shoulder. It was so clear to her now, she loved him. She loved everything about him and wanted to make him happy.

A door opened, and they stepped inside. Hayley's strides were in time with Tate's, and that made her giggle. The farm did bring out the best in people because Hayley hadn't felt this happy in a long time.

There was a low whistle. "She's a stunner."

The room blurred as Hayley sought out the new voice. Was there someone else here? There was a shape in the corner of the room. A wide shape, but the face was all wrong. Contorted. Ugly.

"Tate?" Hayley asked hesitantly.

A hand stroked her hair softly. "Everything is all right, pretty orchid. You want to make me happy, don't you?"

"Yes."

"You'll be a good girl, won't you?"

"Yes."

Her footsteps were no longer in unison with Tate's as she was taken to a soft place to sit. When she was still, her vision improved, and she realised she was sitting on the bed.

"Don't go too far with this one," Tate said. His voice sounded distant, an echo.

"I can do whatever I want with them. You know the rules."

"Well you broke the last one, and even I couldn't fix her."

"That's your problem, not mine. I get to do whatever. You want the police to hear about what's really going on here?"

Hayley's head suddenly felt too large to hold herself upright. She fell back into the bed, and the soft sheets enveloped her. The room smelled like lilies, and the chandelier above twinkled like light on diamonds. There were orchids on the wallpaper, and Hayley thought about her perfect day in the greenhouse. The tall shape of Tate was looking down at her.

"Be a good girl, Hayley. Remember that you would do anything for the farm, wouldn't you?"

"Yes," she said, but it felt wrong, everything felt wrong. The large bulk of the other man stepped out from his corner and moved towards her. She looked back to Tate's tall form, but he was gone and the door was closed. Did she hear the click of the lock? She wasn't sure.

"Get on your knees, bitch."

She would do anything for the farm.

———

Tate was right about the rains. They came and went whenever they felt like it. Difficult to predict, but often a welcome break from the hot sun. It was warm with clear skies as Hayley headed to the food hall with the rest of the workers. She was in a good mood because she would get to see Tate, and she hadn't seen him since she'd helped him in the lab a couple of days ago.

She had to admit that she'd felt a little disappointed that Tate had only handed her a towel to use, rather than the seduction she'd been hoping for, but she still cherished any moment she got to spend with him. It was okay if he didn't love her back. He didn't have to. Her love for him was selfless. He had more important things to deal with than a teenage girl working on his farm. He had to run this place. This wonderful, magical place. She realised in that moment that she would do anything for this place. Anything at all.

"You all right?" Gemma asked, as they sat down on the cushions.

"Perfect," Hayley replied. But then she winced. She had had some funny pains recently. Maybe it was her period coming or something. Her stomach was a bit delicate.

"You look different," Gemma pressed. "Like you've lost weight or something."

"It's probably the heat."

Everyone took a bowl of soup and a spoon. Hayley tried a few spoonfuls, but her stomach was still queasy so she left it. She hadn't eaten much of anything recently.

After the soup was all done and the bowls cleared away, Tate walked barefoot into the room and Hayley saw nothing but him.

"My orchids," he said quietly. Hayley was sure he was looking directly at her. "Everyone close your eyes."

Hayley did so immediately.

Soon she heard Tate's voice again. "Another perfect day at the farm."

Another perfect day.

"We give thanks for the harvest and thanks that we are all here together. Every day is a celebration."

Every day is a celebration.

"The farm deserves protection."

The farm deserves protection.

"Open your eyes."

Hayley opened her eyes and saw Tate looking at her. Her cheeks immediately warmed, and she bit her lip. Maybe she was wrong. Maybe he did like her as more than just an employee.

The session moved forward, and two new backpackers were welcomed. Hayley didn't notice much about them because her stomach was cramping up.

"I have a gift for you," Tate said. He took a basket up off the ground and began making his way around the room. "A flower for each of you. An orchid for my orchids."

Hayley smiled as she waited for her gift. She remembered the day in the greenhouse with Tate. That perfect day. And then...

Get on your knees.

Pretty orchid.

Hayley's hand rose to her mouth. What the hell? She turned left and right. Where had that voice come from? The backpackers looked back at her with confused expressions on their faces.

"Hayley?" Gemma's eyes were wide.

Hayley hadn't even noticed that she'd risen from her cushion. She turned away from Gemma and stared straight ahead with her arms clasped over her stomach.

"What's wrong?" Gemma tried to put a hand on her leg, but Hayley moved away.

She shook her head and whispered. "No." Tate's basket of orchids came closer, and in her mind, she saw orchid wallpaper from another room. She smelled lilies and body odour. The few spoonfuls of soup she'd eaten churned in her stomach.

"Come with me, Hayley." Tate offered her his hand.

Hayley glanced from his hand to Gemma. She shook her head once and then calmed herself.

"It's all right, Hayley."

Tate wouldn't harm her, that much she knew. She took his hand, feeling as though its warmth was a familiar one. He gently led her through the circle of backpackers and out of the meditation centre.

"I have a stomachache," she explained, the words sounding ridiculous. A child's excuse. "I'm sorry." She began to cry, and he put an arm over her shoulders. "I'm sorry."

"Do you trust me, Hayley?" he asked.

"Yes." She wiped the tears from her eyes. "Yes, I trust you."

"Then let me prescribe something for that stomachache."

"Okay."

"Here, let's go to the house for a minute," he said. "It'll only take a moment. Then you can take the rest of the day off if you like. Take a nap. Rest and recharge. Would you like that?"

"Yes."

"Good girl. This way, pretty orchid."

The words made her tense, but she forced herself to keep on

walking. Why didn't she want to come back to the house? Tate must have sensed her tension because he squeezed her a little more tightly. They made their way past the reception and up to the meditation room where she'd had tea with Tate before. But instead of staying in the sparse white room, he turned to an adjacent room and flipped open a small white cover to a keypad that she hadn't noticed before. After tapping in a code, the door opened, and Hayley realised from the hospital bed that this was a sick bay.

"Hop onto the bed for me Hayley."

"W—what's going to happen?" She asked.

"I thought you trusted me," he replied, one eyebrow arched.

"I do... I just..."

"Like I said. I'm going to prescribe something for that stomachache, and you'll feel all better."

Tate unlocked a storage cupboard and rummaged through it. When he appeared with a needle and a bottle of medication, Hayley's eyes widened.

"I don't..."

"It won't hurt."

"I don't think I..."

"You'd do anything for the farm, wouldn't you, Hayley? This is your home. You want to make me happy, don't you? We're a family."

"Yes," she said, hating this, hating the way she felt inside, like everything was a broken mess.

"This will make you feel better. It'll take that stomachache away, and you won't even remember you had it."

25

GEMMA

Blinking back hot tears, Gemma snatched the orchid that Tate had given her from behind her ear. Stalking out of the hall, she shredded the orchid into tiny pieces. *Tate's taken Hayley away with him yet again.*

He'd been attentive to Hayley lately. Checking how she was, having her do special tasks for him. Touching her. Helping her. Like she was some kind of delicate flower. While Gemma worked relentless hours out in the fields with Freddy and the others.

It wasn't fair.

More than anything, she seethed about the attention he gave Hayley and didn't give to *her*.

Why am I so obsessed with Tate? Who cares?

She cared. An unexpected rage bristled through her. She hadn't realised just how deeply she cared until the day Clay asked her to leave the farm.

Maybe she'd fallen for Clay—crazy Clay who needed to see a shrink—but she *craved* Tate. Craved him like a drug. She'd never met anyone like him. For the first time in her life, she felt important and like she was actually special. Only Tate made her feel that way. Tate was the sun watching over the farm, and everything revolved around him. Everyone here wanted to live in the warmth of that sun.

She couldn't leave Tate. Clay thought she'd be going with him. She didn't know how to tell him she wouldn't.

Crumpled, velvety petals fell through her fingers as she looked up in time to see Hayley coming from the house. She'd seemed ill during the meditation, but it must have just been a ploy.

Hayley stepped out into the baking sunshine.

"Everyone's heading out to the springs for the Harvest Friday thing," Gemma told her stiffly. "You'd better get ready."

A small, wan smile flickered on Hayley's face, but her eyes remained vacant. "Oh... I'm just going to go lie down in the cabin. I'm really tired."

Gemma failed to keep her voice steady. "Tired from *what*? You've been given cushy jobs in the greenhouses most of the week."

"I'm just tired, all right? Tate said it was okay for me to stay behind this afternoon."

"Whatever." Gemma wanted to say more, but there was a brittle strangeness in Hayley's tone that stopped her.

Hayley hummed as she headed away.

Just like Ellie. Ellie had often gone vacant in the eyes as she hummed. Gemma felt unsettled for a moment, but then her anger burned the thought to ashes.

She rode out of the gates in an SUV with Clay, Eoin, and Dharma. Hayley remained in her cabin.

Dharma had insisted on taking the wheel. They went in the opposite direction to last Friday, turning east a short distance down the road—this time to Kakadu. She knew of that place—all Australians had. But it was mythical to her, and she had no idea what to expect.

Miss chatty—Dharma—told her that the national park of Kakadu was 20,000 square kilometres in size. They had a long way yet to go. The heat began drumming inside Gemma's head.

The landscape changed dramatically the further they drove in: lush, monsoon rain forest, tangles of vines and red termite mounds taller than two-storey houses.

"How're you guys doing in the back there?" Dharma called to Clay and Eoin.

"You drive like a feckin' girl," Eoin complained.

"You mean, you're getting there in one piece? Damn shame, that," Dharma quipped, winking at Gemma.

"What spots are we headed to?" Gemma asked from the passenger seat beside her.

"Motor Car Falls and Gunlom Plunge Pool." Dharma steered carefully around a muddy ditch. "You'll love both. They're amazing, especially Gunlom. It's like a big, natural infinity pool, looking out over Kakadu. There are fairly long walks to get to each one, so the tourists tend to be the more intrepid types. Like backpackers. We tend to harvest workers while hiking the trails. You know the kind of recruit Tate wants, right?"

Gemma nodded, gazing out at a broad pond studded with water lilies. She knew the drill:

Strike up conversations. Zero in on the ones who are alone, the ones who've just been dumped by their boyfriend or girlfriend, the ones who seem estranged from their families. The ones who can be helped by the warm embrace of the farm.

The long line of cars from Tate's farm parked at the visitor centre. A small thrill of excitement zipped through her. She'd do a good job for Tate today. Show him exactly what she could do. If Hayley kept up with her fragile princess routine, she'd soon fall out of Tate's graces.

The workers all set off on the trail. Clay attempted to walk with her, but she reminded him that they were both being watched by the others and they had to stick to the routine.

She flitted from backpacker to backpacker on the trail, saying hello and chatting with them. She was good at that. She could small talk underwater if she had to. But she had no luck finding the kind of person Tate was looking for.

Gemma fell into step beside a guy with clear brown skin and wavy black hair. He had his backpack slung low over one shoulder and earphones in.

"Hey." Gemma grinned widely.

He pulled his earphones out in surprise. "Hi?"

That was all it took. She knew exactly what to say and what to ask. In five minutes, she'd found out that he was a native New Zealander, he was travelling alone, and he was out of money. Back in New Zealand, he lived with his grandmother and hadn't spoken to either of his parents in the past four years.

He's perfect.

When you identify a recruit, jump in and lead the conversation.

She let him ask her about herself and then she casually mentioned the farm. He didn't show interest—he was on his way to Darwin tomorrow for a job he'd been offered.

When they reached Motor Car Falls, she stayed glued to his side and determined to change his mind. Peeling off her clothes, she kicked off her walking sandals. She wore her white bikini today—she knew it showed off her tan.

She smiled as he watched her winding her hair up into a high ponytail.

Establish a relationship quickly. Do something physical with the recruit, such as touching or a little game.

"Race you to the other side," she challenged.

They dived into the translucent green water of Motor Car Falls together. Laughing, they swam across to the rushing waterfall and onto the rock edge.

Isolate them. Take them somewhere private.

Taking his hand, she took him behind the wall of water.

"Why not come back to the farm and see what you think?" said Gemma, her lips on his ear to be heard above the roar.

He smiled but shook his head. "I need to make money. Real money. Not fruit picking money."

Seduce the recruit.

"The pay isn't bad. And... *I'll* be there." She caught his mouth with hers, kissing him deeply. His shoulders instantly relaxed, and he kissed her back.

A hand closed around her arm. Gemma twisted around to see who was behind her.

"Excuse me," Clay told the New Zealander. "I'd like a word with my *girlfriend*."

The moment was ruined beyond repair. And she'd been certain she had the recruit on a hook.

Gemma climbed out from behind the waterfall, a sense of guilt at the look on Clay's face competing with a seething anger.

"What do you think you're doing?" Clay's jaw muscles tensed as he strode beside her.

"Exactly what I'm supposed to be doing."

"Why? What the fuck does it matter? You don't have to be one of The Chemist's good little soldiers anymore. We're leaving on Monday."

She squeezed water from her ponytail, blowing out a tight breath. "I'm staying."

"You're *what*?"

"Clay, I'm not your girlfriend. You don't even know me."

"You can't be serious." His voice quietened. "Did something happen? Were you threatened?"

"I don't know what you're talking about. It's just what I decided to do. This place suits me right now. The area is nice. I get fed and paid. It's got everything I need."

"After all the things I told you? About Ellie and everything? I haven't told anyone else those things. Because I wasn't sure of anyone else. But *you*... you I was sure of."

"I'm sorry. I hope things work out for you when you get back home."

Retracing her steps to the water, she dived in. There was nothing left to say.

————

That night at the farm, Tate held the party that he always did on Harvest Fridays. It should have been a triumphant moment for Gemma. But it was the opposite.

Dharma and two other girls had brought back guys from the trip today. Gemma had returned empty-handed. She felt Tate's disappointment in her, as visceral as if a knife had been pushed deep into her side. He turned away from her, touching Dharma under the chin and murmuring to her that she was his best recruiter. He glanced at Gemma once more with a look of frustration before walking away.

Gemma had no interest in the party. People, music, and laughter streamed past her as she walked through the house.

Hayley was there, in a long, pale-blue dress that Gemma hadn't seen before. Hayley hadn't been to the shops as far as she knew, so either she'd borrowed the dress from one of the girls or Tate had given it to her. Gemma suspected that it was Tate's generosity.

Hayley stood swaying to the music, sipping a glass of wine. She didn't look sick—or tired. She just had that dazed look that she had all the time now.

Clay wasn't anywhere. Maybe he'd taken one of the cars straight from Kakadu and just kept driving. Gemma had come back in a car with Dharma and the backpacker that Dharma had picked up, this time taking over the driving while Dharma canoodled in the back seat with the guy.

Even though she'd made the decision to distance herself from Clay, the thought of him leaving saddened her. At another time and place, they could have been together. Just not here.

Then she turned and spotted a guy slouched on a chair in a corner, drinking and looking morose. Clay. With a girl. The girl, with her over-plumped lips and huge boobs, looked like she was doing everything in her power to gain his attention. It was the redhead girl that Gemma had seen around the farm a few times. She must have sensed that Clay was single again and decided to pounce.

She guessed that Clay was waiting until Monday, after all, to get his last pay before leaving the farm for good. He needed the money. And perhaps he thought she'd change her mind. *She wouldn't.*

Still, it hurt to see him with someone else.

Everything felt messy and wrong.

Gemma made her way outside. A band of purple clouds bruised the twilight sky. Hundreds of small bats swooped and chattered in the fading light, the sound almost deafening. In the fields, a small group of people was driving a picking machine along an aisle, testing out a mango harvesting method that was new to the farm—picking them at night. Tate was there in the field, watching them, calling out instructions. She'd heard him say earlier he was putting in new fields soon. To grow papaya and dragon fruit. And he was building two new orchid greenhouses. Soon, the farm operations would be going on here around the clock.

Gemma wandered to the cabin, feeling more alone than she ever had. If staying at the farm was what she wanted, then why did she feel like her skin was peeling away from her body and leaving her raw?

She slept for hours, but her sleep was fitful—tossing and turning.

The noise of people returning to the cabins woke her. Dharma was having loud sex in the cabin next door with her new recruit. Hayley hadn't returned from the party.

Throwing on a long-sleeved top, Gemma left the cabin and entered the cooled air of the small hours of the morning. Just past two.

For once, she didn't care about snakes or spiders or bats. She was desperate for a shower.

She tilted her head back in the open-roof shower block as the warm water gushed over her. Bats still swarmed overhead, making their eerie high-pitched calls, but she couldn't see them now. The night was too dark.

What was wrong with her? She wished there were something she could do to make herself feel better, to get the high that Hayley was obviously feeling.

She wanted to disappear. Vanish into the fabric of the farm. Forget herself. But instead she felt lost and angry and alone. She'd disappointed Tate. And in that moment when she thought Clay had already gone, she realised she was going to miss him hard.

Stepping out of the shower, she towelled off and then pulled a sleep T-shirt and old shorts on.

She needed to walk. Clear her head.

Things will sort themselves out soon, and I'll be happy again. I just have to trust.

She passed the well. It reminded her of Clay. It always would.

The house stood in front of her now.

Its grand spaces had completely emptied out. Everyone had returned to their cabins. Apart from two people still dancing.

Breath stilled in her chest. It was Tate and Hayley.

Hayley, in her pretty new dress, was spinning around the floor with Tate, oblivious to the world. Just a single, soft lamp illuminated the two of them, making the scene closed and intimate.

Gemma crept across the grounds and onto the patio. Like a thief marking a house, she hid and watched them through the glass walls.

Everything she wanted was *in there*.

Tate lifted his chin, looking straight at her. He must have caught sight of a dim spot of light on her body just before she concealed herself.

Bowing to Hayley, he ended the dance. He opened one of the

many glass doors that lined the patio and let Hayley out. She ran across to the cabins.

Tate lingered there, making Gemma's lungs hurt from holding her breath.

"You might as well come out, Gemma." He shrugged, a wry smile positioned on his face.

She slid out, unfolding her limbs.

"Come in," he said.

Once she'd stepped inside, he closed the door and extended his hand. "Let's dance."

"But... I'm wearing—" She was acutely aware of the old T-shirt she had on and her sodden hair. *No pretty, pretty party dress for me.* Tate only gave gifts to those who were worth it.

"You're beautiful in your own way. Trust me."

She didn't trust him. She wasn't beautiful.

He took her into a slow-moving waltz. Quiet, seductive jazz music played from concealed speakers.

"Gemma..." He sighed. "I'd like you to try a little harder with the recruiting. I'm going to need more people soon. And I know you can do it. You have the talent. You could do better even than Dharma."

"I—" She stopped. She wanted to defend herself and tell him that Clay had gotten in the way. But she didn't want to mention his name and have Tate unhappy with him. Then again, Clay was leaving, so did it even matter?

"Tell me," he said gently.

"It's nothing. Just, Clay thinks I'm his girlfriend, and I was kind of tripping over him on the harvest afternoon."

"Do you feel the same way?"

"No."

Tate caressed her temples. "Good. Entanglements can get messy on the farm. Gemma, Clay hasn't adequately explained where you both went the morning that he took the car. I can't tell you how disappointed I am."

"It was just into town. For some different scenery."

"The two of you didn't look like people who'd just been on a scenic drive when you returned. No, there was another reason for the trip. And I'd really like to know it." His voice remained steady and soothing, but it was edged with an urgent tone. He touched the back of her head, guiding her in against his chest.

Her heart squeezed into a rhythm that felt chaotic. She couldn't tell him why Clay had really gone into town, could she? It had been private. "It was just a drive."

He kept stroking her wet hair. "Do you like dancing?"

"Yes."

"With me?"

She nodded.

"Good. I'm enjoying this too. Things happen for a reason, don't you think?"

"What do you mean?"

"You finding your way to me tonight. But I didn't really have to explain that, did I? You're smart, Gemma. You've got special talents. You could go far, here. Maybe even run the farm for me one day."

She didn't want to run it *for* him. She wanted to run it *with* him. By his side.

But he would never want her, like that. That was a stupid dream.

All she had was this dance, right now. Like a moth to a flame, she clung to him.

She felt the hurt inside her begin to dissolve. He offered her wine, and she accepted. They drank glasses of red wine together, watching the party lights' reflection flickering on the surface of the pool.

Her eyes tracked the shimmering length of the pool as it vanished beneath the glass doors and out to the patio. It occurred to her that she'd never once seen him swim in it, no matter how hot the day.

"You can be open with me," he said, taking her empty wineglass away and refilling it. "As I am with you. But you haven't told me everything."

"I *have* been open. And I've done everything you've asked of me. I'm still learning, and I mess up sometimes."

"I can forgive you messing up. But I can't forgive dishonesty."

She gulped the wine he handed her, not trusting herself to speak, hoping he would dance with her again.

"Okay, then, Gemma, maybe you should go and get some sleep," he said in a dismissive tone.

It was if a veil had been thrown over her, shadowing her.

She took a step away, placing the wineglass down on a side table. She knew she should have kept walking.

But she turned back to him. "Clay is seeing a psychologist. He's been having nightmares... about dead people. He thinks something is... *wrong*... with this farm."

The words just slipped out.

She held her breath, an ashen taste in her throat, watching a dark expression stitch itself into the lines and hollows of Tate's face.

She wished she could take those words back.

But it was too late.

26

HAYLEY

It was back out to the fields today, and Hayley couldn't stop humming the earworm that had been stuck in her head for several days. It was a pretty song, but she couldn't remember the words, and Gemma was clearly fed up with it.

Her skin had toughened up against the sun's intense rays, turning opal into gold. It brought the highlights out in her hair and the freckles on her cheeks. Hayley had adapted to this place. She'd opened herself up and let it in. When she'd first arrived at the farm, she'd wanted to leave her paranoia, her suspicions, her trauma behind. She'd wanted love. And she'd found it.

Now she was a different person.

The farm was perfection.

Except...

There was sap on her fingers, so she moved over to the harvester to wash the sap away. As she went, Gemma caught her arm.

"Did you see Clay at breakfast?"

It was the first time Gemma had spoken to her all morning, and now Gemma had her attention, she was noticing how on edge Gemma was.

She couldn't stand still, readjusting her weight from one foot to the other. She'd been biting her thumbnail most of the morning which wasn't a good idea when dealing with mango sap, as Hayley had pointed out earlier.

"No, I didn't see him," Hayley said. "He's probably running errands for Tate."

"I overslept," Gemma said. "I thought he might be in the fields but..." Gemma shrugged in an exaggerated way as though overemphasising the fact it didn't matter. But perhaps it did matter.

"I didn't see much of you at the party," Hayley said. "Is everything all right?"

"It's fine." Gemma went back to using her pole to pick the fruit, aligning carefully with the branches so as not to damage the mangoes.

"We've not been spending much time together, have we?" Hayley noted.

"No. You've been with Tate." There was a clipped edge to Gemma's voice that caught Hayley's attention.

"We all spend time with Tate," Hayley replied. "We're his orchids."

"You are, anyway."

"We're a family, Gem. I hope you're all right."

Hayley finally went to wash her hands and then continued on with the fruit picking, that same refrain popping into her mind. Her body fell into a rhythm, and time hurried on as though it had somewhere to be. Hayley was at peace.

Except...

There was a niggle at the back of her mind that she could not figure out. It had no right to be there and Hayley was sure that she had told it to go away. Like any unwanted guest it kept on coming back, knocking at her door impatiently. *Knock knock.*

On your knees.

She hummed the tune more loudly.

"Would you shut up?" Gemma gave Hayley a low-lidded glare that immediately silenced her. "You're as bad as Ellie."

They continued in silence until the morning shift was completed. Hayley and Gemma didn't speak to each other for the duration, and for once Hayley was glad. Gemma made her feel tired these days. Looking at her friend only reminded her of a time before the farm that she didn't want to go back to, and she certainly didn't want to answer the knocking on the door of her mind that she was trying so desperately to ignore.

———

Despite their tense morning, Hayley still followed Gemma to the food hall for lunch and sat with her, Eoin, and Dharma. Perhaps it was because Gemma had brought it up earlier, but Hayley noticed that Clay wasn't with them, which was strange because Clay and Eoin usually stayed together. There was bound to be a good explanation for Clay's absence, so she decided to not question it.

Sure enough, after Gemma asked Eoin where Clay was, the explanation was given.

"He's gone. Up and left. I guess the lad didn't have what it takes to stay." Eoin moved some of his hair out of his eyes and smirked. "It's a shame, like, but it's his call."

"Right," Gemma mumbled. She stabbed a piece of broccoli but didn't bother to eat it, instead she sat there glaring at it. Then she shook her head slightly and seemed to snap out of her anger. "Like you said. It was his call."

"I guess he had some demons to get rid of," Dharma chimed in. "I heard he wasn't all there."

"Is that so?" Eoin turned towards Dharma in interest. "He always seemed all right to me, but you never can tell."

Gemma looked away for a moment but then sighed and went

back to eating. Despite all the bluster, Hayley could have sworn that Gemma was upset.

"I don't know why people leave here." Hayley shook her head.

Eoin nodded. "Why would anyone want to? It's paradise here. This place is everything you want and more. It's amazing."

Hayley agreed enthusiastically, pleased that there was at least one other person who understood. Maybe she'd misjudged Eoin when she'd first met him.

"Listen you two," Eoin said. "The Chemist's got a big job for you tonight. You need to go up to the house at sunset."

"Oh, that sounds exciting!" Hayley remarked.

"He wanted both of us?" Gemma leaned across her meal, her eyes brighter than Hayley had seen them for a while.

"That's what the big man said," Eoin replied with a shrug.

"I wonder why sunset?" Hayley said. "Maybe we're going to be part of the night-picking mango crew."

"Have fun with that," Dharma said with a grin. "It's bloody hard work."

"Could be." Eoin cut his chicken breast in half. "Could be something else altogether."

———

It was dusk before she saw Gemma again, who came back to the cabin with her pad of paper tucked underneath her arm. She put it away inside her bedside table and then finally looked at Hayley.

"Are you ready to go?" Gemma asked.

"Yeah."

There was a new calmness about Gemma, but she also seemed paler than usual, and that thumbnail was bitten down to the quick. She even fumbled with her keys as she locked up their cabin.

"Are you nervous?" Hayley asked.

Gemma let out a low laugh. "I think I am. But this is good, isn't it? Being chosen by Tate? I mean, you should know, you get chosen by him all the time."

"I guess so," Hayley admitted. They began a slow walk up to the house. "I think... Oh, it sounds ridiculous."

"No, go on." Gemma's voice was softer now.

"I think maybe we have a connection. I mean... we haven't *done* anything, but... Well, I just hope he feels the same way I do. I think he's amazing. I think this *place* is amazing."

"I don't think that's ridiculous," Gemma replied. "I think that's truthful. But..."

"But what?"

"Nothing," Gemma replied.

"No, go on. Be honest."

"I think it's great that you both have a connection like that. You should go for it. You really should. And you can handle it, can't you? If he rejects you, I mean. I'm sure he *won't*, but you *can* handle it. Can't you?" She smiled, her voice gentle, but her eyes strangely hard. "God, can you imagine being rejected by Tate Llewellyn? It'd *break* me."

Hayley's own smile faltered. "I can handle it. If it happens." But inside she felt like nothing more than raw meat waiting for a beating.

The glass walls of the house glowed with moonlight. They trod softly over the lawn where the parties are held and past the pool and the patio area where Tate usually had appetisers laid out. Hayley felt like this was home now, whereas when she first arrived she'd felt like an outsider. She walked up to the glass doors and opened them. She had worked up here a few days this week, assisting Tate in the lab and felt at ease walking into the house like this. She wasn't a scientist, so all she did in the lab was wash equipment and... and... water the orchids and... wait. She couldn't picture the faces of the scientists she'd helped. Why was that?

She pushed that thought out of her mind as Tate descended the stairs from the first floor of the house.

"Girls. It's so good to see you both." He walked over to Hayley, placed his hands on either side of her face and smiled intently, his eyes shining with love. When he released her, Hayley let out a little gasp of surprise and disappointment. She wanted his hands on her forever. Then he moved across and greeted Gemma. "I'm glad Eoin passed on the message. It was an important one. What you both are about to do is so fundamental to what I'm trying to achieve here, but I think you're both ready. In fact, I'm sure of it." He stepped back to Hayley. "You, Hayley, have shown me this week that you can handle responsibility. You are willing to do what it takes to make sure this farm continues on. You *care* about the legacy."

"I do," Hayley said.

"And you, Gemma, are keen to show me the same thing. You want to take a bigger part, to prove yourself, to finally once and for all show that you are a part of this family." He took her hands in his. "And I *want* you to succeed."

Gemma appeared earnest as she answered. "I will."

"I have faith in you both," Tate said with a smile. "You are willing to do anything for the farm."

"Yes," Hayley said automatically before she realised he hadn't asked her a question.

Tate moved the back of his hand gently down her face until his finger traced the line of her collarbone. "My pretty girl."

She shivered.

A moment later, Tate seemed to wake up from a reverie and sucked in a long breath. "I won't be going with you tonight, girls. I regret that I have an engagement elsewhere." He glanced out of the glass windows and up at the sky. "The moon is bright tonight." He frowned like that wasn't a good thing. "Nevertheless, I think it's time for you to learn more about the farm. It's time for you to know what we're truly about here." He turned away from them both and called out, "Rodney. You can come in now."

To Hayley's surprise, a large man walked into the room. When she saw him, her blood ran cold. His eyes were like two dull beads in his skull, devoid of emotion. He was an enormous man, as broad as he was tall, with tatty clothing and worn boots. She didn't want to go anywhere with this man.

"You'll be perfectly safe," Tate said. "This is important. This is *for the farm*. Do you understand? If you don't do this, you put the existence of the farm in jeopardy, and I know neither of you want to do that."

"We get it," Gemma said. "But maybe tonight isn't... ummm, Hayley, didn't you say you had a stomachache?"

"What?" Hayley glanced at Gemma in surprise. What was she doing?

Tate's dark eyes found her own. "Is this true?"

"It's nothing," Hayley replied. "I'm fine." She shot Gemma a glare. Her throat was dry from the nerves but she didn't want to let Tate down. Next to her, she noticed a few beads of sweat on Gemma's upper lip. They were both afraid. "Good. I'll see you when Rodney brings you back." A slow smile spread across his lips before he turned and walked away.

Hayley looked at Gemma and hated herself for being afraid. This was for the farm, and she'd do anything for the farm. Gemma's expression was impassive, not giving her any reassurance. Neither did Rodney, who began walking out of the farmhouse and seemed to expect the girls to follow him.

The night had turned cooler than expected, and Hayley was wearing just a thin top and shorts. She wrapped her arms around her body and tried not to shiver. Rodney unlocked a pickup and the girls climbed in. She noticed his hungry eyes as she bent over to pull herself into the truck.

For the farm.

But where are we going?

Hayley's legs brushed up against Gemma's as the truck reversed out of the space and headed out of the carpark. She was on the outside, next to the door, with Gemma closer to the man. That she was relieved about, because the man made her skin crawl and she didn't even want to look at him. Since she'd seen him, her stomach felt twisted up in knots. Her lower body ached as though it had been beaten. Why did he seem familiar to her?

She turned to Gemma. Gemma stared back, her expression stricken.

Gemma began whispering something. "It's *him*. He's the one that—"

"No talking," Rodney cautioned. "This isn't a ladies' luncheon. Tate expects more from you two."

Hayley closed her eyes and suppressed a sob. Crying like a baby was not the way to show Tate that she had what it took to be a member here at the farm. This was not how a member of the family behaved when the farm was in jeopardy. Whatever Tate wanted them to do was important, and if he was ever going to love her back, she had to do this.

The headlights of the truck licked the tarmac of the road. They'd left the compound and that always made Hayley feel strange. Not only that, but she recognised the road as the same one she and Gemma had hitched up from Sydney. It felt like a million years ago. But that experience had changed her, made her realise there were experiences to be taken, beauty to be seen, people to love.

She took comfort from that. From the girl she used to be. The knocking was there, of course, because it never went away, but she was strong enough to ignore it.

The journey was not a long one, but it was a quiet one, and at one point, the truck pulled off the road and onto a driveway which was headed by a long wooden field gate. The truck went over a bump in the driveway, and the headlights jumped onto some sort of skull fixed onto the front of the gate. Large horns came out of the skull like antlers. She shivered again.

Rodney got out of the truck to open the gate.

Gemma grabbed Hayley's arm. "He's the one who hurt Ellie."

In shock, Hayley shook her head. "What do you mean? He was there when she fell?"

"No," Gemma rolled her eyes. "I don't have time to explain—"

"Let's just get through this. It could be dangerous if he knows we know. We'll tell Tate later."

"But what if he hurts *us*?"

Hayley didn't know what to say. She wanted to be back at the farm, dancing with Tate like she had at the party last night. But she knew she had to be strong, so she decided to reassure Gemma as best she could. "This is important, remember? Tate wants us to do well."

Rodney came back and drove the truck through the gate, past an old cabin, and towards a field which held a cluster of outhouses. Finally, he parked the truck, pulled on the hand brake, and opened his door. Hayley's fingers trembled as she opened her door, and for a moment she was embarrassed that Gemma might have noticed. Her flip-flops churned up dust as they followed Rodney towards a large building locked by a thick chain and padlock. She shivered as she waited for him to open the door, and as she shivered, Gemma slipped her hand through hers. Gemma was shivering too.

She wanted to ask questions. What was this place? Why had they come here after dark? Where was Tate? But her voice was gone. Instead her throat was clogged with an unspoken scream. She longed to scream at the top of her lungs or throw up until her stomach stopped cramping, but for some reason she could do neither.

The door was open, and Rodney was walking in.

They went. Two small women. Hayley not much more than a bag of bones, barely layered by the small amount of muscle she'd acquired from working the fields, still not much in terms of physical strength. Skinny and lithe. Her tongue felt thick.

As they entered the strange, large facility, the cold air tickled the hairs on her arms, infiltrated her nose, her lungs. It was scented with the sweet smell of rot.

They followed Rodney as he stepped between old metal benches. No, not benches, they were some sort of conveyor belt. What *was* this place? Gemma was whimpering now, and Hayley's chest felt tight.

You would do anything for the farm, wouldn't you? You would do anything for me?

Yes.

Get on your knees, bitch.

Hayley couldn't breathe. Why had Tate made them come here? What did he want them to see? Why this man, this Rodney who turned her stomach and made her feel dirty just by looking at her? Why hadn't he spoken? She glanced back towards the open door and thought about running away, now, stealing the truck and getting out of here. Driving for as far as she could until she found a safe place. A hospital. A police station. Anywhere with a phone and a friendly face.

But none of those places would have Tate, would they? Or the cabins and the beautiful mansion? They wouldn't have fresh mangoes or lunchtime soup. They wouldn't have a sunrise that bathed the world in orange—a bright, burning star in the sky.

Rodney opened up another door and led them down some steps to yet another door. When this was opened, the smell hit her hard. The air was freezing. Both Hayley and Gemma hesitated on the final step, neither wanting to go into that dark room. Their shoulders were huddled together. Both of them were shaking now, and Gemma continued to whimper. Rodney turned back and stared at them, perhaps hesitating about what to do next. Hayley recoiled away from him. Finally, he grabbed Gemma by the wrist and forced her into the room, which in turn dragged Hayley through the door because Gemma wouldn't let her go.

It was pitch black. Gemma's hand was like a vise around hers. Tenacious. Bone crushing.

Silence.

And then, more of Gemma's whimpering.

The light went on.

The whimpering stopped.

All Hayley could hear was the sound of Gemma screaming.

The big man moved behind them, and a meaty hand wrapped around Hayley's face until she could taste salt on his palm. It was only then she realised she'd been screaming too. Gemma's hand tightened until her fingers felt like they were going to snap.

Hayley closed her eyes, hoping that if she opened them again it would all be a terrible nightmare. A terrible mistake.

But when she opened them, she realised that this was real, and that all of those eyes were indeed staring at her. There they were in a circle. Frozen. Stiff. Whiter than the moon. There they were.

And at the back, facing her directly, were Ellie and Clay.

27

GEMMA

Run...

Lifeless people tethered to chairs.

Run...

Clothes and shoes on their bodies. Flesh tainted blue.

Run...

So young. *So dead.*

Run...

A face she knew well. A beautiful face. Eyes staring blankly.

Clay.

No, no, no, no. It can't be you.

Not here.

I'm inside your nightmare. Of the dead people sitting in a circle.

What is this place? Who are all the others?

The word *dead* started up a chant inside her mind.

Dead, dead, dead. All dead.

Rodney stepped across to a thin, frozen girl and ran a lock of her long, dark hair through his meaty hand.

Stiffly, Gemma turned and forced herself to look at the girl's face.

Ellie.

You didn't go home.

A slow grin pulled Rodney's mouth into a bloodless line. "Don't worry, girls. In another hour, you won't even remember being here. You'll forget *me* too. The Chemist will work his magic on you. Until the next time. It's just a test. To see how good you are at forgetting."

"Forgetting?" Gemma whispered.

"Yeah," he said. "We show you terrible things. Then Tate makes you forget."

"Why. *Why?*" Gemma raged at him.

"You don't need to know that." Rodney smirked as he sauntered over and perched on one of the empty chairs. "Come and join the group, girls. Have a little chat. Pull up a chair."

Hayley shook her head stiffly. Gemma felt her tug on her hand, dragging her backwards towards the door.

Rodney's expression flattened as he glanced at the door and back to Hayley. He jumped to his feet—pitching forward as one foot caught on a chair leg.

For a moment, Gemma stood immobile.

Hayley's voice pierced the air. *Go! Go, go, go!*

Blood buzzed in Gemma's ears. Adrenaline shot through her limbs with electric jolts. She raced after Hayley, knocking hard into her just as she yanked the door handle.

The two of them exploded through the doorway. Gemma spun around, catching a glimpse of Rodney scrambling to his feet and chairs crashing to the floor. She slammed the door shut, fumbling desperately with the door's lock.

"Leave it," Hayley hissed.

They tore away into the cavernous darkness. The only illumination came from the weak moonlight through the windows and from the tiny bulbs of a control panel outside the cold room. She couldn't remember the way they'd come in through all of this machinery and equipment.

They ran in the wrong direction, ending up in an area with a metal grid underfoot. Enormous bull horns were stacked up in a corner. She knew what this place must be—a disused meat processing plant. Right now, they'd run towards what must have once been the slaughter floor. It'd been half-dismantled, but huge hooks still hung down from an overhead conveyer belt. A revolting, sickly odour of rust and death saturated the air, coming up through the drainage grates.

A sharp clang of metal against metal echoed as Rodney threw the cold room door open. Gemma's stomach flipped. She hadn't managed to lock it.

"Hide, hide," Hayley whispered. "He's coming."

"Fucking get out here, you two!" Rodney stomped through the shed, kicking out at something that made a loud clatter on the floor. "Don't make me have to find you."

Gemma ran behind a partition with Hayley. Rodney charged past them.

Hayley pointed at a vertical sliver of moonlight, inhaling a shivery gulp of air. "The door is all the way down there. Let's go."

"Wait." Gemma clutched her friend's arm. "If he turns on the lights, he'll see us. We don't know where he is."

"Why isn't he switching the lights on, anyway?"

"Don't know," Gemma muttered.

As if in response, machinery whirred to life. The overhead conveyer belt jolted and made a grinding sound then began shuffling along its track.

Hayley stared fearfully at the hooks as they swung menacingly on the conveyer. "God... he must be right next to us."

Gemma squinted around the building, trying to see better in the dark. Something was off. He was giving them a clear shot at the door.

She caught sight of a tall shadow passing by the window nearest to the exit. "He must have a remote control. He's playing a game with us. He's down there near the door. Waiting for us."

The control panel she'd seen before flashed in her mind. It'd been directly outside the cold room. She realised it must hold its temperature controls.

"Come on." Gemma pulled Hayley with her.

"Where—?" Hayley gasped, running with Gemma.

Gemma raced to the control panel and began tearing at the looping leads that were connected beneath the panel. "If we destroy this, he'll have to try to fix it. Maybe then we can get away."

Hayley grabbed a metal bucket and started hammering at the buttons and levers.

Rows of fluorescent lights buzzed and crackled and turned on overhead.

Rodney came charging towards them. "What the hell you doin'?" he roared. "Dumb bitches."

Gemma and Hayley rushed away as Rodney went to the control panel. They could see a clear path to the door now. Without looking back at Rodney, they fled.

They sprinted out through the door and into the dark night. And kept running, across the field.

"There's a light on—there!" Hayley gestured frantically towards the low-set farmhouse.

"Wait. We don't know"—Gemma caught her breath—"we don't know if they're bad too. The cold room is on their land, right?"

Hayley whirled around to Gemma, gasping. "The road—we'll find our way there. Get a ride into town."

"Yeah. We need to get into town. But which way?"

"Maybe straight past the house?"

Gemma nodded.

Staying low, they raced around the house, keeping a wide berth.

The howls and snaps of a group of dogs sent chills spiralling down Gemma's back. She heard them jumping up against a metal fence. "They sound vicious. What if Rodney lets them loose? They'll find us and rip us to pieces."

"Damned dogs just gave away where we are too." Hayley's voice rose in desperation.

Gemma tried to make out features of the land. *Fences. The odd tree here and there. Bushes.* Everything looked the same in every direction. "Maybe we should follow along the fence. At least we won't be circling back."

They ran to the fence and ran alongside it, stumbling and falling every few minutes.

"I still don't hear any cars," said Hayley, stopping to look around. "Maybe we're just heading into the middle of nowhere."

Nerves fizzed under Gemma's skin, her stomach so tight she wanted to vomit. "Let's try going a different way. Only, we don't know where he is. We could be going straight to him."

Hayley gripped her arm. "Gemma, he'll kill us, too, if he finds us, won't he?"

Gemma closed her eyes as she breathed out a *yes.*

She could see Clay's bluish face so clearly in her mind. Clay had wanted to leave. *I should have gone with him. He'd still be alive. God, they're murdering people. And no one knows but us.*

Hayley was pulling her again, urging her on. Together, they climbed the fence and raced into the field.

The frenzied barks of the dogs came from a different direction now.

"The dogs..." Gemma whirled around. "They've been let out."

"I hear a car!" Hayley pointed ahead.

They fled diagonally across the dry grass—low, dry bushes scratching Gemma's legs.

A thin road stretched in front of them. A car drove slowly up the road, headlights illuminating the tar. Music streamed from a window that was partially open, a female voice warbling a country song on the radio.

"It's not Rodney's van," Gemma breathed as it drew close.

"Should we—?" Hayley turned to Gemma.

The dogs were closer. Their barks and snarls terrifying. *If we hesitate, it'll be too late and the car will be gone. Can a stranger be any worse than Rodney?*

Wordlessly, Gemma ran with Hayley to the edge of the road.

The pale-coloured station wagon pulled up. "Does the car look safe to you?" Hayley whispered.

Gemma couldn't see in through the dark window. "If we don't like the look of who's in there, we run."

Hayley nodded fervently.

The driver's door opened.

A man jumped out.

Gemma barely had time to recognise that it was Rodney's bulky frame in front of them before he'd swung a rifle up and pointed it straight at them.

"Get in." He gestured with the rifle, swinging it towards the car and then back to them.

They backed away.

"I got the car from the house. From good old Wendy," Rodney told them, looking unconcerned that she and Hayley were readying themselves to flee. "I'm not stupid enough to go searching for you across the countryside. Easier to flush you out."

Hayley shook her head. "I'm not going with you. I'm not." Her voice had grown hoarse with fear.

"Awww." Rodney blew out a stream of air from between his teeth, mocking her. "If you think I'm taking you back to the cold room, you're wrong. That was just a taste."

"A taste of what?" Gemma tried to sound defiant but instead her words squeezed together into a whimper.

"You'll have to ask Tate that." He shrugged. "Anyway, where's your loyalty? Aren't you girls loyal to your precious Llewellyn?"

"You people are killers," Hayley cried. "You killed Ellie."

"I bet you're a bad shot," Gemma told Rodney, making another desperate attempt at bravado. "You smelled like booze on the way here. If we run, you're not going to get us."

"Maybe I won't be quick enough to shoot both of you. But I'll be sure to get one of ya." He swung the rifle from Gemma to Hayley and back again. "Which one of you will it be?"

The dogs' deep barks came closer.

"Just get in," he said. "I'm not going to hurt you."

Hayley stared at Gemma. Any choices they had were gone.

He grinned as they walked onto the road and into the car.

The car reeked of cheap perfume and fast-food chicken—which had to be Wendy's—and Rodney's sweat.

"Lucky you didn't do too much damage to the control panel," he said as he drove away. "I was able to plug the important bits back in." He shook his head in annoyance. "Still needs fixing though. What were you trying to do—thaw out your friends? Trust me, better to keep them iced, so you can go back and talk to them whenever you like." He chuckled to himself.

Rodney left the country music playing loud on the radio, humming along. He swung the car around and drove to the house then made them get into his van.

He headed for the highway. Gemma and Hayley remained silent, clutching each other's hand.

The drive seemed to go on forever.

All the while, panic whirled through Gemma's mind.

What happens when we get back to the farm? Will Tate and Rodney kill us too? I knew Rodney was bad, but not this bad. And Tate... God, Tate's a murderer too.

She raised her head in time to see a highway sign.

"This is the wrong way," said Gemma in alarm. "I just saw the sign for Katherine."

"Just taking a detour," Rodney said.

Gemma scanned the road frantically through the car window.

Rodney steered the car around a bend and into town. It was comforting, at least, to see houses. There were people here.

Hayley nudged Gemma. "Soon as he stops, we jump out and run for help," she said in a voice so soft that Gemma strained to hear.

Gemma gave a slight nod back. She was next to Rodney, and she didn't want him to know that she and Hayley were communicating.

But Rodney kept driving, until they were way out of town. The sign for a town named *Bowman's Creek* was ghostly in the moonlight.

The houses grew sparser and sparser and the land rougher and rougher. Until there was nothing and no one.

He drove down a dark dirt road and onto a property.

"Where are we going?" Gemma demanded.

"You'll see," he said. He got out and opened up their door. "You two get in there." He gestured towards a small shed.

"Help us!" Hayley's scream rang out clearly.

"Scream all you like," he told her. "There's no one to hear you."

When they tried to turn and flee, he was quicker, pushing them in their backs with the barrel of his gun.

The air inside the shed was hot as they stepped through the doorway, still baking from a day of sun on its metal roof and walls. The shed stank of a funky, sour odour that she couldn't name.

Rodney switched on a set of LED bulbs.

Gemma blinked in the sudden light. "What the hell?"

Two large cages dominated the shed—one occupied by large, white birds and the other empty. The cockatoos screeched and flapped their wide wings.

Rodney pushed Gemma and Hayley into the empty cage.

Gemma gasped at the sight of a puddle of clothing in one corner of the cage. *Girl's clothing*.

Rodney seemed pleased with her reaction. "You girls and me can have some fun here. You'll be my birdies."

"I won't be your *birdie*." Gemma pressed her back into the metal bars.

"You've got about as much choice in the matter as my cockatoos do. That is, none," he said. "Anyway, Hayley's my favourite. We've already gotten to know each other, haven't we, little birdie?"

Hayley shook her head, whimpering in terror. "I don't know what you're talking about."

He snickered. "Just because you don't remember it, birdie, doesn't mean it didn't happen."

Hayley stared at him with huge, shocked eyes.

A phone ringtone shrilled above the noise of the birds. Rodney dug in his pocket and fetched his phone.

Stepping out of the cage, he grabbed a set of keys that were hanging on the wall. He locked the cage and walked out of the shed, whistling.

Gemma heard him answer his call as he walked towards his house. "Tate..."

PART III

NOW

28

BRONWEN

"I'm going to..." Bronwen squeezed her hands into fists. "I don't know *what* the fuck I'm going to do."

"Take it easy, Bron," Joe soothed.

"Wait, rewind... a bit more. There. Pause it." Bronwen leaned back on her heels and let out a low whistle between her teeth. She was standing behind one of the security guards at the hospital going over the recorded camera footage of the corridor outside Gemma's room. "Is that Hayley?"

"Same height and build." Joe noted. "But who's with her?" He scratched his chin and leaned closer to the screen.

The girls' disappearance was a monumental fuckup that Super-intendent Jones was never going to let her forget. This case was getting to her. From the creepy shit in White's home, to the freezer room on Denton Road, to the weird pharmaceutical guy at the mango farm, her mind was completely scrambled and frustration wasn't strong enough a word to describe how she felt right now. She knew it was all related, but she couldn't figure out how or why.

Her chest felt tight as she stood there watching the security footage. She was leading an investigation that had grown and grown from the night the two girls had been found on the highway. A large team was waiting for her instructions on what to do next, and every night she found herself buried under the massive load of files generated by this case.

She pressed her weight against the back of the security guard's chair. "Go back and forth again. I want to rewatch them coming out of Hayley's room."

So far what she'd learned from the footage was that a tall guy wearing a baseball cap and brown shirt had entered the room. After a couple of minutes, Hayley emerged with him in jeans and a T-shirt. Then they both went into Gemma's room to fetch her. Gemma was walking but seemed visibly dazed from the way she stumbled along.

"Is Gemma drugged?" Bronwen pointed her finger at the screen. "Have we got more footage of her walking through the hospital?"

"We'll have to look through every camera," the security guard replied. "It might take a while."

"We don't have a while." Bronwen frowned. She'd put out a bulletin over the radio based on Hayley and Gemma's appearance as they left the hospital. If only they'd been able to get a better look at this guy's face, but he'd kept it angled down and out of view with the peak of his hat.

Joe placed a gentle hand on her arm and led her to the back of the room. "Bron, what's up? It's not like the girls are suspects. They're over eighteen. We can't actually keep them in the hospital. I know they're witnesses, but—"

"You saw the CCTV, Joe. It's a kidnap. Gemma has been taken by the guy on that tape, and I don't know why or what Hayley is doing. Didn't you see the way Gemma was stumbling around? She looked like she'd been drugged to me. When we spoke to her earlier, she didn't seem groggy and out of it like she is in the video."

"Maybe she just woke up," Joe replied. "We can't spend too long on this, Bron. We have the press conference coming up that we need to prepare for."

Bronwen shook her head. "Yeah, and that's going to go down well if we've lost our two main witnesses. No, this is important, and there's something else going on." She walked away from the security room. There had to be more to it than a sleepy girl and two friends helping her out. She needed to find those girls now.

———

Needing a break from Joe and his well-meaning attempt to calm her down, Bronwen headed towards the cafeteria and ordered a strong coffee instead. As she tipped two sugars into the dark liquid, she thought about what her next move will be. There were officers out looking for the girls, but right now they hadn't established what kind of vehicle they used—if there even had been a vehicle—not to mention which direction they went in.

She took a seat and removed her mobile phone from her pocket. The last lead she'd been about to follow was a phone call between Hayley and her friend Alice that had taken place back in December. Maybe she should start there. It gave her something to do while the guard went through more hospital footage. She took out her notebook and returned to the details she'd written down for Hayley's friend. She had no time to worry about what time it was in England right now. If she woke them up, so what? They'd live.

It was five rings before someone answered. She asked for Alice and then waited.

"Hello?"

"Is that Alice Marsons?"

"Yes, who is this?"

"My name is Detective Bronwen McKay, I'm a police officer based in Katherine, Australia. Do you know a young woman named Hayley Edwards?"

"Yes, she's my friend." There was a hint of panic in her voice, and the girl spoke more quickly, as though she had suddenly become more focused. "Is she all right? I heard that there was some sort of accident there and she was hurt."

"She's okay. But I'm investigating the incident, and I need to ask you a few questions."

"Okay. If it helps," Alice said.

"We have here that you spoke to Hayley via telephone sometime at the beginning of December. Can you recall that conversation?" It felt strange to be asking official questions over the phone. Bronwen had no way to verify her status, and she couldn't be certain that the girl would even take her seriously, but it was either that or fly to England.

"Yeah, I remember. We didn't talk for long. It was strange to hear from her, actually. She'd been travelling, and we hadn't really been in touch. But then she kept telling me I should go out there because it's so beautiful."

"She wanted you to visit?" Bronwen asked.

"I guess so. She said something about a mango farm, and a guy called Tate, and there were waterfalls. But it was long distance so she didn't stay on the phone long."

"She called you on a landline? No texting, WhatsApp, or Snapchat?"

"Yeah, that's why I found it weird. She could have just sent me a message, but she called me, and it was like she called me just to brag about her holiday. Then she had to go."

"Did anything else about the conversation stick out to you?"

There was a pause on the other end of the line until Alice said, "Her voice had changed."

"Her accent?" Bronwen asked.

"No. Hayley was always pretty uptight. She was quiet, you know. That's why it was so weird when she flipped and ran away. She always seemed so together. But on the phone she sounded different. Spaced out. And she sounded really, really happy. Too happy."

"You think she might have been on drugs?"

"Hayley? Hardly? I don't know what it was. She just sounded weird. Not herself."

Bronwen made a quick note. "Thanks so much for your time, Alice."

"Will you tell her to come home?" Alice said, surprising Bronwen. "I don't think it's good for her to be out there alone."

"I don't either, Alice. I'll tell her, okay?" Bronwen hung up the phone and took a moment to process the information Alice had offered up.

The mango farm seemed connected to all of this. She just couldn't figure out how or why.

As she was tapping her fingers on the table, trying to connect the pieces, a red-faced Joe appeared from the corridor.

"There you are," he said. "The security guard has the rest of the footage pulled."

Bronwen took her coffee with her as they made their way back to that stuffy little room. "Have you seen it?"

"Yeah," he said. "There's not much else to go on. The three of them walked out of the exit at the back of the hospital near the maternity ward. It looks like Hayley puts on a hat as she's walking out."

"Any vehicles identified? Do we know how the guy in the baseball cap travelled to the hospital?"

"It may be a transit van," Joe replied. "The guy knew what he was doing. If the van does belong to him, he parked it under a broken light in the carpark, pretty close to the appropriate exit. The camera didn't pick up any registration numbers."

"Let's update the officers about the van," Bronwen said. "I'm going to try calling Hayley's parents again after I've seen the video."

Bronwen had called them almost immediately after the girls went missing, but neither parent was answering their phone. She was pretty certain that Hayley wouldn't be going back to see her parents after what happened when they visited, but they had a right to know that their daughter had left the hospital. She opened the door into the security room and lifted her chin to the guard as an indication for him to press play. He did.

She watched it. And then she watched it again. Joe was right about the fact that there was little to go on. The mysterious guy kept his head down. But she saw that he was tall, medium build, white, a little on the pale side. Maybe he was English too? The way Gemma's head kept rolling down towards her chest, and the way the guy had his arm around her made Bronwen's stomach lurch. What was going on, and why was this girl being coerced out of the hospital? This sorry event was yet another reminder that they'd never actually found Gemma's family during the investigation. She could call Hayley's family, but where was Gemma's?

They knew so little about the two girls. Hayley had parents and had a home, but she never acted in a way that Bronwen expected of a nice, studious, and quiet girl as described by most of the people who knew her before. Both of the girls were unpredictable and uneven. But then there was always one place Hayley always felt the same about. There was one place she consistently talked about in a positive light. There was one place she always expressed love for. The same place that she knew was involved in this investigation somehow.

Everything leads back to the farm. Maybe it led Hayley and Gemma back too.

29

MEGAN

A sense of urgency pulsed through Megan's veins. Ever since the girls had vanished, she'd had a cold fear growing inside her. If there were other people involved in the cold room murders, then the girls were in danger.

Last night, she'd told Bronwen that she'd found some secret client files that Leah Halcombe had been keeping on Clay Durrell. But in between the search for the girls and preparations for the police/media conferences today, Bronwen hadn't had time to take a look or discuss it with her. Had Rodney murdered Leah because of what Clay was telling her about his nightmares? If so, how had Rodney found out?

Megan shivered in the cold air-conditioning. She'd driven three-and-a-half hours through the roasting heat to Darwin, and she'd just arrived at the media conference centre. On the way in, she'd bought an icy drink to try to cool down. It was now sitting like a frozen pond at the pit of her stomach.

She was here to give a report to the media about Gemma and Hayley's states of mind. There had been a lot of wild speculation about the two girls in the press and that had only gotten worse since they went missing. She'd be clearing up the misperceptions. But first, Bronwen and Joe were to give their address to the media about the *Cold Room Killings* case.

The room had been set up with the chairs in rows, facing the podium and a large screen. Journalists were jostling for the front seats.

I don't envy you two, Megan thought as she watched Bronwen and Joe enter the conference room. The detectives had already briefed a room of police in the morning. From what she'd heard, the room had been filled to capacity. Police from all over Australia and overseas had flown in to hear the details. This case had stretched far beyond their little part of the world.

Now, in the afternoon, Bronwen and Joe were tasked with addressing the media. Whatever everyone in the room was about to hear would soon be ricocheting all around the world—as soon as the journalists had their notes ready. For the families of the victims, they would be hearing a lot of grisly information for the first time.

As well as all of that, Bronwen and Joe would have to explain the disappearance of Gemma and Hayley. From the time they'd been found up until they went missing, the two of them had been painted as a good news story in the media. Young victims who'd experienced horrors but who had escaped. But now they were gone again.

The address began without fanfare. Bronwen briefly explained the case in a matter-of-fact manner and asked that all questions be kept until the address had ended.

Pictures began displaying on the screen. First, there were images of the fallen fuel tanker on the dark highway—flames still bursting skyward. These were accompanied by pictures of Rodney White's car off the side of the road—later found to be owned by a woman named Wendy Williams. Next, photos of Gemma and Hayley filled the screen—hair tangled, skin bruised, and dresses covered in blood. These images had been snapped soon after they were rescued and taken to safety.

A variety of images and video of Rodney White's house, land and aviaries were shown next. The inside of the house was a pigsty. The land was bare except for junk. Two cages stood inside a large shed, each about two metres square and four metres high. Large, sad-looking birds—cockatoos—were huddled together in one of the cages. Dirty straw covered the floors of the aviaries. There was nowhere else for the girls to have sat or slept. It would have been itchy and prickly and uncomfortable to sleep on. The aviaries were dark. Not much sunlight getting in at all. The ventilation would have been awful. How did the birds survive, let alone teenage girls?

Megan's stomach tensed as the video camera display stopped for a moment on a crumpled pile of girls' clothing in a corner of an unoccupied cage.

Next came a catalogue of items belonging to Rodney's rape victims. Six victims in total. Rodney had apparently been careful not to show his face to them, always wearing an old balaclava. The last rape had been years ago, and none of the victims had been held for longer than three hours, as far as police could tell. The victims had been identified, and their rape cases now solved. Rodney had been the perpetrator. The investigation was continuing, to discover if there had been additional victims.

Joe announced that they were moving onto the cold room. His voice sounded drawn and flat—very unlike Joe.

The cold room presentation began with photographs. Full colour. Dead persons sitting in a circle. Strapped to chairs.

The faces had been blurred out, but images filled Megan's mind anyway—faces drained of colour and eyes devoid of life.

The victims were all young, as had been reported on the news. Megan caught a glimpse of the only older person—a woman wearing a floral blouse and pink skirt. Red hair in a neat bob. Sunglasses in her blouse pocket. Sensible shoes. Leah Halcombe. Most likely, those were the things she'd dressed herself in the day she died—not knowing those would be the clothes she would end her life in.

The silence that blanketed the room was so thick it was almost smothering.

The pictures were confirmation that serial killers existed, because here was their handiwork. It was something so far outside of the normal world that it was hard to grasp. It was a bucket of ice-cold water thrown on your face while you were sleeping.

Bronwen informed the media that they could describe these visions of the cold room, but they wouldn't be provided with photographs, and out of respect to the victims' families, members of the media were not to describe any of the victims personally. With that, she ended the media address.

Question time came after that. The first question came in a brash tone from a journalist asking how Gemma and Hayley had been able to leave the hospital so easily and if the police had found them yet.

As question time was ending, Megan slipped around to the back-stage area. She came out and gave a brief address to the media about Gemma and Hayley. She spoke about two frightened but brave girls who'd been through the unimaginable, hoping her words would clear up some of the more ludicrous speculation that was being tossed about.

With her part in the conference done, she hoped to catch Bronwen and Joe for a chat about Leah. But they were now in discussion with a roomful of detectives.

She walked out of the hall and back into the furnace-like heat outside. Tourists in colourful summer clothing thronged everywhere as she drove through the busy streets of Darwin. It was a pretty, green city, ringed with ocean. The scenery was welcome after the dark images she'd just seen in the hall.

She headed onto the Stuart Highway for the long drive back.

Some details niggled at her. There a very damning case against the dead Rodney White, but when and why had he gradu-ated from raping women to murdering a range of people? The second type of crime was inherently riskier than the first. She knew that people who committed these terrible crimes sometimes started getting bolder and bolder and committing worse atrocities. But still, it wasn't good practice to make assumptions about people's motives.

As soon as she was home, she stepped into the shower and washed away the dust of the highway. But she couldn't clean the images of the cold room and birdcage from her mind.

She put on an old, comfortable cotton dress. She had work to do.

A knock came at the door. Answering it, she found Jacob standing there, clutching a bunch of flowers. She'd forgotten he was flying back to Australia this morning—she'd been too caught up with everything. He looked good, in jeans and a blue shirt and cleanly shaved. Last time she'd seen him, he'd been in a crumpled coat straight from the microbiology lab, his beard the victim of an uneven shave. Today, she was sure it was herself who was looking worse for wear.

"I know you said you don't like cut flowers, but these looked nice." He shrugged casually, but his smile was a little sheepish.

She combed her fingers through her wet hair. "Thank you. Hmmm, do they come with wine and dinner and chocolates? I mean, if we're being all traditional?"

He grinned. "No, it's just the flowers. And me."

She laughed, taking the flowers. "Then come on in."

Jacob followed her inside and perched on one of her kitchen stools. "Hey, this absolutely can be dinner and wine, if you'd like."

"I was just kidding. Dinner would be nice, but I'll have to take a rain check. I've got some things to do tonight."

"That's a shame." He looked at her reflectively. "Are you sure this is okay, me turning up like this? You know, if you're seeing someone else—"

"Jacob, I'm not seeing anyone."

"Just so you know, I wouldn't blame you if you were. Or if you thought I wasn't putting any effort in. I've been away a lot."

"Noted." She attempted a lighthearted grin. This was how Jacob and herself had run their relationship so far—they joked with each other, never venturing into the serious kind of dialogue that committed couples had.

He looked as if he had something else to say, but a tight ball of nerves formed in her chest, and she carried the flowers to the kitchen bench. The exchange had felt awkward. Were they at the stage where they were ready to have the conversation about becoming exclusive? She didn't know if she wanted that.

Opening one of the two cupboards in her tiny kitchen, she fumbled about, searching for something that resembled a vase. She didn't own any. Settling for a water jug, she took it to the sink.

"Have you heard about the cold room murder case?" she asked him, deciding to steer the conversation back to safer territory.

He nodded, frowning and seeming confused at the change in conversation. "Yup."

"I was asked to speak with the two girls who escaped from that guy. And they're missing now. I've got some notes to go over—I want to see if there's any clues to where they might have gone. Haven't had a chance yet. I went to a media briefing up in Darwin today." She filled the jug with water and dropped the bunch of flowers in.

He came and sat on a stool at the kitchen bench. "Heavy stuff. Do the police have any ideas?"

"Not really. The girls originally came up to the NT to do fruit picking at Llewellyn Farm. There's a small chance they might have met up with some friends they made there." Megan didn't mention the fact that it seemed that Hayley and an unidentified man had taken Gemma by force. So far, the police were holding that piece of information back from the public.

"Llewellyn Farm? Is that the one owned by Tate Llewellyn?"

"Yeah. You've heard of him?"

He shrugged. "He's been at some of the pharmaceutical events

I've been to. And I remember a lab of his in the same building that we had one—in Thailand."

"I guess that makes sense. I mean, I keep thinking of him as a fruit farmer. But he's also a chemist. And his father does own a pharmaceutical company." She paused. "Can I get you a cold drink? Ginger beer? Or a coffee?"

"Ginger beer sounds great. Interesting stuff Llewellyn was researching."

"Oh yeah? Like what?" She fetched two bottles of ginger beer from the fridge and gave him one.

"He had dozens of rats," Jacob told her. "They were researching memory recall."

"Memory recall? For what purpose?" She sat beside him on a stool.

"Hmmm, not sure. No, wait, I think I do. I chatted with one of the Thai lab techs in Llewellyn's lab one day. She said the lab was for post-traumatic stress disorder. Testing drugs to see if they could make the rats forget a specific psychological trauma."

"That *is* interesting."

"Knew that'd get your attention. That kind of thing is your field. How would they make the rats forget a memory?"

Megan thought for a moment, toying with the bottle caps she'd just removed from the ginger beer bottles. "I'd like to know what the experiments were about, exactly. But memories can be altered, even without drugs. We think our memories are reliable and sorted in filing cabinets in our brains, but they're not. Each time we recall a memory, it's plastic and can change."

"Well, I didn't find out much," Jacob said. "Llewellyn came into his lab and shut me down super quick. He was polite, but he showed me the door, more or less."

"Weird. Hope they weren't mistreating the rats or something. Do you think there was something he didn't want you to see?"

Jacob swigged his beer. "I didn't see anything out of order. The rats were looking a bit dazed, but y'know, that could have been part of the experiments."

"Hmmm, so what happened with his research?" she mused. "I mean, I'm guessing the tests weren't successful?"

Jacob shook his head. "The Thai lab is still functioning, as far as I know. I saw Llewellyn there just four or so months back."

Megan stared at him. "That guy has a finger in a lot of pies."

Bronwen had told her that Tate Llewellyn was running a sizeable mango farm and some kind of perfume testing that went on every day —and now she'd learned that he was actively conducting memory research with lab rats.

Just where, exactly, did his real focus lie?

30

BRONWEN

It was seven a.m., and Bronwen woke from a cot in the corner of her office. She made her way to the showers, grabbed a towel from her locker, and ducked under the lukewarm water. This was the third night in a row that she'd slept at the station. Going home and having a nice warm bath would be nice. Maybe she could order in and eat a Chinese feast on the sofa in her pyjamas. Those were the things that dreams were made of, not falling asleep on top of crime scene photos.

Throwing herself into a case wasn't unheard of, but she'd never gone this long without a rest, and now the little herb garden she'd been cultivating on the porch was beginning to die. Joe had a girl-friend to go home to, but for Bronwen, her modest house was her haven. Quiet. Unquestioningly hers and sorely missed.

But it was worth staying at the station, because Bronwen had been examining her notes on Leah Halcombe overnight and had to admit that Megan was right: Leah didn't fit the profile of the other victims. She was a professional woman with a decent job. Why would she be mixed up with so many young drifters? If you added to that the fact that one of her clients, Clay, was a young troubled guy who *did* fit the profile of the other victims, then there was definitely something unusual about this whole situation. One thing that seemed likely was that Leah only ended up in the freezer room on Denton Road because of her connection to Clay.

It all leads back to the farm. Where do young drifters go? They find work picking fruit at places like Llewellyn's.

The shower was a short one, just enough time for a wash. She dried swiftly, pulled her hair up into a tight bun, and slipped into a spare suit she kept at the office. She had to remember to ask someone to dry-clean her worn clothes so she could keep ahead of this schedule. Never had Bronwen felt this kind of pressure. The super wanted this case done. Every time they spoke, he talked about White. *It's clear Rodney White is the perp here, McKay. No? What's taking so long to close this case? The commissioner is on my back about this one. Don't you know who Llewellyn is? We can't keep investigating the guy.*

Every time they met, he refused to acknowledge that the case was far more complicated than that. Yes, Rodney was with the girls at the time of the accident, and yes, they had identified him as their attacker, and yes, he was the person renting the slaughterhouse on Denton Road. She wasn't denying that Rodney was a murdering scumbag, she just thought he wasn't the only one. And now she had to find those girls, get them back, and figure out who else was involved.

"Good morning, sleepy head." Joe strode into her office carrying coffee, which he placed down on her desk. "It's the good stuff from the coffee shop in town. Extra strong."

Bronwen lifted the safety lid from her coffee and sipped greedily.

"I come bearing other gifts," Joe said, his eyes sparkling.

"Pastries?"

"No, well, yes, actually, but that isn't the gift." Joe reached into his top pocket and removed a sheet of paper. "Came in from the JoP this morning. The search warrant for Llewellyn Farm."

"Joe, I could kiss you."

"Come on, Bron, don't be gross."

———

"What do you think Brad Pitt of the Mangoes is doing on that farm?" Joe said, licking the last of the Danish from his fingers.

"Joe, use a napkin and keep those mitts off my glove box," Bronwen snapped. They were on their way to Llewellyn's with a search team following directly behind them. The farm was a big place, and it was going to take some time to comb through it. "Killing backpackers? Keeping the girls somewhere? I dunno."

"What's his motive?" Joe finally used a couple of napkins but then screwed them up and threw them on the floor of the car. "Rich guy likes to kill? He's got a lot to lose, hasn't he? And why work with a man like Rodney—a total lowlife?"

"I honestly don't know. We're missing something, but I don't know what it is. Seriously, Joe, are you gonna pick them up?"

"What?"

"The napkins." Bronwen rolled her eyes. Her stomach had flipped over several times this morning, and she'd been unable to finish her pastry. Since this case started, she'd lost three kilos and needed a new belt.

They pulled onto the property, parked up, and climbed out of the car. Bronwen touched the search warrant in her pocket and hoped to God they'd find something. She needed it after blundering through that damn press conference yesterday. Try explaining missing witnesses to a room full of journalists hungry for details. She needed the win, but she was exhausted.

It was early, barely eight a.m., but the receptionist greeted them cordially. Bronwen asked for Llewellyn before turning to the team to help split up the officers for a thorough search. The farmhouse was a priority, seeing as this was where Llewellyn lived, but they also had to search the dormitories, outbuildings, and the fields. It was going to be a long day.

"Detective McKay. Detective Kouros. It's so lovely to see you both. But what on earth is going on?"

She'd half expected Tate Llewellyn to come downstairs in silk paisley pyjamas, but he was already fully clothed and without a hint of sleep in his eyes. She'd forgotten just how good-looking the bastard was, but this time it didn't move her. She was prepared for it.

"It's a little early for all this, isn't it?" he said, smiling broadly. "Sophie, would you mind getting the officers some coffee?"

"Sure." The receptionist slipped away from her post while Tate Llewellyn stepped closer.

He placed his hands in his pockets and leaned against the reception desk.

"Mr Llewellyn, we have a warrant here issuing us the right to search your property." Bronwen took the piece of paper and spread it out on the reception desk.

He bent over the paper with a smile. "Interesting." Then he leaned back and clapped his hands together. "Well, good luck with your search, officers. I'm not exactly sure what you're looking for, but I'm confident that our operation is completely legal. We have a strict 'no-drugs' rule on the premises, and my employees are well aware of that rule."

"Even still," Bronwen said, "we'll begin the search now." She turned and smiled at him. He lowered his chin and met her eyes with his own.

————

Bronwen took her coffee in a small room with comfortable chairs. Sophie handed her a printed list of all employees from the last five years, and she began to work her way through the list, looking for names matching those of the bodies found in the freezer room. She'd sent Joe to organise the search teams while she kept an eye on Llewellyn.

She worked in silence for a while, trying not to get distracted by the way Llewellyn insisted on tapping against the arm of his chair. She wouldn't give him the opportunity to rile her. As she worked, she received updates when a zone had been searched and cleared. Every time a zone ended, Tate smirked, as though he knew the police would find nothing.

Eventually, he said, "I can save you some time, detective." He placed his elbows on his knees as he stretched himself forward in the chair opposite. "I recognised some of the names from the news. Clay, for instance, worked here for a time. Ellie too. I'll be reaching out to their parents to help with the funeral costs. It's the least I can do."

"How generous of you." Bronwen refrained from rolling her eyes. "Why do you think at least two people from your farm have been murdered?"

"Honestly, I think someone is pursuing these people because they are easy targets. I hate to put it that way, but many of our employees are young wanderers running away from abusive families or a broken home. They come here to work, but they happen to be people who may not be missed. It's incredibly sad, but that's the way it is."

He wasn't fooling her with his bleeding-heart act. "Then the killer must be someone from your farm."

"That's not true," Llewellyn replied. "My employees are free to come and go off the farm. They go kayaking, hike the Kakadu Park. They go into Katherine or Pine Creek sometimes too. They could be discovered anywhere at any time. The murderer doesn't have to be at the farm at all."

"But your farm is the consistent link in this case," Bronwen pointed out. "Both Hayley and Gemma were here for a time, and now at least two of the bodies from the freezer room too. Everything leads back to your farm, Mr. Llewellyn. Why is that?"

He shrugged. "Like I said before, the people here are often vulnerable." He let out a heavy sigh and leaned back in his chair. "Anyway, I thought you had your killer. What was his name? White? Didn't he die?"

"He did," Bronwen said. "Which is a shame, because now we can't ask him if he had any accomplices." She finished her coffee and turned back to the list of names, rubbing at the growing ache of a headache forming at her temples. It wasn't good coffee, too bitter, but hopefully it would keep her awake after a bad night's sleep in her office.

"Why would a sick, twisted individual like Rodney White need an accomplice?" There was an odd shift in the tone of his voice. It had turned rhythmic, soothing. Bronwen tried to ignore the way his voice made her feel even sleepier. "More coffee?"

She held out her cup and allowed Tate to pour her another.

"Tell me about what's troubling you, detective."

"The girls' stories don't match," she said. "I can't trust them as witnesses. The upkeep of the freezer room on Denton Road must be expensive and time consuming. Plus, it doesn't fit the chaotic nature of Rodney White. He's messy and dirty, but the freezer room is neat. The bodies are placed carefully. Why?" She frowned and lifted her head from the paper. Had she really said that out loud? That was far more detail than she should be telling a suspect.

"It sounds like you have quite a case on your hands, detective. Perhaps you need a sounding board to figure out what's going on. You know, I might not have much experience, but I am willing to listen—"

Bronwen's phone began to ring. She glanced at the screen and saw that it was Megan. "Would you excuse me a moment?"

"Of course."

Bronwen took her phone and coffee into the hallway. "Megan."

"Hi, Bronwen. Sorry to bother you at work. I wondered if there was any news on Hayley and Gemma?"

"Nothing so far. We're searching Llewellyn Farm to see if they're here. So far none of the teams have found them, and we're almost halfway through the search." As she said the words she realised how deflated and tired she felt. Her head was fuzzy, and she was having trouble concentrating.

"Listen, this might be nothing, but I wanted to pass it on. You remember that biologist I was seeing?"

"Oh, Mr Incommunicado? Yeah, what about him?"

"He met Llewellyn at a pharmaceutical event and apparently he owns a lab in Thailand."

"Huh, small world."

"Yep. He's conducting some pretty cutting-edge research. Attempting to alter the memories of lab rats. Jacob told me one of Tate's lab tech's said it was for post-traumatic stress applications. I was thinking about it all last night and, I don't know, I just felt like maybe it's connected to the case in some way."

"There is a lab on the premises," Bronwen replied. "I'll get the search team to check for drugs."

"That could be a good idea," Megan said. "It just seems odd, doesn't it? Going from working on memory drugs to owning a mango farm? Thought it might be worth looking into."

"Yeah. That's true."

As Bronwen hung up the phone, she stared down at the coffee cup in her hand. She felt spaced out and woozy, and her hands were shaking as she put the phone back in her pocket. This felt like more than lack of sleep. Sure, this case was the toughest she'd ever been through, but she'd never experienced this kind of dizziness while on the job before. And now Megan was telling her that Llewellyn had a history of experimental drug trials. That was suspicious in itself.

Rather than head back into the room with Llewellyn, she decided to go downstairs, find some sort of container, and have the lab test the coffee in her mug. If he'd... if he'd drugged her...

"Detective McKay? Are you all right?" Llewellyn's voice came from behind her, but she ignored him and kept going, trying to remember how to get back to the reception. There were stairs in front of her, but they seemed impossibly steep.

"Hey. You're not all right at all, are you? You're dead on your feet."

A strong hand hooked underneath her elbow and turned her around. Bronwen found she was too weak to pull herself away from him, but she must have bumped against the wall because she felt a sharp jab in the flesh of her arm.

"Was there a screw?" she frowned, trying to turn to look at her arm as Tate continued to keep hold of her. Llewellyn Farm didn't seem like the kind of place to have screws or nails sticking out of the walls. What was that sensation she'd felt? Her eyelids drooped, and her knees buckled slightly.

"Here, let me take that cup from you. Look at you. You're dog-tired, come on." He walked her back into the room, managing to keep her upright. "Here. Lie down on the sofa. Rest for a while. Joe can finish up, can't he? Have a nap now, there's a good girl. And, Bronwen, no one called you on the phone at all, did they? You didn't speak to anyone, you just fell asleep right here on this sofa for a few minutes. That's right, nestle down. Get comfortable. You're safe and well, Bronwen. Everything is fine."

31

HAYLEY

She didn't like this room. It was too small, and there were no windows. It made her think of Rodney's cages and the birds squawking outside. In this place she felt like she was trapped again. But she had to keep reminding herself that this was different, because this time it was for a good cause, and she knew she was going to be okay. Hayley was down here to protect the farm, and that was what mattered.

Tate had explained it to her very carefully before they came down to the basement room, making her understand what she had to do. She had to stay out of sight until the police finished searching for her and Gemma. You see, Hayley made a mistake when she brought Gemma back to the farm. Bringing Gemma back wasn't the mistake; in fact, having her back at the farm was a good thing. But she'd done it by force, and that was the bad thing. Gemma didn't always realise what was good for her, so Hayley had to make the decision for them both. This time, however, she'd risked too much. She and Eoin had taken Gemma from a public place with cameras tracking their every move. Tate had sat her down and explained exactly why she shouldn't have done that.

"Hayley, my pretty orchid. You're so loyal. But you've been a little fool, sweet girl. The police will be looking for you now. You're involved in the biggest murder investigation of the last few decades, and now you'll bring the police to my door." His knuckles had turned white as he'd clenched his fists tightly by his side. Then he'd taken a deep breath, reached out, stretching those clenched fingers until they splayed out, and stroked her face. "I'm going to have to hide you now. There's no time for anything else."

"I'm sorry," Hayley replied, biting back tears. "I thought we had to come back to you. I brought Gemma back to you because I thought that was what you wanted."

She'd glanced across at Gemma, still bound, glaring at her with furious eyes. Hayley glanced away. Gemma never knew what was good for her. Hayley had seen her make one reckless decision after another.

While they'd been in the hospital, Gemma had kept saying things to the police that didn't make sense, like being in Rodney's cage for months. None of that was true, and Hayley couldn't understand what she was doing and why. All she knew was that Gemma was ruining it all. She thought that if she brought Gemma back to Tate, he would make her realise that her place was here at the farm with Hayley. Gemma would understand one day, she was sure of it.

Tate wrapped a lock of her hair around his finger. Gently, he began to pull. "You're more loyal to me than anyone else here." He pulled a little harder. "I know that. But it doesn't change the fact that you made a mistake." His fingers tugged hard on her hair, until her eyes began to water, then he let her go. "Come with me, and I'll show you where to hide. You, too, Eoin. Bring Gemma."

He'd taken them to the back of the glass-walled house into a room that Hayley had never been in before. This had to be part of Tate's living quarters. She'd always assumed that he lived in the area nearest to the glass patio doors by the terrace. Now they were heading deeper into the house.

"This is the second wing of the house," Tate explained. "My favourite part."

It was a stunning area. The open space had been divided into a library and a lounge by a grand water feature designed to imitate a waterfall. Black marble stone shone through the running water, twinkling as the ripples caught the ceiling lights. It was in a step formation, with the water travelling down to a grate in the floor. Tate moved across to the wall, lifted the cover of a small box and flipped a switch. The water ceased immediately, leaving only the smooth black steps. He bent down and pressed the third step from the bottom. There was a click, and the step lifted up to reveal a trapdoor underneath. As Hayley let out a little gasp of shock, Tate entered a number in a keypad and the trapdoor opened to reveal another set of steps leading down into darkness.

"In you go, Hayley," Tate had said. "There's a light switch on the left."

She turned back to Gemma and saw her friend's eyes wide with terror. Gemma was truly terrified, and Hayley was surprised to see her like that. Okay, so she'd forced Gemma back to the farm, but she hadn't thought she'd be *this* afraid. Maybe she was all mixed up after what had happened with Rodney. Hayley still hadn't recovered all of her memories, so she couldn't fully remember what Rodney did to them, but as far as she knew, Gemma remembered everything and it had messed her up.

"It'll be okay, Gem," she'd said, trying to reassure her friend.

Hayley's stomach had tingled with nerves as she took the first step into the darkness. Her fingers groped out to find the switch, and for a moment her breath caught in her chest. In her mind she saw the bodies from the cold room again, all arranged in a circle, Ellie staring at her, and she panicked, almost coming back up the stairs. *Ellie.*

The light came on and down she went. There was another door to be opened. Once she opened that door, she realised she was in some sort of panic room, which had a television, a sofa, a bed, food, and basically everything needed to survive a zombie outbreak. As her eyes roamed around the small space, she also noted another door, closed. But before she'd had time to wonder where it led, she'd glanced back to see Eoin dragging Gemma down the steps, and then the door had closed.

How long had they been down here since then? She'd played several rounds of gin rummy with Eoin, which he always won. Gemma was no longer gagged, but Hayley had been too afraid to remove her wrist ties in case she attacked them. Gemma sat in the farthest corner with a sullen look on her face.

"He's a murderer, you know," Gemma said, eyes low and dangerous. "You're helping a murderer."

"We're protecting the farm," Hayley replied.

"You're delusional," Gemma snapped. "You don't remember any of it. He *changed* your memories, you idiot. You're just a pawn he uses in his game, and now you're not useful to him anymore. You're a liability because the police are after us both. We're both liabilities. We're going to end up dead like Ellie."

Ellie.

"Gemma, the cold room was all Rodney," Hayley said. "Rodney's dead now. Everything is going to be okay. Tate just needs to make sure we don't bring too much attention to the farm with the police and everything."

"Listen to the girl, Gemma," Eoin added. "The Chemist knows what he's doing, okay? Just sit tight now."

"Why are you paying attention to anything that sexist pig says?" Gemma nodded towards Eoin. "He's not your friend, Hayley. I'm your only friend. Think. Why would Tate be worried about the police finding us here? How would that hurt the farm?"

Hayley didn't want to think about it. She wanted to be back on the mango fields picking fruit or out on the terrace with the other backpackers, laughing and singing. The farm was the only place she'd ever been happy, and she needed to remember that.

"Gemma, stop worrying, okay? We're going to be fine. Once everything has blown over, we can go back to working on the farm like before."

Gemma shook her head. "No, we won't. We'll be put in the ground. Look at this place. It's the lair of an evil, murdering psycho. Why else would he have a secret room, for God's sake?"

Eoin scoffed.

"What are you laughing at?" Gemma demanded. "You're dead, too, Eoin. You know too much."

"Fuck off, will you?" Eoin swiped the cards from the table and stood up from the sofa, his frame looming over them both. "I've had about enough of your lip."

"Eoin, stop!" Hayley rushed to her feet, positioning herself between Eoin and Gemma. His hands were balled into fists, and a ripple of tension worked its way along his jaw. "What are you doing?"

"She's getting on my last nerve. I'm putting the gag back on."

"Don't you dare," Gemma said. "I'll bite your fingers off."

"Jesus Christ." Eoin rolled his eyes in frustration. "It wasn't worth bringing this fucking gobshite back, was it?" He turned to Hayley. "I don't know what you were thinking, but she's going to ruin this for everyone."

"She's not," Hayley pleaded. "She just needs to come around. Once Tate has talked to her properly, she'll remember how good it was here. Eoin, please, let's just sit down and play cards again, yeah? You were winning."

"Wake up, Hayley. Get out of fantasy land," Gemma said.

"That's it, I'm gagging her."

Eoin shoved Hayley out of the way and tried to pull the rag up from around Gemma's neck. But Gemma was true to her word, biting down on Eoin's fingers until he yelped.

"Feel like a big man, huh?" Gemma cried at him. "Forcing me to shut up, just like *you* were forced to shut up and take it? In your cabin that night, forced to be a pretty boy? You know what he did. He liked the feeling of control—whether it was boys or girls."

Eoin's eyes darkened with rage.

He wrapped his hands around Gemma's throat. His face was bright red now, and tendons bulged from his neck. He pressed his thumbs hard against Gemma's neck as she squirmed underneath him. Hayley didn't understand what Gemma had said to Eoin, but she knew one thing. He was going to kill her. He was actually going to kill Gemma. This wasn't right. None of this was supposed to happen.

After a moment of panicked hesitation, Hayley pulled herself together and grasped hold of Eoin's arm, digging her nails into his flesh. She was sure that if she jolted him out of his stupor, he would realise what he was doing and stop. But it was taking longer than she thought.

"Eoin!" She slapped his face. "Eoin, stop, you'll kill her!" She balled her hand into a fist and punched him squarely in the nose. A little blood burst from the blow, Eoin fell backwards, holding the bridge of his nose with his finger and thumb, while Hayley dropped to her knees to make sure Gemma was okay.

Hayley's stomach flipped when she saw the red bruises on Gemma's neck. Gemma's throat rattled as she wheezed in and out, desperate for air. But at least she was alive and conscious. Hayley rushed to get Gemma a glass of water from the tiny bathroom cubicle at the back of the bunker.

Gemma took a sip and then leaned her head back against the wall. "Do you see"—she rasped, the words seeming to take all her energy—"who you have aligned with?"

32

BRONWEN

The super was a big guy, almost as red in the face as Joe, but definitely less fit. Usually, when Bronwen was stuck in a room with him, she found herself drawn to the neck rolls that spilled over the collar of his jacket. Today, however, she found it difficult to raise her eyes from her tightly knitted hands resting on her thighs.

"In all my years on the force I've never seen such a cock-up as this." Spittle flew from his mouth as he talked. When he wasn't leaning across his desk like a bull over a matador, he was pacing his office from one end to the other.

"I know, sir—"

"Not another word out of you!" A short, stubby finger bobbed up and down in the air between them.

Despite the super's weight gain since he passed fifty, he was still a formidable officer with a past on the force that couldn't be dismissed. Superintendent Jones took down Jimmy Flint, the drug lord of Katherine. Jones was decent, and Bronwen hated this spittle-soaked dressing down so much that she felt a stress headache coming on.

He rocked back on his heels and sighed. "You're on this case because you're reliable, McKay. What happened to you? I can't have a lead officer fall asleep during a search! Any evidence found in a search like that would be laughed out of court! The suspect—from a family worth billions for God's sake—had to find you a fucking pillow! He sat there and watched you take a nap like a toddler!"

Every time Bronwen thought about it, she felt a combination of strange emotions. Firstly, she felt sick. Then she felt oddly calm. Then she panicked, because she knew it was her career on the line.

"Then the search turned up nothing. Not even a fucking spliff, which I find pretty hard to get my head around. Who tipped them off? That's what I want to know." He shook his head. "If you ask me, those girls went there. I don't know if they're still there, but they definitely went there and he knew you were going after him."

"Sir, can I say anything yet?"

He threw his hands up in the air as though through with the whole sorry situation. "Oh, what the ever-loving shit do I care anymore? Fine, what do you have to say for yourself?"

"I know that your first instinct will be to take me off the case—"

"You're damn right it is," he said.

"But the thing is, I'm the highest-ranking detective you've got, and you can't afford to lose time by transferring someone from elsewhere. I know this case inside out, and I can still be useful. I know I fucked up. I was exhausted. I'd been sleeping in my office." Bronwen allowed her head to drop. "The pressure got to me for a minute, I'll be the first to admit that, but you have to keep me on the case."

Jones regarded her with one last, long stare. "You're staying on the case. But you're taking a day off."

"Yes, sir. Very good."

"And, McKay, listen to me. The commissioner wants this over, we both know that. He's putting pressure on me to wrap this thing up with Rodney White as the guy." He paused, licked his lips. "This is between you and me. Right?"

"Right." Bronwen fiddled with the cuff of her jacket.

"He's under pressure from Llewellyn senior. The two play fucking golf together, when senior isn't in London or New York, that is."

"Jesus, I had no idea."

"Well, you do now."

"I've been thinking about it, sir, and you know, I think we've pursued this Llewellyn angle as far as it'll go. Maybe I was wrong about an accomplice after all." Bronwen pressed her fingernail down on the flesh of her thumb. She wasn't sure what to believe anymore. Her head was pounding, her stomach wasn't right, and there were times when she felt spaced out and dizzy. Was she coming down with the flu? "The evidence is stacking up against White. He made deliveries to the farm, which would explain how he found his victims. He rented the slaughterhouse. He had the girls with him when he died." Bronwen shrugged. "Maybe I let my judgement get clouded by my suspicions about Tate."

Jones sighed. "I don't know anymore. The commissioner is putting more pressure on us than usual, and I'll be honest, that makes me wonder if there's something going on, given his relationship with Llewellyn senior. But what can I do? He's the commissioner."

Bronwen paused for a moment, thinking. Then she said, "Sir, this case will be over by the end of the week. I guarantee it."

Jones grimaced. "Just don't fuck it up again, all right?"

———

Bronwen's day off hadn't gone quite according to plan. She'd headed home, fallen asleep, and dreamt the strangest dream. In her dream, everything seemed to make sense. Rodney was the man she was after, and his death meant that the case was solved. She was free. But then she'd woken up and remembered the complexities that had been frustrating her since the first day on this case. But every time she thought about one of those annoying details that didn't fit, a small voice at the back of her mind kept saying: *it could all be so much easier if you just accept the truth.* And then she thought she heard Tate Llewellyn tell her to "sleep tight."

In the mirror, she examined a bruise on her arm. It'd been there since the day of the search. Every time she thought about the search at the farm, she felt deeply ashamed of herself, so much so that she wanted to vomit. Right now, she remembered how she'd woken up by rolling off the sofa onto the carpet, with Tate standing over her smiling. Had that been the cause of the bruise?

She'd barely eaten since that day, shedding even more weight. Soon she'd be skin and bone.

She sauntered into the kitchen, poured a coffee, and took it out onto the porch. Yep, she was right, the little garden she'd created was dying off from lack of water. She took her watering can and started drip-feeding water into the pots, one at a time. But as she reached for her secateurs to begin pruning away dead leaves, her phone rang.

"It's Joe. Look, I know this is some sort of scheduled day off and everything, but the long-haul driver, Adam Johnson, just woke up from his coma."

She told Joe she was leaving, put away the watering can, dressed in a suit, tied her hair back, and made her way to the car. When she reached the ward, Joe was waiting with a coffee, but she shook her head.

"How long has he been awake?" she asked.

"It started two hours ago apparently. He was pretty out of it to begin with. But the docs say he's come around a bit and seems to understand his surroundings. The family are with him now."

"We're going to have to rudely interrupt," Bronwen said. She rubbed her eyes and tried to prepare herself to question the guy. For some reason, she couldn't get the sleep from her eyes, but the thought of drinking more coffee didn't appeal.

"You look a bit..."

"What?" Bronwen let out an exasperated sigh. She wasn't in the mood to be reminded that she looked tired.

He raised his eyebrows and shook his head. "Nothing."

It wasn't often that they snapped at each other. After all they spent long hours together in difficult, life-threatening situations. They'd become pretty comfortable with each other over time, but today the atmosphere was heavy with something unspoken. Since Bronwen had fallen asleep at Llewellyn Farm, she couldn't shake the feeling that Joe didn't trust her anymore. He had a right not to trust her. Bronwen wasn't sure she trusted herself.

She walked into the room on shaking legs. The bright lights hurt her eyes and she didn't feel at all like herself.

"My name is Detective Bronwen, and this is Detective Kouros—"

"Detective McKay," Joe corrected.

"Right. I'm Detective McKay. We're leading the murder investigation and wanted to ask Mr Johnson a few questions."

"My dad has only just woken up," a young woman about twenty years old pleaded. Her eyebrows lifted, and Bronwen could see the red rings around her blue eyes. The girl's hand gripped hold of her dad's. Next to her stood an older woman dabbing her eyes with a tissue, mascara stains left on the white surface of the material.

"I realise that, Miss Johnson. We wouldn't ask if it wasn't important." Bronwen folded her arms and tried to concentrate. The folding of her arms probably appeared to make her stronger and more formidable, but in reality it was a poor attempt to stop herself from falling apart at the seams.

"We'll be back soon, Dad."

"Love you, Adam," said the older woman who must be the wife.

Bronwen stared at the floor as the two women stepped out of the room. Of course this bothered her, she would have to be a sociopath to not feel guilty about throwing loved ones out of the room to conduct an investigation, but it was more important to find out the truth. Jones was a pretty straight-up supervisor, but even he muttered the words *sometimes the ends justify the means* on occasion.

"How are you feeling, Mr Johnson?" Bronwen sat herself down on the chair nearest the bed.

"Like I've been in a coma," he replied.

Joe flopped down in the seat next to her. "We're sorry you've been through that. Can't have been pleasant."

"I woke up in hospital with tubes sticking out of everywhere," he replied. Then his voice dropped. "Not to mention the burns."

Bronwen tried not to focus on the bandages covering almost all of the man's skin.

"We'll let you rest soon, Mr Johnson. We just need you to help us establish what happened the night your tanker caught fire. Can you talk us through what you remember?"

"I can," he said. His tongue flicked out to wet his lips. "If you'll bear with me. Talking isn't easy with these bandages."

"Take your time," Joe said.

"All right. Well, I was driving along the Stuart Highway heading towards Kakadu. It was late, sometime around midnight, and the road was dark. I came over the peak of a hill when I saw these two girls standing in the middle of the road, waving their arms like mad things, with some guy running behind them. There was no time to brake; they were too close. I swerved sharply, and the tanker flipped." He paused. "Water, please."

Bronwen reached across to the table, lifted a glass of water, and held it closer so that he could suck through the straw.

"Thank you," he rasped. He cleared his throat and continued. "I was upside down, and the tank was on fire. I remember pressing my seat belt and falling onto the roof of the cabin. That was when I hit my head, but I didn't pass out. The heat was terrible." He closed his eyes. "I could barely breathe."

"Take your time," Bronwen repeated. "There's no rush."

"I'm all right," he said. "I'd just rather forget all of it."

Bronwen passed him more water, and he accepted.

"I started to wind the window down in the cab so I could crawl out. The girls got to me just as I managed to get it down. They pulled me out and took me away from the tanker. Where are the girls? I'd like to thank them for that. I don't blame them for being in the road. That man obviously scared them. What happened to him?"

Bronwen ignored the man's questions. "Can you give us a description of the man?"

"Big," Johnson said. "Tall *and* wide. I couldn't offer you much detail about his facial features, but my mind went straight to ugly when I saw him. That's all I remember: that the guy was big and ugly as sin."

"What happened when you got out of the tanker?" Joe asked. "Where was the man then?"

Johnson thought for a moment. "I didn't see him, but by this point I was in and out of consciousness. I just remember the girls dragging me away. One of them leaned down to me, and I remember her taking my pulse, so I guess I wasn't with it at that point. After that, all I remember is waking up in the hospital."

Bronwen's mind finally sharpened, and she realised why Joe had asked that particular question. When they'd first questioned the girls, they'd claimed that Adam Johnson had fought off Rodney to save them. This version of the story was different again. She shook her head very slightly. What if Johnson wasn't remembering properly? He had just woken up from a coma.

"Can I confirm that you didn't see this man," Bronwen held up a photograph of White, "after exiting the vehicle?"

"That's correct," the man said. "But I sure saw him before. He's definitely the guy who was chasing the girls. Did he hurt them?"

"Thanks so much for your time, Mr Johnson," Bronwen said.

33

MEGAN

She'd been up since five in the morning painstakingly going through the stacks of secret files that Leah Halcombe had left behind, fuelled by coffee and a desperate race to find out more. She had papers spread from one end of her dining room table to the other.

There was one file in particular that had her interest—what it contained was nothing like the usual psychologists' notes. It wasn't a client file but a file about the place where the client had worked—which in Clay's case was the farm.

Leah had described an event called *Harvest Friday*. She'd called it *mind programming*. Psychologists tended to shy away from such terms. Many didn't even believe in mind programming, or brain washing, at all. This file contained a page of frenzied scrawl —with heavy red marker underlining some terms and circling other terms:

Chanting, isolation from friends and family, a sense that the past no longer exists. Charismatic leader. Loyalty to the leader at all costs. Drugs used for dependency or to alter perceptions.

Megan chewed absently on the end of her pen. Leah obviously

considered the farm a cult. But could a mango farm that employed seasonal workers really be hiding a cult?

She flipped through pages of speculation about cultlike activities at the farm, finally stopping on a page about Clay. The page contained a mind map of circled sentences, with links drawn between the circles. She'd repeatedly circled one line about Clay:

Nightmares of frozen dead people. Scientifically correct details. Is it real or just dreams?

Everyone knew now that it was real. From Leah's notes, it was evident that Clay had seen the cold room at several points before he died. But why did he think he was just dreaming about it? Perhaps it was an avoidance device—his mind making him believe that the cold room didn't exist.

The thought of Tate's experiments with the lab rats jumped into her head. If there was a connection, what was it?

She flinched as a pair of hands landed lightly on her shoulders. Jerking around, she looked into Jacob's face—his expression a mix of bemused and concerned.

"Hey." He kissed the top of her head. "You were up until midnight with this stuff, and now you're into it *again*? It's Saturday."

She sighed, relaxing and squeezing her bleary eyes shut. "I know. I just... I just need to understand what's really going on here. This is big—in all directions." Her eyes blinked open. "Hell, what am I doing? I shouldn't be sharing this stuff with you. It's kind of confidential."

He massaged her shoulders, glancing down at the files. "Hey, so this is about Llewellyn and his farm? Well, I can be your friendly microbiologist consultant. I've got lots of contacts who can dig a bit further into what he's been up to. You need to know anything? I'm your man."

She felt an awkward pause after he spoke the words, *I'm your man*. Because it was seeming like he *was* her man. He'd come to see her as soon as he'd flown in. It was starting to feel like they were a couple. She glanced down at the masculine shape of his fingers as they clasped the top of her right arm. She loved his hands, especially his beautiful knuckles and clean, square fingernails.

I just don't know if I'm ready to jump into a relationship with you, Jacob.

Leaning over her, he touched a page that was lying on the table. "Leah thought the farm was running a cult?"

She nodded, looking up at him.

He raised his eyebrows. "Wow." He picked up a transparent plastic folder. The name Clayton Durrell was written on the front of the folder in permanent ink. "What's in here?"

"Not sure. I haven't even gotten to *that* yet."

He sat on a chair beside her, taking a sip of her coffee.

"I'll grab you a coffee," she said, half rising.

"No. I'm fine. This has gotten my interest. I can see a list of chemicals inside it—that's my field." He opened the folder and slid out a creased piece of paper. "These are some very unusual chemicals. Zeta interacting protein?" He browsed the internet on his phone. "Why on earth would Llewellyn be keeping stuff like this at the farm? In large quantities too."

"What is it?"

He inhaled deeply as he read the information on his screen. "It's a protein synthesis inhibitor."

Megan shook her head in disbelief. "That kind of inhibitor would interfere with memories..."

"Yep." He kept reading. "These enzymes were apparently used in experiments with rats. The rats were made to forget a painful memory, of a series of noises that led to their foot being shocked. The protein synthesis inhibitor is injected, and then a single memory can be isolated and wiped out—such as just one of those sounds."

Megan's forehead pulled into a worried frown. "You know, Bronwen said the lab he has at the farm is pretty big for a hobby perfume operation..."

Jacob chewed on his lower lip for a moment, as if thinking. Picking up the folder again, he carefully drew out the remaining item —a small glass vial. The vial was empty, a crack running along one side of it. "Damn, whatever was in here is long gone. I could have taken it away and tested it."

She sighed in frustration. "Clay must have been stealing these items to show Leah."

"I bet this vial contained at least some of the chemicals on that list."

"So... if he has no lab rats at the farm—and I don't think he does—then how is he testing his drugs there?"

For a moment, they held each other in an anxious gaze.

"Megan," Jacob said carefully, exhaling a slow breath. "This might have just gone a few steps further past the crazy cult thing. If it was dangerous for Clay and Leah to know what they knew, it's dangerous for you too."

She met his gaze. "I know..."

"Get these files down to the police station," he said. "*Now.* I've got a couple of hours of field work to do today, but I'm not leaving you here with dynamite on your hands."

"Okay. I'll go. You make yourself at home. Have a coffee. Make yourself some breakfast. Whatever strikes your fancy."

He smiled. "The thing that strikes my fancy is just about to walk out the door."

She hoped she wasn't blushing. But she was pretty sure she was.

Glancing down at her watch, she checked the time. "I thought it was later. It's only seven. Bron won't be at the station yet."

"Call her."

"I can't. She and Joe are barely getting any sleep as it is."

He sighed. "Well, I'm not leaving here until you do."

"No. *Go.* You've got work to do."

"Come here." Gently, he guided her from her seat and into his arms. "I'm serious. I'm not going anywhere. I can get my stuff done anytime today."

He kissed her again.

Within minutes, they were in bed.

It was different to every other time she'd been with Jacob. He was so... *tender*.

Afterwards, when they were lying naked and wrapped up together, he began drifting into sleep, and she realised how exhausted he must have been with the long days in the heat with his fieldwork. But he'd come straight to *her*. He hadn't even stopped for a rest.

She snuggled on his chest. It felt natural, being here with Jacob. It occurred to her for the first time that she could be happy with him.

How did this even happen? How did I go from not knowing how I felt to knowing this?

He ran a lock of her hair through his fingers. "Smells nice," he murmured drowsily. "I love your hair. I love everything about you..."

Her breath caught. She raised her head, astounded by the sincerity in his tone. His words were sleepy and his eyes closed, but she was in no doubt that he was serious about what he'd just said. She was trying to find a reply when he spoke again.

"Tonight, I'm taking you out to dinner," he said. "No ifs or buts. I won't get in the way of your work, but you have to eat sometime. May as well be with me." He grinned, still without opening his eyes.

"Sounds great," she said, breathing easier now. "I'm paying though. You bought the Chinese last night."

"Hmmm, in that case, we're going to the most expensive restaurant in town." He winked.

His breaths began drawing out longer and deeper, and he fell asleep.

She watched him for minutes then rested her head on his chest again, listening to his steady heartbeat, growing drowsy with him. A bubble of warmth grew around her. It was just Jacob and herself, floating on this small island together.

Abrupt thoughts shook her from the peaceful lull she'd been in.
Leah's files.
The farm. The memory drug.
The girls.

Tilting her wrist, she eyed her watch. Bronwen would be arriving at the office soon. She wished she could just stay where she was, but she had to go.

Leaving the bed, she went to take a quick shower then dressed and headed down to the station.

Both Bronwen and Joe were in Bronwen's office, looking decidedly more groomed than they usually did.

"Meggie," said Joe in his booming voice. "You got something? You look like you've got something."

Megan nodded, her right shoulder weighed down by the mass of files in her carry bag. "Yep. A *whole lot* of something."

"You'd better pull up a seat, then." Bronwen indicated towards an empty chair. "But I'll warn you, we're rushed for time. We'll be in a meeting with the superintendent from ten a.m."

"Okay, that explains why you two are looking so damned smart." Flashing a grin, Megan took a seat with them. "Does a meeting with the super mean that you've had a breakthrough? Any news of the girls? Or... did something turn up during the search of Tate's farm?"

Bronwen and Joe eyed each other hesitantly before Bronwen spoke.

"We've still got no trace on the girls," Bronwen said. "The search turned up sweet nothing. Tate's as clean as a whistle. Or if he's got anything incriminating there, he's managed to get it off the farm before we got there." She paused, toying with the cuff of her shirt. "The search wasn't my finest moment, all told."

"Oh?" said Megan.

"Bron's the best detective in the NT," Joe cut in. "But sometimes she lets others get to her and she forgets how damned good she is."

"You *are* looking tired," Megan told Bronwen with concern. "I mean, underneath the sleek hair and crisp clothing. So, who's been getting to you?"

"It's just *everything*," she replied quickly, giving Megan the impression that she wasn't telling everything. "When all this is over, the three of us have got to go out and have a meal together. Like we used to." She studied Megan's face for a second. "You, my dear, are glowing. Something you want to tell us?"

"Jacob," Megan said.

"Mr Incommunicado himself?"

"Yep."

"What happened?" Bronwen's eyebrows pushed upwards.

"I don't know." Megan exhaled. "I don't even know. Things between Jacob and me just suddenly got... special."

"Nice." Bronwen shot Megan a grin.

"Glad to hear it," said Joe. "I like the guy."

Megan was sure she was beaming like she had a schoolgirl crush. "So, the search turned up absolutely nothing?"

"Nope," Joe answered. "And we went over the place with a fine-toothed comb. Can't say it doesn't have a weird feel there though. All those happy fruit pickers. Some of them seemed a bit spacey."

"Well, you know, that's just what I wanted to talk to you about." Megan pulled out the stack of folders and placed them on the desk. "These are Leah Halcombe's files. I've spent two days going through all this—and I'm still not done—but there are some things in here that you two need to know."

Joe leaned back in his chair. "Lay it on us."

"Okay, these notes make it clear that Leah thought that the farm might just be a front," Megan started. "A front for some kind of cult. And you know how I told you that Tate was doing memory research in a Thai lab? Well, there's a possibility he's also conducting research at the farm. It looks like he might have the drugs there. We need to get a sample of the chemicals."

"We got samples already," Joe told her. "We rushed the analyses.

They were easy to break down. It's all just orchid extract and perfume bases. And some of the usual kind of chemicals kept on farms."

Megan bit down on her lip in frustration. "What if he's hiding the other stuff somewhere?"

Bronwen gave Megan a kind but weary smile. "We could go back, but we're under some pretty heavy pressure not to do that. Problem is, it's a murder investigation. Plus, we've got two missing witnesses on our hands. Those two things are where our focus has to be. Even if Llewellyn's stashing some kind of unusual chemicals there, unless they're connected with this case, we don't have a clear reason to go back there. Plus, he's a chemist, and he could pretty easily explain away a lot of that kind of thing."

"I'm not explaining myself properly," Megan said. "If he's using mind-altering drugs on people, that has to be criminal, right?"

"Is there direct evidence of that in those files?" Joe asked.

Megan gave an uncertain nod. There wasn't much. "There's a sheet that lists the chemicals. And a vial—but it got broken and the contents leaked out, unfortunately. But Leah had done quite a bit of investigating. She thought maybe Tate was using the drugs to run a kind of cult there—"

"Leah was doing all that on her own?" Bronwen broke in. "So, she didn't consider it a police matter? Things tend to get messy when people try to play detective."

There was something a little odd in Bronwen's tone. Megan couldn't quite pinpoint it, but there was a vague *drift* at the end of every sentence Bronwen spoke. It was barely perceptible, but it was there. Like, a slight upward inflection as if she were asking a question. Bronwen always spoke so precisely. Maybe it was just fatigue.

"I think Leah was trying to gather evidence," said Megan, worrying that neither of them was taking the detective work of a deceased psychologist seriously. "But we know that Clay was seeing

Leah, right? It seems that he was the one trying to bring her the evidence. That has to mean something?"

"We've been pursuing that angle," Bronwen replied. "And it *is* interesting that Clay brought these things to Leah." She softened her tone. "But it could be leading us down the garden path. That poor kid, Clay, might really have had severe mental health issues. There's a hell of a lot linking the murders to White. Tate told us that Rodney White made a few odd deliveries to the farm in the past. He might have just decided to start picking off random people from the farm. Leah might have just gotten in the way."

There it was again—that vague *drift* as Bronwen finished what she was saying.

"Okay," said Megan. "But what if Tate is actually trying to run a cult there and using his drugs on people?" The words sounded ridiculous as soon as she'd spoken them, especially with Bronwen and Joe looking at her with those sceptical expressions.

"We'd need some pretty heavy-duty evidence of that, Meggie," said Joe in a kind voice. "It'd be a strange direction to take the investigation into."

Bronwen blinked then rubbed her eyes. "Ah, if only White hadn't had the bad manners to go and get himself roasted at the scene, we might have been able to get a signed confession out of him. But a dead killer tells no tales. We're just going to have to pin a post-humous serial killer medal on him."

Megan felt a buzz of alarm under her skin. "Are you thinking that White is the sole perpetrator?"

"No, we're not there, yet," said Joe. "There's—"

"But it's totally within the realm of possibility," Bronwen cut in. She sighed, shaking her head. "I really wish we had something on Tate, Megan. That guy... he's slimy as hell. Wouldn't surprise me if he has some kind of racket going on. But is he involved in this case? I just don't know." She lowered her eyes, and rubbed her arm, seeming distracted for a moment. Then she raised her head again. "Serial

killers most often work alone, and they're usually pretty unremark-
able people. Like I said, the evidence is stacking up against White.
Forensics also found a match with White's DNA on some of the
bodies from the cold room. Unless we've got something compelling
that links the murders to another party, we could just be muddying the waters."

Megan felt as if she'd been stung. *Muddying the
waters?* Bronwen hadn't said it to her in a harsh way, but still, it
seemed as if Bronwen wasn't taking her seriously. Normally,
Bronwen gave what she had to say quite a lot of consideration.
Maybe it was just as Bronwen had said—everything was getting to
her. This case was beyond horrific, and she didn't blame her friend
for buckling under the weight of it. And she'd detected it yet again—
that *drift* at the end of Bronwen's words. Even Joe had given
Bronwen a confused glance. She must be exhausted and not quite
herself.

But Megan didn't have time to think on it because Bronwen was
already pulling herself to her feet.

"Sorry that we don't have more time right now," Bronwen told
her with a heavy sigh. "Joe and I need to prepare for our meeting. Ah,
so not looking forward to that. Thanks for coming in. We'll certainly take a look at those files."

Megan said her goodbyes and headed back to her car. She was
confused and anxious. Maybe she'd put forward her argument all
wrong. The files hadn't even been opened. She wasn't sure what she
wanted Bronwen and Joe to do about the material that Leah had
written, but she'd wanted *something*.

———

She drove along the road that led back to her apartment.

Jacob was back there, probably still asleep.

She imagined crawling back into bed and falling asleep beside him. Everything within her wanted to do that. To return to his warm body and the solid, steady beat of his heart as she rested on his chest. It'd been hard to leave him. Besides, she really needed sleep. She'd stayed up so late reading the files that she was exhausted—this morning she'd been running high on the shock of the stuff in Leah's files and the surprise of falling hard for Jacob.

Instead, she swung the car off to the side and switched off the engine. Her shoulders were trembling, and she didn't know if it was because of anger or frustration—or both.

Rodney White was about to be named as the *Cold Room Killer*—posthumously. And Tate Llewellyn was going to continue on—doing whatever it was that he was doing at his farm with those memory drugs. Whatever had happened to the girls and wherever they were, Megan was certain that Tate must have had a hand in it.

She told herself to go home. Leave it to the police. Stop trying to *play detective.*

But instead, she found herself slipping her iPhone out of her handbag and browsing the internet. There it was—the website for Llewellyn Farm. At Deep Springs. A picture of a massive, sunny mango orchard adorned the home page, with images of healthy, sun-kissed workers picking mangoes underneath it.

Happy fruit pickers, Joe had called them.

The police weren't going to go back and find out what was really going on there. And they weren't going to get a sample of the drugs that Tate was brewing up.

Someone needed to do both of those things. As a psychologist, she'd be in a better position to judge whether the workers at the farm were a bit too *happy.* She wanted to go there and see it all for herself. Maybe even, if Tate's defences were down because she wasn't the police, she might be able to find a sample of the memory-altering drug.

Before she knew what she was doing, she'd called the number on the screen.

"Llewellyn Farm, Sophie speaking," came a bright voice on the other end of the phone.

"Hello, Sophie, could I speak with Tate Llewellyn?" Megan said.

"Oh, Tate's busy. Are you interested in fruit picking?"

"No. I'm Megan Arlotti, from the Northern Territory Department of Health, specifically, mental health services. I need to talk with Tate."

"Putting you through," came the swift but guarded reply.

Tate sounded unconcerned when he answered the call. "Hello, Ms Arlotti, you're looking for me?"

"Yes, I am," said Megan. She stalled for a second, trying to ensure she kept any quiver out of her voice—because she was about to tell an enormous lie. "Sorry, I was just looking at my notes. It seems we've had some complaints about the treatment of workers at your farm. From a number of families of former farm employees."

"I see. How can I assist you?"

"I've been asked to put together a report for the department. But I wanted a more rounded perspective. One of their complaints are what they called your meditation sessions. I thought perhaps if I could take a look at those sessions and—"

"We have a meditation session happening at lunch today. You're welcome to attend, if you can make it here. Lunch is at eleven sharp."

"I'll be there. Thank you."

She ended the call, heart hammering, no longer trusting herself to keep her voice even. It was true that she was employed by the Department of Health, but she'd made up the rest.

Switching the engine back on, she headed in the opposite direction.

Llewellyn Farm was over an hour away. She had a whole hour to put a lid on her nerves and figure out what she was going to say to Mr Llewellyn.

34

GEMMA

Gemma sat huddled in a corner of the underground room, staying as far away from Eoin as possible.

He would have killed her if Hayley hadn't hit him—she was sure of that. Her jawbone was still sore from the stranglehold he'd had on her neck yesterday.

At least the ties were off her wrists now—Hayley had undone them after Eoin's attack.

Eoin and Hayley were sleeping in their chairs. Heavy silence claimed the room but for the steady hum of the refrigerator. She was beginning to feel entombed in the bunker. If Tate chose to never come back and open up the exit, they had absolutely no way out. And if he chose to stop piping air down here, the three of them would be dead within days.

Hayley woke, stretching. She looked sleepily across at Gemma. "You okay?"

When Gemma didn't answer, Hayley came to sit beside her on the floor. "If it helps, I'm finding it hard being down here too. I don't even understand why we have to be in this room."

"Get away from me," Gemma cried. "You think I can just forget all the things that you've done, but I can't."

Hayley recoiled. "I wish you'd stop saying that. I haven't done anything to you. I'm on your side."

Gemma bent her forehead down to her knees, shutting Hayley out. "You wouldn't have forced me back here if you were on my side. You only stopped Eoin from hurting me because you thought Tate wants me kept alive."

Hayley started to answer but stopped short as a low mechanical buzz sounded, and the heavy door began lifting. Daylight spilled down the stairs.

Waking, Eoin jumped to his feet. "*Thank fuck.* I can't stand another minute in here."

Tate, dressed in a casual suit, came down the steps. He surveyed Gemma and the others coolly then smiled. "Unfortunately, I'm going to have to ask you for your patience a little longer. Gemma, come with me."

"What?" Eoin fumed. "Why does *she* get to get out?"

Gemma drew back into the wall, her eyes fixed on Tate's lanky figure. "Where to?"

"Just upstairs. To the meditation room," he answered.

"I'm not going there," Gemma told him. "I'm not."

Hayley touched her shoulder. "The meditation room is a *good* place. We always came out of there feeling good, didn't we? Stop trying so hard to fight everything."

"You know *exactly* what he does in that room." Shivering, Gemma wrapped her arms around her middle. "I'm going to be sick."

The smile faded from Tate's face. "Gemma... it's time for you to remember who you are."

Gemma stared at him in shock. "I don't know what you're talking about."

"Of course you do. After all, you've been with me since you were seventeen," Tate told her calmly.

"*What?*" Gemma shook her head vehemently. "No. That's not true."

"You were an unloved, underfed runaway with nowhere to go," Tate continued. "I found you on the streets of Sydney and gave you a home."

Hayley sprang to her feet. "Gemma? What's he saying?"

Gemma eyed her in confusion. "He's lying."

"You were the best at telling me what was happening among my recruits back then," Tate said. "And you were my best recruiter. You sent dozens of people to me. And, of course, you brought me Hayley."

Hayley cried out, her eyes huge and her hand flying to her mouth.

"Oh, that's rich." Eoin exhaled a sharp, angry breath. "All this time, little miss innocent has been fooling us."

Tate crossed the room and reached for her hand. "Gemma... wake up."

Gemma let him help her to her feet, as if she were incapable of refusing. She felt her mind ticking over.

Tick, tick, tick.

A switch seemed to blink off inside her head, and her mind filled with blackness. As if the TV show she'd been watching had suddenly been switched off.

"It's time to remember everything," Tate said. "Time to remember who you really are. Now, tell me, who are you?"

A new reality swelled inside her.

She watched a scene play inside her head:

A young girl arriving at the farm, stepping out of an expensive car and staring up at the dazzling shine of the sun on the mansion's windows. The girl was scared and half-starved. But the man who'd brought her there had been kind and reassuring.

He'd been her saviour.
He'd become her mentor.
She'd loved him.
She remembered everything now.
The man was Tate.
The girl was her.

The things she'd believed Hayley had done were the things that *she* herself had done.

She was the bad one.

———

Tate led her from the underground room and closed the door behind them. She blinked in the harsh and sudden daylight. She rode the service elevator with him in silence and followed him to the meditation room.

For a second, just before he closed the door, she caught a glimpse of the farm beyond the enormous glass window. Workers streaming between the obedient rows of mango trees. The sun glistening yellow on the leaves.

She was certain she would never step out there again. She understood now why she'd been so terrified of returning to the farm. Because somewhere in the depths of her mind, she knew what she'd done and she knew that Tate would kill her because of it.

Her body grew numb as she sunk into a chair, enveloped by the clinical whiteness of the room. The room was cold, hard, terrifying. It was an insane asylum, an execution chamber.

He locked the door.

"Excuse me a moment," he told her, pulling back the bifold doors on a row of cupboards. Six surveillance screens were revealed, all showing locations around the farm. "Can't be too careful, considering what's been happening lately. I need to keep an eye on everything."

She'd seen the screens before. Tate had never pretended that the room was a meditation space when it was just him and her alone.

He turned, surveying his row of surveillance monitors. Each screen flicked to a different scene of the farm every minute. He watched Dharma dancing in the field, and a smile played on his lips. He'd always watched them, from up here in his glass tower.

She knew that Tate adored beauty. Girls like Dharma and Hayley. And the rare orchids he nurtured in his greenhouse.

Tate took a syringe and a bottle of liquid from a drawer. He drew the liquid into the syringe and flicked out the air bubbles. Tremors zipped down her arms and into her fingers. She tried not to look at the syringe, knowing it was meant for her.

He turned to her. "I can see it in your eyes that you're remembering everything."

She didn't have an answer to that. She felt as if she'd been turned inside out and was now raw and exposed.

He cast a look at her that was almost paternal. "You know, you have the distinction of being the only one who my memory drug didn't work on."

"You... used me," she whispered. "You knew I'd do anything for you, and you took advantage."

She pictured herself at age seventeen. She'd run away from home. That was when Tate had found her—she'd been curled up asleep in a park in Sydney, with only a thin jacket to cover her. She'd woken to find him looking down at her—a handsome man wearing a gentle smile and a smart suit. He brought her all the way to his farm. She thought she'd found a family. Tate had trained her for months, patched up her broken mind with promises, and then he'd sent her back to Sydney to recruit others. He'd assured her that when she'd proven herself—when she'd sent him enough quality recruits—she could come home to him. She'd been away from the farm for just over a year when she met Hayley. Hayley had been the high-quality recruit who'd been her ticket back to the farm.

"Of course I used you," he said. "You were a flower in full bloom. You can't blame me for plucking such a beautiful specimen."

"I'm not beautiful." Her response was automatic.

"Perhaps not physically. But I'm most interested in people's minds, Gemma, and you have a beautiful mind. A pathological liar who can make herself believe anything she desires."

Yes, she was a pathological liar. When she was seven, a teacher at school had called her a *dirty little liar*, right in front of the other kids. A year later, a psychiatrist had diagnosed her with *pseudologia phantastica*. The psychiatrist had seemed oddly excited by the fact that Gemma's lying went far beyond the usual, into the delusional. Another psychiatrist had diagnosed her with a personality disorder. She didn't have total control over her lies. They would spin like spiderwebs all over her mind—spinning and respinning, until all she could see in any direction were the webs.

There were two Gemmas. The first Gemma knew the truth. But the second Gemma had the power to silence the first. The second Gemma could invent a story and make it so true that the first Gemma would believe it. *Almost.* The first Gemma always retained some awareness of what was real, but she went along with the charade. Even her thoughts were the thoughts of the second Gemma—usually. It was easier to do what the second Gemma wanted.

"I didn't know about the freezer room when I brought Hayley here," she cried at Tate. "I didn't know about the dead people. I didn't know about the rapes. I didn't know about any of that. I just thought the farm was a big family. It seemed like the most pure thing I'd ever found. Except... *it wasn't*." The words came from deep inside the real Gemma, twisting and bitter on her tongue.

A slow, curling smile dimpled Tate's sculpted jaw. "But when you *did* find out, you made a decision, didn't you?"

She didn't answer.

"You're trying to block me out, even now. You're trying to tell yourself a new story. I won't let you do that. After you saw the cold room for the first time, you decided to join me, didn't you, Gemma?"

Exhaling slowly, she nodded.

"It was a night of firsts. It was also the first time I tried my memory drug on you—as well as Hayley. I was successful in erasing the memory of the cold room from Hayley's mind, but not from yours. I'd been able to take that memory from every test subject before—including Ellie, Clay, and Eoin."

Her body grew limp at the mention of Clay's name.

"And when I discovered that you had retained the memory, we made a deal," he said. "You would remain with me and continue to help me, despite knowing all that you did. And you said *yes*. You chose to stay with me, Gemma."

"I was terrified."

"But you overrode your fear."

That wasn't true. She hadn't overcome her fear.

What she'd done was to invent a new story. She'd made herself believe that Rodney and Hayley were behind the murders in the monstrous cold room. Because she hadn't been ready to accept that Tate could do such a thing. *Not Tate, her mentor, her saviour, the man she adored.*

She'd made herself believe that she had to stay and protect the man who'd saved her.

Tate didn't understand why she'd been able to resist his drug, but she knew why. It was because while Rodney was driving them back to Tate that night, she'd altered her memory of the cold room. Tate hadn't been able to erase a memory that she'd altered so completely.

"I don't know why I stayed with you," she whispered in a broken voice. "I shouldn't have. Please, I promise I'll go away and I'll never tell. I haven't told the police anything. And I won't, either. I'll make myself believe that I never saw a thing."

"I could almost trust you on this, Gemma... *almost*. Except you made one wrong choice, didn't you? And that choice sealed your fate."

"It was wrong of me. I won't make such a stupid mistake ever again."

"Sadly, actions are more telling than words." His eyes grew flinty, cold. "If you hadn't killed Rodney, things would have stayed on course. The farm would have continued to fly under the radar."

"He was going to rape Hayley," Gemma told him between gritted teeth.

"And that's regrettable," he agreed. "But it wasn't as if he hadn't done so before. And a murder on the highway was going to be an extremely messy affair, and you would have known that."

"It was the heat of the moment. I won't ever—"

"It's too late for your promises. You've demonstrated that you can't be trusted." He sighed. "Everything has been shot to pieces. And now the damned tanker driver has woken from his coma. I would have arranged it so that he never woke if I could, but he had family that never left his side."

She swallowed. "The driver will tell a different story to the one I told."

"Tell me what happened. The real story. I need to know exactly what happened a week ago on that highway. If the police come back to me—and I have a pretty good idea they will—I have to be fully prepared. I need you to tell me exactly what happened the night of the accident. I haven't heard any of it from you yet, and I need to know every last detail."

"You're going to kill me, anyway." She eyed the hypodermic needle in his hand. "And you'll kill Hayley too. I don't have to tell you anything."

"You owe me, Gemma. I gave you a place to stay and call home. You always knew what the price was. Complete loyalty. But you didn't give me that."

Her lower lip quivered. "Do it, then. But not Hayley. Don't hurt her. You can make it so that she never remembers. And then you can send her home."

"Oh, I fully intend to send her home. But I'll destroy her mind to the extent that she'll want to take her own life. I've been forced to do that a few times to past employees of the farm. That's the unfortunate consequence of testing on humans. It gets messy."

A gasp stuck tight and hard in Gemma's throat. She hadn't known that he could do that. "No, please. You can just make her forget returning to the farm. I'll tell you what you want to know."

He studied her for a moment with cold, predator eyes. "Okay. I'll make that deal with you."

"You promise?"

"Of course."

She wrapped her arms around herself, trembling again.

"Are you cold, Gemma?"

She shook her head. "I can't feel... anything."

"Tea? It'll help you relax."

"I don't want your tea. Ever again..."

"Then please begin."

She forced herself to remember all the things she'd been shielding herself from. It was physically painful as the memories returned—like her skin being flayed from her by invisible whips.

In a voice that sounded emotionless to her ears, she began talking. "The night that it all started, Hayley saw a rape happening in one of the cabins. It was... Eoin. Rodney raped Eoin."

"Eoin didn't tell me that," Tate remarked.

"He might have been... ashamed," Gemma said. "Hayley ran to tell me. She was scared and confused. And it was obvious that seeing Eoin's rape had jolted her memory. She recalled Rodney doing the same things to her. She begged me to run away from the farm with her. I tried to calm her, but she wouldn't listen. She stole one of the farm's SUVs, and she drove off."

"Good girl." Tate nodded. "Please... continue."

"You know the next part of it," Gemma said. "I went straight away to tell you that Hayley had stolen a car. You sent Rodney and me after her."

He nodded. "Tell me everything that happened after that."

"We found Hayley down the highway," Gemma said. "She'd crashed the car into a tree. She was barely conscious when I pulled her out. That's how she got her concussion. Rodney pushed the wrecked car far off the road to hide it, into the bushes. He tied Hayley's wrists and shoved her into his van. I sat beside her."

Gemma's heart began hammering. She'd locked these memories away and now they were flashing back into her mind all at once. "We were supposed to go straight back to the farm. But Rodney decided that he was going to teach Hayley a lesson for running away. He drove the van off the side of the highway. He opened up the door on her side, and he started pulling her out. He was going to rape her. She was tied up, *defenceless*, for God's sake."

Shaking, she could almost smell the filth and grease inside Rodney's van. "Hayley was screaming and fully awake now. He had a knife at her throat. He was sticking his disgusting tongue in her mouth. I couldn't... I couldn't let him do it. I leaned across Hayley and grabbed the knife from him. Then I stuck the knife straight in his chest. Rodney's blood went all over us."

Gemma was completely transported back to that night. She no longer saw the white room around her. Everything went dark. "Hayley kicked at Rodney with both feet, and he fell backwards. She trampled him as she ran from the car. I ran after her. Everything would have been okay if Rodney had stayed down. But he didn't. He got up and chased us onto the road. That's when the fuel tanker came over the peak of the hill. The driver flipped the tanker, and it skidded straight for us. It exploded into a fireball."

Her breaths quickened, and she began hyperventilating. "Rodney grabbed me. But I got him off-balance and pushed him straight into the fire. He went up in flames. Hayley and I watched him burn, and we didn't even try to help him. We were glad. But I knew that the explosion would bring the police, and I needed to explain Rodney's dead body. I asked Hayley to help me drag the driver out. I untied her, and we went and pulled the driver free."

"I see," said Tate. "So, the driver wrestling with Rodney was just a story you made up. Please... slow down. You're getting difficult to understand, Gemma."

Gemma nodded, trying to still her erratic breathing. Her head felt faint. Everything was spinning. "I took Hayley back to the car with me. Before she knew what was happening, I injected her with the memory drug. Rodney had the drug kit that he always kept in his van. I used the methods that you taught me, Tate. I had to insert new memories into her mind. I needed a story to explain Rodney's dead body and our cuts and bruises, as well as the rope marks on Hayley's wrists. You taught me to take a real and true memory and then twist it. And so that's what I did."

She remembered the raw pain in her throat and eyes from the heat and smoke from the blaze. She remembered the pain inside her, knowing that she'd brought Hayley to the farm in the first place, knowing what Tate and Rodney put her through, knowing that she'd just stopped her from escaping.

"I told her that we'd only been at the farm for two weeks," Gemma continued. "And I told her that we'd been kidnapped and locked up in a birdcage at Rodney's house for the other two and half months. Rodney did lock us up in there once—after the first time he took us to the freezer room."

"So, that's what took him so damned long that night."

"Yes. We weren't in the cage long. But it was enough to construct a false memory in Hayley's mind. You taught me well, Tate. And I made her remember the times he'd raped her. Those times were real, but I got her to believe that they had happened in the birdcage. After that, I knew I needed to look as if I been tied up by Rodney, too, and I made rope burns on my wrists."

Tate eyed her with a look that almost seemed impressed. "I told you, Gemma, you're a clever girl. A brilliant mind. You could have been the one to run this place one day. Such a shame, because after killing Mr White, that is never going to happen. Your one big mistake."

"My one big mistake was in ever trusting you."

"We're running out of time. I interrupted you. What happened between then and when the police came?"

"I buried Rodney's drug kit, because I knew the police would search the van. Then I just sat there in the van with Hayley, while the police were coming in cars and helicopters. And during the time I was waiting, I made myself believe the story that I'd just told Hayley. I made myself believe that I was the innocent and that Hayley was the one who knew everything. Because that was the only way I could live with myself."

She raised her eyes to him. "That's all. You know the rest."

Tate squeezed her shoulder, sighing. "You made a tangle out of what could have been so simple, Gemma. You should have just let Rodney do as he desired. I could have then simply taken the memory away from Hayley upon her return to the farm."

"It's not that easy, though, is it?" Gemma cried. "Dreams and nightmares still break through. You can't erase everything. It always leaves a trace..."

He shrugged. "My drug is getting better with every test. Hopefully, I'll soon find a way of leaving people's minds undamaged when I remove their memories."

Gemma's skin prickled with cold shivers. "I once saw you as some kind of god, Tate. Like the sun itself. I somehow forced myself to accept the bad things you were doing because I knew they were part of your experiments. You needed terrible things to happen to people, and then you'd see if you could take their memory away. I even made myself think that the freezer room was unavoidable.

Sometimes your experiments made people die. Or they betrayed you and you had no choice."

"I did what I had to do," he insisted. "At first, I had to inject the memory drug directly into people's brains. It sometimes didn't go well. I refined my methods over time." He raised the hypodermic needle.

Her throat almost closed up. "Your experiments were wrong. *So* wrong. As much as I loved you, I was terrified of you. Part of me always understood how wrong all of this was. But I was afraid, and I went along with it. I hate myself."

Her mind went numb as Tate brought the needle close to her arm. "Where will you put me... after I'm dead?"

His expression turned unexpectedly gentle. "Maybe in a field, somewhere that wildflowers grow. That would be fitting, wouldn't it? You were never a hothouse orchid. You were too fierce for that."

She bowed her head. "Tell Hayley I'm sorry..."

Across the room, the display on one of the surveillance screens swapped to showing a car driving in through the gates.

Tate tutted in annoyance. "I told her to come at eleven. Can no one manage to follow directions?"

A camera closed in on the woman's face as she stepped from her car and looked about with an uncertain expression.

Gemma recognised the psychologist from the hospital.

Megan.

35

MEGAN

A burst of heat hit Megan as she stepped from the car. Sweat instantly wet the back of her neck. Terror coiled low in her stomach.

How am I going to pull this off?

Llewellyn Farm appeared eerily empty of people, apart from the music filling the air. A long stretch of flat ground led to a huge mansion-style house. From this vantage point, the whole place looked as picture-perfect as it did online, with its green mango tree plantations.

Scanning the grounds from left to right, she then noticed a small scattering of workers harvesting fruit, some of them absently nodding along to the music that blared as fiercely as the sun.

A woman zipped towards her in a cart that resembled a golf buggy. From another direction, a young man with a walkie-talkie headed her way on foot. He stopped as the woman reached her first.

It was all innocent enough—the people who ran the farm coming to greet her. But at the same time, it seemed almost military in speed and precision. Obviously, they kept a close watch on who came in and out of the gates.

With a close-lipped smile stretching her narrow, milky face, the woman parked the buggy next to Megan's car. Megan guessed she worked in an office here and didn't get out in the sun much.

"I'm Sophie. Llewellyn Farm's manager. I'm assuming you're Megan?" Without waiting for a reply, she turned to the man with the walkie-talkie. "S'okay Freddy," she called. "I'll take it from here."

The man nodded but didn't move from his position. He remained there watching on.

Sophie extended a hand in greeting. "Hope you found us without too much trouble." She raked back wisps of blond hair from a face that was unblemished but for some fine lines.

Megan shook her hand. "It's quite a distance out from the main road, but apart from one wrong turn, I made it okay." Giving a short laugh, she braced herself to tell a lie. "Look, I'm sure that everything's fine. But the department has to follow up on the complaints it receives. You have a lot of international backpackers here, and backpackers make up a big percentage of the seasonal harvest jobs. I'm guessing the government doesn't want any negative publicity."

"Of course. If I could get you to come this way, I'll get you out of this maddening sun. Mr Llewellyn will be coming to meet with you shortly."

Megan walked beside her to a set of greenhouses. The air inside the greenhouse that Sophie took her into was far more humid than the air outside. Megan would have almost preferred to stand in the hot sun and bake. Rows of bright orchids ran from end to end in the greenhouse, some of the orchids under separate glass housing, as if they were museum displays. One side of the greenhouse was attached to a large building. Through an open door, Megan caught a glimpse of a room filled with lab equipment and felt a cool stream of air.

A woman wearing a hairnet peeked out at Megan from the room and then closed the door quickly.

Sophie crossed and then uncrossed her arms, her brief smile seeming more of a twitch than a friendly gesture. "So, can you tell us some details about the complaints you've received?"

"I'm afraid I'm not able to give specific details, as they could be identifying. But as I said over the phone, it's to do with concerns about cult-like events and teachings."

"Crazy," Sophie scoffed. "It's a mango farm, for goodness sake. But we certainly don't need nonsense like that floating about. It's a good thing you're here to clear things up." She bent to pick up some pieces of broken ceramic pot from the floor. Megan detected a vague mocking tone in the last thing Sophie said, giving her the uneasy impression that Sophie wasn't taking her seriously.

She decided to start taking down some notes and try to appear more official. Her pen was missing from her clipboard. Amid the anxiety she'd felt in the short trip with Sophie, she must have dropped it. Already, she was looking like an incompetent ninny.

"Just a sec. Dropped my pen out there. I'll go grab it." Megan headed for the exit.

Pieces of ceramic clattered on the floor as Sophie dashed up behind her. She grasped Megan's shoulder. "I forgot to offer you a cold drink."

"I'm fine—"

"We have cold tea, cola, filtered water? Or kombucha? Kombucha is popular with the backpackers."

"Cold water would be nice."

Reaching past her, Sophie closed the door that Megan had just opened. "Sorry, we have to maintain a certain humidity for the orchids. I'll radio Freddy to bring us some drinks. And a pen for you."

Just before Megan had turned back, she'd glimpsed Tate's house. Two people had been exiting a room on the top level. Through the all-glass frontage, she'd seen a tall man in a white shirt and a young, slightly-built girl. He'd had his hands on her shoulders, her dark hair sweeping low as she dropped her head. For that moment, Megan could have sworn the girl was Gemma. The house was a short distance away and she couldn't see facial features, but there was something distinct and familiar in the uneven way the girl sloped her shoulders and lowered her head. Megan was well-trained in body language, and this girl was so... *Gemma.*

36

GEMMA

Gemma stepped ahead of Tate into the service elevator at the back of the house.

Dead girl walking.

That's what she was.

She had blood roaring through her veins and breath in her lungs, but not for long. Megan arriving at the farm was a brief reprieve. Tate couldn't have a dying girl lying on the floor of a room upstairs while he was busy with a visitor. It was too risky.

They rode to the bottom floor, and Tate opened the underground room again.

Gemma avoided Hayley's eyes as she entered. She couldn't bear to see the hurt and accusations she knew would be there. She wished Tate had just gone ahead and given her the injection upstairs.

Tate crossed the room to Hayley, bending to cup the side of her face with his hand. "Why so sad?"

Hayley raised her head to him. "I'm just... confused. Gemma was never a friend."

"Gemma just wasn't one of us, that's all," he said. "Some people simply can't learn. They're too wild. But *you're* one of us. You're a very special hothouse orchid." His hand lingered for a moment, trailing across her temple. Then he turned to Eoin. "Both girls need to relax. The hothouse orchid and the wild orchid have had a rough time. Please administer these sedatives." He set the kit that he had brought from upstairs on a sideboard. He then pulled out a small drawer in his kit and handed two vials to Eoin. "This one for Hayley, and this one for Gemma. You know how to inject these safely, right?"

Exhaling hard, Eoin nodded. "Anything to shut them up."

"Do it quickly. No messing about, okay?" Tate told him. His gaze swept over Gemma, and he walked back to her. He touched her hair. "Do this for me. Life doesn't have to be such a struggle, you know."

Gemma stared back, swallowing.

It was an insanity, but somehow, it would have been easier to die knowing that he loved her. But he didn't. He never had. *You don't kill people who you love. You don't intentionally hurt them.* She felt the dizzying light that had been Tate go completely dark.

In the hollowness that opened up inside her, she was ready for death. She deserved this. He was right—she'd been loyal to no one.

The smile faded from Tate's face, and he strode towards the door of another room. He tapped numbers onto the keypad and retrieved something from the room that Gemma couldn't see.

He left quickly.

When Tate was gone and the bunker was closed again, Eoin turned to them, a smirk indenting his cheek. "I get to shut two women up at once. Usually that only happens in bed." He carried the kit over to Gemma. "*You first.* Maybe I'll like you more when you're asleep."

Gemma eyed the two vials that he held in his right hand. Her breath stilled. "They both have the blue label."

"Yeah. Blue." He shrugged.

She licked lips that had gone dry. "The blue is just for me. The yellow should be for Hayley."

He shot her a wary glance. "I'm not playing around with The

Chemist's drugs. These are what he gave me, and I'm using them. Can't wait to put you to sleep."

"*Forever*," she said. "Because you'll be putting us asleep forever with those. The one with the blue label is lethal."

Hayley gasped then shook her head vehemently. "That's crazy. She's lying again. You can't trust her, Eoin. I don't know why Tate brought her back here." She walked to the furthest corner of the room, balling herself up on an armchair.

"Yeah. That's a load of old shite, Gemma." Eoin gave an incredulous grin. "Tate didn't ask me to kill you."

"He didn't have to," Gemma told him. "The drug will do that all by itself. It takes about fifteen minutes to put you into a deep sleep and about half an hour for your heart to stop beating. Tate didn't have time to wait for me to die upstairs. He has a visitor."

Eoin rolled his eyes. "You're saying Tate took you away to murder you?"

It seemed such an ordinary thing, to hear it like that. It *was* an ordinary thing, to Tate. "Yes," she replied in a dead tone.

"Bollocks." Placing the kit on a table nearby, Eoin drew liquid into the syringe from a blue-labelled vial. "They're just sedatives. Sit tight, and you'll be sleeping like a baby in no time."

Desperation welled inside her. "Hayley wasn't supposed to die. He promised me. Eoin, you have to believe me. There are three different types of drugs in that kit. The one with the yellow label is a sedative. The one with the blue label is lethal. The one with the green label is the memory drug."

"What the fuck is a memory drug?" he scoffed.

"The memory drug makes you forget bad things. Tate doesn't like us to have bad thoughts. He even gives us bad memories and then takes them away. I don't know why."

Eoin started laughing. "You're off your nut, you know that?"

"It's true," Gemma insisted. "Clay had nightmares about the cold room. The drug failed to work completely on him. Same for Ellie. You're one of the successes. Congratulations."

He made a mocking sound from between his teeth. "Yeah, right. Tate had nothing to do with the cold room. The people in the freezer got snap frozen by Rodney White. The guy was gone in the head."

"That's what Tate wants you to believe. But Rodney was just Tate's assistant."

"Shut it," Eoin hissed. "Hold still, and let's get this over with— like the good little girl that you're not."

She whirled around to face Hayley. "I swear I'm telling the truth. Look, I'll tell you what really happened three months ago, the first night we were taken to the cold room."

Hayley refused to look at her. Gemma took a few faltering steps towards the back of the room, where Hayley sat with her arms wrapped around her knees.

"Tate had Rodney take us there," Gemma told her. "We were made to stand and look at dead people. We saw Clay and Ellie, dead in their chairs. We managed to escape, but not for long. Rodney forced us back into his van, at gunpoint. He took us to his property and put us in his aviary, in the shed at the back of his house."

Hayley's eyes were cold and angry as she raised her head. "I remember the aviary, but that's *not* how we got there."

"It's *exactly* how we got there," Gemma said. "You don't remember because Tate stole your memories afterwards. Tate didn't know Rodney put us in his birdcage, so he didn't take that part of your memory away."

She unlocked her arms from her knees, fingers trembling. "It doesn't even matter. What matters is what Rodney *did*. All the things he did. In that cage. I don't remember everything, but I can still feel his disgusting hands on me."

Gemma shook her head. "No, that's not what happened—"

Jumping to her feet, Hayley's hands formed fists. "Don't tell me none of that happened. Don't you dare—"

Tears wet Gemma's eyes. "Yes, Rodney did those terrible things to you. That's true. But not there. Not in the cage. We were in there for just a few minutes. Not months or weeks. *Minutes*. Tate called and demanded to know what was taking Rodney so long. Rodney was forced to bring us straight back to Tate. He didn't touch us. We were at the farm for the whole three months."

Hayley was crying now too. "Then where... where did Rodney do those things to me?"

"In the house. In *Tate's* house. Under Tate's direction."

"No," she cried out. "Stop. Just stop. You're nothing but a liar."

Gemma turned as Eoin moved up alongside her, his expression dark. "You're sure of that?"

Gemma nodded.

His breaths came short and sharp as he seemed to struggle with his thoughts. He kicked out at a sideboard, the wood cracking into a deep dent. "I've had it," he raged. "I've had it with everything. This is where my loyalty to anyone on this damned farm ends. I'm looking out for number one now. And I'm not staying down here like a sap any longer."

"You really think there's a way out of here?" said Gemma. "Tate wouldn't be so careless."

"Well, he wasn't careful to cover up his key presses when he opened the supply room," said Eoin. "I watched his code. 197890. Like I said, I owe no one my loyalty anymore. Not even The Chemist."

Gemma stared as Eoin marched up to the keypad on the supply room and punched in the numbers. With a click, the door unlocked.

He strode into the room.

Gemma ran in behind him.

He turned. "I didn't tell you to follow me, you damned sheep."

Ignoring him, Gemma scanned the room. If they *could* get away, it would be her only chance to save Hayley—and herself. A mere moment ago, that was an impossibility.

Eoin cursed as he stomped about, messing up Tate's careful order. "How the hell do we get out of this hole? I can't find anything. I thought there'd be a remote control or something."

Gemma kept frantically searching.

The supply room was crammed full of large lab equipment on the floor and files on the shelves. A small fridge held vials of drugs. A computer and monitor sat on a high desk, the screen showing that Tate had been looking up flights to America earlier. He'd obviously been in a rush today, leaving his computer switched on. Gemma knew that he was normally so vigilant with everything.

Eoin was right. There was nothing here they could use to get out. They were essentially entombed until Tate returned.

Frustrated, Eoin stormed out of the room.

Gemma peered inside a file filled with more USB computer drives than she could count. *What does he keep on all of these?*

Taking out one of the drives, she inserted it into the computer. The drive contained digital folders that were labelled with dates and cities. Sydney, Melbourne, London, Rome, Amsterdam, Baltimore, New York, San Diego.

Does Tate document all his travels?

She clicked on a file in the folder that was labelled Baltimore.

A video flicked onto the screen.

Tate sat at a table in an upmarket hotel room. An older man sat across from him, dressed in a well-cut suit. A girl slept on a sofa across the room—thick dark hair splayed across a cushion. She looked like a teenager, maybe about fifteen years old, with high cheekbones and childlike smooth skin.

"Are you sure she won't remember the event?" the man asked Tate.

"There's no guarantee for a hundred percent wipe," said Tate, "But she won't remember enough of the details to be convincing in court. And she'll contradict some of her earlier statements to the police. That's all you need. Judge Mitchell's son is safe."

"Will she remember anything about the rape?" the man pressed.

"She'll no longer consider it *rape*," Tate said.

The man shook Tate's hand. The video ended just as the man opened a suitcase on the table. Gemma caught a glimpse of wads of money inside.

Was this what Tate had done all those times he was away from the farm?

He'd told her that in the end, his testing and research would be for good. He'd said that because of him, anyone who wanted to rid themselves of a traumatic memory would be able to do it. She'd known his methods were wrong and that people died.

But he wasn't helping people.

He was doing it for money. And more than that, he was obsessed with power. Power in the business world. Power over his farm. And power over the victims he kept in his cold room. She'd been to the cold room with him a handful of times. He'd killed his victims with a slow poison, arranging them into a sitting position as they finally lost consciousness, so that rigor mortis didn't make it impossible to pose them afterwards. He'd sit with his frozen victims, speaking to them like they could hear him. It was as if they had been witnesses and confidantes to all his misdeeds. And then he violated them again, using them as objects of horror to shock people with—his test subjects from the farm.

A cold shiver passed through her body.

Gemma looked through the other USB drives. A drive labelled *Ellie* caught her attention. She inserted it into the computer.

There were dozens and dozens of video clips of Ellie in folders, stretching back twelve months.

She clicked on one dated six months ago.

It showed Ellie walking into the cold room. Gemma instantly knew where it was, even though none of the dead people were shown. The camera focus remained on Ellie.

Gemma watched as her eyes lit on the scene in that room.

Screaming.

Covering her face.

Trying to run.

The video stopped. When it started again, Ellie was in the meditation room, struggling, restrained by Rodney.

Tate injected her with a syringe. Rodney left the room. Tate gently sat Ellie on the armchair. She seemed suddenly dazed and confused.

"I want to go home," she whimpered.

"Why do you want to go home?" Tate asked her.

"I don't remember. There was a circle... people... chairs. I feel... scared."

"A circle? What kind of circle? Were they people at a meeting, perhaps? It's normal to feel scared when meeting people for the first time. It was a meeting, wasn't it? At the job you had before you came here? Yes, you told me before. You worked for a tourism company. Was that the first time they held their meeting in a circle? That must have been a little disconcerting."

Ellie nodded vaguely. "I'm glad I don't work there anymore."

"Me too," Tate said. "It's much better here for you, with everyone who loves you."

"Who loves me here?" she mumbled.

"I do," he told her. "And so does everyone else. We're your family. We're here for you."

He held her, stroking her hair. "Ellie, you are the most fragile of orchids. You need a lot of care. It's lucky you found your way here to us."

Gemma stopped the video, browsing through the *Ellie* files until she came to the one with the most recent date. She played it.

Ellie was sleeping in the reclining position on the white armchair in the meditation room. Her long dark hair hung damp around her shoulders. Her wrists were wrapped in gauze, blood seeping through.

Gemma inhaled a deep, silent breath. It was the day Ellie had cut her wrists. She remembered that now. When Tate had used his drugs to make Hayley forget the suicide attempt, Gemma had made herself forget too.

Someone else walked into the view of the camera. *Sophie.* She was clad in gym gear, her blond hair pulled back in a severe ponytail. She put a hand to Ellie's forehead. "She has a high temperature. I'm guessing the knife she used was a bit rusty."

Tate sighed. "This wasn't supposed to happen. I miscalculated and pushed her too far. But it's not a waste. She taught me a lot. I've refined my treatments because of her." He paused, shaking his head. "We'll have to dose her with antibiotics and see how she does."

"Tate," said Sophie, looking alarmed. "We can't. She'll want to go home for sure after this. And we can't predict what she'll do or what she'll remember."

"You're right of course. But I hoped that if I kept trying, I'd find a way to completely remove those memories."

Sophie didn't look convinced. "Better to try it on someone new, right? The treatments are only meant to be one-time events. Not multiple. I mean, it's impressive that you've managed to remove Ellie's memories so many times, but it's become too risky. And maybe... choose your test subjects more carefully."

Tate frowned deeply. "What do you mean by that?"

"Someone's got to say it. So far, your formulation has only worked well on very young, very vulnerable people. And even then, the subjects have breakthrough memories. It's not ready for the market, yet you're selling it as if—"

"I didn't expect that kind of disloyalty from you, Sophie," he said tautly, his expression growing hostile.

She softened her tone, a hint of fear sending a quiver through her voice. "It's not disloyalty. I'm just worried. About things like *this*." She gestured at Ellie. "I *know*, Tate. Much more than you think I do. I know about the orchid formulation. It's just hype. It's just what you tell your clients to make it sound like you've created a unique drug.

I've known that ever since you hired me to work in your lab. You're just using the same brain protein inhibitors that other researchers already know about." She took a deep breath before continuing. "The only thing you're doing differently is you're experimenting on humans."

He clutched her arm. "Stop there."

She wrenched her arm away. "I've been loyal to you, Tate. I wasn't long out of uni when I came to work for you. But I applied myself to being a damned good lab assistant. And when I found out what else you were doing, I didn't run to the police. I came on board. Through thick and thin, Tate. Thick and thin."

"You've been an excellent assistant. But you're stepping way outside of your role here." He enunciated each word from between his teeth, obviously incensed.

"Am I? I think I'm taking on a huge share of the risk. And I think it's fair that I have an opinion on what happens. You know I didn't agree with Gemma coming back here."

"Gemma's loyal to me."

"Is she? Can you trust her? She's a risk, Tate. A huge damned risk. That's the way I see her. She was asking me some pointed questions about what's happening with Ellie. You know, it's lucky that she didn't meet me last time she was at the farm. But she might still manage to work out that I've been working for you for years, and I—"

"Sophie. You worry too much. Let *me* worry about things like that. Everything is okay."

Sophie let out a measured sigh. "Okay. All right. But it's time to let Ellie go. We can't keep her. It's gone too far."

For a moment, Tate looked as if he were going to get angry again, but then he pressed his lips hard together and nodded.

Gently, he brushed Ellie's cheek.

Taking a blue-labelled vial from his kit, he drew liquid into a syringe and injected it into Ellie's limp arm.

Ellie roused from her sleep momentarily then drifted back, her words growing incoherent until she finally stopped.

Gemma heard a sharp intake of air behind her. She pivoted.

Hayley stood watching on, horror rising in her eyes. "*No. No, no... this is wrong.* Tate wouldn't..."

"Yes. He *would.*" Gemma said. "I didn't understand what he was doing, but I do, now. He wasn't trying to make us forget all the bad things in our lives. That wasn't it at all. He was... testing his drugs on us for profit. We were his lab animals."

Gemma twisted around, looking for Eoin and finding him to the other side of her, standing back in the dark recesses of the supply room. "Did you see that?"

"I saw enough," he replied darkly.

"Then you know I wasn't lying. This is who Tate is."

His expression grew strangely distant. "You're right. I didn't understand what he was doing to us. He's a fucking scary individual. You don't mess with people like that." He paused, a look of wild terror making the muscles in his jaw draw tight. "Don't take this personally, but I'm going to have to do what he asked me to do."

He launched towards her, a manic look in his eyes, sending a stool skittering across the floor.

37

BRONWEN

It was a small bruise, fairly insignificant, and yet a deep shade of purple that she couldn't stop obsessing over. Despite the slight reprieve in her long hours, Bronwen still hadn't managed to find any rest, and at night she woke up thinking that she felt Tate Llewellyn's lips next to her ear, whispering...

"You wanted to see me, detective?"

Bronwen pulled her thoughts away from the purple mark on her arm and directed her attention to Audrey, their head of forensics. The doctor seemed impatient, tapping her finger against her ribs as she stood with her arms folded tightly across her petite body. Stress had seeped its way into every department at the station. No one was immune.

"Anything new in the lab? It's a big job sorting through the mess from Denton Road," she said.

Audrey narrowed her eyes, obviously disappointed that Bronwen had interrupted her work for this. "We're working our way through. But you know we'll call you as soon as we find anything." Audrey shrugged. "Is there anything else you needed?"

"Do you mind if I sit?" Bronwen asked. She'd gone down to the lab to ask this because she wanted it to be private. She didn't even want Joe to know about this. Not yet. Not until she was sure.

"Go ahead," Audrey said, perching on the edge of her desk. Her expression softened, sensing Bronwen's discomfort.

"I'm guessing that everyone here knows about how I passed out on the job during the Llewellyn Farm search." She made sure her sleeve was rolled up high and held out her arm. "I woke up with this bruise. It was barely noticeable at first but now it's very visible. What do you make of it?"

The doctor leaned closer, and Bronwen could tell that her interest had been piqued. Gently, she held Bronwen's arm while examining further.

"Have you had any vaccines recently? Any medication?"

Bronwen shook her head.

"That's the kind of bruise I'd expect an inexperienced doctor to make when administering a drug. They often result from a blood test, but in this case it's not in a position I would expect for a blood test." She let go of Bronwen's arm and frowned. "It's tiny, but you can see the pinprick from the needle. How is it possible that you have an injection bruise without knowing about it? You on the heroin again, Detective McKay?"

Bronwen smiled thinly as she rolled her sleeve back down. "Good one." But despite the smile and the retort, beneath her hopefully calm exterior, Bronwen felt dizzy. Her heart began to beat faster and the remnant of a memory jumped into her mind. She'd felt something odd that last day on the farm—a sharp jab on her arm.

"Listen, you should get a blood test and definitely an HIV test. The blood test might pick up on any drugs in your system. It's a long shot, but perhaps we can find out what you were drugged with. I have my kit here in the lab."

Bronwen rolled her sleeve back up. "Just don't leave another bruise." She hoped that Audrey didn't notice that she was trembling all over.

———

Audrey, probably feeling guilty about that heroin joke, had given Bronwen a lollipop after her blood test and told her the results would be in a few days later. She was going to rush it through, handling it personally, which was a big gesture considering the job they had going on.

As Bronwen made her way back to her office, the walls felt as though they were closing in on her. Her mind refused to sharpen, and she couldn't stop thinking that everyone was watching her. She'd never felt so naked and exposed.

And it was all because of *him*. The bastard had drugged her during the search at the farm. He'd stuck a needle in her. Violated her. Made her believe she'd fallen asleep. She noticed some of the officers look up from their desks as she walked through the station, probably noticing her pasty skin and yellow complexion. God she was a mess. Bile started to rise up from her stomach. She barely made it to the bathroom before retching up her breakfast into the communal sinks.

Luckily, the bathroom was empty, so she rinsed the water away, splashed her face, and chewed on five mints from her bag. *Get a grip, McKay.* So, he'd drugged her? So what? She was alive and kicking, and she needed to turn this *shame* into an anger so fierce that she would win this war at all costs. Judging by the last conversation she'd had with the super, he was on her side, and she could always rely on Joe. There was a good team around her. What was she whining about?

Now was the time to act. If she didn't do something, Rodney White would end up taking credit for every crime involved in this case, leaving Llewellyn free as a bird. But she *knew* Llewellyn was involved and now he was toying with her. This was personal.

Bronwen held her head up high on the way back to her office. She shut the door, moved across the room to her desk, and began looking for the files Megan had dropped off the other day. She'd been so off with Megan, and now she felt terrible about it. With everything that had been going on, her head had been all over the place. When Megan had come into the office, she'd heard this *voice* telling her to move the investigation away from Llewellyn. But what if it was Llewellyn himself fucking with her mind?

Working its way through the fog of her mind was another memory of Megan. *Mr Incommunicado.* Wait, they'd spoken on the phone at Llewellyn Farm, just before she'd fallen asleep. What had Megan said? That Llewellyn had been working on a memory drug? That was it. That was when she'd felt the pinprick, except it hadn't been a pin. It had been a needle. He'd administered this drug to her during the search. The fucker had changed her memories.

Where were the files?

"Bron, you got a minute?"

Her heart slammed into her ribs at the sound of Joe's voice. She spun around to see him in the doorway with the files in his hands.

"Learn to knock, Kouros." She might've rolled her eyes, but she was glad to see him, and even more relieved to see the files. Plus, she could tell from his bright eyes that he'd discovered something.

"I couldn't stop thinking about what Megan said." Joe dropped the files on Bronwen's desk, opened at a specific page. "She kept talking about how Llewellyn was up to something with this memory drug thing. So, I read through them all, and I think I have something here."

"How much coffee have you had today?" Bronwen asked, noting he was even more enthusiastic than usual.

"More than you by the look of it. You okay? You look like something my niece dressed up as last Halloween."

"Cheers, Joe. What you got for me?"

He turned back to the files. "I almost missed it. In Leah Halcombe's notes, she mentions how Llewellyn has friends in high places. Well, no surprise there, right? He's from a rich family. He's rubbed shoulders with judges, politicians, businessmen and women from all over the world. She mentioned a few names: Robert Glossop —an MP based in London—known for a rape scandal that mysteriously disappeared, Jack Chen—a tech billionaire—accused of a sexual assault before the girl changed her mind for no good reason, and Laura Blatt—a multimillion heiress in her thirties accused of statutory rape of a minor... until the fifteen-year-old boy changed his testimony." He looked up from the files. "I've checked the internet, and there's no reference to Llewellyn with any of these people. It's weird, as though he's been careful not associate with them in public. But if we believe what's in these files, and with Megan talking about a memory drug—"

"He's selling it," Bronwen interrupted. "He's selling the drug to rich people who want to cover up a crime. The memory drug erases the memories from the victim. How did Leah Halcombe find this out?"

"According to her notes, it's from the testimony of the boy at the farm. Clay."

"That's not enough evidence."

"Apparently, the kid saw the meetings on a few recordings."

"The computers were checked during the search but they didn't find anything," Bronwen said. "Fuck."

"We've got to convince the super we need to raid that damned place," Joe replied. "A take-no-prisoners raid this time. Before the warrant runs out."

Bronwen closed her eyes and sighed. When she opened her eyes, she rolled up the sleeve of her shirt. "He did it to me. He injected me with the drug. Whatever happens, we're nailing this bastard."

Joe's expression turned dark, almost frightening Bronwen for a moment. She wasn't used to seeing him so riled up about anything. "Yes. We are."

She just hoped that Audrey could find traces of the drug. They needed some sort of miracle to close this case against Llewellyn.

38

MEGAN

Megan sipped on the bottle of water that Freddy had brought into the greenhouse a few minutes ago. The icy liquid slipped straight down into her stomach. She was suddenly desperate to pee, but she couldn't guess whether it was the water or the anxiety rippling through her middle.

She didn't know how she was going to do what she'd come to the farm to do. All she knew was that she had to try.

Was it really Gemma she'd glimpsed through the plate-glass wall of Tate's house? It could have been any teenager with hair like Gemma's. Maybe she was just so desperate to find the girls that she was manufacturing things in her head.

Still, when she pictured the girl in her mind again, she could have sworn it was Gemma.

Freddy had left as soon as he'd brought the drinks for Sophie and herself. He'd had a goofy grin on his face as he'd joked about an incident in the orchard earlier, but his eyes had remained guarded. Odd.

While waiting for Tate to arrive, Megan asked Sophie a few general questions. She jotted down the answers, pretending to have an interest in the operations and employees of the farm.

She was both relieved and nervous when Tate strode in through the door.

Sophie stopped mid-sentence. "Ah, here he is. Over to you, Tate. This is Megan Arlotti."

Immediately, Megan understood the description Bronwen had given of him a week ago. His shirt was crisp and his hair styled perfectly. He reminded her of those male actors from the noir films of the forties. She'd recently watched a string of old movies with Jacob. Tate had that same kind of presence.

When he shook Megan's hand, his palm felt cool and dry. "Pleased to meet you. Ms Arlotti. I trust that we can clear up whatever it is that's causing the bother."

Sophie coughed and cleared her throat. "The department has apparently had complaints from former employees—about us running a cult. Can you believe it?"

A look of amusement creased Tate's face. "Must be a couple of backpackers who've had some bad party drugs or something. You can return to work, Soph. I'll take it from here."

"Certainly." Casting a tight smile in Megan's direction, she left the greenhouse.

Tate's gaze swept over Megan. "Are you fond of orchids?"

The question caught her off guard. "They're very pretty. You seem to have every type imaginable."

He shook his head, smiling. "No, I'm afraid it isn't possible to have every type. I have grand plans to build something much larger in which to house them, but it still won't be adequate. I admit to being a victim of *orchidelirium*."

"Excuse me?"

"It's a term from Victorian times. Orchid collecting first became a thing then, and it became well-known that collectors acquired a kind of delirium. You see, orchids have a special quality that drives their collectors to insanity."

The effect of his soothing voice, together with the overwhelming humidity and scents of the flowers, was making her mind blur around the edges. She wondered if the measured way he spoke was deliberate.

He delicately touched a nearby flower. "There are almost twenty thousand named species, and more are being discovered all the time. A collector will never own all there is to own, and most will never be able to afford to. The most expensive orchid of all time—the *Shenzhen Nongk*—sold for hundreds of thousands of dollars."

"I didn't know that," she replied. She hugged the clipboard. He'd effortlessly taken over the subject of conversation, and she couldn't let him do that. "Perhaps we should begin. If you could show me what happens where around your farm, especially the meditations that we've been told about, that would be a good start."

"I'd be happy to show you around. Naturally, I'm very proud of what I've built up here."

He led her across to the production room that was attached to the greenhouse and opened the door. "This is where we extract elements from the orchids that go into the making of perfume. It's just a hobby of mine, but it's very rewarding. Orchids are very difficult to capture in an essence, and so we are attempting to capture the impossible. But that makes it all the rarer and more precious, don't you think?"

Tate led her outside then, to his golf buggy. He took her on a quick trip around the mango fields and grounds, pointing out machinery and cabins and fruit sorting buildings.

He stopped in front of a large hall. "This is where the employees have all their meals. Twice a week, I give them a pep talk."

She turned to him. "What kind of pep talk?"

He shrugged. "Just a bit of positivity to keep them motivated. Most of them are a long way from home. And days of fruit picking in the hot sun can be challenging. We don't actually have many workers at the moment as it's off-season. We only have about a fifth of the usual number."

Extending a hand, he helped her down. "You know what? I'll

give them a treat today and let them knock off work half an hour early. Then you can observe a session without waiting around any longer. How does that sound?" A generous smile showed his even, white teeth.

"Sounds good to me," she told him.

Stepping from the buggy, he walked away out of earshot and made a phone call. Seconds later, the music stopped, and the sound of a buzzer rang out.

Confused workers turned to one another in the orchard.

"Early lunch today, everyone," came Sophie's voice over the loud-speakers. "Compliments of Tate."

Tate touched Megan's back lightly as he guided her towards the hall.

Rich scents of spices had saturated the air inside. Coloured light sparkled from a large leadlight glass square in the ceiling.

She walked with him into the kitchen. Tate introduced her to the three workers who were in there. The three of them were energetically stirring steaming pots of soup and adding ingredients.

The girl named Dharma tucked a lock of frizzy hair behind her ear, grinning at Megan. "It won't be ready for a while yet, I'm afraid. We got caught out with the early lunch call."

"No problem," said Tate affectionately. "Creating a beautiful meal takes time, and how could someone like you create something that's anything less than beautiful?"

The girl seemed to blush.

Out in the hall, workers were streaming in. Each one grabbed a cushion and sat down. Megan had to admit that although they looked exhausted, they seemed happy. They really *were* a match with the pictures online.

"You're about to view one of our talks," Tate told Megan. "Feel free to sit and have lunch with us."

Tate crossed to the front of the room. "Enjoy your early reprieve from the fields." He smiled, his eyelids fluttering shut. "Close your eyes. Let your body relax. You have worked hard and deserve to rest now. Let's focus on each breath and let the weariness leave us. Breathe."

Breathe, came a chorus.

Tate, his eyes remaining closed, continued with the meditation.

Megan stepped from the main part of the hall towards a larder room. The area was private enough. She needed to make a call. Slipping out her phone from her pocket, she called Bronwen.

"Megan—hello," answered Bronwen. She sounded tired and perhaps a little anxious.

"Bron, can I have a minute?"

"Shoot. But I'll warn you I'm pretty flat-out right now."

Megan took a breath before saying, "I can't be certain, but I thought I just saw Gemma."

"You did?" she said with surprise. "But you're not sure?"

"It was at a distance."

"Where are you?"

"The farm."

"*The farm?* You mean Llewellyn's?"

"Yes."

"Hell. Why?"

"I know it's wrong of me, and I know I shouldn't be here. But after reading Leah's files..." She sighed. "Look, I told Tate a lie about the department getting complaints from some former workers. I just wanted to come and check things out for myself. Bronwen, I'd really like you to read those files. Lots of the things that Clay Durrell told Leah ended up being true. There's every reason to believe the rest of what he told her, and—"

"Hold on. Listen. Don't say any more. You need to get yourself out of there. We have reason to believe that it's not safe."

"It's not safe? What—?"

"Just find an excuse to leave. Say you're feeling ill or whatever. Just *go*."

Megan fumbled for words, stunned at the sudden flip in Bronwen's attitude towards the farm. She'd been almost blasé last time they'd spoken. Even her voice was different—back to Bronwen's usual direct tones.

"Have you discovered something new?" Megan said, a small surge of hope rising in her.

"I can't say right now. Please, go," Bronwen replied. "Oh, and Megan, leave quickly but don't let on that anything's wrong. I don't want him tipped off."

"Okay. Got it." Putting her phone away, she headed back to the hall.

The group was still sitting and meditating with their eyes closed. Tate was watching on with an encouraging smile on his face, his ear to his phone.

Maybe she could just leave—and then phone Sophie with an excuse when she was on the road. Say she was sick or something. Yes, that sounded easier.

But when she turned to walk out of the hall, Sophie was there near the door.

A frown stippled Sophie's forehead. "Is everything all right?"

Megan shook her head, giving herself a second to think. She could hardly say she was sick now. She needed a different excuse. "I'm terribly sorry. Just got an urgent call. One of my clients has gone off his meds, and he has his wife and kids bailed up inside their house —with a knife no less. I'm going to have to run."

She spilled the words out to Sophie, almost stuttering in her haste. It was a real story, but it had happened six months ago.

"Oh, that's terrible! I'll drive you back to your car."

Megan gave her a grateful smile. She didn't want to get back into a buggy with Sophie, but it'd seem odd to refuse it, seeing as she was meant to be in a hurry, and it was quite a distance by foot.

Sophie started chatting about the mango harvest as they walked out and into the buggy.

Instead of heading directly to the gate, she veered towards the house. "I'll just grab you some information about our farm operations. The office is on the bottom level of the house."

"I'll get that next time," Megan hastened to say. "I'm in a bit of a rush."

"It'll just take a second." The cheery voice gone, Sophie drove the buggy around to the back of the house and parked it.

Another buggy cut across in their direction. It was Freddy again.

Megan tensed. The farm seemed even emptier than when she'd first entered the property. Everyone was now in the hall. Behind the house was just miles and miles of nothing. Just scrubby red bushland.

Sophie jumped from the buggy. "Come through."

"It's okay. I'll wait here." Surely this couldn't be what it seemed? It was only Tate who posed a possible danger, right? Not his staff.

Freddy pulled up alongside. Megan cast a sidelong glance at him. His expression was cold and intent.

Something was very wrong.

The keys in the ignition caught her eye. Before she could act, Sophie snatched the keys out. In an instant, Freddy was beside Megan, his hand closing around her upper arm.

This isn't happening to me. It can't be.

Freddy tugged her towards the back entry of the house while Sophie watched on.

They're kidnapping me. They're really kidnapping me.

Struggling, Megan whirled around to Sophie. "What are you doing? I'm sure you don't want to force me in here. I was actually on the phone to the police when I was in the hall."

Sophie's expression turned brittle. "I know. Tate asked me to watch you. I overheard your entire conversation."

Freddy tightened his grip. Sophie took her bag and checked her pockets. Her phone and car keys were ripped from her.

Freddy pulled her into the house and along a hallway. The

hallway opened into a private lounge area with a library. A waterfall washed down over gleaming steps of black marble.

Sophie turned the waterfall off, and then tapped another screen that made a loud click. Stooping, she raised a step in the marble and then a door. Megan stared down into a set of dark stairs.

Her heart skittered.

Freddy prodded her back. With legs of jelly she walked down the steps.

A young man stood in the middle of the room. He glanced warily from Megan to Sophie and Freddy. "Who the hell is *that*?" His accent was Irish.

"Never mind," replied Sophie sharply. Turning her head, she gestured towards a dim area to the side of the staircase. "How long ago did you give them the injections?"

The young man shrugged. "Don't know, hey. Maybe ten minutes."

Megan followed Sophie's gaze, inhaling an abrupt breath as she caught sight of two girls lying face down on the floor. Their hair had tangled together—their limbs at odd angles—as if they'd been crawling across the floor in painful spasms. Two syringes sat on the table near them.

Gemma and Hayley.

Dead.

39

MEGAN

Megan cried out loud. Anger flamed white-hot in her chest.

The police hadn't found the girls in time. Neither had she. Everyone had failed them.

In death, Gemma and Hayley faced each other, their hair half fallen over their still faces.

Who are these people? How can they do such terrible things?

It seemed that Sophie and Freddy were waiting for something. A minute later, Tate entered the room. Megan understood then that they'd been waiting for him.

Tate closed the marble door behind him. A brief look of regret flickered in his eyes as he stared at the two bodies on the floor, but his expression quickly sharpened.

When Tate glanced at Megan, there was none of the charm he'd exhibited earlier. He looked ruffled, no longer as self-assured, his lips drawn into a taut line. She knew with all certainty that he intended to kill her too. The overheard phone conversation had sealed her fate.

Her heart pounded like a fist against her ribs.

The young Irish man crossed his arms. "I swear I did what you said. Gave them the sedatives and all. It went belly-up somehow. Not my fault."

"Well, that's not looking good for you then, is it, Eoin?" said Tate coolly.

Eoin's jaw slackened. "What the hell are you saying?"

"What I'm saying," said Tate, "is that you've just caused the death of two people. Aside from that, we have some problems. And you're in it up to your neck. What I need to know is, are you with us, or not? Make your choice."

Swallowing, Eoin nodded. "I'm in with you all the way."

Sophie eyed Tate, nervously scraping sweat-soaked strands of hair from her forehead. "You promised that things wouldn't blow up like this. The police weren't supposed to have Leah's files. Rodney said he destroyed them, right?"

A vein jumped in Tate's temple. "She must have hidden the real files. White wasn't smart enough to realise the ones he found were dummy files."

"The police know too much now," said Sophie, her voice thin. "They're sure to want to do another search." She sucked in a shrill breath. "God—the *recordings*. I'm on some of those."

"They won't find this room," Tate told her. "They didn't before. They won't now."

Sophie shot him a horrified glance. "This room? You encrypted the data online, right? We spoke about—?"

Tate ran a hand in jagged lines through his hair, ruffling the perfect waves. "Anything you put online can be compromised, for a price. Don't worry. I've got this. Okay?"

Sophie nodded stiffly. "Okay. But you know they'll look harder this time. We've got two dead runaways on our hands. And a fucking police psychologist."

Megan realised then that they'd probably known who she was as soon as she'd contacted them. But they had gotten one thing wrong. She wasn't a police psychologist. She was just a psychologist who'd stepped way past her professional boundary lines. And now she was about to pay the ultimate price. Just as Leah had.

One thought rang clear: *survive.*

"The police are on their way." Megan's words rushed out. "You have to let me go."

"You should have thought more carefully before you invented a fake reason to come here," Tate told her icily.

"This is insane. You're making things far worse," Megan countered.

"Thank you for your diagnosis," he said. "Now keep quiet, or we'll make you quiet."

He turned his attention back to Sophie. "It's all right. Everything's wrapped up watertight. We just need to manage the current situation. Let's take a moment to consider our options."

"We don't have a *moment,*" Sophie snapped.

He met her gaze with irritation. "If you want to do something right, you don't rush."

"You don't understand, Tate," she said. "It's not just the current situation we need to worry about. It's this whole place. *The employees.* If the police know about the memory research, then they'll question every single worker, one by one. And if too many of the workers have the same exact nightmares, then what do you think is going to happen?"

"That's understood. Completely." Tate straightened his shirt and collar, as if putting himself in order. "But there isn't anything that can't be fixed." Leaning his back against a cabinet, Tate seemed to remove himself from the others and sink into deep thought.

Sophie and Freddy had a heated exchange—Freddy backing Tate up and telling Sophie to be patient. Freddy dropped his hold on Megan, gesticulating angrily at Sophie. Eoin stood alone, staying silent.

Megan sensed the seconds ticking away faster and faster.

Walking to the girls, she dropped to her knees next to them. "I'm sorry," she whispered. "You deserved much better. *So much better...*"

When she raised her head, she found Tate gazing at the girls, an abstracted look on his face, as if he were looking at mere objects.

Tate faced Sophie. "This is what we're going to do. We're going to solve all the issues at once. We're going to have it that Hayley and Gemma went crazy and poisoned everyone. They're here, and the police suspect they're here, so why not put them in plain sight?"

Poison everyone, Megan mouthed silently, a cold stone forming in her stomach. She stared from Sophie to Tate in horror.

Sophie's mouth dropped incredulously. "Dead girls can't poison anyone."

"They're not dead yet," Tate told her. "It's a slow acting medication. And untraceable."

Megan watched on in shock as Tate crossed the room and knelt on one knee, as if he were about to propose to the girls in some macabre gesture. Picking up the wrist of each girl in turn, he held two fingers to their veins. "I have a heartbeat on Hayley. And Gemma too." Tate was surprisingly gentle as he replaced their arms on the floor.

You're both still alive. Megan reached to touch Hayley's shoulder and the top of Gemma's head. "Call an ambulance," she pleaded. "And don't do this. *You can't.*"

Ignoring Megan, Tate stood. "Everything fits. The girls have shown police that they are troubled liars. They claimed to have been chased by Rodney White on the highway that night, yet he was the one who ended up dead. We'll have it that Rodney White was running a secret cult together with some of our members. And Hayley and Gemma were among his willing acolytes. They left the farm to go and be with him on his property. Forensics is going to find that their ridiculous story about being kept in his aviary is false. And there was no wrestle between the tanker driver and White—the driver will surely tell the police as much. It was Gemma who pushed the bleeding Rodney into the flames."

Sophie nodded, but she still looked dubious. "So, the girls plotted to poison everyone here as some kind of tribute to their dead cult leader? How on earth do we pull this off?"

"There have been rumours of a cult running around here for years. It's even in that dead psychologist's files. We can use that to our advantage," Tate said calmly. "After we carry out the plan, we'll tell the police that the girls arrived at the farm this morning. We'll be emphatic that we told them we'd have to contact the police. This only enraged them. Next thing we knew, they'd stolen chemicals from the supply shed and poisoned the lunch. Unfortunately, people died before we had the merest clue what was happening. And afterwards, the girls drank the poison straight, as a suicide gesture to their leader—Rodney."

Megan's breath caught fast. The plan was brutal, unimaginable. But he'd spoken as if this was just some ordinary business meeting.

"Okay." Sophie exhaled a long breath. "What do you want me to do? Which poison? The same one that Gemma and Hayley were given?"

"No," he said. "It's too slow. And it must be ingested with food, not injected. We have a large quantity of pentobarbital here. Lots of farms do, to euthanise sick animals. It won't be questioned that we have it in storage. It's bitter, but it doesn't take much to do the job. But give me a minute, if you will. I need to figure out which poison is the best choice and then formulate quantities."

He shot a sharp look at Eoin. "You're looking a bit pale. You're still with us, right?"

"Yeah, man. All the way." Eoin met Tate's eyes but then looked away.

Megan could tell that the boy was terrified and struggling to hide it. Because of that, he would be killed too. She guessed that Tate would use Eoin for as long as he needed to and then dispose of him.

Tate wrote down some things on a notepad, his pencil moving quickly on the page. "Okay, we have things sorted." He showed Sophie what he'd written. She nodded.

"Sophie and Freddy," he said, "listen carefully. Go directly to the supply shed. Select what I've written here. Be sure to smash the cupboard to look as if the girls broke into it. Leave some of their hairs about for DNA evidence. Then head to the kitchen. Help with the lunch, ensuring that an exact dose goes into each plate. Dharma won't question it. She knows we put drugs via eye droppers in every lunch. Get the kitchen hands to serve out all plates. One of you stays in the kitchen and one of you stays in the hall. Ensure that no one so much as has a taste of the food. Tell them you're going to say a meditation or something before everyone eats. Then have everyone begin eating at precisely the same time. They'll die quickly."

"And then return for Gemma and Hayley?" Sophie asked. She tossed a glance in Megan's direction. "And *her?*"

"Yes," he told her. "You, Eoin, and Freddy will bring the three of them to the hall. They'll die in the kitchen. Be sure to get the girls' fingerprints all over the drug containers. You and Freddy must wear disposable gloves the entire time. Then of course, raise the alarm. Call the police. Sound hysterical. Sophie, you say you were in the office at the time of the vicious attack by the girls. And Eoin and Freddy, you'll be fixing machinery in one of the top fields. None of you had any idea what Hayley and Gemma were doing in the kitchen."

"How do you know this is all going to work?" said Sophie anxiously.

"Of course it will work." A hard edge moved into Tate's voice. "If you do it right."

"What's your part in it?" Sophie asked him with a slight tone of suspicion. "What are you going to be doing?"

"I need to prepare this room, in case the police find it," he told her. "As you said, they'll be more thorough this time. I'll have to destroy the recordings. And clean out all the vials and drugs. There isn't much left. Most of it was already taken away before the police search. Then I have a private flight to catch."

Sophie shook her head hotly. "You can't run out and leave us with this mess."

"Learn to shut up," Freddy told her. "Tate knows what he's doing. You're just slowing us down with all the questions."

"It's under control, Sophie," Tate said. "I have business to attend to. And it fits in well—Hayley and Gemma knew that I was going to be away, and they took their chance to do this terrible thing." Tate was almost smiling as he unlocked a drawer in the same cabinet that he'd taken the notepad from. He pulled out two handguns, handing them to Sophie and Freddy. "Trust me, you won't need these. But if they'll make you feel more secure, perhaps you should take them. You've both had enough practice at the range by now."

Tate walked Sophie and Freddy across the room, speaking assurances to them in a low voice. Sophie stopped to yank handfuls of hair from Gemma and Hayley's heads. For a second, her eyes met Megan's glare.

Sophie and Freddy vanished up the stairs. Tate opened the door for them.

"Eoin," Megan said in a whisper that she hoped Tate couldn't hear. "He's going to kill you too. Please. Get help."

But Eoin just eyed her coldly.

The door closed.

Tate spun around. "Eoin, keep a close eye on Ms Arlotti. Won't be long now. Everything will be sorted, and we can all move on from this."

Megan remained sitting on the floor by the girls. She wouldn't leave them until she was forced to.

Soon, almost everyone at the farm would be dead. Herself too. There was a chance Tate's plan would work. And the girls would forever be blamed for the murders.

Her mind spun in tight circles of panic.

She thought about her family and all the people she loved. Her parents. Her sister and her newborn baby.

And Jacob. This morning, she'd fallen in love with him. *No*, this morning was just the first time she'd been sure of it.

She hoped he knew.

40

BRONWEN

40 minutes earlier

Bronwen smoothed down her hair and stared at herself in the mirror. There was no time for this. No time for last minute throwing up in the bathroom. No time to doubt herself. Megan was at the farm, and that was bad news. She splashed her face with water for a second time, shoved a stick of chewing gum in her mouth and left. On her way back to her office, Joe caught up with her, his jaw set tightly.

"The super doesn't know?"

He shook his head.

"We're going anyway," Bronwen said.

Joe lifted his eyebrows. "Oh, I know."

As they headed out of the station, Bronwen tried to ignore the heavy feeling in her stomach. She'd urged Megan to get away from the farm, but she'd also recognised a steely determination in the psychologist's voice and was worried about the consequences of that. Now that Bronwen understood exactly how dangerous Tate was, Megan's presence could spook him into doing something hasty.

How many deaths had Tate been responsible for? There were the bodies in the freezer room—people who figured out too much about him, unlucky souls who got in the way—but what about out in the world? If Tate sold his memory drug to the rich and powerful, what did that drug allow all these people to get away with?

There was no food in the car today, and neither were in the mood for their usual banter. Joe was as solemn as she felt as they drove out of the carpark.

Eventually, she broke the silence. "There weren't any weapons on the farm. We know that from the search."

Joe shook his head. "I don't think we can trust that search, Bron. He's a rich guy; he can afford to have a hiding place for his toys."

"We had the blueprints—"

"Doesn't matter. He hid those girls, and we searched every inch of that place. That means he could have anything hidden. We get there, check things out, and get Megan away from danger. I don't know if we can arrest the bastard for something, but I sure as hell want to."

Bronwen nodded along.

"But," Joe continued. "If there's a sniff of trouble we call in backup."

"Agreed."

Joe shook his head. "We couldn't have waited to get approval from higher up, Bron."

"I know," she replied. "Megan."

"And the girls," Joe said. "We owe it to them too."

Bronwen tilted her chin down and pressed the accelerator. What they were doing was reckless, but it was the right thing to do. She thought about Hayley and Gemma in the hospital, traumatised, confused, and so young. Little did she know then that they'd most probably been drugged and manipulated by Tate Llewellyn. She'd always known this case was a complete and utter mindfuck, but it'd taken her to a place she hadn't expected. It'd led to her own violation. And now they'd uncovered a rich and powerful psychopath.

She gripped the steering wheel and ignored the squirming sensation in her stomach.

41

HAYLEY

Ten minutes earlier

"Eoin, keep a close eye on Ms Arlotti. Won't be long now. Everything will be sorted and we can all move on from this."

We can all move on from this.

A soft but cold hand stroked her hair a couple of times then stopped. She gently opened her eyes and looked straight at Gemma who was also awake. Hayley watched Gemma's eyebrows lift in question. She knew it meant: *now?*

Hayley responded by mouthing: *no.*

They needed to wait, but her heart was thumping hard and she was sure that anyone in the room with them could hear her heart.

Hayley wasn't unconscious or dying. She was ready, and so was Gemma. But they had to find the right moment to strike.

Tate thought he could sweep everything under the rug like it was nothing but dust. The murder of innocent people. *Sweep sweep.* The rape of young women. *Sweep sweep.* Memories altered. *Sweep sweep.*

But she remembered now, she remembered it all, and she wasn't going to allow herself to forget.

It'd started when Eoin had wrapped his fingers around Gemma's neck. Watching that act of violence had awoken something in her, beginning with a deep pain in her abdomen, and the churning of her stomach. When Eoin had finally let Gemma go, Hayley had looked at him and remembered something. She remembered him on a bed in a different room with an altered version of Eoin sprawled out on the covers, naked from the waist down, with tears falling down his face.

She glanced at Eoin now. The three of them had a plan.

Since the accident with the tanker, her damaged memory had come and gone in fleeting glimpses. However, despite her confusion, throughout all of it the one constant had been how nothing bad had ever happened to her on the farm. Then why was this terrible memory of Eoin from the farm? And then there were more memories. A bed. Why was she thinking of this bed? For some reason, she knew this bed was in the mansion, in Tate's private residence...

There was no reason for Hayley to ever be in Tate's private quarters, and she certainly couldn't recall a day she had ever been in any of the bedrooms. She sometimes drank tea with Tate in the meditation room where he held a few meetings with staff or meditated with a chosen few of the backpackers. She'd helped out in the lab from time to time and visited the orchid greenhouse. Why was the bed familiar to her?

Aside from the memory, there was the feeling that this familiar bed gave her when she thought about it. Churning, sickening distress. She wanted to scream.

What had surprised Hayley was that now that this memory had resurfaced, her body and her mind had decided to enter into survival mode. She sharpened for the first time since she could remember, and she'd made herself think: what had really happened this summer at the farm?

"Eoin, you have to do something." It was Megan's voice, whispering. "He's going to kill us all." There were shuffled footsteps and the sound of more breakages. "Act now while he's distracted. Do it now, and you'll be able to save us. Now, while he's destroying the evidence."

Hayley imagined another voice in her head.

Get on your knees.

But she didn't. She got to her feet instead and whirled around to press a hand over Megan's mouth.

Megan's eyes stared up at her, bulging from their sockets. She trembled beneath Hayley's hand.

Hayley put a finger to her lips and quietly whispered: *shhhh*. She nodded to Eoin then reached down and tapped Gemma on the shoulder. Megan was right. This was the best opportunity they'd get while Tate was distracted with the evidence, and they didn't have long. Gemma rose quietly. They were ready.

Now that Megan understood, Hayley removed her hand and patted the woman on the shoulder. Perhaps she could help them if they needed help, but this was hers and Gemma's and Eoin's responsibility to finish. They'd bought into this lie, and they'd lived it, and for that she felt like an accomplice to every crime Tate had committed. She had to make sure he wouldn't hurt anyone ever again.

Hayley watched the open door that led deeper into Tate's bunker. That must be the supply room where Gemma found the USB sticks with Ellie on them. Poor Ellie. Her stomach flipped with sadness and fear. She glanced at Eoin and nodded, communicating for him to go first. Now that she remembered what had happened to Eoin she understood where his anger came from, not that she condoned it. He was an uneasy ally and someone she didn't completely trust, but he was also a lot taller and stronger than Hayley and Gemma. They needed him to take Tate by surprise.

Eoin had only pretended to give them Tate's drug. Instead, they'd made a plan to fight back. But they hadn't had much time to work out how they were going to achieve it, and they still needed to get the code for the door and somehow get out of the bunker.

Eoin took a step forward, moving slowly and quietly towards the open door. There was a light on inside the room, showing Tate's shadow as he moved around. There was a whirring and crunching noise as he fed computer equipment into a trash compactor. Hayley moved her head so that she could see further into the room. There were piles of empty vials, their contents emptied into a tiny sink in the corner. Tate had his back to the open doorway, his guard down, so completely trusting of Eoin, who had never betrayed him. But that was Tate's problem, he was a narcissist, and he thought that he was always one step ahead.

Not this time.

Eoin wrapped his arms around Tate's torso, dragging him back into the main area of the bunker.

"Get him down on the ground," Gemma instructed. "Tie him up in my corner. The ropes are still there."

Tate tried to fight against Eoin, but Hayley and Gemma rushed forward to clamp his arms and legs. It was strange, seeing him panicking and flailing, like a child having a tantrum. It took away some of the glamour and stripped him back to the entitled piece of shit that he was.

"Stop!" he shouted desperately.

His body thudded against the ground as Eoin threw him down. Even Megan hurried over to help them tie him up.

"Sophie!" he screamed.

Gemma slapped him around the face as Eoin tied the ropes. "Sophie isn't here."

"Eoin, untie the ropes." Tate, red in the face, stared down at his bound feet. "Hayley. My sweet orchid."

Gemma slapped him again, and Tate's face fell to the left. "Aren't I your orchid too?" Her eyes flashed with anger.

"Of course you are, Gemma. You're my favourite, and you always have been."

As Gemma leaned away from him, Tate began to laugh, and Hayley knew that he was just playing with her like he always was.

Tate's eyes found Hayley's, and he smiled sweetly. "I'm not sure why you're doing this."

Hayley picked at a piece of dry skin on her lip. "You gave me to Rodney."

It hurt to say the words out loud. Pieces of Hayley seemed to break away as she realised that throughout all of her life people had been using her. First it started with her parents, who weren't terrible people but had forced her into a life she hadn't wanted. They'd never given her the *actual* life she'd wanted: warmth and love. No, her schoolwork was always too important. Then it was her boyfriend who'd tried to use her when they'd run out of money. Instead of finding work or going home to face the consequences, he expected Hayley to abandon her principles for him. She'd almost done it for him. She'd considered going through that humiliation rather than lose him.

And then Tate, the worst of all, the most disgusting person she'd ever met, except for Rodney White. He'd used her and broken her. All of these pieces were falling away because of him. Hayley felt hot, angry tears in her eyes. This hurt. Remembering all of this hurt because she'd thought what she had with Tate was real, and only now was she realising just how stupid she'd been.

Now, as she looked at this man, this crumpled human being, she realised that it was all an illusion he'd orchestrated. He'd charmed her, and then he'd drugged her and kept her drugged to keep her submissive. He'd taken her memories away, given her body to another man, traumatised her and killed her friends.

There was no air in the bunker, only the stale scent of body odour. She raised her head and sucked in a long, slow breath, slowly relaxing the muscles of her body.

"Hayley," Tate said, desperately.

"Hayley?" Gemma's voice was questioning. "What do we do now?"

Hayley paused for a moment, contemplating Gemma's question, and then she said, "Where are his drugs?"

42

GEMMA

Instantly, she understood what Hayley was planning.

Tate had destroyed all the vials of drugs in the supply room. But there was still the box of vials that he'd given to Eoin. He'd had that little metal box of drugs ever since she'd known him. It was the thing he'd wielded power over them with.

Now, they would use it to wield power over *him*.

She ran out to the table where the metal box sat. There were usually nine vials in the box. And nine syringes. Two used vials and syringes lay next to the box—the two lots of lethal poison that Eoin had pretended to use on Hayley and herself. Eoin had tipped the poison down the sink.

There were seven more vials in the box. One more lethal dose, three of the relaxant drug, three of the memory drug.

She carried the box back to the supply room.

Eoin and Hayley had Tate securely tied to the chair now.

Tate's gaze flicked over the box in Gemma's hands. "You might as well destroy them too." A nervous tone underlined his words.

"Why, Tate?" Gemma asked. "Scared we might use them on *you?*"

The vein above his left eye pulsed, and he didn't answer.

Hayley took out a vial from the box. She hid the vial in her fist. "I wonder which one I have? I guess you'll soon find out."

"What do you want?" Tate hissed from between his teeth.

"The code for the exit door," Hayley told him.

"I can't tell you that. I'm sorry." He shook his head.

Hayley opened up her hand and showed him the vial resting on the palm of her hand. "It's blue."

Tate fixed his gaze away from the needle, saying nothing, but his eyes clouded.

Desperation hammered inside Gemma's chest. Everyone in the hall had minutes left to live—and none of them knew it yet.

Taking the vial from Hayley, she stepped to the bench. She drew liquid into the syringe and then brought the needle up against Tate's eye. "You know what this will do. Give us the code. *Now.*"

He flinched. "I did my best for you. I gave you a home. I fed you. Made you feel wanted. *Gemma... Hayley...* it wasn't meant to go like this. You don't understand. My research is important. And you—you were a part of it. You were *special*—"

Fear and cold rage twisted through Gemma's body. "*Don't.*"

"You used us." Hayley's bottom lip quivered. "Every step of the way. Every—"

Megan grasped Gemma and Hayley's shoulders, her voice urgent. "He's stalling. He's trying to draw you in. He knows Sophie and that man will be back here soon."

Breathing hard, Gemma nodded.

"Where's his phone?" Megan dropped her hands from the girls' shoulders. "We need to call the police."

Eoin pointed to a mangled object on the floor. "It got busted when we tackled him."

"Doesn't he have a laptop or something?" Megan cried.

Hayley shook her head. "He already destroyed it."

Megan gasped in desperation.

They needed to get out and get to the hall. *Now.*

The sound of a loud smack reverberated through the room as Eoin hit Tate in the jaw. "I'll kill you, I swear. Tear you limb from limb, you evil bastard. For Clay and Ellie."

Tate took the punch without protest, his eyes growing absent.

An image tore up Gemma's mind. Tate had once told her how millions of tiny seeds burst from each orchid pod and tumble away in the wind. That was how it was right now. A short, frenzied burst of time, of seconds. And then it would all be over.

"He should die the same way he made the others die. A slow, painful death." Gemma barely recognised the brittle voice as her own. She needed Tate to believe that she was about to inject him.

A sheen of sweat on Tate's forehead and temples caught the overhead light. "Untie me. Then I'll unlock the exit. You can go save your friends."

"What are you trying to pull on us now, *Chemist*?" said Eoin.

"I'm just trying to make the best of things," Tate answered. "You can do what you want, and I'll be leaving. Directly."

Eoin exhaled an incredulous breath. "No honour among crims, right? You're happy for Fred and Sophie to take the blame, while you vanish from the face of the earth."

"Don't trust him," Megan warned in alarm. "This might be a trick."

Tate ignored her. "Picture this. Within the past several minutes, Sophie and Freddy would have sourced the chemicals from the supply shed. They might already have it at the hall by now. Lunch is being ladled out. A group of hungry, tired workers is waiting for the last meal they'll ever have."

Gemma exchanged glances with Hayley and Eoin. A silent communication bounced between the three of them. *Tate's loyal to no one. He'll try to protect himself.*

"We'll untie you, Chemist," said Eoin. "We'll go with you to the door and leave at the same time. If you try anything, I'll make you sorry."

Hayley nodded. "Do it."

"I need my briefcase," Tate said. "It has my passport and wallet. And I need the contents of that medical kit and syringe destroyed. You will understand that I can't leave them behind."

Casting a wary look at Tate, Gemma emptied the box and syringe into the compactor. The glass made a grinding noise as it was crushed. Water gurgled as it was all carried away into the pipes below.

"Okay. Done," Gemma breathed.

Eoin unknotted the ties from Tate's body and let them fall away. "Watch yourself, Chemist."

They walked with him to the exit, two behind and two in front.

Gemma held her breath as Tate tapped in the number for the keypad.

The slab of marble lifted, light washing in.

Hayley and Gemma stepped out onto the upper floor first, then Tate. Megan and Eoin followed.

Tate gave a polite nod to Gemma and Hayley. "I wish things had turned out differently."

"Me too." Gemma plunged the needle of the syringe that she held directly into his arm.

His mouth went slack, eyes widening in a sudden, confused panic. He stared down at the needle hanging from his arm.

"I didn't put it into the compactor, Tate," Gemma told him. "It's all about tricking someone into believing something that is slightly true, but not completely true, right? You taught me how to do that."

"Sorry, Chemist." Eoin wrestled him back into the underground room.

———

Gemma rushed out of the house alongside the others.

"Wait." Megan held up a hand, catching her breath. "Are there any other guns?"

Eoin shook his head. "No. They took the only two. The rifles are kept on a shooting range."

"Okay," Megan breathed. "Then we've got nothing. No defences. You three stay here. Find a phone and call the police. I'll head over and warn the kids in that hall."

Hayley clutched Megan's arm. "Thank you. But this is our fight."

Gemma sprinted away with Hayley and Eoin—Megan's desperate calls for them to come back fading away.

The hall loomed ahead—squat and windowless.

Eoin broke away and headed around to the side entrance by the kitchen.

The huge double-doors of the main entrance were open.

Gemma squeezed Hayley's hand as they reached the doors. For a moment, they both hesitated.

Hayley's expression was grim. "Whatever happens next, we're in this together."

They stepped inside, breathless and gasping.

A heavy silence claimed the room, apart from the low, tinkling music coming through the speakers. Multicoloured light from the stained-glass ceiling windows spilled down as always but in this moment heightening the surreal look of the scene below.

Bowls of food upturned.

People lying everywhere, unmoving.

Twisted limbs, fingers outstretched.

Hayley spun around to Gemma, her skin ashen and mouth open in a silent scream.

Too late.

The people were all still—either dead or nearly dead.

A woman moved from the deep shadows beside them, next to the wall.

Sophie.

Gemma recoiled. Sophie must have been standing there guarding the door in case anyone tried to leave.

Sophie eyed them in shock. "What the hell? Where's Tate?" She pulled out the gun from her waistband.

"Tate's dead," Gemma told her. Her stomach clenched with fear and horror. Sophie and Freddy had already killed everyone. And now they'd kill them too.

Sophie made a choked sound. "What about the others? Eoin and that Megan woman?"

Hayley stared back with hate in her eyes. "Gone. And they called the police."

"Fuck." Sophie's breaths sounded fast and tight.

Freddy strode into the room from the kitchen, gun raised. "They're lying. We didn't hear a car leave. I made sure to take all the car keys, to make doubly sure no one could get away on wheels. They didn't call no one either. No landline phones here. And all the mobiles are in that basket. We're safe." His gaze flicked to Gemma and Hayley. "So, you two were just playing dead, huh? Shame it was all for nothing. Get up here to the kitchen. That's where you're goin' to die for real."

He still held the gun on them. It was all over. Gemma's knees weakened as she walked. They could have tried to escape the farm, but they'd made their choice.

Sophie stepped behind them, her gun at their backs.

A slight movement wavered in Gemma's side vision. Nearby, a girl lifted her head, just barely. Her face rigid with terror. Dharma. She mustn't have eaten the food.

"I only had a sip," Dharma silently mouthed. Something caught Dharma's attention. and she turned her head to look directly up the hall towards the kitchen.

Eoin was stealing up behind Freddy, a large kitchen knife gleaming in his hand.

Gemma held her breath.

Sophie noticed Dharma moving and then followed the direction of her gaze. *"Freddy! Turn around!"* she screamed, running forward.

Freddy spun on his heel.

Eoin charged at him.

Jerking his gun up, Freddy shot twice. Eoin stumbled back and then collapsed in a thud that resonated through the hall.

Gemma faced Hayley, exchanging frantic glances with her.

"You weren't supposed to shoot him!" Sophie raged at Freddy. "How are we going to explain someone being shot?"

One of the workers roused slightly and groaned. It was Lucas—a guy who'd worn tie-dye T-shirts and his hair in a top knot every day that Gemma had ever seen him. Greenish vomit trickled down his chin.

Cursing, Freddy stepped across the bodies to Lucas. Sophie stood in a rigid pose, watching Freddy.

Hayley eyed Gemma and pointed at the doorway. Gemma nodded briefly and then gestured at Dharma. This was their chance —*their only chance*—to get out of the hall.

Dharma half rose from the floor, her eyes huge.

Together with Hayley, Gemma edged across to the door's opening—Dharma running silently towards them.

Freddy made a hard kick at Lucas's head. Lucas fell silent again.

"Relax. *Relax,*" Freddy told Sophie. "We can still rescue this situation. We'll put the guns in the girls' hands after they're dead. They're crazy bitches, right? Went nuts and used guns as well as poison. It still fits. We're still okay." He exhaled a long, loud breath. "I'd better go round up that idiot psychologist. You stay here and stick with the plan. Make them eat poison. Not long until we're done here. Keep yourself together. Right?"

Gemma focused on the open doorway. *Run for it.*

"Don't even think of it, ladies." Freddy's voice boomed through the hall.

Gemma froze alongside Hayley, turning to look back over her shoulder.

Freddy had his gun aimed, a stupid smile on his doughy face. "I never miss my target."

Sophie whirled around to them, her face bloodless as she marched to the doors and closed and bolted them. Freddy ran out through the kitchen.

Waving her gun about, Sophie looked almost maniacal now. "What were you doing? We've got to stick to the plan."

Dharma grasped Gemma's shoulders, trembling, trying to balance herself, but swayed about like a drunk. Gemma held her weight as she sank to the floor.

Sweat beaded on Dharma's forehead and temples, high spots of red in her cheeks. Gemma realised that Dharma wouldn't have been able to run to safety, even if they'd been able to escape the hall. The single sip she'd had of the soup must have been enough to make her very ill.

"Sophie," Dharma rasped in a shivery voice. "I don't understand... any of this. Freddy's making you do it, isn't he? He's gone crazy. Just... let us out of here."

"I can't," Sophie replied tightly. "It's gone too far. I'm not going to be the one taking the blame for anything that's happened here today. No way in hell. We've got to see this out and stay with the plan."

Gemma took a bold step towards Sophie. "There's no plan anymore. Tate is dead. He took control of you ever since you started working for him, didn't he? Just like he took control over me. We can end that here."

Sophie shook her head, her thin lips twisting. "Tate didn't have control over me. Not for a single day." Stepping over to a bowl of soup, she nudged it with her foot in Gemma's direction. "Time to have your lunch, girls."

43

BRONWEN

At first, Bronwen couldn't figure out what had changed as she drove through Llewellyn Farm, but then she realised it was the stillness. Her gaze trailed over the lush mango plantations, searching for the usual happy workers going about their day. Even though it was out of season for fruit picking, she expected to see at least a few employees milling around checking on the fields, but the entire place was deserted.

"I don't like this," she said quietly, watching Joe nod his head out of the corner of her eye.

But she didn't slow down, despite her gut telling her to turn around and get out. What if Megan was hurt? What if the two girls needed her help? The stubborn part of her hungered to see this through to the very end. She was sick of the pressure from her super, sick of awkward and confrontational press conferences, sick of being blamed for not closing this case. She was sick of opening a newspaper to see her name alongside a picture of the Cold Room Killer. She wanted it over.

Perhaps this was the end, now, and that was why all the hair was standing up on the back of her neck. She took a deep breath as she pulled the car into the carpark next to the glass mansion, but as she was exhaling, several loud cracks sounded out across the compound.

"Fuck," Joe exclaimed.

Bronwen snatched the radio unit from the car to request backup as Joe opened the door. Swearing under her breath, Bronwen wrestled with her own door and hurried around the vehicle to join her partner, her weapon pulled from its holster.

"Joe," she whispered. "You know that was gunfire. Maybe we should wait for the backup?"

"Megan," he replied. And that one word was all she needed to hear. Megan wasn't an officer like her or Joe, but she'd worked on the case and that made her one of them. They couldn't leave one of their own in danger.

Bronwen shook her head. "Fuck that bastard. Come on then. This way. The sound came from further away than the house. I think it was over there by those outbuildings."

Crouching low to the ground, Bronwen levelled her Glock, racked the slide, and surveyed the area as they moved quickly towards the shots. She tried not to think about having to use her weapon. Though she practiced and her aim was good, she'd only discharged once on duty, and that one time she'd missed her first shot at a drug addict as he'd run at her partner with a knife. On the second shot, she'd hit him in the chest, almost killing him. It wasn't a memory she often allowed her mind to linger on, but now, as she headed towards danger, she couldn't help but think about it again.

Her old partner had been injured in the foray that time. What if something happened to Joe? No, don't go there. Concentrate, she thought.

There was no sound, not even a breeze, certainly no gunfire. The sun seemed to hang above them, relentless, uncovered. The back of her neck dampened, sweat trickling down behind her ears.

Bronwen kept her sight on a long hall now less than ten feet away. Is this where the gun shots came from? She'd seen the plans of the farm during the search, and knew this particular structure was the food hall. With the rest of the farm deserted, it made sense that there were people inside. But there were no windows, only sky lights, which meant there was no way of checking who could be hiding in the building without opening a door.

Glancing towards Joe to check he was ready to cover her, Bronwen edged towards the door of the hall, placed her hand on the handle, and pulled it down. It was locked.

"Can you hear that?" she whispered. "Music."

Joe nodded, his face grim, lips pulled thin.

The music was soft and tinkling, completely out of place considering the circumstances. How many of the backpackers could be in there? What about Llewellyn? Was he the one with the gun?

"We need to take cover," Bronwen whispered. She indicated a ute parked a few feet away. "Behind there?"

He nodded in agreement.

Neither of them turned their back on the hall as they moved away, treading carefully backwards. Bronwen felt the pattering of her heartbeat and heard her breath whistling through her nose. In one quick movement, she wiped the sweat from her forehead before placing her hand back on the Glock.

Just as they reached the truck, Bronwen heard a noise coming from the side of the hall. Footsteps and another gun shot. She ducked down, running behind the vehicle to take cover, before slowly edging her head out to see what was going on.

It was Megan, running for her life.

"Megan, over here!" Bronwen yelled, lifting her gun ready to cover her friend if needed. Her teeth gritted hard together as she concentrated.

"The soup," Megan shouted, almost tripping over her feet. "They poisoned the food! Two guns. Tate is in—"

Another shot sounded out, and Megan hit the ground. As her body fell, a jolt seized its way through Bronwen's muscles. Before she even had time to process what had happened, Bronwen was racing out from behind the ute towards Megan, her eyes locked on the blood pooling in the gravel, finger on the trigger, ready to shoot. *No, no, no, no, no, no, no.*

Crack.

Bronwen felt a thud and then heat in her left shoulder. She fell back, almost down to the ground. And then she saw a man coming towards her, his handgun raised. Bronwen lifted her own weapon, but it was too late. Another shot rang out. She flinched, waiting for the hit, but instead the man keeled over and slumped onto the gravel, blood blooming from a wound on his back. Bronwen gasped, trying desperately to get air back in her lungs. Her whole body was rigid and cold, and when she raised her hand it shook uncontrollably.

"Bron!"

She turned her head to see Joe hurrying towards her, his bulk moving faster than she'd ever seen. He dropped to his knees and examined her shoulder.

"No. Megan." Bronwen nodded her chin towards the psychologist who lay lifeless on the ground. "Bloody good shot, Joe."

He only grunted as he moved towards Megan, his fingers groping at her neck. Then he swore, and his head hung low.

"She's gone?"

He nodded.

It wasn't fair. Megan hadn't signed up for this. She was a psychologist, not an officer. She didn't deserve to die like this. The sight of her dead friend breathed life into Bronwen's rigid muscles. Tate Llewellyn and his cult needed to be stopped. She sucked in two long, deep breaths and pulled herself back together.

"Megan said the food is poisoned. We have to get in. Llewellyn is going to kill them all." She struggled to her feet and Joe got up to help her.

"Not a chance, Bron. You're injured. Megan's dead. We need to wait for backup."

"Megan said there were two guns. You just shot one of the gunmen. That means there's one armed person in there and two of us. My shoulder is hurt, but it's my left arm and I can still lift my gun. Check it over, the bullet barely hit me."

Joe did as she said and nodded. "You're right. It grazed the arm. It's deep, though, Bron. You're losing blood." After fashioning a quick tourniquet using material from his shirt, he bent down to check on the man. "He's dead." He stood up, taking the gun and placing it in the holster for his service weapon. Then he shrugged. "Might need it."

Bronwen took her walkie-talkie and requested an ambulance, informing the station of Megan's death. "There are people hurt inside the barn. The food has been poisoned. Kouros and I are going in."

She ignored the response, gestured for Joe to follow her, and began moving slowly around the side of the food hall.

"We don't know what kind of gun they have left," she said. "Could be a shotgun or an automatic weapon. We could still be outgunned."

"Then we have to be quicker."

Joe sounded determined, and that helped Bronwen stay strong as she edged closer to the back door of the food hall. She tried to remember the blueprints of the farm to help her. Wasn't there a kitchen inside the hall? There must be a large canteen-style kitchen for the staff to prepare food. Only this time, they had a Jonestown situation going on.

There were sounds coming from inside. Carefully, Bronwen moved closer to the wall and took a moment to listen.

Deep within she heard a woman's voice yelling, "Eat it! Now!"

Fuck. She had to act fast.

"This is the police," she shouted at the top of her voice. "Everybody out of the hall with your hands up."

They positioned themselves either side of the door. Quickly, Joe tested the handle. It was locked.

Silence.

Then. "We have hostages. We want a car, and we want to be allowed to leave."

Bronwen recognised the voice immediately. It was Sophie, the cool and collected receptionist who had brought her coffee on the day of the search. Now the pieces fell into place. Sophie was Llewellyn's accomplice. Loyal to the cause. Perhaps she was armed too. But if Sophie and the man who killed Megan were armed, that must mean that Llewellyn didn't have a gun. Had Megan been mistaken about the number of gunmen at the farm? Before she died, Megan had been about to say something about Llewellyn. Bronwen had assumed it was to tell her he was in the food hall with the others, but now she wasn't sure. She turned to Joe, trying to decide on her next move, but he just shrugged.

"This isn't a negotiation," Bronwen shouted back. "This is your last warning. Come out with your hands up."

Silence again. Her pulse thumped with adrenaline as she waited for a response. Time was ticking away, and with it, the opportunity to save the people inside the hall.

"We need to get in there." Joe moved closer to the door and raised his eyebrows. "I reckon I can kick it in."

She checked over the door, examining the hinges and the lock. It was a regular wooden door, a little worn, fairly old, like the building itself. The food hall was a converted barn with some of its original features. The structure wasn't built for protection; it was a storage place. Maybe Joe was right. She nodded, and he took a few steps back to give himself a run up.

Well, she'd been right about one thing. They were approaching the end of this case. After all the buildup over the passing weeks, this was how it was going to end—in a barn, with blood pouring out of her shoulder, her friend dead, her partner kicking in a door. What was behind that door? She sucked in a deep breath, ignored the pain in her shoulder and focused.

Bang. Bang. Bang.

The lock gave away, and it swung inwards. Both Joe and Bronwen took cover on either side of the open doorway. A gun fired in their direction. Not an automatic weapon though. That was something. It sounded more like a handgun.

Bronwen peeked through the doorway, but there was no one there. She stayed low as she stepped into the kitchen. Keeping her firearm level caused her pain in her hurt shoulder, but she ignored it, creeping silently through the outbuilding. Joe behind her. She didn't have to see him to know he was there and would cover her if it came to it.

"Just eat it!" she heard Sophie screaming. There was the sound of pottery clattering on the floor. A girl let out a cry of pain.

Bronwen hurried through the kitchen and out into the communal area. What she saw almost knocked her back with shock. There were bodies on the ground. Perhaps a dozen or more. The place smelled like spices and the sour acidic lining of the stomach. She saw upturned bowls all over the floor, as well as vomit on the clothes of the people lying still beneath her feet. She wanted to turn back to her partner, to gauge his reaction, but she had to be careful here. Someone in this room was still armed.

She forced herself to focus on the few people who were conscious. Finally, she came face to face with Sophie. The woman's eyes were wide and panicked, her lithe arm shaking as she pointed a handgun towards a young girl. *Hayley.* And next to Hayley was Gemma. She'd found them at last, and what a way to find them. But there was no Llewellyn.

The girls were sitting on the floor with their hands in the air. In front of them were two bowls of soup. The poisoned food.

When Sophie turned to Bronwen, there were tears rolling down her cheeks. "They won't eat it," she said desperately.

"Are you all right, Sophie?" Bronwen asked, manoeuvring herself further into the hall so she could get closer to the girls. Joe did the same, but on the opposite side.

She wiped away the tears with her sleeve. "I'm supposed to make them eat it. But they won't eat it."

Bronwen didn't like this. Sophie was clearly broken, and that made her completely unpredictable. She could turn that gun on anyone in the hall.

"She's working for Tate," Gemma said. "Be careful. She's dangerous."

"You don't have to make them eat anything, Sophie," Bronwen said quietly. "It's over now. Come on. Hand the gun over to me. Let's stop this before anyone else gets hurt."

The receptionist stared at her with bright, glassy eyes, and Bronwen saw how much she truly did want it all to end. But then she turned back to the girls and lifted the gun until it pointed directly at their faces.

"You don't want to do that," Bronwen said calmly. "You don't want to hurt them."

"That's what he told me to do. He told me to make sure they ate the food. And then everyone would think they did it, and the farm would survive."

"Hey, look at me a moment, Sophie," Bronwen said, hoping to gently reason with her.

She pulled her gaze away from the girls and did as she was told.

"Now look at the rest of the hall here," Bronwen instructed. "Does it look like the farm is going to survive?"

Sophie's shoulders sagged as though she was completely defeated. Her arm holding the gun dropped to her waist. But as Bronwen was about to approach to take the weapon from her, Sophie lifted the gun and aimed.

44

GEMMA

She jammed her eyes shut as Sophie raised her weapon. Gunfire exploded through the hall.

Someone fell heavily to the ground.

Did Sophie shoot the detective?

Did the detective shoot Sophie?

One of those things was true. Gemma didn't want to know which. The detective could be lying there dead, in a pool of her own blood. Sophie could be about to shoot them or pour the poisoned lunch down their throats. If she kept her eyes closed, she could believe what she wanted to believe.

All she could hear now was the tinkling music.

Someone clutched her arm.

"Gemma!" It was Hayley.

She forced her eyelids open.

Hayley turned from her, staring in terror at the scene before them.

No one else was standing.

Sophie was struggling and failing to get to her feet. She'd been shot somewhere in her middle, crimson blood staining her white shirt. Her gun was lying a short distance away—it must have flown from her hand.

Detective McKay was slumped on her side on the floor. Blood had seeped through her shirt and onto the floorboards. Was she dead?

Someone was crawling towards Sophie.

Dharma.

Sophie's eyes flew wide open as Dharma reached her. Dharma's fist closed tight on Sophie's shirt—her other hand grabbing a nearby plate. Gasping, Dharma threw the plate of soup over Sophie's face.

Sophie screamed hoarsely. Wrestling herself out of Dharma's grip, she scrambled across the floor and grabbed her gun.

Dharma drew back.

A large man came running towards them. Detective Kouros. Gemma hadn't even noticed that he was in here before.

"I'll kill her," Sophie croaked, pointing her gun at Dharma's temple. With her left hand, Sophie clawed at her own face, trying to scrape the liquid away.

"Don't be stupid," the detective told her. "You're badly hurt. It's over, Sophie. Just—"

"Put your gun down, or I'll put a bullet in her," Sophie said. "I'll do it. Gladly. Bitch just threw poison on me."

Detective Kouros's gaze skated from her to McKay and back again. He lowered his gun.

"Get up," Sophie hissed at Dharma. "If you try anything, you're dead."

Dazed and swaying, Dharma got herself to her feet.

Keeping her gun pointed at Dharma, Sophie half loped, half limped towards the kitchen, one arm around her stomach. Dharma looked back at them with a stricken expression as she was forced to walk alongside Sophie.

Sophie made crazed sounds as she made it to the kitchen. Gemma knew she was terrified that the poison on her face was working its way inside her eyes, mouth, and nose. *Good.* She deserved to know what it felt like.

The sound of water running in the kitchen sink echoed through the hall. Sophie must be desperately trying to wash the poison off.

Groggily, Detective McKay roused. She wasn't dead.

Kouros ran to her. "Bron!"

"I'm okay," she murmured. "Got off balance when I tried to shoot Sophie. Hit my head on the damned floor."

He helped her sit. "I know. And you *did* shoot Sophie. I was in the wrong position. I could have shot the girls."

"What do we do?" Hayley's eyes were huge and filled with fear. "We've got to get Dharma away from that woman."

Kouros exhaled heavily, an anxious look in his eyes. "Bron, you okay to cover me? I'll try going out and around the outside to the kitchen door. She won't get away. I promise you that."

"Yeah. Let's do this." McKay grimaced in pain as Kouros helped her to her feet. "I'm fine."

Kouros unlocked the double doors. Harsh daylight flooded in.

He ran out.

"You girls stay well back," McKay cautioned.

Gemma turned to Hayley. Hayley shook her head firmly.

"No," Gemma said in a low voice to McKay. "We're with you."

The detective didn't argue. She headed off towards the kitchen.

Gemma and Hayley followed her.

Thin cries of terror were audible in the kitchen as they drew closer.

Detective McKay held out her injured arm, holding Gemma and Hayley back as they peered inside the doorway.

Sophie had filled a jug with water and was about to splash it on her face—her face and hair already wet. She was panting hard, her eyes glazed and skin chalky, looking as if she could barely stand.

Dharma was on her knees, vomiting.

Kouros stepped in through the external kitchen door, gun raised.

Sophie looked from Kouros to McKay. The jug slipped from her hands, crashing to the floor and splintering into dozens of pieces.

She fell, writhing in pain.

Until she became silent.

45

BRONWEN

"This is it," Hayley said. "This is where Tate is."

Bronwen found that her throat was thick with emotion when she opened her mouth to reply. "Okay, Hayley. We'll take it from here. You can go back to the ambulance."

"I don't know what you'll find though," Hayley said. "He destroyed it all. He crushed it. There's nothing left."

Bronwen's stomach sank. "What do you mean?"

"I think we got to him too late," she said. "All of his drugs and all of his files will be gone."

That sinking sensation of dread made Bronwen feel exhausted, and as though a heavy weight was pressing down on her shoulders. She rubbed her eye, now sore from her tiredness. If there was no evidence left... Tate with his money, connections and slippery character... She didn't even want to think about it.

"That's not true." Gemma's expression was grave as she unfolded her palm to reveal a memory stick. "I saved this. Tate was about to crush it in the compactor. He used to record some of his meetings or... tests."

Bronwen picked up the small item and tucked it away in her pocket. Her head was still fuzzy with blood loss and stress.

"And this," Gemma said, producing a small vial of clear liquid with a blue label.

Bronwen reached out to take the second item, noticing a shift in atmosphere as Hayley sucked in a sharp breath.

"You didn't administer it?" Hayley said, her gaze directed at Gemma.

"I couldn't. I'd be just like him if I did."

Hayley squeezed Gemma's arm. "It's okay, I get it."

Bronwen regarded both girls and then lifted the vial. "What is this?"

"It's poison," Gemma said. "I made Tate believe that I'd injected him with it, but I gave him a sedative instead. I think you'll find that helpful. He used it on all the people in the cold room."

Bronwen nodded.

"Thank you." Bronwen held the girl's eye contact and nodded. She knew what they'd both been through, and her heart ached for them. Her eyes trailed down to the bruises on Gemma's neck, and a shiver wormed its way down her spine.

She watched briefly as the girls turned and walked away. It had been a long journey since she'd first seen the two of them, small and thin, propped up with cushions on hospital beds; their stories so wildly different that she'd wanted to tear her hair out. Now she understood what had been going on. Tate had messed with their heads until they didn't understand their own thoughts. She'd gone through some of it herself and understood a little of what they were feeling, and now she was about to face the man who had done that to her.

"Are you ready?" Joe asked. There was concern on his face, which meant that Bronwen wasn't hiding her fear particularly well.

As she heard the sound of a helicopter outside, she took a scrap of paper with a code from her trouser pocket and tapped in the number.

No doubt the helicopter was checking the area for any more back-packers who might have been outside the food hall. It was a mess down there. Bronwen didn't know if the people collapsed in the food hall were alive or dead. She also didn't know what she was about to find in this bunker.

A door opened after she typed in the code, and the two of them descended into Tate's secret bunker. This is the reason why they couldn't find the girls during their search. The arrogance of the man was quite extraordinary. Not only did he use his money to research a memory drug and then sell it to high-profile people, but he thought he'd get away with this in Australia, a rich, developed country. He thought his money was a buffer to allow him to do whatever he wanted.

But he was wrong.

There was a lingering odour of chemicals down in the hole. She checked to make sure Joe was propping open the doors. She also checked to see there were officers following down with them. Bronwen was not at her best, and she knew she couldn't deal with Tate alone. *There are times when an officer needs a team, and this is one of them.* She was still dizzy with pain from her injured shoulder, and the knock on her head after shooting Sophie. So, as they approached the inner door, she gestured for two armed officers to go first.

"I don't know what the super is going to make of all this," Bronwen said quietly to her partner.

Joe shook his head. "I can't stop thinking about the loss of life. All down to this one guy. How is that possible?"

The inner door opened, and Bronwen braced herself for what was about to come. She'd heard about charismatic cult leaders influencing mass suicide or mass murder. Charles Manson. Jim Jones. She just never thought it would happen here. Not like this.

"Detective McKay, how nice to see you."

Llewellyn's dark brown eyes followed her movements as she

stepped into the main area of the bunker. She saw that he was tied up just like Gemma and Hayley informed her, and that he was groggy. His eyelids appeared to be drooping, but he was clearly fighting against unconsciousness.

"Oh, but you're injured. What happened?"

"One of your employees shot me."

"We don't condone violence here at Llewellyn Farm," he said. "I do hope the culprit has been arrested. Who was it? Out of interest."

"Freddy," Bronwen said. "He's dead now."

"Ah," Llewellyn replied. "I think Freddy might have concocted a terrible plan to kill everyone. If you could just untie me, and perhaps get me some urgent medical attention, I'll tell you everything."

"You're lying," Bronwen said. "Unless Freddy built this bunker. Unless Freddy maintained a state-of-the-art laboratory. Unless Freddy sold memory drugs to rich people all around the world. He doesn't quite strike me as the type."

"It's such a shame when you offer an opportunity to a young man and he takes advantage of your facilities." Llewellyn shook his head sadly.

Bronwen pointed towards a second room where she could see broken glass and plastic all over the floor. "What's in there?"

"You know, I gave Freddy the code to this place in confidence," Llewellyn said. "And then he used it to store all kinds of terrible things. I don't know what's in there. I think he destroyed it all."

Bronwen stepped into the small room and kicked a few of the discarded items with the toe of her boot. "I think you're in luck, Mr Llewellyn. There's an essential piece of evidence left. This will no doubt show us Freddy up to all kinds of bad things." She took the memory stick out of her pocket and opened her palm, mimicking Gemma.

Llewellyn frowned at the memory stick in her hand, and quick as a flash, his expression changed. His face morphed into an expression that could only be described as completely blank; devoid of humanity; eyes empty, and mouth slack. "Hurry up and arrest me so I can call my lawyer."

————

Bronwen sat in the back of an ambulance. She didn't want to leave the farm, not yet, despite Joe and some of the medical staff telling her to go to the hospital. Most of the air ambulances had left now, transporting the people from the food hall to get the medical attention they needed. She was pleased to find out that they were unconscious, not dead.

That meant Sophie was alive too. Perhaps Bronwen and Joe could get some truth out of her if they couldn't get it from Llewellyn himself, who was now also on the way to hospital. They had the memory stick and the lethal drug, both of which Joe was taking back to the station, and now the rest of the officers were combing through the mess in the bunker.

But Megan had paid the ultimate price and that seemed incredibly unfair to Bronwen. As a police officer you accepted the dangers involved, and though you would never think something like this could happen in their corner of the world, she also accepted the chance that she could be killed in the line of duty. Megan did no such thing. She had been pulled into this through unfortunate circumstances, and all Bronwen could think about was that first day in the hospital when Megan had come in half-asleep after spending the night helping her sister give birth to a baby. Megan had a family who would miss her, and the world didn't feel right without her in it.

She sighed, letting out a long, exhausted breath. Now that the initial chaos was over, a new stillness had descended on the farm, one a lot less foreboding than when she and Joe arrived a few hours ago. After receiving treatment, Bronwen sat with her legs over the side of the ambulance floor, taking in the sight of this place one last time.

Now, maybe, just maybe, Bronwen could go to sleep without waking with a nightmare.

Nothing, though, could change the fact that Llewellyn had stolen and twisted her memories, and that was one thing she was going to have to live with. It was a small price to pay, she decided, as she sipped water and stared at the glass building in front of her.

46

GEMMA

She studied the space around her.

Square room. Painting of a meadow on the wall. Yellow flowers on the windowsill. Bars on the window.

A week had passed since the day of the poisonings. Gemma had been transported to a psychiatric hospital soon after that day. Her government-appointed barrister had gone hard with presenting her as being mentally ill to the court, to avoid her being sent to prison before the criminal pre-trials began. Tate, Sophie, Eoin, and herself were the only ones who were expected to stand trial. Freddy and Rodney were dead. The other people that Tate had been connected with overseas had scattered like cockroaches.

The barrister had told her that the prosecutor was preparing to have her charged with being an accessory to Tate's multiple murders. If she were to be convicted, it would mean several life sentences. She'd spend her whole life in jail.

Shivers passed down the length of her body—cold and painful as they reached her feet and hands. She had no clue what was going to happen to her. Was she *guilty* or *not guilty*? She couldn't even figure that out in her own mind.

She flexed her fingers then pulled a blanket tightly around herself, staring out at the yellow roselike flowers in the trees outside. *This hospital is obsessed with yellow flowers. They grow them everywhere. I bet they think the colour yellow helps tame disordered minds.*

The ward held a grab bag of psychoses, schizophrenia, delusions, and depression. And it held *her*—everything that was Gemma.

But who am I? I don't know. I just don't know.

It wasn't the first time she'd been in a psych ward. But this time was different. This time the staff feared her. Some of them treated her as if she were a devotee of a deadly cult, with horror in their eyes. Maybe she deserved that. She'd allowed herself to get swept up by Tate. He'd been so smooth, so assured, and at the same time making her feel like it was the farm against the world. He made her believe that sometimes people have to die in order to make a safe space.

She knew what the hospital staff were thinking: *What did she do? How many people did she recruit to that death cult? Did she kill people? Does she know how to hypnotise people and steal their memories away?*

The staff avoided her, mostly. They gave her pills and meals and slipped away.

It wasn't true that she didn't know who she was. She did.

She was a poison orchid. She was one of Tate's many poison orchids—deadly little flowers who he'd grown in his garden and cultivated to do his bidding.

She stepped across to the window, dragging the blanket with her.

The one bright thing from the day of the poisonings was that all the farm workers had survived. And Eoin survived his gunshot wound. He was still recovering in a hospital—she didn't know which one. They wouldn't tell her, nor was she allowed to talk to him on the phone. They were both seen as possible criminals, and criminals weren't allowed to chat.

Dharma had gone into hiding somewhere and was refusing to talk to the media. The last Gemma had heard, she was on suicide watch, unable to accept that the farm she'd known had been a lie. She'd been one of Tate's most prized poison orchids, only she hadn't known it.

Gemma had only been out of the psych ward twice since she'd arrived. Once to attend Megan's funeral, at which she'd witnessed the raw outpouring of grief from Megan's parents and her boyfriend, Jacob. And she'd been out once for a police interview. Those police hadn't been kind, unlike Detectives McKay and Kouros. They'd been trying to get her to admit to a love affair with Tate and involvement in the murders.

It was true she'd loved Tate. She'd loved him with a burning passion. And she'd known about the murders. That was as good as being involved. She was *bad*. She should be convicted of everything the police wanted to throw at her.

She felt *cold, cold, cold*. Dead cold. Frozen like the victims in the freezer room.

A sheen of moisture covered her eyes. The yellow flowers in the trees outside seemed to turn into mangoes and the garden into an orchard. She could see Hayley and Ellie out there picking fruit, laughing together. But she couldn't quite hear the music. And the farm wasn't the farm without the music. Then Ellie vanished, and it was just Hayley. Gemma recoiled as Hayley turned to stare at her. Then Hayley, too, vanished.

Hayley. Together, they'd been through nightmarish horrors. Worse, Gemma had lured Hayley into that world.

It had been Gemma who'd planted the fruit-picking leaflets in the Sydney bar where she and Hayley worked. Then she'd given just enough signals for sleazy Sam to take the bait and make a pass at her just before she knew Hayley would be entering his office. She'd known exactly how Hayley would react. She'd set everything up perfectly.

Gemma had been good at what she did. Tate's best recruiter.

Tate's favourite. For a time.

But everything fell apart when she brought Hayley to the farm. In every possible way.

In Gemma's mind, she'd become Hayley, and Hayley had become herself. Hayley had been the bad one, the crazy one. Even before that first day Tate had sent them to the freezer room, her view of Hayley had twisted day by day. Hayley had been a friend, a sister, an adversary, a competitor in the race for Tate's affections. She'd wanted to *be* Hayley, to have her innocence, to have an intact, loving family surrounding her. And to have grown up in the beautiful house Hayley had described, not in the mouldy old dumps that Gemma had.

She turned sharply as someone entered the room.

It was that detective, Bronwen. Her shoulder in plaster and her arm in a sling. "How are you, Gemma?"

"I'm fine," she said reflexively. Moving from the window, she went to sit on her bed.

"Sure? You're not feeling sick? You've got a blanket on, but it's a stinking hot day out there. Whew!" Bronwen scraped back damp strands of hair from her flushed face, exhaling noisily.

"I'm fine, really. The aircon must be up too high."

Bronwen's eyes softened. "When I get time, I'd like to come and sit down and chat with you. Not as a police officer. As a friend. Joe and I have been taken off the case. We're seen as having too much involvement in that last day at the farm to be impartial. Would that be okay? A little chat? Maybe on Sunday?"

Gemma nodded hesitantly. Was it a trick? Why would Bronwen want to bother with her?

"Great." Bronwen smiled widely, showing her evenly-spaced teeth. "But for now, I tracked someone down that I think you might want to meet up with again."

"I don't want to see anyone," Gemma was quick to say. She was certain Bronwen had brought Hayley here. Seeing Hayley would hurt too much.

The person Bronwen had brought didn't wait for Gemma's answer. He stepped around Bronwen and into the room.

Gemma swallowed the stone that had lodged hard in her throat. She hadn't expected this. She hadn't expected the one person it would hurt the most to see. This was more painful than seeing Hayley, more painful than anything.

"Hello, Gemina." Her brother Ryan walked across the floor.

A sad grin flickered on his face. Scruffy, sun-streaked hair hung across his blue eyes. A three-day-growth stubbled his chin. He looked so much older than when she'd last seen him, maybe eighteen months ago. Even his voice was deeper.

Giving a brief wave, Bronwen left the room.

Ryan sat beside Gemma on the bed. "Hell. I just heard. *Everything*. That cop found me in Central America. She traced me from place to place until she pinpointed me—using other people's travel blogs. I've been living without internet, in a small village in Guatemala." He paused. "Sorry for leaving you on your own, Gem. I shouldn't have done that."

"You didn't leave me on my own. I ran away," she replied stiffly. "I was seventeen. I didn't need a guardian anymore."

He shook his head. "You were still a kid. I should have come looking for you. I gave up on you and went off and did my own thing."

"I wanted you to give up on me. I never needed anyone, Ryan."

"That's where you're wrong. You needed so much more than what you got."

Her childhood came rushing back to her. *Her real childhood.* The truth was that she was poison long before she ever met Tate. He just cultivated what was already there.

For the first time, she told herself her own story. She heard it inside her head, loud and clear, a wash of painful memories flooding through with it:

Mum vanished when I was six. I made her unhappy, and I know that because she never came back. We found her years later, shacked up in a caravan with a delivery guy from our town. She still didn't want anything to do with me.

Dad was already ill when Mum left. Lung cancer. One morning, when Dad was coughing up blood outside on the patio, Mum raged at me for spilling lime cordial on the kitchen floor. Fluoro-green liquid running into the cracks and grout of the floor tiles. She said I made everything a hundred times worse than it already was. Ryan had stuck up for me, telling her I was only in kindergarten. He was eleven— almost twelve—then. Mum had always liked him better. She said she never should have had me.

It was when she left us that I started lying. Making my life sound bigger and better than what it was.

I changed my story often. Sometimes I'd say my mother was travelling overseas for work. Sometimes I'd say my father was rich and other times he was an abusive alcoholic.

None of it was true. But I discovered that I could make myself believe anything. My lies weren't lies, exactly—because I could make them true in my mind. It was a little trick, a wonderful talent—something I nursed all to myself.

Dad died when I was twelve. Ryan, aged eighteen, was appointed my legal guardian. I made his life hell, always running away from home and telling people he was hurting me.

Eventually, I ended up on Tate's farm. At Tate's urging, I sent Ryan a brief text message to say that I was happy and not to come looking for me. I'd found my new home.

"Ah, sis'," said Ryan, his voice hitching sadly. "I think you might have got yourself into too much trouble this time. I don't know if anyone can get you out of it."

He hugged her, and he sobbed.

For a moment, she thought she was crying too. But then she realised she was just humming.

Finally, she could hear the farm.

A snippet of a song played in her head. One of the songs she always heard blasting over the farm's loudspeakers. A song about summer days under the sun. She could really hear it. She could feel the warm, sultry air on her skin, and she wasn't cold anymore.

The air was always yellow at the farm.

Golden yellow.

EPILOGUE

HAYLEY

So, there it is, the final part. One long year later, and there's the last image to complete her scrap book: the cutout of Tate Llewellyn in handcuffs on his way to prison. It had been a long trial, one that she'd aided with her witness testimony, and finally he'd been convicted of murder. The murder of Ellie, of Clay, and all the other backpackers who went to him in the hope of finding a new life. Who wanted happiness and love but instead ended up in the cold room. Hayley had once thought she'd found all the happiness she needed at Llewellyn Farm, but it had been a lie, of course.

She skips back several pages to look at photographs from a happier time that had been printed in the newspaper during the trial. One of the boys had taken them. Maybe Freddy. There was Ellie sitting with her arm draped over Hayley's shoulders, mouth smiling, eyes not. It seems obvious now that Ellie was haunted, but at the time Hayley hadn't noticed anything. She'd been too wrapped up in her own problems to see the pain in someone else's life.

In a photograph on the opposite page, Hayley sees herself sitting on the grassy ground next to Eoin, the light of a campfire giving their faces an orange glow. She hadn't seen him since that terrible day. Eoin had been so arrogant and cocky. He'd thought he was using the farm to his own advantage, but really, he'd been the used one. Chewed up. Spat out. Never the same again. She didn't know where he was now. She liked to think he'd gone back to Ireland.

And there was Gemma, cuddling up next to Clay, a wide grin on her pretty face. She remembered the day they'd flown to Katherine in the air ambulance. The helicopter had already made several trips with the injured backpackers after Sophie and Freddy forced them to eat the poisoned soup. Not enough of it, though, because they all survived. Sophie survived the soup, too, but inhaling it as she did caused her ongoing health problems. She went to jail alongside Tate, convicted of lesser charges.

Hayley had held Gemma's hand the entire journey in the helicopter. Their relationship had certainly been rocky, and even now she couldn't help feeling a little betrayed by all the lies Gemma had told. But that seemed like a million years ago now.

Forgiveness isn't coming easily. Life is too short to hold onto negative feelings, but at the same time, forgiveness isn't a quick fix. It's easier to forgive Gemma and Eoin, but when it comes to Tate, well... that's a lot harder. And then there's Rodney. Most nights she dreams about Rodney White's hands on her body. She hears the word *orchids* whispered to her like a caress.

Since the mass-murder attempt at the farm, Hayley moved back to England, while Gemma was undergoing her criminal trials. The prosecutors tried to turn Gemma into more of a villain than she was. But nothing stuck. Gemma was young, vulnerable, and easily manipulated by Tate. After her time in the psychiatric hospital, Hayley found out from Detective McKay that Gemma was now studying to become a psychologist.

In the media frenzy that followed, it emerged that Gemma's father had died several years ago and that led to a downward spiral in her mental health. Perhaps that's why she created so many different stories, to avoid the pain of that passing. While Hayley was rejecting her family, Gemma was trying to pretend she still had one. Hayley touches the photograph of Gemma and then closes the book.

The detective still sends her emails every now and then, asking her if she's doing okay. There are photographs of Bronwen in the scrapbook too. The woman who would not give up, who saved them in the end. And then Megan, of course, who made the ultimate sacrifice.

Hayley gets up, stretches out her legs, moves over to the window and opens the curtains as wide as they'll go. The sun hasn't quite emerged from the horizon yet, but she can see the sky turning a pinkish blue. She raises her arms and stretches harder, releasing the tension in her arms and shoulders. Her skirt lifts from the cold wooden floor of the bedroom. Then she steps out into the hallway.

They'll be waiting for her, so she has to hurry. Her stomach rumbles with hunger, but she can't eat yet. That's for after.

She loves this house. It creaks and complains with every step, but it's theirs and theirs alone. They need to hire a roofer and replace the cracked toilet. There's money to be spent, which she doesn't have, but that doesn't matter. What Hayley has instead is faith and hope. Her family is growing, and that means soon the work will be done.

Her long skirt trails the floor as she hurries down the steps and out into the fresh air. Out here the stars are brighter because there are no street lamps. They abandon their mobile phones because there's no signal. They plant seeds to grow food because the shops are so far away. The smells of nature are stronger. On a whim, she turns around to look at the old stone house from the little courtyard outside. One of the windows is cracked. The hinges on the front door are rusting. None of that matters. This old farm is where she's supposed to be, and she's happier now than she's ever been before.

But the sun is beginning to peek out from behind the distant hills which means she has to hurry. Now isn't the time to bask in the natural beauty her home county of Yorkshire delivers on a daily basis; now is the time to skip up the tallest hill to a field that they acquired along with the farm. She'd bought it with savings and with help from her family. Her new family.

"Good morning, Sister."

The chorus of voices greet her with joy and love. Despite a slight chill in the air, Hayley has never felt warmer. She smiles at the group of people before her, old and young, tall and short, racially diverse, and yet all her family. A small family for now, just fifteen of them, but all so loving and warm that she could smile with them all day.

She takes her place within the circle, sits down and crosses her legs.

"Another beautiful day on the farm."

They echo her.

One day she'll make sure that Gemma comes to join them. It's only right; Gemma needs a family, she deserves one. Gemma would make this place whole.

"We give blessings for our family."

As Hayley hears the words spoken back to her, she feels deeply loved.

We hope you enjoyed our story,
POISON ORCHIDS.

The book was written over two years, in between our personal projects. It involved an enormous number of hours and plot wrangling.

We loved the idea of the raw, wild beauty of Australia's Northern Territory contrasted against the refined and ordered (but brutal) world of Tate Llewellyn and his hothouse orchid collection.

It's wonderful to finally share the story with our readers!

Sarah and Anni

ABOUT SARAH A.DENZIL

Sarah A. Denzil is a *Wall Street Journal* bestselling suspense writer from Derbyshire. Her thrillers include the number one bestseller *Silent Child*. Sarah lives in Yorkshire with her husband, enjoying the scenic countryside and rather unpredictable weather.

SAVING APRIL
THE BROKEN ONES
SILENT CHILD
ONE FOR SORROW
TWO FOR JOY
ONLY DAUGHTER

Find out more about my books here:

sarahdenzil.com

ABOUT ANNI TAYLOR

Anni Taylor lives on the Central Coast north of Sydney, Australia, with her wonderful partner, amazing sons and a little treats-wrangler named Wookie.

Her first thriller, THE GAME YOU PLAYED, and her subsequent thrillers, have all been chart-toppers in their categories. Anni enjoys nothing more than diving into writing the next dark story!

THE SIX
THE GAME YOU PLAYED
STRANGER IN THE WOODS

Find out more about my books here:

annitaylor.me

ACKNOWLEDGEMENTS

Huge thanks and appreciation to our first readers for your valued feedback:

Linda Gonzales, Lena May, Jessica Printz and Declan from Writerful Books.

Many thanks also to our ARC readers for reading our story before its release.

Printed in Great
Britain
by Amazon